WORLD WARRIOR

Harris Brooker

Kindle Direct Publishing

Copyright © 2020 Harris Brooker

All rights reserved

The characters and events portrayed in this book are fictitious. Any similarity to real persons, living or dead, is coincidental and not intended by the author.

Harris Brooker reserves the moral right to be identified as the author of this work.

No part of this book may be reproduced, or stored in a retrieval system, or transmitted in any form or by any means, electronic, mechanical, photocopying, recording, or otherwise, without express written permission of the publisher.

Typesetting by Laura Kincaid

Special thanks to Laura Kincaid, who without her copyediting skills and constructive criticism, I would be lost.

And special thanks to my friends and family for their advice and encouragement.

ISBN: 9798569514472

Cover design by: Yellow Tractor
Printed by Amazon, in the United Kingdom

A LITTLE AUTHOR'S INTRO

My name is Harris Brooker and I live in the north east of Scotland. As you'll soon discover, nature is my world – my way of enjoying and seeing positivity in a world that's often so negative. This story came to me during a fateful holiday to Florida back in October 2003, when I was only eleven. Roundabout this time I'd left my curriculum support unit and had been integrated into mainstream school.

It was only then that I'd been told about my Asperger's syndrome. Self-esteem had been at an all-time low. I lost contact with most of my friends, and the learning environment that had seemed so cushy back there was now strict, with few peers to relate to.

This trip was a beacon of light in such a turbulent time. It was the first time I had ever left Europe. It was before I was really into wildlife in the diverse way that I am today. This trip was mostly about the major theme parks around Orlando. But I still enjoyed the egrets, vultures, pelicans, lizards, alligators and armadillo I saw there.

Funnily enough, this story is set mostly at the opposite end of Florida to where I visited. I'm not sure exactly why I made it that way, but it just felt right and seemed to work out all the same. Nor does this story resemble what I really did in Florida – I can assure you, it was much less dramatic than what you'll find here.

Here's to all who have ever felt different at school. To anyone who has Asperger's syndrome or any other condition. To anyone who has ever endured indifference and injustice. Know that there is a light at the end of the tunnel. Anyone can use their pain to fight for something better.

PROLOGUE

Scott Wallace was a very rare person, about to be shaped by extreme circumstances that would change his life forever.

Prior to this change, he'd been a happy, carefree child. He had lots of friends, two loving parents, a nice house in the countryside and a well-protected schooling environment where all his learning needs could be catered for.

His family weren't particularly well off. His father Sean was a farmer and his mother Mary was a part-time nurse in nearby Aviemore, and they had a few money worries. Their rent was high and demanded weekly by the landlord. Two out of every three weeks it wasn't paid on time.

But any disadvantages were made up for in a very important way. He'd had the room and autonomy to roam the hills and forests that surrounded his Speyside home, in the heart of the Scottish Highlands.

Out of all his assorted interests, this wild space facilitated his dearest: natural history.

Everything, especially birds, but also mammals, reptiles, amphibians, fish, all manner of invertebrates, plants, fungi, history, geology and even astronomy – but generally speaking, everything that was endemic to Earth, Scott loved with a passion.

Nearly every weekend, he wandered the vast forests of Scots pine, in the grand scale of the Scottish landscape – a small remnant of what Scotland used to be. Whilst still considerable in size to someone wandering its length, it had once been a wilderness large enough to be populated by lynxes and wolves and bears and the fearsome Pictish tribes that did battle with the armoured Romans. Whilst those animals and tribes were long gone, and the forest had shrunk to less than five percent of its original cover, Scott enjoyed the best treasures it still retained. Many of which were envied elsewhere.

But Earth's history has taught us many times that peace and tranquillity don't last forever.

At the age of twelve, Scott's world would change completely.

What was this change? Why was it so terrible? How could anything alter the psychological state of someone so rapidly?

Scott lived in a world of his own, wrapping his individuality around him like a cloak. He was happy that way; life was idyllic as far as he was concerned. He had everything he wanted, and the future was bright. How on Earth was he supposed to see it coming?

He woke up at two thirty in the morning, left his room and knocked on his parents' bright-red bedroom door, opening it as quietly as he could. His parents, now vaguely aware they weren't alone, stirred from their sleep and opened their eyes to look at him, standing there in the darkness.

Mary reached for her bedside lamp.

'What is it, Scott?' she asked blearily, wincing from the brightness.

'I'm going out,' he replied. 'I'm going to look for Scottish wildcats.'

'Where are you going for that?'

Scott knew where the place was, but because it had no name, he was unable to make it as clear to them as he'd have liked.

'I have to go deep into the forest,' he said. 'There's a boulder-strewn slope there that I've seen on previous outings. I thought it might be a good bet – they like that kind of habitat. It's quite an open area, so I thought I would have a better chance of seeing one there than anywhere else.'

Mary frowned. Sean, however, seemed more negotiable.

'Just keep your phone on,' he said. 'Just in case we want to ask how you're doing. But otherwise have fun; I hope you see one.'

Scott was aware that having a phone on him that might ring and disturb any wildlife he found might be a handicap, but he accepted the conditions.

'Thank you,' he said. 'I'll aim to come back for nine.'

With that, Scott left them to sleep.

He came down their sole flight of wooden stairs, through the black-tiled kitchen and peach-carpeted living room to the porch. He put on his walking boots, turned the copper door handle and locked the door behind him, compulsively trying the handle at least ten times before he was satisfied it was secure.

He walked along the access track that stretched out from his house. In daylight it was a modest place; a detached building made of granite with four single-glazed windows on each side, screened from the nearby public road towards Aviemore by some thirty-metre-high sycamores. He then climbed over a half-rotted wooden stile into one of his father's grassy fields. Some sheep lifted their heads, watching him with gleaming eyes. Unperturbed, he walked the half kilometre to the other side of the field, climbed over another wooden stile – this one in better nick – and quickly crossed the main road to where the dark forest lay waiting.

He took an overgrown deer path that he'd used many times before, heading uphill into the darkness. The forest was very quiet, the only noise being Scott's footsteps on the soil and leaf litter. The moon blazed overhead and the few stars that Scott could see through the canopy shone like beacons in the night sky. Light pollution was so low that stargazing was a very rich experience here; even the bluish streak of the Milky Way could be seen quite clearly.

Scott continued deep into the heart of the forest. It was now four thirty in the morning and the sun was still to rise. He'd reached the boulder-strewn slope and crouched patiently behind the root plate of a fallen Scots pine, crossing his fingers that the Highlands' rarest denizen would appear. There was no guarantee that it *would* appear of course; wildlife sightings, especially of the rarest of creatures, were unpredictable, and wildcats were notoriously elusive. It was the only creature in his Eden that he'd never seen.

He had his black night scope raised to the boulders; if there was any eye-shine, the night scope would pick it out.

Two and a half hours passed. Nothing appeared. The sun gradually rose, softly illuminating the surrounding forest. A few blackbirds began to warble, announcing the dawning day. A robin whistled softly. Scott craned his head towards the canopy, but they were too high up for him to see.

Suddenly he heard a twig snap. He spun round and held his breath. Something was in the trees about ten feet off the ground.

Scott waited.

Whatever it was descended from a straight-trunked Scots pine and onto the wet mossy boulders. Seeing that it was now light enough to use his spotting scope, Scott carefully put his night scope away and raised the other to his eye.

He gasped. It was a wildcat! He could see its black stripes, grey fur, thick face and brownish lower jaw; the tail looked like a club. Scott counted the bands on it – about three with no stripe down the middle. Scott took particular care to note these features, as Scottish wildcats interbred heavily with domestic cats, diluting the wildcat gene pool and causing them to tiptoe ever closer to extinction. With so many hybrids around these days, finding any that were pure was becoming increasingly difficult, perhaps impossible.

Even though this individual looked very much like the real thing, Scott knew it was impossible to be a hundred percent sure of its purity without a DNA test.

The wildcat stood stock-still, its ears pricked for any suspicious sounds. Once it was satisfied it couldn't detect anything, it crept along the boulders, pausing periodically to sniff for any signs of its prey. Scott's excitement was overwhelming; he was struggling to breathe. He'd spied this place out with his own initiative and he'd scored. Watching the wildcat doing no more than tread across the wet mossy boulders of its Highland home was what Scott lived for.

There was a sudden loud bang from uphill. The wildcat jerked its head and Scott groaned – Bernie MacDonald, his landlord's gamekeeper, was out shooting. He heard more gunshots and even a faint trace of other voices, whooping for joy. Scott had forgotten that today was the twelfth of August, popularly known as the Glorious Twelfth – the start of the grouse-shooting season. There was a grouse moor just over this hill, where his landlord ran a shooting estate, attracting wealthy clients from across Scotland and the world.

The noise made the wildcat scamper away into the undergrowth, never to be seen again. Scott was elated to have seen his first wildcat but annoyed with how the encounter ended. Bernie of course didn't know he'd spoiled something special, and wouldn't have cared even if he had.

Scott got to his feet and walked up the hill towards the moorland, wading through the knee-high stands of rough, brown heather and twisted green bilberry branches, overshadowed by more towering Scots pines. He heard more blackbirds and raised his scope to catch sight of their slender black bodies – their yellow-ringed eyes and bills.

He then saw a robin. It was on a low branch only five metres from him, watching him nonchalantly with its beady black eyes. Scott grinned; it never ceased to amaze him how bold they were. He often saw them in his garden and whenever he wanted to do a party trick for friends and family, he'd tempt one to take a peanut straight from his hand. It made them laugh every time.

He caught the orangey flash of a red squirrel,

scurrying up a tree trunk in its search for pine cones. It disappeared into the canopy and, presumably having not found any to its taste, hopped onto another tree and faded from view.

About an hour later, he reached the top of the hill and came out onto the vast moorland, stretching towards the horizon. He raised his scope. Some red deer were grazing; five stags and six hinds – the largest land animal in Britain, standing at least a metre and a half at the shoulder. They had striking chestnut-orange coats and the stags bore large sets of antlers spanning a metre or two, now covered in velvet which they would shed in two months' time for their autumn rut. The hinds bore no antlers, and were slimmer faced and necked than the males.

He scanned the moorland for anything else of interest but found nothing.

Scott's attention suddenly switched to the sky. Something soared over his head, a raptor of some kind with just short of a half-metre wingspan. Scott took a few seconds to lock onto it. He made out a long dark greyish tail, black barring against a broad white breast, culminating in a thickset head.

'Goshawk,' he said aloud. It was one thing he rarely saw on his travels; only twice before had he seen this elusive and much declining bird of prey, and that last time had been in more or less this same area. Unlike its commoner relative the sparrowhawk, it usually shunned areas close to humans, preferring undisturbed forest (and forest-edge) habitat, hunting small birds and mammals by keeping watch from perches. Once a victim was spotted, it would burst forth to catch them with long sharp talons.

The goshawk was flying away from him and into the distance. Scott wished he'd been able to see its eyes, which would have been a fiery orange surrounding black pupils. On a sparrowhawk the irises were yellow (though juvenile goshawks can have yellow eyes too, only adults have the orange eyes). He watched it go, crossing his fingers that it would choose to circle back round again for another look, but it carried on, without stopping.

There came a loud bang, and to his horror, the goshawk fell. He saw a curly-haired, windswept pied spaniel approach its fallen body. It took it in its jaws and headed back towards some people coming to meet it. Scott raised his scope. At the front of the group was Bernie. With him were five other figures. None seemed to be doing anything to stop him.

This is the last straw, Scott thought angrily. *Bernie's gone too far this time.*

'Bernie!' he shouted.

The burly gamekeeper turned his thickset head. Scott was at least three hundred metres from him, the glare of the sun behind him.

'Who are you?' Bernie shouted throatily.

Scott came closer. He only noticed at that point that everyone in the group was armed with shotguns. Bernie's five clients all looked to be between fifty and sixty years of age, with greying hair, green jackets and tweed trousers. Each wore a bemused expression on their faces.

'What the fuck are you doing disrupting my shoot?' growled Bernie, contorting his thick chubby face.

'You know goshawks are protected, right?' said

Scott accusingly, nodding at the dead raptor he held. The once proud bird's eyes were closed, its neck half twisted from its socket.

'So what?' Bernie scoffed, 'It means more grouse for the rest of us. I hate raptors; I don't know how people can make such a hullaballoo about them. Now fuck off, Scott – don't you do my head in again!'

'You're in big trouble, Bernie,' said Scott. 'When I tell the police what you've done, you're going to jail, and there's no way out this time.'

'Don't you *dare*!' Bernie waved his shotgun at him threateningly.

'See! Pointing a gun at me, how original,' he said sarcastically, 'If you shoot me, good luck hiding the fact!'

One of the clients, a pot-bellied man with a grey beard tried to intervene.

'B-Bernie,' he stammered, 'this is getting out of hand...'

'Shut it!' Bernie shouted.

His clients shrank back. The dog broke into a fit of barking and growling.

Bernie seized Scott by the collar, getting right into his face and baring his cigarette-stained teeth.

'Don't you forget, my boss owns your parents' house. He's been looking for any excuse to get rid of you lot and this could be the perfect opportunity. If you keep your mouth shut, you get to carry on living there, simple as that. Fail to do that and we'll make sure you suffer.'

He batted Scott's shoulder with the muzzle of his shotgun. Scott's courage evaporated.

'OK, please!' he pleaded. 'Let me go! I won't say

anything; just let me go!'

'You're not going to tell a soul, are you?' said Bernie.

Scott's eyes were red with tears. He could only shake his head in a flurry.

'Alright.' Bernie pushed him away and he fell against a mound of heather. 'I don't want to see you here again. If I do, I'll shoot you.' Scott's tears hadn't diffused his anger. 'Now get out!'

Bernie's clients all stared at him as if he were a monster. They had all been nonchalant about the goshawk killing, but threatening a boy was a step too far.

'Come on,' said Bernie, 'let's shoot some more.'

'I think we're good for today,' said the client that had tried to intervene. 'Come on guys, we can try elsewhere.'

Scott, meanwhile, headed back to his house. When he came through the front door two and a half hours later, he slumped onto the beige sofa, burying his head in a silk cushion with a badger sewn on it.

Sean was already at work. Mary was just about to leave for hers when she noticed Scott in this position.

'Scott?' she asked. There was a tremor of anxiety there. 'Are you OK?'

Mary Wallace took twenty minutes to drive from the house to her nursing practice in Aviemore. She hated having to work on a Saturday, but the colleague who usually had this shift was off on maternity leave.

She drove through the town, past a small train

station and a selection of restaurants, outdoor shops and supermarkets before arriving in the small residential area where the practice lay. She walked through the automatic doors, passing the reception and a waiting room, before walking down another corridor towards her office, where she took a few precious minutes to organise herself.

Life here could be very fast. Having a quiet moment to yourself was rare and unpredictable. Apart from a half-hour lunch break, there wasn't much to break up her 9 a.m. to 8 p.m. working day.

There was a knock at the door.

'Come in,' said Mary.

Bernie came in and took a seat opposite her. For the majority of patients, she'd normally have been more welcoming, but even before what had happened with Scott, he wasn't her favourite.

'So, Bernie, what can I do for you today?' she asked with some effort.

'It's my backache,' said Bernie. 'It's been bothering me for the past three weeks.'

'Any ideas what's caused it?' she asked.

'Not a clue.'

'You do quite a lot of heavy lifting, don't you? Do you take regular breaks?'

'Perhaps not.'

'Well that would be something to consider,' she said. Her professionalism was straining.

'Is there anything you can prescribe?' he asked.

'I can prescribe you anti-inflammatories,' she said. 'And just try to take more regular breaks from lifting, and follow the correct lifting procedures. You may just have some ligament damage – nothing that won't heal in time.'

They talked for some time, well over fifteen minutes, thanks to Bernie droning on about his days on the moors and his personal bag record. Mary was summoning her courage. Bernie eventually announced he was leaving. This was her last chance.

'Scott told me everything,' she said, her kind professionalism gone.

'Told you what?' said Bernie, frowning deeply.

'He told me that you killed a goshawk and threatened him. Is that true?'

'That's a lie,' said Bernie. 'I was taking a shooting party onto the moors. I don't know where he made that up from. Your son's always had it in for me.'

'We'll find out the truth,' said Mary. 'Either here or at the station.'

The next day a rumour spread through the community – that her son was a disruptive delinquent; that he needed discipline for interfering with a shoot; that he was a scumbag influenced by dysfunctional family dynamics. It was fuelled by out-of-proportion stories of past disputes the family had had with Bernie's boss.

Their landlord, Gordon Banning, wasn't much kinder than Bernie. He had a cold, industrial demeanour and was known for his parasitic property dealings.

For example, whenever something broke and needed fixing, Gordon didn't lift a finger and insisted that his tenants pay for it themselves – every time. These were habits that drew complaints of negligence, which Gordon grew increasingly tired of. It was unlikely Scott's family were the only tenants to feel this way, but out of fear of losing their homes, they kept silent.

Until the case came to light, Scott had been completely unaware that there were people around who secretly disliked him – and it wasn't just Bernie or Gordon. Other adults whose children attended the same class as him cited his odd, eccentric and sometimes challenging behaviour with their children as being related to some inadequacy of his parenting. In actual fact he had Asperger's syndrome, the very reason he'd been put in that class in the first place.

The community ultimately took Gordon and Bernie's side, intimidation became their weapon of choice and the pressure it created caused Mary to lose her job.

Eventually Scott's family were successful in bringing Bernie and Gordon to court. Bernie was found guilty of the goshawk killing and jailed for two months. It would have been twice that if Gordon hadn't agreed to pay a fine of £2,500.

Gordon's passive complicity over Bernie's actions was lambasted by the judge. But there was no punishment the judge could give Gordon for any of it, and the jury found Gordon not guilty of negligence, a verdict that horrified Scott's family. To Gordon, the trial was a passing annoyance that did nothing to change his demeanour, so there was no real victory for Scott's family.

With a strained reputation and a landlord that no longer wanted them, they were evicted. Unable to find work or housing in the immediate area, they were offered the chance to move in with Scott's aunt and uncle. They lived in Aberdeen, a city on the east coast about three hours' drive away. Scott lost his friends, his Eden, his autonomy and his normality.

The concrete jungle was no place for him; the nature he knew was absent and he wasn't allowed to roam as he once had. They'd move to an area of the city known as Balnagask.

Aberdeen was a city known for its oil industry, an industry that had brought increased prosperity and jobs, but Balnagask was considered a rough part of town, having not benefitted from the boom, and stabbings, drug deals, robberies, burglaries and antisocial behaviour were a weekly – sometimes daily – occurrence.

There was his aunt and uncle (both of whom didn't work due to health problems); two cousins (one worked in the oil industry but the other also didn't work, for reasons unknown); and another unrelated lodger known for his alcoholism and drug dealing.

The rent, which was expensive to begin with, was partly paid by the sole earning cousin, but most of it was paid by their lodger's drug dealing. A means of earning that was only tolerated in case the sole legitimate earner of the family lost their job, which was very possible in the oil industry.

With eight occupants crammed into what was actually a two-bedroom house, six of whom didn't work for one reason or another, Scott found it almost unbearable. He had to sleep on a urine-stained mattress next to the lodger and share the bed space with his empty beer cans, needles and packets of heroin, cocaine and marijuana – the latter of which would be smoked well into the night. Let's not forget the 9mm pistol he kept under his pillow that Scott had sometimes seen stowed in the back of his trousers.

Scott barely slept a wink in that place, not just because of the smoke or the fear of being shot; he was terrified that, given the lodger's connections, the flat would be burgled. And on one occasion that was exactly what happened, the perpetrator fleeing with some cash and a desktop computer belonging to the lodger.

This made him lethargic, anxious and angry, and it spilled over into his school life. To Scott, school was the definition of hell. With no support for his learning needs, he was thrust into mainstream secondary school without consultation or, it seemed, any concern for his well-being. Despite its reputation, the family consoled themselves with the logic that he was older and therefore ready to be given the same chance as his peers – that he would manage this change and be successful and so, however stressful, it would be best in the long run. But this new environment was very different.

The care and protection that he'd known before was gone. And with that, the happiness, social life and all the things young people took for granted had also vanished.

Then there was the workload – it seemed so technical and so unachievable that he wondered how he could even learn anything. But the most terrible change was just how different the people were in this mainstream environment: the other students *and* the teachers. He didn't connect well with the other students at all; none of them were like the friends he'd once had. Most of them ignored him, and he didn't really care, but at least ten of them had a very different use for him.

This particular Monday began just like any other: he'd come in at 9 a.m., sat through ten minutes of registration, then fifty-five minutes of maths – which he hated, not just because he had difficulty with the subject, but the teacher, Mr Barnsley, berated him for it and his punishment was double homework in long division, to help him 'get the picture'. The next lesson was English – not much better.

He got a roasting for that one too, simply because his maths class had been made to stay behind after the bell went. Mr Barnsley had insisted on giving a disparaging speech on how pathetic everyone was for a full five minutes before letting them out.

After English, there was a fifteen-minute interval, then fifty-five minutes of German and forty-five minutes of science.

Then the lunch hour came, something Scott looked forward to more than anything else in the school day. Afterwards he'd only have fifty-five minutes of geography and forty-five minutes of history to go, which wasn't too bad – these subjects, at least, he found interesting.

After science had ended, he'd descended a flight of stairs from the school's tower block to the main entrance hall, then headed through another corridor past the toilet blocks, which took him to an exit to the courtyard playground. Most pupils would be in the cafeteria by now, or taking to the streets to buy something from the shops or at least socialising in the social room.

Scott, however, had a particular bench he liked to sit on, a brown oblong structure that was in desperate need of a new paint job. Like many things in the school, it was falling apart; despite the oil money, public schools right in the heart of the inner city somehow missed out.

'Oi, Scotty boy!'

Scott turned, his mouth still chewing over part of his cheese sandwich.

Ten boys had appeared, each wearing casual clothes that went totally against the school's uniform policy, which said that all students must wear either a black or a grey jumper (preferably the school's black one), with a white polo shirt underneath, black or grey trousers (again preferably the school's black ones) and black or grey shoes. Each of these boys wore red jumpers instead, complimenting a rebellious palette of tattered blue jeans and white football boots.

It was Blake Mitchell that had shouted. Scott didn't know the names of the other nine boys, but they followed Blake obsequiously, as if they were his loyal servants.

'What you deein' by yourself, eh?' he taunted, sniggering to his pals.

Scott ignored him.

'I said, what you deein' by yourself?' Blake asked, offended.

'Just having lunch,' said Scott irritably. 'Can you leave me alone?'

Blake seized his open lunch box and the banana, crisps, chocolate bar and two orange juice cartons fell onto the concrete. He stepped on one of the cartons, showering Scott's trousers with juice.

'Whoops,' said Blake, tossing the lunch box over his shoulder.

Scott was bewildered. His eyes filled with tears.

'Aww, you gonna cry, Scottie?' said Blake, seizing him by the jumper and pushing him back onto the bench. Scott cried out in pain.

'You gonna *cry*, Scottie?' said Blake, shoving him again. This time Scott fell on the ground. More laughter. Blake checked his surroundings, looking up around the school walls for cameras. He found none.

'Now for the best bit,' said Blake and kicked Scott in the groin.

Scott howled in pain, curling up in a foetal position.

'What are you waiting for, lads?' said Blake.

Scott was struck from all sides, tightening his foetal position harder each time. The boys were having great fun, made better by some of the most popular girls turning up, including one that Scott fancied, each breaking into whoops of laughter.

Scott didn't move. Blake got on top of him and drew a kitchen knife from his belt. 'Keep watching, girls – I'm gonna take a sample of him,' he said.

Scott rose up and sank his teeth into Blake's hand, and Blake cried out in pain. Scott kicked him then quickly scrambled to his feet, jostled through the wall of boys and ran.

Blake and his friends were soon in swift pursuit, but Scott was so badly hurt, his stamina failed him.

'Thought you could bite me, did you?' snarled Blake. He seized Scott's shoulder and stabbed him in the back. Scott screamed and fell to the ground, unable to move and bleeding all over.

Blake stood there for a moment, stunned at what he'd just done, but he recovered swiftly.

'Next time you're getting a shooting!' he shouted. He and his mates ran off. The girls joined them.

A pool of blood surrounded Scott. He screamed for help for what seemed like an eternity. Then he blacked out.

The next thing he knew he was in a hospital bed in the dark with Mary sound asleep nearby. He took three weeks to recover. His parents were furious. Despite their pleas, Blake and his pals were never punished.

Scott's teachers were unsympathetic. Mr Barnsley insisted that Scott was making up the allegations against Blake, and Blake was allowed to continue his studies – not that he did much studying. That was the end of it. Mr Barnsley then asked Scott to not cause a fuss again; it was bad for the school's reputation apparently.

The injustice was overwhelming. Scott felt that the school system was the biggest bully of all, and it took over a year for his parents and a psychiatrist to talk him out of staging a school massacre.

So Scott decided to deal with his feelings a different way. Over the next three years he learned karate, fencing, archery and even the use of firearms, through a local rifle club on the outskirts of the city where he shot at paper targets from half a kilometre away.

By now his childlike innocence had all but gone, replaced with a new adult extremity. By now he felt ready for a war. Yet apart from that one incident with Blake, he never hurt anyone. Even with all those skills he never even attempted what he'd initially threatened. What got him through such tough times was knowing he had the tools to tip the balance at any time.

Then when the chance came, he made the most

important discovery he'd ever made. Scott had found a new Eden of sorts, more urban, but it had wildlife of its own that he wouldn't have had on his Highland doorstep.

One Saturday morning Scott decided to sneak off to the coast. He discreetly left the apartment whilst everyone slept, walked past a row of tenement blocks, each with cars parked outside the various doors, past his school and up another row of tenement blocks sloping uphill.

Then he passed the police station with its brick walls and blue and white pendent sign – *the fat lot of good it was*, he thought bitterly.

The slope flattened out and he passed more houses until he reached the edge of a huge green park studded with trees and marshes, with an area of wood chippings, containing the chutes, swings, see-saws and climbing frames that entertained the city's screaming children.

He came to a steep cliff with an old red foghorn perched at the top. At the bottom of this stone-studded clay cliff was an abandoned boathouse, about the size of a small warehouse.

Beyond that was a jagged rocky shore, studded with dull white barnacles. Roosting there were turnstones, plump, little waders known for their habit of shifting stones whilst foraging. There were also redshanks – greyish brown waders with long orange legs – and next to them the larger, cryptically coloured curlews, brown feathered with black spots, bearing their long scythed bills.

Next to the curlews were purple sandpipers – greyish purple waders the size of sparrows, bearing short curved bills, dull orange in colour. Each species sat there, huddled together on the rocky shore, somehow tolerating the monotonous splash of the surf.

Scott panned his scope to the right of them. He came across a small rocky island, black and bare of barnacles with numerous herring gulls – large grey-backed birds whose screams culminated into a seven-noted laugh.

Four cormorants sat at the top of the rocky island – large glossy black birds with thick, hooked bills, which were a dull grey, surrounded by yellow facial skin. One was a juvenile, similar to the adults with a white belly surrounded by brown plumage.

Scott scanned the light swells of the sea. What he was after was something more unpredictable, yet Torry Battery was one of the best areas for them in the whole of Scotland, if not the world. He couldn't see any yet. But with the fine July weather in full swing, seabirds were an abundant alternative.

Fulmars were everywhere, soaring the waves with their metre-wide wingspans. They looked gull-like in colour and appearance: white headed, white bellied, their grey backs mottled white. Their bills bore tubed structures, designed to smell food from miles away, a feature that related them more to albatrosses than gulls. The name fulmar was a Norse word meaning 'fowl gull'. It was well named. They had a habit of spitting oily fluid at anything that got too close to their nests.

Taxonomically speaking they weren't gulls. No, Fulmars were a kind of petrel, a name given to small to medium-sized birds with that kind of bill.

Scott noted the gannets, large seabirds of pure white upper parts, whiter even than the herring gulls nearby. Their wingtips were black and pointed. Their heads, which were harder to see from several kilometres away, were yellow and their bills were long and tapered. Scott followed their flights, watching them fold their wings and dive into the water like missiles. A few seconds later they'd pop up like a cork, sometimes sitting for a while before taking off with a pitter-patter of black webbed feet. They'd be after mackerel or similarly sized fish. They'd take their catch back to Troup Head, the sole mainland colony in Britain 40 miles to the north, or to the world's largest colony at the Bass Rock, 76 miles to the south.

Greater black-backed gulls, mixtures of black-backed adults and last year's browner youngsters roamed with the smaller herring gulls and the even smaller black-headed gulls (this species was not black headed at all but brown headed and was much daintier in its proportions).

Scott saw a long line of birds flying together and identified them as guillemots, pigeon-sized birds that looked black and white from this distance (more brown and white up close), with long bills and protruding feet. Often dubbed the penguins of the north, they were actually members of the auk family, the same family that puffins belonged to, and like their more colourful relative, these birds could fly underwater, for the shoals of silvery sand eels and sprat they favoured.

Scott saw a movement, a slight break in the low waves that looked unnatural. He watched the area closely, wary that it could just be a trick of the waves. Then it happened again, and soon the water foamed with activity. Five fins now pierced the surface, then went under.

For Scott this meant mission accomplished. They were bottlenose dolphins, but not just any bottlenose dolphins. These dolphins, found mainly on the northeast coast of Scotland, could grow to four metres long, twice the size of the ones from warmer climes, and were darker skinned.

They surfaced again, closer to shore this time. Then one of them breached high into the air, showing its whole body from beak to tail. Scott raced down a steep track to catch up with them.

The individuals in this pod seemed to be mostly adults, but Scott thought he could see a smaller, paler calf amongst them. From the few glimpses he managed, he could make out pale lines around its body, foetal folds for when it was compressed inside its mother's womb. It must have only been months old at most.

The dolphins continued on towards the harbour, Scott running to catch up – until he collided with something, or rather someone. The man was dressed in a blue boiler suit with a white hard hat and thick heavy-duty boots. He raised a dirty-gloved hand to stop Scott going any further.

'You can't go this way son,' he said.

'Why?' Scott asked. He tried to peer over the technician's shoulder and caught a glimpse of a large grey object. It was being taped off by some policemen.

'What is that?' Scott asked, straining to get a proper look.

'We don't know,' said the technician. 'I found it this morning. The police are taking precautions just in case. It's not a bomb, in case you're wondering; bomb disposal have been able to confirm that at least. I've no idea what it is, but whatever it is it's too big for us to move.'

Word quickly spread, crowds began to gather outside the cordon and the police were kept busy holding them back. As the day wore on, it was announced that the object would be airlifted the following day to a secure location. Where that was they wouldn't say. The nearest helicopter for the job was on the other side of the country.

When night fell, a violent storm erupted, the rain and force-nine wind lashing at the cordon. A lone policeman stood before it, his back to the rocky shore, cloaked in his reflective jacket, his pied policeman's hat wrapped in a clear waterproof cover. His radio crackled into life.

'Sergeant Murray, do you read me, over?'

'Go ahead, sir, over,' he replied.

'The weather is taking a serious turn for the worse,' said the commissioner. 'It's not forecast to get any better until morning. I'm authorising you to stand down, over.'

'Is anyone else coming to keep watch, over?' asked Sergeant Murray.

'Negative,' said the commissioner. 'It's too dangerous – the wind is getting stronger. People get blown off their feet in conditions like this. Stand down now. That's an order, over.'

'But it will be unguarded, over,' said Sergeant Murray.

'There's nothing we can do about that,' said the commissioner. 'Consider the situation, Sergeant – it's dark and the weather is stormy. I think it's very unlikely someone will come along and tamper with it, and no one has been able to open it – if indeed it can be opened. We'll find out its secrets in due course, over.'

Sergeant Murray grimaced, taking a look around for any signs he wasn't alone. He saw the sea, whipped up by the wind into a foamed frenzy. The waves splashed the rocky shoreline, spraying water wide across the grassy path. He looked towards the cliffs covered in tussocks of grass and gorse. They towered black above him. The rain hit him in the eyes. He sighed.

'Understood,' he said.

'Very good,' said the commissioner. 'Don't worry, Sergeant; there's nothing more you can do. Go home and see your family or join us at the pub for a pint. Up to you, just stand down, over.'

'Alright, sir,' said Sergeant Murray. 'Leaving now, out.'

Sergeant Murray walked up the cliffside path, then along the paved road where his yellow-and-blue panda car was waiting. It glistened, even in this light. Professional and conscientious, as all good cops should be, he took one last long look around before driving back into town.

Scott peered up from the gorse bushes. He'd snuck out after everyone had gone to sleep. There was every risk someone would wake up and notice he was missing – they could already be looking for him now – so he would have to act fast, investigate this object and get out.

Scott grimaced as the gorse spines scraped his clothes and emerged from the bush noisily, taking a few seconds to dust himself off. He felt nervous. The place was deserted. If he was caught, he had no idea what would happen, and the thought of getting into trouble terrified him to his core – yet not enough to dissuade him from his course.

The object was only about forty yards away, but every step felt like a mile.

It made no sense. Why did this thing have to be guarded at all? Why were such lengths being taken to get it away as fast as possible? Was it dangerous? Was it some top-secret government technology? Did someone high in authority know something everyone else didn't?

When Scott was within touching distance, he took one last look around, then turned to the object. It was about the size of a car, grey and almost egg shaped.

Scott touched it, enjoying the smooth texture of the metal, then jumped as the object gave a soft hum, green lights flashed and, with a hiss, a panelled door slid open.

Scott couldn't believe it; the excitement was overwhelming.

He took another look towards the cliff and peered inside. It was very cramped and dark, with only a small green light in the far corner. He reached inside and his fingers brushed against something. He thought it was a wall. Then it shifted slightly, bumping against him. Scott frowned.

With an unseeing hand, he grasped something thin and metal. It felt like a handle, and Scott pulled it towards him. It was a cuboid metal box, plain grey, no bigger than a briefcase. There was a black button on the front that Scott pressed. With a hum and a hiss, it slid open. Scott was totally engrossed – he forgot about the rain and the wind; he forgot about the risk of being caught; he forgot about his family still sleeping in the flat.

He pulled out something – a slightly smaller box. When he opened it, he found an assortment of mechanical parts, none of which he could recognise.

Next to it was a leathery bag, no bigger than his school bag, and a helmet, about the size of a cyclist's, with some wide clear goggles. He put them to one side and felt around the bag for a zip. But he couldn't find one; he could only feel two holes from either side, and inside those, the texture of leather and metal.

The helmet suddenly glowed red. Scott was so taken by surprise he let go of the bag. The red light went off.

'What on Earth was that?' said Scott to himself.

He put the helmet on, wondering what had made it glow. He heard buzzing, like an electrical current, then the bag began to vibrate, and from those holes two scythe-shaped objects protruded, spanning two metres. They looked like— no – surely he had to be imagining things.

Scott had no idea at that point what he'd found, but he wanted to keep it and speak of it to no one. He would take it home and keep it safe, and investigate later. He closed the door of the object and, under the dead of night, smuggled this mysterious thing back to the flat. He had no idea how he was going to keep it hidden, but he would find a way.

Little did he know, this was the start of many great

things to come.

CHAPTER 1
Miami

One year had passed since that life-changing day in Torry Battery, and for the first time ever Scott Wallace was going abroad.

The family had won a competition hosted by a local travel agent. All they'd had to do was correctly answer a single question: which of these cities lies closest to the Everglades: A, Tallahassee, B, Orlando, or C. Miami. The lucky winner would be drawn at random and win an all-expenses-paid trip to Miami, including flights, accommodation, rental car and spending money. Thousands must have already entered and Scott hadn't seriously been expecting to win. So when they did win, it was a great cause for celebration.

On top of that the school holidays had started twenty days earlier than usual. Whatever the reason for this early start, Scott welcomed it with open arms.

They'd set off early in the morning, flying from Aberdeen to Amsterdam, and from Amsterdam they were in the air again heading towards the city of Miami.

He'd sat in his economy seat, gazing out of his circular window over the vastness of the Atlantic Ocean, lying in what could only be described as an incredible state of calm. It was a chance to get away from it all, both home and school.

His expectations were humble and modest: a fabulous trip with wildlife to watch, a new place to explore and an escape from the stresses of life. No school, no lessons, no homework and no bullies.

When they landed, it was straight to immigration, baggage collection and outside. From the moment he stepped into the open air, the difference between the climate here and at home became clear, the warm air spiced with humidity. He looked to the right: there were palm trees everywhere, decorating the road margins. They were coconut palms, a species that was, ironically, not native to most places it was found in, including here. In actual fact they came from the Indo-Pacific.

He looked left. The full moon illuminated the grassy runway, and the skyscraper lights shone like Christmas lights against the horizon. He'd only been in Miami for half an hour yet he'd already fallen under its spell. He wanted to get out there to the swamps, to the scrub, to the sea, to the reefs – everywhere that was wild.

After locating their hire car, they made their way to their holiday house, which took some time because of the traffic, darkness and unfamiliarity of this colossal city. Scott was tired but excited. He wanted the night to pass as quickly as possible, for morning to come and for his first adventure in the New World to begin.

After two hours they arrived at their white bungalow, at about 1 a.m. It was spacious, with a massive garage, a floodlit private swimming pool and a garden with thick green grass – kept that way by a sprinkler.

Scott quickly chose a master bedroom with big double-glazed windows overlooking the spiky lawn and the wild bushes beyond. His bed was so huge, you could have fitted two or three people into it – not that he had any siblings to share it with. The en-suite bathroom had a shower, toilet, sink and small jacuzzi with some tiled steps leading into it. He took a few minutes to examine them all, before he climbed into bed and slept like a log.

Never before had he slept as deeply as this. Usually his slumber was full of troubled thoughts and worries of schoolwork, bullies, teachers and romances that had failed to blossom, but not tonight. Tonight they were full of excitement and curiosity at the innumerable adventures that could be had within the coming month.

But there was something else about this place that made him wonder.

Although they were in the wrong place for Disney World, some 150 miles up the Turnpike, Miami looked like a magical kingdom. One with so many secrets and possibilities that just about any dream you wanted could come true.

Scott's dreams were big and ambitious; was it possible that they too could come true right here? In all likelihood, probably not. But fate and destiny are as extraordinary as they are unpredictable. Was it possible, *just possible*, that this time, they would?

CHAPTER 2
A Chance Encounter

His first day in paradise. Scott knew exactly what he wanted to do with it. His parents had opted to do something else that day, a shopping trip and then a trip to the beach. They wanted to go sunbathing. They had little interest in nature.

His parents weren't keen on Scott being alone, certainly not in a strange place, but Scott was fearsomely stubborn. So after some rather heated, nervous negotiations he was left alone. He didn't really have a plan as such, other than to wander the suburbs, looking for birds.

After they'd left, Scott left the villa and stepped out into the Floridian sunshine. Within seconds he heard the rattling *'pipirre'* of a grey kingbird. What a sight it was, like a kingfisher on steroids. It was about the size of a crow, with a grey back, white underbelly and a thick long bill that seemed almost cavernous – an adaptation to catch insects in the air.

It sat there on the wire, making tiny swivelling gestures with its head. The sight of a butterfly grabbed its attention and it took off to pursue it. As Scott followed its swooping flight, he noticed to his astonishment a path leading into some woodland scrub. It took him so much by surprise that he forgot all about the kingbird and its pursuit of that butterfly.

He blinked, then looked along the edge of it, left and right. Was it just a piece of undeveloped waste ground that nature had claimed for itself? It looked deceptively small, but how small?

He noticed an interpretation sign, set into a concrete block. The interpretation board was itself photogenic, with only white filling in the gaps between pictures and drawings.

'The Sea Marshes Reserve,' Scott read aloud. 'Managed by the US Fish and Wildlife Service for the benefit of the flora and fauna of this rare remnant of coastal scrub and reed beds – home to a variety of waterbirds such as great blue, little blue, green and tricoloured herons—'

He stopped reading, distractedly casting his eye towards a drawing of a green heron fishing in its watery world, with a hand-drawn wetland backdrop. Next to it were drawings of alligators, red-eared slider terrapins and many more creatures.

Scott was madly into wetlands, third only to the sea and forests. There was something about them that made his heart race. Perhaps it was the prospect of seeing something elusive that always tempted him towards them. He didn't have very many at home, and those he did were of varying quality. This was Florida after all – there was probably going to be something worth seeing here.

Scott couldn't resist following the trail. You could almost call it a rainforest: lizards and colourful beetles scuttled and crawled across the leaf-strewn trail; some frogs croaked and hopped through the foliage. He couldn't assign a species name to any of them.

Birds seemed absent at first, but he quickly came across his first along the trail – an eastern towhee. A small sparrow-sized bird with a black head, beaded red eyes and a white and orange breast, it didn't stay long, flitting away into the bushes, but it would mark the start of so many new things. These were fairly common in this part of the world but unusual by his standards.

Suddenly indigo and painted buntings appeared, darting in and out of the bushes. Both no bigger than the towhee, the indigo buntings were a deep bluish purple all over, whilst the painted buntings really were painted – each with palettes of blue backs, green breasts and red bellies. Two individuals within the flock had more or less the same colours but were duller. They were youngsters.

Some northern cardinals could be seen whistling in the canopy, birds that were bright red all over except for a patch of black near their conical bills. Now birds were all over the place, and his identification skills were really being tested. Scott didn't know American birds nearly as well as European ones, but then that was always the joy of a challenge – identifying things he didn't recognise and adding to them to an ever-increasing list.

The trail and the bushes ended abruptly, and up ahead there was a boardwalk leading across marshes and tree-tall reeds. Strange sounds were coming from them, and wild with curiosity, Scott ran on.

He saw someone up ahead with a pair of binoculars trained on some anhingas – long-necked, black cormorant-shaped birds nearly a metre long, with sharp, dagger-like bills.

Scott approached quietly; the anhingas stayed

where they were, sunning themselves, splaying their wet wings to dry. The birdwatcher casually turned their head to the left and jumped upon seeing him.

Scott jumped too, less severely, but chivalry replaced his fright. The anhingas took flight, uttering calls akin to a comb being crinkled. Scott felt bad.

'I'm sorry,' he said, 'I didn't mean to scare them away.'

'It's OK.'

He stared. She looked no older than his fifteen year old self, and he judged her to be incredibly beautiful, with silky blonde hair that fell to her shoulders, rounded cheeks on a face that glowed with sunlit radiance, a full mouth and wide sparkling blue eyes. She was slim and athletic-looking, wearing a thin black-bordered blue thermal that tightly defined her arms, legs and torso. She smiled.

For the first few seconds Scott was too stunned to smile back, and when he did he came out of his trance.

There was a delicate, awkward silence. Her smile shortened, and her eyes were wide with a nervous niceness, as if trying her hardest to be polite whilst being lost for words.

'I'm Scott by the way – Scott Wallace,' he said at last.

'My name's Sophie,' she said offering a handshake. 'Sophie Patterson.'

He smiled. He was terrible with eye contact, only managing to look at her forehead, a habit that he'd learned over the years to facilitate any kind of conversation.

He tried to find something else to say. He was starting to hyperventilate.

'So do you...?' he hesitated. 'Do you come here often?'

'Every chance I get. I just love this place. Nature in general is what I like best. It sets me apart from others at school. It's an in-service day today, so I thought why not come and do what I like best?'

Scott frowned, not sure what else to say, and there was another awkward pause. Luckily he didn't have to break it.

'Are you from around here?' she asked. 'I don't think I've seen you at school.'

'I come from Scotland,' said Scott. 'I'm here on a vacation with my family.' He took care to use the Americanism.

'Great,' she said. 'How long are you staying for?'

'Most of the summer holidays – at least a month.'

'Where are you staying?'

'At 22 Fisher Street.'

'That's not far from me; I live at 29 Fisher Street.'

'Wow.' Scott's enthusiasm skyrocketed.

'So is there anything you're looking for in particular?' she asked. 'We've got white ibises, great blue herons, tricoloured herons, soras, Virginia rails, even a few king rails.'

The weight of her knowledge fell on him like a tonne of bricks.

'Would it be OK if... um... Can I... join you?' he asked nervously.

'Um...' She thought about it for a moment. 'Sure.' She grinned.

'Excellent.'

Scott had never had companionship like this before, not even in his happier era in the Highlands. He'd almost always birded alone. His parents had accompanied him once or twice, but even then they'd never really paid much attention. Discovering this attractive girl here was probably his best find, more than all the wildlife here combined.

'See that big bird flapping its wings?' said Sophie.

'He's hunting.'

'Hunting?' asked Scott.

To him it looked as though this large heron-shaped bird was merely stretching its wings and prancing through the shallows, but then its bill pierced the water, quick as a heartbeat. Scott didn't even see the little fish – it had already been swallowed.

'Reddish egrets hunt by dancing,' she explained. 'It scares the fish from their hiding places and into the open.'

The reddish egret was indeed reddish, at least down to its neck, where the red gave way to a body of purplish grey. With its two-toned bill, it struck the water again – this time it caught a large eel which it struggled to swallow.

Sophie laughed. To the egret, the eel must have been a cumbersome catch. It seemed to have trouble even holding it, let alone swivelling it into a better position for swallowing. This carried on for some time until the egret juggled it into just the right direction, then slowly began to swallow it.

Scott looked on, crossing his fingers. The egret's throat bulged enormously, so much so it nearly spat the eel out. It paused for a few seconds, catching its breath. Another juggle. Down went the tail. The egret's expression became rather goggle eyed, the look of someone experiencing indigestion.

'My anhingas are back,' said Sophie.

The same birds that Scott had disturbed earlier were perched on a mangrove bush. They spread their wings, shook them slightly and presented them to the Floridian sun.

Scott gaped in amazement. Their prehistoric proportions made him picture archaeopteryxes, one of the first dinosaurs to grow feathers. In fact all birds were living dinosaurs, but these anhingas seemed to pay homage to that fact better than most.

'Oh, there's some ospreys in the sky,' said Sophie, raising her binoculars.

'There's what?' said Scott. He'd heard her fine; he just couldn't believe it.

Scott hadn't known they existed in this part of the world. He'd known some breeding pairs in the Highlands, spending hours watching the parents come and go from their massive nests, raising their chicks on a diet of brown trout. They were a rare bird at home, and seasonal, but here they were not only common, they were abundant. Scott counted at least fifty of the large brown and white raptors circling the blue sky. Some were hovering. It made Scott wonder...

'Is there another lake out there or something?' he asked. The ospreys would only hover whenever they were hunting for fish.

'The estuary itself is out there,' she said, 'but I want to stay for a little longer. There's more here that I'd like to show you.'

She trained her binoculars on a patch of reed beds adjacent to the mangroves. On the muddy banks she spied some of the reserve's most exciting inhabitants.

'I see five rail species over here, Scott,' she said.

'Five?'

Scott was used to seeing two, maybe three at most, but that was a rare treat. Scott raised his binoculars to the muddy bank and was instantly enthralled. First there were the crow-sized common gallinules. They reminded Scott of the moorhens he knew at home, only these were slimmer bodied with more elongated red bills, tipped yellow.

He noticed some coots dabbling in the water – greyish black birds with white bills, similarly sized to the common gallinules, though as far as coots went, these seemed smaller than the European ones at home, with red knobs on their foreheads and streaks through their mandible tips.

'Do you see the American coots?' she asked.

'Oh yes,' said Scott. He didn't know there were any coots on this side of the Atlantic. He noticed others that were less familiar.

'What about these ones?' he asked. 'Just in front of this common gallinule?'

These two were smaller than the rest, no bigger than tennis balls. One of them had a grey breast, barred belly and a brown back, fringed with white feathers. The brown extended onto the forehead, which led to a black face and a yellow cone-shaped bill. The one next to it was about the same shape but seemed browner, lacking the bold colours of the other.

'Soras,' said Sophie. 'An adult and a juvenile together.'

They probed the mud for anything edible, the adult managing to catch a small crayfish, the juvenile catching nothing.

'What about the other two?' asked Scott. 'You said

there were five.'

'They're side by side,' said Sophie. 'Do you see? Further to the right from the soras. There's a bend in the shore and on that finger of land, that's where they are.'

Scott soon found the location.

'Do you recognise any of them?' she asked.

Scott considered, some nearby common gallinules giving him an idea of scale. Both were slightly smaller but patterned completely differently. Scott shook his head.

'This one with the grey cheeks, brown breast and black barring on its back, that's a Virginia rail,' she explained.

'Right,' said Scott, intrigued. That was another thing he'd never heard of until today.

'The taller, thinner, more reddish one next to it, that's a king rail.'

Scott felt an overwhelming urge to hug her.

Both rails were probing the mud quite contently, seemingly oblivious to their presence. Many rail species were particularly shy and quick to disappear when humans were near, but the distance between them was just about right and they enjoyed incredible views of these denizens of the reed bed.

When they'd disappeared back into cover, Sophie signalled that it was time to move on, that the best of this pool had already been had.

They followed the walkway further, and as they did so, the reeds grew sparser, and a nice pool of water opened up, teeming with great blue herons – large metre-high birds with deep blue backs, black-and-white heads and reddish bellies. There were tricoloured herons – with their namesake trio of slate-blue backs, white bellies and yellow legs and bills – and miniature green herons – with backs of frosted green, green crowns that gave way to purplish red breasts and orange legs. All were wading in the shallow water alongside masses of egrets, ibises and wildfowl.

Scott searched for as many species as he could and counted at least twenty in this one pool. He'd tried to keep his expectations modest, especially on his first day, but they'd been exceeded already.

Then they reached the estuary where a wooden platform marked the end of the route. Now Scott could see why the ospreys had gathered here – the estuary waters were rippling, and many a time the ospreys were successful in catching fish. Beyond the estuary was a fierce, pounding surf zone and beyond that the Atlantic itself.

'Unbelievable,' said Scott, after it had all sunk in.

Sophie turned. 'I feel that way every time I come here,' she said, 'ever since I was small.' She sighed. 'But they're going to demolish it,' she said suddenly.

'Who is?'

'Richard Kennedy,' said Sophie.

The name meant nothing to Scott. 'Who's that?'

'A real-estate tycoon.'

Scott was bewildered. 'Why?'

'He wants to build a luxury mansion, privatise the nearby beach and build some resort facilities for himself and some VIPs.'

'VIPs?'

'I don't know who.'

Scott sighed.

'He used to work with my father in the police,' said Sophie, 'but last year he went into real estate. All because he wasn't being paid enough apparently. He's been unsuccessful in a handful of other places he's tried closer to the city, and now he's triumphed in what's supposed to be a nature reserve.'

'I'm so sorry.'

Scott had been forcibly removed from his Eden before, but at least it had never been threatened with demolition.

'If he has his way, these reed beds will be drained, the mangroves destroyed and it'll become just another place crowded with people who couldn't care less about wild spaces. It's the only remnant left today, at least locally. They say there's nothing rare here – surveys have been done – and sure, that may be true, but it was valuable to me and to the community. A green space in the city – that's rare enough, don't you think?'

Scott nodded. He knew he had to do something. He knew that if he didn't, he would never see her again and nothing would develop.

Scott swallowed nervously. 'Do you like cruises?'

Suddenly he felt trapped by his obligation and realised he hadn't thought this through. He hadn't been here twenty-four hours and didn't know his way around or where or what places of interest existed. But surely cruises had to exist here – it *was* the tropics after all. It was the only wildlife experience Scott could think of to both demonstrate his own enthusiasm (since the marine environment was one of his favourite things) and to give her a chance to be somewhere she wouldn't normally be. He didn't even know how much it would cost and he didn't get a lot of spending money. He'd only just met this girl. Was it too much too quick?

Sophie turned. 'Very much,' she said.

He began to hyperventilate again.

'Were you thinking of taking me on one?'

The adrenaline rush was so huge, he could only manage a painful nod, so pitiful it looked like the gesture of a dog awaiting punishment. Scott had dreaded this moment. It was all or nothing and past experience told him with an air of fear that it would be the latter.

Sophie looked thoughtful for a moment. *This was it*, he thought – she'd guessed what his intentions were. Just say the N-word and he'd be running home in tears, throwing himself into his room and never wanting to see her again.

'I like the sound of it,' she said. 'I could do with a break from schoolwork anyway.'

Scott's negative bubble burst.

'What did you say?' he asked breathlessly. He'd heard her perfectly fine; he just couldn't believe it.

'I said I like the sound of it,' she repeated and frowned. 'Did you think I wouldn't want to?'

'Well yeah,' said Scott sheepishly. He was so flustered that he couldn't keep the silence. 'I know this is a bit random but—'

'It's OK,' she interrupted him, 'I'd love to. I don't get to do it very often, especially with a fellow enthusiast.'

Scott knew the answer by now, but paranoia wanted him to be sure.

'So you'll come?' he asked.

'Definitely,' she replied.

'When are you free?'

'Let's see. I've got something on tomorrow; that's no good. So that leaves Saturday. How about that?'

'Sure,' said Scott. Though he actually *wasn't* sure.

Today was Thursday and he would have only a couple of days to prepare. He didn't even know where to start. Already he was making plans and promises that he was uncertain he could deliver on.

They came out of this Eden and onto the street, where he told Sophie he was going to do a little bit more exploring.

'I guess I'll see you then,' she said. 'You know where to go?'

'Yes,' he replied. If she meant her address then he was telling the truth; for the cruise port itself he was lying. She didn't seem to notice; instead, she beamed at him again.

'See you later, Scott.'

'Bye.'

Then she was off, her blonde hair glistening in the sunshine. There was an elegance and beauty to her walk that captivated him, and Scott just stood where he was, watching every step. A feeling of longing was rising in his stomach, an impatience for the cruise to come and for everything to be OK.

As if on impulse, Sophie stopped and looked behind her, and saw that he was still there. Before, he'd experienced girls who'd misinterpreted this behaviour as something predatory, but Sophie somehow seemed to know better. She flashed him another farewell grin and gave him one last wave. Shyly Scott waved back. Then she disappeared around the block.

OK, you've done enough, Scott, he thought. *Let's leave it for now.*

He felt triumphant but also overwhelmed at the great ambition he'd created in the past few minutes. The first thing he had to do was organise it. But how?

He wandered around for a while longer, gathering up all the leaflets he could find, then returned home and ploughed through them all. There were a myriad of attractions around here: the Miami Sea Aquarium, Merritt Island National Wildlife Refuge, Cape Canaveral, Cocoa Beach. Then he found it: Miami Day Cruises Ltd. 'Come and enjoy a spectacular day with us at Miami Day Cruises. Venture out to sea in perfect comfort, with a pool, sun lounge, bingo and so much more.' Not that that interested him. 'Stop at Cutlass Reef and snorkel its crystal-clear waters, complete with coral reefs and tropical fish. Watch green turtles as they cruise by, but don't forget to look out for dolphins and, occasionally, whales. Only $90 a ticket per person – come and join us now.'

Scott was thrilled until he read the cost. He simply didn't have that kind of money, and as a tourist he wouldn't be allowed to work. He considered asking his parents for the money, but it would involve telling them his plan. It was an insurmountable obstacle and a complete disaster. How was he supposed to tell Sophie – undoubtedly the most beautiful and like-minded girl he'd ever met – that he couldn't deliver? Scott had never dated a girl in his life; he barely had any experience, and the little experience he did have had been awful. He'd either been rejected or laughed off every time. But now was his chance to change that.

A thought came to him as he stood there, and he wandered into his parents' room, where he spotted a white chest of drawers backed up against a white wall. He rummaged through it and soon found several ten-dollar bills. He counted it out – $200 in total, though he only needed $180.

Scott leaped with joy. Yet as he held the green bills in his hands, he felt troubled. They were his parents and they loved him very much, but they would be so annoyed with him.

CHAPTER 3
The In-Laws

Scott made good use of the intervening time. He did some more birding in the Sea Marshes Reserve, visiting the spot he'd been to with Sophie in the morning, then taking a different path in the afternoon. It led him into some thick forest, and at the end of it he was alarmed to discover that some demolition work was actually taking place.

There were excavators, harvesters and foresters cutting away at the trees, leaving behind a bare landscape about half a mile long. Someone dressed in a dark business suit and tie was there; Scott thought it might have been Richard Kennedy, perhaps coming to oversee his pernicious proceedings. Whatever it was about, he was chatting and shaking hands with the workmen.

Scott scanned the denuded landscape – not a single living thing other than man moved. Scott had never been so angry to see natural beauty tarnished, not since the day Bernie had shot the goshawk, but he knew he couldn't go about it the way he had last time.

For now, Scott had to grit his teeth and leave them to it. On the bright side though, he'd managed to go downtown to book the tickets. His heart had been in his mouth as he'd handed over the cash, knowing with a tightening feeling in his stomach that he was past the point of no return and the two white laminated tickets were his.

When he got home from the reserve, he found something had been posted through the letter box. It was an odd item; it wasn't a proper letter – not one sealed in an envelope at least. The paper was there on its own with a handwritten note.

'Hi, Scott. Meet me tonight at 8 – you know my address, Sophie.'

It wasn't much to read, but he reread it over and over again because he couldn't believe it. He looked around him. It was a stroke of luck that his parents hadn't noticed it first. Then his gaze fell on the clock in the next room and he realised he only had two hours.

He had a shower, shaved, changed his clothes, brushed his hair and brushed his teeth. These things he'd once considered trivial, but he'd never had more motivation to do them than now. Quite often when he was told to prepare for a special occasion, he often questioned whether there was much point in it, just because there were almost never any other people his own age to impress, and his self-esteem was often too shaky to see the benefit of making this standard the norm.

But as he prepared himself, he knew that at this particular special occasion, there would definitely be someone to impress, and that was all the motivation he could possibly need.

He attempted to leave the house unnoticed – but both parents spotted him.

'Where are you going, Scott?' Mary asked.

'I'm just going to look for raccoons,' he said. There was some truth in that, – he'd never seen a raccoon before and it was one creature on his list that he had a chance to find in these suburbs.

'When will you be back?' she asked.

He didn't want to answer that question.

'How about an hour and a half?'

He had to compromise. It wasn't much time, but it would sound modest enough.

'You haven't got your scope with you,' Sean remarked.

'It's too dark for the scope,' said Scott. 'I've got a head torch with me.'

Scott's heart began to palpitate – they need only check his pockets to discover that he was lying.

'Alright,' said Mary at last, 'take care.'

He tried not to walk away too quickly. He could feel both their gazes on him.

He closed the door behind him and set out into the night. He wouldn't have needed a head torch anyway – there were street lights everywhere illuminating the way. Thank goodness they didn't catch onto any of that.

When he found her house that night, his first emotion was sheer admiration. It was a huge white structure, with a patio leading up to a set of double doors, and the whole house had a slight sloping gait etched into the ground.

Over a tall wooden garden fence, Scott could only just make out some sprinklers showering the tropical grass in bursts of spray. He could see a big swimming pool, which was now floodlit, surrounded by deckchairs, and a few sparse shrubs here and there.

Just across the road from the house was a small lake with a thick fringe of cattails. From those cattails, the eye shine of roosting black-crowned night herons gleamed at him. There was more eye-shine from the other side, and it made him jolt.

On a thin muddy strip lay an alligator, jaws ajar. It was big, at least four metres long, its scaly tail curled at its side, like a cat in the comfort of its own house. Scott tried not to look at it. It was only about six metres away and he didn't fully trust it to maintain its statue-like pose.

He approached the door and rang the bell. He felt so nervous and so excited. He heard footsteps coming down the stairs, and his heart raced. Bolts clicked open, the door handle bent and when it opened, he was confronted by a huge man – broad chested, beer bellied and at least six feet tall, with thick brown hair and a rounded chin on an otherwise square clean-shaven face. He regarded Scott with a defensive frown that instantly put him on edge.

'Who are you?'

He was very quiet, but his probing nature felt like a thump to the gut. Scott wanted to ask him the same question, but he had a feeling he already knew.

'Sophie asked me to come here. My name's Scott Wallace.'

'How do you know her?'

'We met at the Sea Marshes Reserve a few days ago; we started chatting and she said she liked birds as well so—'

'Is this a joke?' he asked accusingly. 'The last boy who came here said the same thing and look what's happened!'

Scott had no idea what he was talking about.

'She invited me here,' Scott pleaded.

'What's going on, David?' An older woman came to the door. She was in her fifties, he thought, with a rounded face, slim figure and shoulder-length curly blonde hair, some of it turning grey. She wore a white sleeveless vest and her bare arms had a faint suggestion of freckling.

'This boy says he's come to see Sophie, but I've never heard of him.' Her father glowered at him. Her mother seemed a little more open.

'I'm Sally, Sophie's mother.'

'Pleased to meet you,' said Scott, not knowing what else to say.

'Shall I call her down?' Sally asked.

'Yes, thank you,' said Scott.

She leaned backwards. 'Sophie, Scott's here.'

'He's here?' Scott heard her muffled voice from upstairs.

She quickly appeared at the top of the stairs.

'I knew you'd come,' she said. 'Uncle Wilson, he's here!'

A second man came in; he looked about the same age as her father. His brown hair was short, revealing a wrinkly forehead, and he too had a rather rounded face, though more from being heavyset than anything else. He wore a pair of rounded spectacles and had a thick bristly moustache, and his smiling demeanour really set him apart from her dad.

Scott was ushered into the living room. It was a work of art with four white couches, white walls, a pinkish carpet, a widescreen TV and hanging lights that dangled with the elegance of a chandelier. There was a long pause. The visit hadn't started off as he'd imagined and he wondered if he was going to get chucked out before the occasion had even begun.

'What did you say your name was again?' asked Sally.

'Scott,' he said.

'And you're from *Scot*land I hear?' she said. 'It's obviously in the name.'

'I suppose,' he replied sheepishly. Scott didn't always know how to react to jokes.

'So where about in Scotland are you from? Do you live in some forest or up a hill or where?' she asked. 'I'm sorry; I don't know it at all.'

'You're not too far off,' said Scott, easing himself into the conversation. 'I used to live in the Highlands in a house just outside a place called Aviemore. There's plenty of forests and hills nearby, which I used to like walking in whenever I had the time. My father used to be a farmer and my mother used to be a nurse.

'A nurse?' said Sally. 'I'm a social worker. I was interested in nursing at one stage, but I decided I was better at counselling.'

'I see,' said Scott. He felt his apprehensiveness grow again, wondering where the conversation would go next. He'd trained himself to keep a straight face at least.

'You said your parents *used* to be those things?' asked Sally. 'What do they do now?'

'They don't work anymore,' said Scott.

'Why's that?' asked Sally.

'It's a long story,' he said.

Sally chuckled. 'Don't worry, we don't mind long stories – we've got one too.'

All eyes were on Scott, Sophie eyeing him the most curiously out of all of them.

'It all started with my landlord and his gamekeeper,' he began. 'When I was out one day I saw his gamekeeper shoot a goshawk, a bird of prey protected by law. I went to confront him and he threatened to tell my landlord and have us evicted if I spoke out. My mother treated the gamekeeper in question, and when she confronted him he badmouthed us to the community.

'The pressure caused her to be let go. We took them both to court and the gamekeeper went to jail and our landlord agreed to pay a fine, but we also wanted to bring him to account for negligence.

'We didn't manage that one and that was when he got rid of us. The only place we could go was to my aunt and uncle's house in Aberdeen, one of the nearby cities' and I've lived there ever since.' There was a stunned silence. Scott felt it best not to elaborate further.

'So what are you doing in Miami?' asked Sally. 'On vacation?'

'Yes,' said Scott.

'Are you staying locally?'

'At 22 Fisher Street,' said Scott. 'Until August.'

'I heard something about you being interested in birds,' she said. 'Tell us about that.'

Everyone was watching him. He swallowed.

'It's something I've done all my life, but I'm actually into all areas of natural history. I also like diving and snorkelling, amongst other things, but wildlife is my biggest hobby without a doubt.'

'Well that's good,' said Sally. 'Sophie has obviously found another fanatic.'

Scott felt his confidence climb. He spilled the beans.

'I'm planning on taking her on a cruise tomorrow.'
'A cruise? How did you manage that? Have you got tickets?' said Sally.
'Right here.'
'What time are you setting off?' she asked. 'When will she be back?'
'We set off at ten in the morning,' said Scott. 'Then we'll get a cab back at ten at night – if that's OK?'
She paused. Scott realised too late that his parents would never approve such a plan, but then Sally nodded.
'I hope you look after her,' she said. 'It's a mother's right to worry about their daughter's safety when they go off with a stranger.'
'That's alright,' he said, not knowing what else to say.
'I think it's a great idea,' said Uncle Wilson. His accent reminded Scott of a cat's purr. 'I hope you have a wonderful time. Money's a little tight just now, so I really appreciate what you're doing.'
'Thanks,' he muttered nervously, forcing a nervous smile.
Sophie's father, who hadn't said a word throughout the whole conversation, got up and left, his aloofness still present, so Scott spent the next while chatting to just the three of them, telling them more about his past adventures. After a while, people started doing different things and the conversations became more casual.
Scott glanced at his watch – over an hour had passed and he only had twenty-five minutes to go. If he was back late, Mary would demand to know what had happened. When Sophie came to talk to him again, he

felt his nervousness increase. He was under pressure to get back home, but also under pressure to *mentally* prepare for tomorrow.

Scott took himself aside, excusing himself by saying he needed the toilet, trying to think what to do about it. He had only minutes to think.

'Uncle Wilson, can I have a chat with you privately?' he asked.

'Certainly,' he replied.

The older man led him up the stairs to where the bedrooms were located. Nobody else was up there.

'So what's up?' he asked with great sympathy.

'Well…'

It was difficult to say anything, Scott was even beginning to wonder if this was a good idea.

'Do you know if Sophie is seeing anyone?' he managed finally.

'As in…?'

'Yes.'

Scott felt like he'd indicted himself. Uncle Wilson's expression changed ever so slightly, still friendly but with an air of seriousness and wisdom.

'I had a feeling you would ask this,' he said.

'And?'

Uncle Wilson sighed. 'I'm not sure, Scott; she hasn't mentioned that to me. She *is* very popular with the boys so I would just be cautious.'

It wasn't quite the reaction he wanted to hear.

'But… do you think I have a shot with her?'

'Definitely,' said Uncle Wilson. 'You're pretty compatible I think.'

'Perhaps I'll ask on the cruise.'

'Perhaps that's a little early,' he said. 'You only met

yesterday.'

He saw Scott's dismay.

'If you want my advice, Scott, Sophie is a very nice albeit complicated girl. She's very popular, but if you want a chance I say take your time, don't rush in all at once – allow it to grow at its own speed.'

Scott took a while to compose himself, but the advice made sense.

'Thank you, Uncle Wilson.'

'No problem.'

The doorbell rang. Uncle Wilson jerked his head. 'I'm going to go and see who that is,' he said.

In fact, Sally Patterson had got there before him, but as soon as she saw who was at the door, she made a rapid bid to close it again.

'Wait a second,' said the visitor. 'Can't we talk first?'

Suddenly everyone was there to witness this visitor. Scott recognised him at once. The man's head was somewhat vertical, with short blonde hair that was slowly turning grey; he looked to be between forty and fifty years old.

'What do you want, Richard?' asked David. 'Can't you see you're not welcome here anymore?'

Richard Kennedy straightened his tie and smiled mockingly at his former colleague.

'Why do you have to be that way, David?' he asked. 'We used to be so close you and I. Why treat me this way now?'

'You know perfectly why, Richard,' said David. 'Does my daughter's favourite nature reserve mean nothing to you?'

'I came because I noticed someone had been

watching us,' said Richard. 'I'd spotted him with Sophie yesterday and wanted to know who he was.'

Scott suddenly felt self-conscious and made a vain attempt to hide behind the others.

'Haven't you got what you wanted, Richard?' said David. 'You wanted a job that paid better than your deputy's salary. You're a millionaire – you could build your stupid playboy mansion anywhere, and you chose to build it on my daughter's nature reserve.'

'I did try other locations in the city,' said Richard, 'but they wouldn't let me. This will be *the* location for this new residence.

'That decision was made final last year, with overwhelming support from the planning authority. They approved it on the grounds that business deals within the city would be easier if the tycoon himself had a decent place to stay, and where better to put it than a place that many of us in business would classify as unproductive land.'

'Do you hear yourself?' said David. 'It's an amenity. People enjoy going there for fresh air and nature.'

'There's nature and fresh air in other places,' said Richard. 'Birds can fly, right? They can fly somewhere else, can't they?' He smiled.

'Very funny,' said Sophie sarcastically.

'Anyway, why don't I come in and have some cookies and coffee – that'll be nice, won't it?' said Richard.

'Don't think we're going to let you come inside,' said David. 'We already have one visitor to contend with right now.'

'I'm sure one more won't hurt,' said Richard. 'Come on.'

He sidled past his former colleague, and before anyone could stop him, he was in the kitchen putting the kettle on and helping himself to something in an overhead cabinet.

'Cookies,' said Richard. 'Perfect.' He opened the packet and downed half of it. The others watched with bemusement.

'Want some?' he asked, shaking the packet in their direction. Nobody said a word.

'OK, well let's all have some coffee – a cappuccino will do for me.'

He searched the cupboard and couldn't find any coffee, much to his surprise – not even instant.

'Are you kidding me?' he asked. 'All I've got is hot water.'

'Because you're *in* hot water coming in here like this,' said David. 'Get out of my house now!'

'OK,' said Richard, 'I know you're upset. I get it – the nature reserve means a lot to you. I understand. I sympathise deeply with your issues. But we both know that power and money make you successful – that's all I'm doing.

'We've always cut down forests and drained wetlands to make new developments; otherwise how would we have the city of Miami as we know it? How would we have our dear country, the United States of America, functioning as well as it does in the world today? Come to think of it, how does anywhere in the world function without losing a few trees and marshes first?'

'Everything has its place in this world, Richard,' said Sophie. 'Everything has value; surely you'll know people who can vouch for that.'

'But some things have more value than others,' said Richard, 'like money and connections.'

Sophie apparently felt it was pointless to mention that these had little to do with nature; she stayed silent.

'I got plenty things of value, I've got the money, I've got the connections,' he said, chuckling, 'and I've got VIPs that will benefit handsomely from this development. It's just as much for them as it is for me.'

'Who are these VIPs?' Scott asked, speaking for the first time.

'That's classified,' said Richard, 'but they've promised me everything. A new place to live, more money and more babes. I would have thought you'd have sympathised with the latter, David.'

David suddenly lost his temper.

'That's enough!' he shouted. 'Get out of my house right now or I'm going to get my shotgun.'

'Threatening your former colleague, that's a very serious offence, don't you think?' said Richard. 'I could have you arrested for that, but because your inability to see the bigger picture has diminished your sense of responsibility, I'll let the matter go.'

He was surprisingly calm.

'Please leave!' Sally spoke for the first time since answering the door. 'This isn't helping anything.'

'Alright, I'm going. But I'm sure we'll meet again,' he said slyly. 'Bye for now.'

'I damn well hope not,' said Sophie after she'd closed the door. She sat on the foot of the stairs, Uncle Wilson trying to comfort her.

Scott glanced at his watch. He had five minutes before his parents would expect him back.

'I better go,' he said.
'You're leaving?' asked Sophie.
'Yes, curfew, you see,' said Scott. 'I'm really looking forward to tomorrow – you and I are going to have heaps of fun.'
He opened the door and made a move to go out.
'No doubt about it, Scott,' she called after him.
'And, Scott?'
'Yes?'
'Thanks for taking me,' she said. 'And sorry about... you know?'
'That's OK,' he replied.
Scott waved back at her and disappeared into the night. He wanted to go against Uncle Wilson's advice. For all he knew, someone much better than him would get her if she wasn't taken already. It was a hard and daunting-enough task for anyone, with or without a social difficulty, with or without good looks, and like most wildlife, it was never guaranteed.

CHAPTER 4
The Cruise

Scott wasted no time. He got dressed, had breakfast, brushed his teeth and packed his things. Within minutes he was out. He paused for a second, wondering whether he'd remembered to lock the door behind him. He looked around to check whether anyone was watching and tried the door handle. Nothing happened. He tried it again, and again, and again as if unconvinced that it was actually locked.

He started to fret; Sophie would be waiting for him and he had to get away. He also had to get away before his parents could see what he was up to. They suspected he would probably go out in their absence, but if they saw him going to Sophie's house, or worse saw them together, it would probably spell trouble.

He walked away. One thing he'd had to practice over the years was dealing with compulsive tendencies like this, and he'd found it was a good idea to take a break for a few seconds and try again.

He tried again, and after the fifth try, he almost bent the handle out of shape. He tried it again, ten more times, more gently this time. Perhaps they wouldn't notice the damage; he could explain to anyone who cared the issues he dealt with.

The door hadn't opened in all the tries he'd made,

so at last he was convinced all was well and walked away for good.

Suddenly he found himself rushing, hating himself for getting caught up in his stupid compulsions. He'd had many compulsions during the course of his life, but one of his worst had been checking his school bag fifty times to make sure he still had his jotters and pencil case – one bad technology teacher had inspired that one. Whilst his compulsions weren't severe enough to be classified as OCD, they were still irritating for him.

When Scott arrived to collect Sophie, he was relieved to see that she was ready. One anxiety gone, now they had to get on that ship.

It took about an hour's walk to get to the harbour, but before he knew it they were making their way onboard a massive white cruiser. It was pitted with windows, and a huge wooden deck extended to over a third of its whale-sized length. Even a blue whale would have bowed down to this giant.

Boredom was clearly not in this vessel's vocabulary. There were four floors of facilities: restaurants, seating areas, plenty of window seats, with swimming pools and Jacuzzis on the top deck.

With everything that the cruiser offered, it was no surprise that the queue was very long indeed. Passengers one after the other were preparing their tickets for inspection, a hubbub of excited voices all around, indistinguishable from one another. Then their tickets were checked and they were courteously welcomed aboard.

Scott had been on a few boat trips in the past; on those rare days when he wasn't either in the forest or the hills, he was either on the coast or on the sea. He'd been to Orkney, Shetland and the Hebrides in his summer holidays, the three occasions when his parents had saved up enough to go away. All three had involved ferry crossings, and he had been fascinated with the many seabirds and cetaceans he'd seen along the way: white arrow gannets, razorbills, guillemots – the penguins of the north – orange-billed puffins, diminutive harbour porpoises, yellow blazed common dolphins, majestic minke whales... just some of the many citizens of the sea that Scott had known on those journeys.

And now, as then, his instincts summoned him to the upper deck. He never gave it any thought as to whether that would be where Sophie wanted to go first, but her purposeful stride suggested his instinct was shared.

They stood at the railings with at least a hundred others, all excitedly awaiting departure.

Even though they were aboard, his heart thumped with apprehension. He wanted the cruise to be a success and for them to see some great things. He was more sure that would happen now. He knew there would be a price to pay for the means he'd used to do this, but even that wasn't his greatest worry.

'Are you looking forward to this, Scott?'

Scott jumped. He had a look in his eye like he'd temporarily forgotten where he was.

'Um, yes,' he said.

His diaphragm hadn't quite descended.

Sophie gave him a friendly frown. 'Are you alright?' she asked.

'Yes, yes,' said Scott, collecting himself. 'I just... can't believe I'm here, that's all. It's all so new and I'm a bit nervous.' He quickly improvised. 'It's not Scotland, after all.'

'I understand,' said Sophie.

'I haven't quite got over the feeling of being in America; it just seems so big compared to Scotland.'

'So you just feel a little homesick?'

'Sure.'

As a matter of fact Scott didn't miss home at all.

'I wouldn't worry about it, Scott; you'll love America when you get used to it.'

America itself had nothing to do with it.

Scott felt the floor jump and vibrate, and the engines bubbled the water into a thick foam.

Scott didn't even realise they were moving until he saw a steady trail of that foam rippling out behind the ship, steadily getting longer.

His excitement accelerated. Normally he had trouble with eye contact, but in this case he couldn't help but meet Sophie's eyes and let out a whoop of joy.

◆ ◆ ◆

Five miles offshore and the action got going. The very first bird he saw was the enormous and well-named magnificent frigatebird. It glided expertly on a wingspan at least two metres long with barely a flap. This one, a male, was almost completely black save for a red throat, which at its nest it would inflate to attract a mate.

Sophie was used to seeing these of course, but her wonder seemed renewed upon seeing Scott's reaction to them.

'I take it you've never seen one of these before, have you?' she said. The breeze and chug of the engine forced them to speak louder than normal.

'Never,' Scott admitted.

Sophie suddenly seemed to be on a role. Once again, she assumed the role of the guide.

'Keep an eye on their backs,' she said. 'Watch the sunlight catch it.'

Scott watched. Their backs appeared jet black, but as he watched them fly, they gleamed a glossy purple.

'Did you see that?' said Sophie.

'Yes.'

'The magnificent frigatebird has a purple sheen,' said Sophie. 'It tells it apart from another species further west, the great frigatebird, which has a green one.'

Scott might have embraced her for that, if more didn't appear. Brown boobies, with their long, tapered bills flew low over the waves, with white-tailed tropicbirds, the swallows of the sea, gliding with them.

'Spotted dolphins!' came Sophie's exhilarated cry.

Atlantic spotted dolphins were a species only found in the tropical Atlantic, smaller than the bottlenose dolphins that Scott knew in Aberdeen. They were bow-riding, using the pressure waves of the ship as a ride, occasionally demonstrating their athleticism by breaching into the air.

Scott quickly considered his situation. He'd taken Sophie out here to give her a good time, but it seemed that their roles had reversed.

Then like children bored of a game, the dolphins switched their attentions elsewhere and left.

'I have to ask, Sophie,' said Scott suddenly, 'how did you get into nature? You really know a lot about it.'

'Thank you,' said Sophie.

His compliment sent her into a flush, and she

seemed to take a while to recover from it.

'It's hard to say, but I think the Sea Marshes Reserve being close by definitely helped. My mom especially gave me a lot of encouragement. We often went to the seaside when I was younger, then one day I went out too far in my inflatable boat and I was surrounded by dolphins. I was able to get myself back to shore, much to the relief of my parents, but that first experience really planted the seed.'

◆ ◆ ◆

A few hours later, the ship stopped at a reef, which was what all the snorkelers on board had been waiting for. An intercom crackled into life.

'This is your captain speaking. We're just making a small stop at Cutlass Reef so any of you who fancy a swim or a snorkel, now's your chance. Make sure you don't swim too far from the boat for safety reasons and we wish you a pleasant stop.'

When Scott poked his head under the waves, his eyes widened instantly at the rainbow of colour below. The water was like a Jacuzzi, instantly relaxing the senses. The stag horn and brain corals stretched before him like a metropolis, while the white feathery crinoids waved in the current.

Fish were everywhere and in a variety of colours and sizes. Sergeant majors, with their four blue stripes of rank, gleamed through the clear water. There were French grunts – fish with yellow and white lined scaling that drifted above the reef; blackbar soldierfish – like goldfish on steroids huddled together in hidden crevices; rock hinds – small fish with green spots against white skin that peered warily up at them; and wondrous blue and yellow French angelfishes milling around. A single green moray eel stared out from its coral crevice, gulping as it respired.

Of all the things they saw that day, a green turtle caused the most excitement. Its shell was grass green with algae, and its scaly flippers flapped with ease through the blue water.

Two hours didn't seem quite enough, and not surprisingly everybody groaned when the captain told them to come back aboard.

'That was great!' said Scott, dripping wet but exhilarated beyond words. He staggered aboard, his legs taking their time to reacquaint themselves with dry land.

Sophie was equally thrilled. Her high spirits and appreciative smile were contagious, and Scott found his nervousness drying off faster than the water on his skin. But they weren't done yet.

It started with a huge gathering of seabirds. Magnificent frigatebirds were massing like vultures at a carcass; Franklin's gulls were there dressed in their black, white and grey suits, hovering and alighting; bulky brown pelicans sat expectantly; and the diminutive black Wilson's storm petrels hovered and waltzed over the frenzy. That must have been why they were here – for all these birds there was food at this dinner table.

Enormous bluefin tuna lunged at the other defenceless fish, skimming and boiling the water. It all happened so fast. A blue marlin leaped out of nowhere, stunning everyone, its javelin nose swishing left and right. It must have been at least five metres long, with blue striping contrasting a dark body.

The baitfish, whatever species they were, were leaping clear of the water to escape, and the birds really went at them – even if they escaped the jaws of the tuna or the marlin, the birds would be waiting for them.

Something lunged, its huge gape draped in baleen. It blew its vapour high into the blue sky, then dived, the water rolling off its sleek grey skin. The last of its body to disappear was its tiny dorsal fin – three quarters the way along its back. It apparently rang a bell in Sophie's mind.

'Bryde's whale!' she exclaimed.

It was another thing Scott had never seen – there were no Bryde's whales in Scotland. He was used to smaller minke whales – it was usually the only baleen whale species he saw.

The whale surfaced three more times, but it was quite clear that the activity was slowing down. Then, before they knew it, the birds were dispersing. They hadn't seen the tuna or the marlin for half an hour, and the last sighting of the Bryde's whale was of it distantly, fifty metres out.

Afternoon merged into evening.

They stayed up on deck for the rest of the cruise, scanning out to sea for any more marine mammals and chatting at the same time, their conversation becoming richer every minute. Sophie's world awareness of wildlife became more and more apparent to Scott the more she spoke. She talked about her past adventures elsewhere, in the Everglades, in Vancouver and Guyana. Before long she was spelling out her enormous bucket list of destinations.

'I love nature so much, Scott,' she said, 'that if I

had the money to travel the world to enjoy it all, then I would.'

'Me too,' Scott agreed. 'I'd love to go with you if I could.'

He felt the flush in his chest worsen upon saying that.

Sophie smiled nervously. 'I guess you could.'

There was an awkward silence. He didn't dare look her in the eye in case she read his thoughts.

Sophie seemed at a loss as to what to say next. She tried to smile appreciatively, though he noticed she seemed to look away from him a little.

Scott thought quickly.

'I hope this has been a memorable trip,' he said at last.

'It has, thank you,' said Sophie.

Scott wasn't the best at reading body language, but she seemed to shudder nervously when the conversation continued.

'What was your favourite thing about today?' he asked.

'Definitely seeing the Bryde's whale,' she said. 'It was one whale species I've tried to see for years and never quite got lucky enough. I've seen humpback whales before but never a Bryde's – until today.'

There was a chirp to her voice on those last two words that got him instantly hopeful.

Their conversation picked up again, and they had another truly fabulous talk about world wildlife – a talk that to him was as special as seeing that wildcat in its Highland home. Rare, unpredictable and beautiful.

The peace between him and nature had never been stronger.

CHAPTER 5
The Everglades

Last night had ended wonderfully, and Sophie had wanted to see him again the very next day. Scott couldn't believe how well things were going. Uncle Wilson's advice had prevailed and he hadn't asked her out, but at least she was still his friend.

He told his parents he was going out to do some birding, which he was, but he didn't specify where. They were going back to the beach, intending to stay there all day, which would have left him home alone again, that is if he *were* home.

It was 5 a.m. As he walked down the friendly street towards Sophie's house, he took stock of just how lucky he'd been. Things were going to change – no longer would he be friendless; no longer was his Asperger's a barrier to a real connection. For the first time ever, he'd found a kindred spirit.

'Hi, Scott,' Sophie called.

He looked over to see her standing at the door, a blue rucksack strapped to her back.

'Ready to go?' she asked.

'Where to?'

Sophie had deliberately kept it a surprise until just now.

'Just to the outlying countryside – there's good

birding there and I'd like to show you more of our native species. Would you like that?'

Scott couldn't say no. A full day would be needed. That explained the 5 a.m. start.

Minutes later they were taking a bus from Fisher Street. They passed through residential areas for the next half hour, before being taken along the extensive South Miami-Dade Busway, past groves of palm trees, houses and retail parks. It followed this for about twenty minutes before joining the 9336 Highway.

For the next hour it took them out of the city, past pine forests, sawgrass prairies and swamps, then passed the Everglades National Park Headquarters and local marina, before finally stopping at the Flamingo Campground. It was home to a huge campsite and the start of the seventeen-mile Everglades Coastal Prairie Trail, their first priority for the day.

Birds were numerous, and within minutes they'd come across an abundance of red-winged blackbirds – males with resplendent red and yellow scapulars, calling metallically – a harsh '*wack-wiaack*'. Duller females bore yellow superciliums, pointed bills and dense black barring all over, with yellow throats tucked under their chins.

Killdeers – pied plovers with double breast bands – fluttered; lots of long-billed yellow and black eastern meadowlarks sat on fence posts; smooth-billed anis – black birds with bulging bills related to cuckoos – sat atop the scrub oaks; and common and boat-tailed grackles – each with iridescent green, brown and black feathers – strutted across the path.

Scott soon spotted something of his own, and with his telescope zoomed in on a bird of prey – a red-tailed hawk. It had a brown back, whitish brown breast and a dark red tail and was sitting on a fence post, swivelling its head in search of prey.

On the sawgrass prairies themselves, limpkins – medium-sized brown birds with long curved bills – and the tall slate-grey sandhill cranes had gathered. In the grass, some bobwhites whistled softly, yet their plump quail-like bodies remained hidden.

'So what's special about this particular trail?' Scott asked.

'It's the Cape Sable seaside sparrow,' said Sophie. 'It only lives in the Everglades. It's a subspecies of seaside sparrow. They call it the goldilocks bird because its habitat conditions have to be just right: in grassy prairies dominated by hairawn grass. There should be plenty of it along here.'

It was another twenty minutes before they came to any significant stands of hairawn grass. They were about as tall as reed beds. In the autumn they would be flowering, pink spikelets clumped at the top of their stems, but at this drier time of year they were a dull yellow.

Suddenly there were far fewer birds to see, and the atmosphere grew quieter, but there were still red-winged blackbirds calling.

They walked the path for another thirty minutes, mindful that it went on for miles. There was no sign of a Cape Sable seaside sparrow anywhere. With the day growing hotter, they headed back. The red-winged blackbirds were still calling.

Scott paused for a moment; he hadn't had a good look at anything in this hairawn grass thicket and some red-winged blackbirds would be better than nothing.

As he did so, a small greyish-brown bird appeared briefly, vanishing back into the thicket as quickly as it appeared. Scott heard it call: a rising '*wiaack*'. It didn't spark Scott's interest; he assumed it was a female red-winged blackbird, but then the bird reappeared and this time Sophie saw it.

'That's it!' she said. 'That's the sparrow.'

'Is it?' said Scott.

He would have dismissed it if Sophie hadn't been there. The Cape Sable seaside sparrow clung to a stem of hairawn grass, partially shaded by the thicket. Scott could only just make out a pale belly. The rest of it looked dark. He gritted his teeth, hoping the bird would come out more openly. He'd had cases before of birds doing precisely this, and they'd shown better only as they were disappearing into the vegetation, never to be seen again.

Another bird came out and perched on another stem against the sun. Scott grimaced, shielding his eyes with his palm.

'Let's creep slowly to the other side,' said Sophie.

They edged round. The anticipation was terrible – any second they could both fly away and be lost.

But the two sparrows lingered, and they both enjoyed incredible views of this rare and range-restricted subspecies. The pale bellies contrasted with dense dark streaking, with greenish grey backs and brown feathers, while their heads were grey with black stripes down their faces and yellow lores adjacent to their conical grey bills.

The sparrows dropped onto the path and started picking seeds and insects, not unlike the house sparrows Scott knew at home, who loved to loiter near picnic tables for scraps. The morning was fading so they headed back to the campsite to figure out what to do next.

They decided to take the Old Bear Road not far from the marina, hoping to join another trail, but they came upon something else – a building slap bang in the middle of nowhere. Scott grew wary; it was surrounded by two rows of chain-link fences crested with barbed wire.

There were steel gun towers, and men with Alsatians patrolled the perimeter.

'What is this place?' asked Scott. It was deeply unnerving to him that such a place could appear so unexpectedly.

'It's the Miami Correctional Facility,' said Sophie. 'People even younger than us get sent here for committing serious crimes, all the way up to murder.'

Scott blinked.

'You don't want to know the end of it, Scott; it's not a nice place.' She grimaced. 'Come on – I don't want to linger here.'

Scott paused to give the installation one last look. It was certainly a foreboding place – the men in the gun towers were armed with M16 rifles slung over their shoulders. It made him shiver. He wandered away.

When late afternoon came, they took the bus back to Fisher Street. It had been an incredible day and Sophie's energy hadn't dissipated. No sooner had they got off at Fisher Street than Sophie's suggestions began to spill out.

'Would you like to do something this evening?' she asked. 'We have raccoons in the suburbs. There are barred and great horned owls around too, and the Sea

Marshes Reserve sometimes has common nighthawks now and then. We've got about four or five hours of light left; we could do some snorkelling, just off the beach...'

Scott was intrigued. 'Are there sharks around here?' he asked.

'Yes there are,' she replied. 'I've seen bull sharks and tiger sharks off the beach on a few occasions. It freaked the hell out of me.'

'What about great whites?' Scott asked.

'There are actually.'

'Have you seen any?'

'Once before, at this place north of the beach called the Deep Drop. I went diving there with my dad and it swam right past me, almost within touching distance. When it left me alone, I felt exhilarated. I was scared but I've had a fascination with sharks since then.'

'Do you have scuba gear available?' Scott asked.

She nodded.

'Could we go there?' Scott asked. 'To the Deep Drop?'

Sophie raised an eyebrow.

'We could, while it's still light,' she said. 'I wouldn't want to linger there after dark, but I've got lights that we can take. I take it this means you actually want to see one?'

'I would rather,' said Scott.

'You're saying that now,' said Sophie quizzically, 'but you could feel differently when you're in there.'

'I know,' he said, 'but could we try?'

'Yes,' she said. 'I've only seen one there once, but who knows how regularly it happens? There's a cliff we can keep our backs to, just in case anything decides to ambush us.'

'Great,' said Scott, 'I'll just have to come up with an excuse for my parents.'

CHAPTER 6
The Deep Drop

There was no bus link to the Deep Drop so they had to take a cab. It took them along Fisher Street towards the beach, then north for about twenty minutes before reaching their destination. Sophie paid the driver forty dollars, and after a quick thank you he drove away.

They descended down a steep bank and onto a beach, then onto a long wooden jetty. They wasted no time getting changed.

Since there was a hidden rule called 'ladies first', Scott helped Sophie get kitted out first: wetsuit, dagger, mask, oxygen tank, dive computer, tethers, flippers and belt. Then Sophie did the same for him. Scott shivered.

'It'll be dark in four hours, so we'll try not to hang around too long. If we see a shark, great, but whether we get one or not, we'll want to get back to land in good time.'

Scott descended down the rusty ladder.

'I'm curious, Scott,' she said suddenly.

Scott took out his respirator. 'Hmm?'

'What did you tell your parents to get them off your back?'

He sighed sheepishly. 'I told them I would be going out to search for owls.'

Sophie chuckled. 'Did you say when you'd return?'

'Nope.'

The depths opened before him and his spirits quailed. He shivered, but Sophie put an arm round his shoulder and nodded. Beneath his face mask, Scott trembled with apprehension, facing downwards at the blue void below. His eyes played tricks, and every flicker below was shark-shaped. Scott tested their tether. It held strong.

With their backs to the cliff they hovered there, suspended in an otherwise blue space. It was of the utmost importance that they were on their guard. A shark could appear from any direction, and they weren't the only creatures out there.

Scott was scanning anxiously above, around and below. He visualised the creature appearing suddenly out of the blue, the sudden size and ferocious face trembling his soul with the power of an earthquake, its jaws seizing and shaking him till he was cleaved.

Sophie had told him over and over again on the cab journey that shark attacks were actually very rare – that you were in fact more likely to be killed by a falling coconut. It was a nice, comforting thought – when you were on dry land listening to all the facts – but when you were in *its* world, suddenly you weren't so sure.

The shark, after all, knew its world better than you did, it had eyesight approximately five times better than you and could be watching you from ten metres away and you'd never know, perhaps not even once it got you.

Sophie nudged him then, giving him an enormous fright, and a torrent of bubbles came out of his mouthpiece. Sophie held him steady to calm him down then pointed upwards. He braced himself.

Out came the great white shark – a female at least six metres from head to tail. The sight was terrifying and unforgettable: the white underbelly, the gills, the grey back, the falcate fin, the massive tail sweeping powerfully from side to side. There were the black eyes and, of course, the jaws, equipped with sharp triangular teeth capable of shearing whatever they desired.

With terrifying grace, the shark turned its attention towards them and swam closer. Scott's heart hammered against his ribcage – at just three metres away they made eye contact. It swam right at them as if about to strike. Scott couldn't move.

But a split second later it altered its course and flanked around. Sophie tapped him again, this time gesturing that it was now behind them.

The shark circled them once more, then swam under their trailing fins. Scott felt Sophie grab him as it came up again, *circling* again. Scott met Sophie's eyes for an instant and saw her anxiety reflecting his own. Then even more spectacularly, it swam over their heads, almost close enough to touch. They craned their heads to watch it pass and away it went. They waited at least fifteen minutes, but the shark never returned.

Scott felt a huge rush of relief, and with it came a sense of wonder and exhilaration – and even a twinge of sorrow. Increasingly it was the case that humans were posing more of a threat to sharks than sharks were to humans. Millions were caught in fishing nets around the world every year, and sports fishermen took their share too, keen to impress their mates with their trophies.

The water hadn't yet darkened and they were victorious, despite some quite serious odds against them. Sophie had picked the best time to do this, and Scott was grateful for that now.

It was time to head for the surface. Scott began to ascend, but to his puzzlement, Sophie didn't rise with him. She was looking at the surface, transfixed. Scott followed her gaze and saw something far above them – which then dived towards them. Scott thought the shark had come back. He met Sophie's eyes and they stayed where they were to watch it descend.

Its body was long and bulbous, and it was far too close. Suddenly its once slow, calm demeanour changed and it began to thrash its head before baring rows of conical teeth.

Sophie dashed for safety, but the sperm whale grabbed Scott by the leg and took him down, pulling Sophie along with him. She drew her dagger and desperately tried to cut at the tether, until the whale's strength snapped it.

Scott was terrified and disoriented; the pain and pressure on his leg was intense. The whale took him deeper, and the deeper it got, the darker it got. He could no longer see the whale that was taking him to Davy Jones' locker.

He felt desperately for his dagger.

He finally drew it – only to drop it! He clawed frantically at the open water – it was only seconds – and in two or three agonising empty grabs he caught it by the tip of the crossbar. He stabbed the whale's blubber, the blade sinking in by about two or three inches. It worked – the whale released him. Thinking fast, he released some air for ascension, expecting at any moment to be smashed by its tail.

Scott was running out of air; he couldn't see his dive computer, but he felt he must have only minutes left. Scott swam in the direction he thought was up, and up he went, even though he was never going to make it. If he wasn't devoured, he would likely drown, and even if he reached the surface, he would almost certainly get the bends.

He caught a glimpse of the surface – a slight golden tinge – but he was slowing down. He eventually stopped in midwater still about thirty metres short, his contracted lungs screaming like a banshee. He couldn't move, he couldn't think, he couldn't do anything. He felt himself sinking, his vision blurring. He was drowning. Most of his air was gone, and what he had left came out in an uncontrollable torrent of bubbles. Scott started gulping like a fish at the water, and in it came, fully flooding his throat.

Something yanked out his mouthpiece. He coughed and spluttered and some of the water was jettisoned out of him.

He was vaguely aware of a slow ascension, like he was being guided to Heaven itself. The next few minutes were like a dream, though he wouldn't remember any of it. It was broken when he felt a new sensation against his face, one with a warm touch and much less resistance. Scott still wasn't fully aware of everything.

Sophie pulled out his new respirator and held onto him, trying to gauge his consciousness.

Now it was getting dark; they'd totally lost track of time whilst they were down there, but it must have been hours.

Down in the depths it had been chaos, but the surface world remained peacefully oblivious to their ordeal. The lights from the city twinkled from afar, the sky was clear and though it was still twilight, the first stars of the Great Bear were beginning to show.

Scott sat up and stared at Sophie with an incapacitating speechlessness.

'Um,' he began.

'Are you OK?' she asked.

He tried to stand up and cried out with so much pain he slumped back down.

'Just stay here,' she said. 'I've called an ambulance.'

'Oh, Sophie,' said Scott. 'That was amazing! *You* were amazing! You saved my life! How did you – how could you have—?'

'It's complicated,' said Sophie.

'But you risked your life for me.'

'You were in danger; I had to do something. We're friends, Scott, and that's what friends do.'

There – he had it. Uncle Wilson's advice had prevailed and they were now the best of friends.

Scott had a mountain of explaining to do. The bad news was that his cover story was, in the most spectacular way imaginable, in tatters!

CHAPTER 7
In Tatters

Scott had never come this close to death. But he'd never been in this much trouble either. Although the doctors had been civil with him, being a minor they were legally obliged to inform his parents what had happened, despite his protests. He lay in a bed, with a thick white mattress and duvet cover, flanked by a set of ringed steel bars.

Despite their professionalism, the anxiety of the doctors and nurses really showed. There'd been an urgency to get an X-ray done, and even when it had been done, there'd been an anxious wait for the results. He'd been given a hundred stitches, he'd managed to avoid being put into a decompression room and was told he was very lucky to be alive.

He should have been relieved that he'd been saved, and in truth, he was. Sophie had been excellent this whole time, given the circumstances.

'I'm so sorry, Scott,' she said, 'I didn't think this through well enough.'

Her hand made a motion towards his, so brief he thought he'd imagined it.

'At least it wasn't the shark that did it,' he said. 'How could anyone expect a sperm whale?'

'I suppose.' She sighed. 'What am I supposed to tell

Mom and Dad?'
'I'm wondering the exact same thing,' said Scott. The nervousness hit him full on. 'Oh God, I'm not looking forward to their visit.'
The door to the ward opened sharply, and Sophie's dad stormed in.
'Come with me, young lady!' he demanded.
'But, Dad!' Sophie protested.
'Now!'
She glared at him.
'I have to know that he's going to be OK,' she said.
'Well I don't care,' he replied gruffly. 'Come with me now! There's a place in hell for guys like him!'
Sophie met Scott's eyes and stood up reluctantly.
'I'm sorry, OK,' she said.
Her father dragged her out of the ward.
Scott began to cry uncontrollably. It was over. They were never going to be together. *Both* of their families would ensure it. He could only imagine what arguments they'd have. The most likely outcome would be that if he wasn't sent home, at the very least they'd be barred from seeing one another. Perhaps her father would involve the cops and ask for a restraining order. He grimaced painfully at the thought; it wasn't even that kind of issue yet Scott felt it was going to happen anyway.
He saw movement outside and this time both his parents were there.
'Scott!' Mary cried in anguish. 'What happened? Are you alright?'
'I'm fine,' said Scott irritably.
They both took seats around him. Despite her worry, Mary assumed the role of interrogator.

'How did you get into this situation?' she demanded. 'A shark, a sperm whale, nearly drowning – and this girl!' She faltered. 'I don't even know where to start!'

Sean joined in. 'Perhaps we should start from the beginning,' he said. 'Who is this girl and how did you meet her?'

Scott sighed. 'Her name is Sophie Patterson. She lives at 29 Fisher Street and we met in the Sea Marshes Reserve earlier this week. She likes birds and I really liked her so I—'

He realised too late that he was digging his own grave.

'What did you do?' his father demanded.

'Took her on a cruise,' he spilled.

'A cruise?' said Mary. 'How much was it?'

'A hundred and eighty dollars.'

Mary's jaw dropped. 'A hundred and eighty dollars! Where did you… get that kind of money?'

Scott didn't want to answer that question. He'd heard that the wisest reply to most things was silence.

Not this one.

'Where did you get the money?' asked Sean, with a reinforced anger.

Mary worked it out. 'Did you… have anything to do with the money missing from our drawer?'

He looked away.

'Unbelievable!' she exclaimed.

'Look, I'm sorry alright!' he said.

'Let's come back to this,' she replied. 'The doctor and the police told us that you were diving with this girl looking for *sharks!*'

'*Great white sharks*,' said Scott pedantically.

His parents stared at one another.

'And we saw one too!' he added defiantly.

'Don't you realise you could have died today?' said Mary.

'Perhaps I'm already dead,' said Scott, 'if this is where I am.'

'That's enough, Scott!' said Mary.

'It wasn't even the shark that did this,' he said passionately. 'It was a sperm whale – *Physeter macrocephalus*!'

He said the Latin name so loud the entire ward stared at him.

'I know you're trying to be clever,' said Sean, 'but it's not going to work.'

Scott ground his teeth.

'Scott,' said Mary, 'once you're discharged, we're going to have to have a very serious conversation about this, and some punishment will be in order.'

'What if I don't agree?' he said.

'Then we'll make sure that you do!' said Sean. 'I'll even stay at home and babysit you, and prevent you from wandering off.'

'Leave me alone now,' Scott demanded. 'Let me sleep.'

His parents glanced at one another.

'Leave me!' Scott shouted. 'I don't want to speak to you – go away!'

At last, he had his way. They got up and left.

Scott wondered why he hadn't drowned? He might have preferred that to what was in store for him later. He shut his eyes, and hoped they would never open again.

CHAPTER 8
Mayhem

Scott was grounded, and he wasn't allowed to see Sophie again – the family would stay at home today to make sure of it. It was a decision Scott despised, but he intended to violate it anyway and sneaked out to see her as soon as he was able, mindful that her father wouldn't want him anywhere near her. But he was in for a surprise.

It didn't occur to him that Americans didn't have the same holiday system as he did at home. Suddenly he remembered that Sophie had mentioned it before, but even so it *was* a surprise to find out that Sophie was actually going to school today – and at five past eight in the morning, which to him was unbelievably early!

The first he saw of this surprising truth was a long yellow school bus with automatic doors rolling up beside her house. Scott couldn't help but feel annoyed that he hadn't been told or at the very least had the chance to say goodbye. He could see Sophie at one of the windows next to some people, possibly her friends, but only just.

It was a cramped bus filled with students, some quiet, some uproariously rowdy. Even the bus driver looked young enough to be a student, and he acted like one too, playing music so loudly you'd wonder how he'd hear the traffic.

    The rough social interactions between them all looked even less civilised than what Scott was used to at home, with constant capering and dog piling, and loud guffawing that made him wonder how anyone got peace of mind.

    Somehow Sophie didn't seem to mind, and she looked too deep in conversation with someone to care. Scott tried waving at her, but it was clear she would never notice him. There was nothing he could do. He watched the school bus leave the street and turn away out of sight.

    Fisher Street fell silent. The heat was rising. He turned towards the lake where the alligator lay. It didn't appear to have moved a muscle since Scott had last seen it.

    He walked home dejectedly then swam in his own pool for a while, doing practically nothing but relax for the next few hours. Sean and Mary were sleeping on the job. Scott had lunch, did some more birding and that was about it. A quiet day.

◆ ◆ ◆

Sophie Patterson was having a quiet day of her own. But at least there was something new to talk about. She'd been conversing with her friends constantly about Scott, explaining that he was a new friend and a fellow enthusiast. She'd wisely left out the details of last night's disaster.

    She went to her first lesson of the day – and she dreaded it, not for the subject of maths but for its teacher – Mr James Hockley. Sophie hated him with every fibre of her being. He constantly picked on everyone, though mostly on those who were either disinterested in maths or not doing well enough, regardless of their level of effort. He would often give out double homework without a second thought, a practice that made him deeply unpopular. Even the other teachers found him unpleasant, and despite calls from several senior educational figures to sack him, the principal had chosen to keep him, citing the fact that he was the best maths teacher in the school and that there were hardly any other replacements. Worst still, there'd even been rumours that he'd taken an unsavoury interest in some of the students, but they'd never been investigated.

Sophie was trying her best to concentrate; she had exams to study for, and she had others to help do the same. But today all lessons would end early.

Sophie heard something from outside that culminated in a roar that made everyone's heads turn to the window. At first no one thought anything of it – the classroom window overlooked a baseball field, where the school team practised at this time. But when an even louder roar erupted, Mr Hockley went to the window to investigate.

He peered out, and everyone else peered out from behind him. The baseball team were in fact silent, staring transfixed at a mass gathering behind the school gates. There was a loud rat-a-tat-tat and a surge of yelling. The mass gathering, a group of at least two hundred, swarmed into the school grounds like a horde of bees.

Suddenly there was chaos – everyone began to scream, run and hide. Sophie could barely take it in, but all of a sudden she realised it wasn't just her class. Every classroom within earshot was screaming in terror. Windows smashed, doors were broken, shots were fired and people surged in.

◆ ◆ ◆

Scott lay on his deckchair soaking in the sun's rays. He listened to the grey kingbirds and the cardinals calling.

Then he heard a siren. He raised his head, frowned and lay back down again. Then he heard another siren, and a few seconds later the atmosphere was deafened with them. Scott ran to the fence and saw convoys of police cars racing along. A huge crowd had gathered, screaming at the cops to pull over.

Everyone across the twenty-four houses that he could see were out in the open, staring across towards the city. Scott saw a plume of smoke billowing into the air like an industrial chimney. He even thought he heard a distant scream.

He ran inside and locked the door. As he panicked, he came across the note Sophie had given him and was surprised to see something on the back of it he hadn't noticed before – a mobile number. Perhaps she could tell him what was going on; he knew she was still at school but he had no one else to talk to, and he didn't feel like asking any strangers.

Scott dialled the number; he could hear ringing. He pressed the device to his ear. The connection was poor.

'Hello?'
'Sophie, is that you?'
'*Scott?*'

She sounded flabbergasted.

'Yes it's me. Something seems to be going on. There's police cars and smoke – I don't suppose you know what's happening?'

'Scott, I can't talk!'

'Are you in a lesson?'

'No, something's happening here – there are guys pouring into the school. I've barricaded myself and some others in the classroom. They have guns.'

Scott instantly made the connection. His thoughts raced.

'Are you alright?' he asked.

The connection almost cut out. There was a loud bang.

'What was that?' he demanded.

'They're breaking in,' said Sophie. 'There's too many of them!'

His heart raced. 'OK, Sophie, sit tight, I have an idea.'

Sophie was incredulous. 'What?'

'There's no time to explain,' he said. 'You've got to trust me.'

'OK.'

There was another loud bang, and he heard a shot at the other end.

'I gotta go, Scott.'

The line went dead. Scott knew what he had to do.

He searched every cabinet, found what he was after, then strapped it to his back – no bigger than a small rucksack yet the most important thing he'd ever owned and the most secret. Not even his parents knew about it.

Both parents remained dormant as he stole past

them.

    'Hold on, Sophie,' Scott said to himself. 'I'm coming!'

◆ ◆ ◆

Outside, the police blockade looked on, officers crouched behind their cars and vans, guns pointed, unable to advance. A shadow moved ahead of them. The massacre was obvious – the central open-air square lay strewn with bodies. Those closest to the exits must have run out only to be gunned down. Where were the attackers? Where was Sophie?

    Scott was spotted and the gunfire started. There was gesticulation and disbelief amongst the thugs. Their weapons were raised to the sky, but their shots flew wide of the mark. To the shock of anyone looking, Scott swooped down on a pair of scythe-like wings, just shy of a metre wide, to return fire.

    There was a commotion from inside, and more thugs piled out to greet him. Springing from his knees, he took to the air again in an instant, returning fire. He flew another fifty metres, swooping down to pick up a rock the breadth of his chest and hurled it at the thugs below, blasting three of them off their feet. He heard some commotion from a nearby window. He saw it open and the torsos of two people jutting outwards, as if contemplating escape via this means. Scott flew towards them, both boys gaping as he drew level.

    'Can you guys use some help?' he asked, as if their encounter was no big deal.

    'Uh sure,' said one of them. He was blonde, round cheeked, blue eyed and slim but still with the broad frame of a footballer. His friend – large stomached, with a purple jacket, and almost bald save for a thin shaving of brown hair – addressed him.

'Who are you?' he asked.

'Your salvation,' said Scott. 'Do you guys know a girl called Sophie Patterson?'

'Uh yes,' said the blonde one. 'We're friends of hers.'

'Can you help me find her?'

'We could but there's too many of them,' said the other friend. 'We'd never make it.'

'Don't worry, I have a plan. Take these.'

Scott handed them two of his pistols, holding on to another two he'd taken from the house. Both of them stared at him. They now had two pieces of power against a side stronger than they were.

They opened the window wide enough for Scott to get through. The leather wings dragged against the window frame as he scrambled inside. In this classroom, twenty students were huddled together with a very frightened teacher. They'd barricaded themselves in with their tables, but it wouldn't hold. It was just minutes away from being breached.

'You two spread out to opposite sides of the room; everyone else hang tight,' said Scott.

A table toppled with a tremendous crash. Scott had his hands to a whistle strapped around his neck, standing poised and ready for action.

'Will this plan work?' said the blonde one. 'There's like twenty of them out there.'

'It'll work,' said Scott firmly.

He felt a tension rising within him. The barricade came loose.

'Cover your ears!' Scott cried.

'What?' said the blonde one.

Before Scott could repeat the order, the door burst open and he blew on the whistle. It wasn't the typical shrill of a normal whistle, but an immensely loud one equivalent to a stereo at full volume. Scott gesticulated.

'Fire!'

Both boys somehow managed to understand. Bullets flew and the thugs began to fall. Some were raising their weapons. Scott blew again.

'Move up!' he cried.

Both boys kept firing and the thugs began to retreat. Scott pressed home the advantage. He took to the air and dragged a table through the crowd of twenty thugs, knocking them all to the floor as if they were skittles. A leg of the table broke off as he slammed it against the wall. He struck the remaining thugs until they lay still and beckoned the others to come out.

'Take up their weapons,' he said.

'But who are you?' asked the blonde one.

'My name's Scott Wallace,' he said. 'You?'

'I'm Wayne Taylor,' said the blonde one.

'And you?' he asked his friend.

'Dave Tate,' he replied, grimacing as he took a shot of his inhaler. 'Sophie's class is this way.'

They advanced a couple of metres to where there was a bend in the corridor and stopped short.

'It's that third door on the right,' said Dave. 'Is there anyone there?'

Scott peered round. 'All clear.'

They got past the first door, then the second.

'Contact!' shouted Dave.

Nearly fifty of them came out at once.

'Fall back!' shouted Scott.

A heated exchange of rounds followed, in the time it took to retreat five metres, ten thugs crumpled and nearly twenty of theirs. Dave swore, taking another shot of his inhaler.

'Where did these guys come from? Were they waiting for us? They gotta have been waiting for us,' said Wayne.

'Maybe they heard the shots we fired earlier,' said Dave.

Scott peered round. Rounds flew.

'There's far too many of them,' said Scott. 'There's about forty of them and five of us left.'

'Can't you blow on that fucking whistle thing you had earlier?' Dave asked frantically.

'It takes a while to charge up after a couple of uses,' said Scott.

'Fuck!' Dave shook his head.

'Then how do we get past them?' said Wayne.

Scott thought quickly. 'We need help.'

'From where?' said Wayne.

'From outside,' said Scott. 'The cops. What's stopping them from advancing?'

The others blinked.

'I noticed a blockade out back, but I don't know if any of them got through,' said Scott. He instantly had a plan. 'Keep them engaged until I return.'

'*What*?' cried Wayne hysterically.

'Whatever's stopping them from coming in, I have to deal with it,' said Scott. He turned to Dave, 'Do you think you can hold them?'

'For how long?' he asked.

'As long as you can,' he said. 'If all else fails just get out of here. We can regroup.'

'But what about Sophie and the others in that class?' Wayne asked. 'What if they break through?'

Scott's thoughts raced. 'Just stay here as long as you can.'

Scott couldn't waste any more time. He took off out a window and across armies of thugs patrolling the grounds. He found the police blockade. The SWAT teams were huddling behind their armoured vehicles. Several of their members that had evidently tried to advance were either dead or dying. More blasts of gunfire came, bonging ominously against their metal. From the sound of them, they were machine guns of some kind, mountable ones capable of firing hundreds of rounds a minute.

A police sniper fired a shot, but Scott had no idea if he'd hit anyone. The enemy retaliated and he was peppered in the stomach. Scott wasn't sure if he survived it; he could watch no longer.

Instead, he swooped into action, taking out several of them with his pistols. Another police sniper fired. It hit a thug in the head. Scott pressed home the attack and took out the remaining thugs.

Shots whistled and suddenly Scott was dodging more bullets. When he saw who was firing, he was furious.

'STOP IT!' he shouted. 'CEASE FIRE!'

He whizzed this way and that, screaming at them in exasperation.

'MOVE UP!' he shouted.

With their mistake realised, they quickly did so.

Scott flew back to the others.

'We've only managed to down two more since you left,' said Dave. 'Are the cops moving in?'

'Yes,' said Scott. 'They'll be here soon.'

The stand-off continued for what seemed like an eternity. In the next hour, Dave took down two more and there was still no sign of the cops.

Scott saw the light on his Aquilacry go green.

'OK, guys, my whistle has charged up. We've only got two blasts, so if we're going to make it to that door in time, we'll have to move fast.'

The others reloaded with their last magazines.

'Covering fire!' he shouted.

They fired in unison. A split second passed. Scott blew.

Both sides were crumpling from the noise, yet both pressed on. The first door was passed.

'Again!' shouted Dave.

Scott blew once more and they made it to door two. Somehow they pressed on again. The whistle's effect wore off.

'Keep going!' cried Scott.

There was no going back now. They took down three more and burst through door three! Some more covering fire. Everyone made it in.

They barricaded themselves inside, noticing the remains of a previous barricade withered to dust.

'There's no one here,' said Scott. He couldn't believe how long it had taken him to notice that.

He stared at the others. 'Where could they have gone?'

'I don't know,' said Wayne.

There was a loud bash from the door. Scott checked his ammo and asked the others to do the same.

They only had twenty shots left between them, and it sounded like there was another army of them outside.

'We'll have to escape,' said Scott.

'How? We're four floors up,' said Wayne.

Another bash.

Scott smashed the window and looked outside.

'You've got to be joking,' said Wayne.

'We have to go,' said Scott. 'We'll use the ledge.'

Another bash.

'We'll be sitting ducks,' said Wayne.

Dave nudged him. 'Fucking do as he says.'

Another bash, and a plank of wood clattered. Scott fired through the gap, hitting one of the thugs in the shoulder.

'Come on!' he shouted.

The others scrambled through the broken window and onto a sloping ledge no wider than a foot. They barely made it along a few inches.

The thugs burst through, and some fire came their way. Scott returned it.

'Keep going!'

This was really bad. Wayne was right.

Scott spent his remaining bullets, hitting only two out of the teeming mass that had now piled in.

They could barely hold on, their trainers trying vainly to get a grip of the sloping surface.

Somebody slipped and fell, the gutter he grabbed hold of ripped and he dangled from it like a rope. The thugs saw what had happened and fired. The guy hanging from the gutter was shot in the head and fell four storeys below.

Dave gaped in horror. Bullets flew at him, and he returned fire. The thugs shrank back.

Scott thought quickly. 'Hold onto each other's backs,' he shouted.

A shot rang out, somehow missing them.

'Now!'

Scott held onto the other guy whose name he didn't know, with Wayne and Dave somehow managing to lock arms, then took off, a human stack trailing beneath him. They made it to the ground, and by the time the thugs realised what had happened, they were running for the nearest building – the gymnasium.

Dave tried the door. 'Fucking hell, it's locked!' he cried.

The thugs began to fire again.

'Come on you fucking—' Dave shouted. At the same time, the door opened, causing him to fall flat on his face. The humour was lost in their frantic struggle to get inside. They slammed the door behind them. More pupils and a few teachers were hiding there, frozen with fear.

'Does anyone know Sophie Patterson?' Scott called out.

Most of them were far too frightened to talk. But a few people raised their heads in response.

'I do.'

Three boys approached them. One of them was thin with curly cinnamon-coloured hair, wearing the blue school uniform. Another was dark skinned, with plaited hair, also wearing the same school uniform. The boy next to him was short and unkempt, with greasy brown hair and a small nose, wearing brown trousers frayed at the bottom. On his back was a little girl who looked no older than five. Scott wondered what she was doing in a high school.

'Do you know where she's gone?' Scott asked.

'No, do you?' said the shorter one.

'We went to her class,' said Dave. 'There was no one there. Do you have any other ideas, Nigel? Is there any other group of survivors you know that have made it out?'

'We haven't left this place since it happened,' said Nigel. 'Maybe.'

'Is any help coming?' said the cinnamon-haired boy. 'It'll only be a matter of time before they discover us.'

'The cops are coming, Olav,' said Dave. 'Scott helped them advance but our position was overrun and we couldn't stay in her classroom. I don't know how long they'll be.'

Scott addressed Olav. 'I need to find her. Is there really no other place they could go?'

'Why don't we just wait here?' said Olav. 'Like Dave said, the cops are on their way. Why don't we just wait here until they come for us?'

'The thugs literally saw us come in here,' said Scott. 'We have to keep moving, and we're out of ammo.'

The other boy, who he would later learn was called Rickey, suddenly tensed. A bullet had shot between them. Scott spun round. A pinprick of daylight speared through the door. Then another.

'Move!' he cried.

They ran on, and seconds later the door was breached. Everyone fled, those at the back being gunned down. A hundred yards later they were out, running on. Then there were more gunshots and people running their way. They were surrounded.

'Now!'

Someone leaped from behind the thugs and kicked one in the face. Scott turned and saw another do the same. Then, most spectacularly of all, another leaped in and took down six in a matter of seconds.

'Are you OK, Scott?'

He stared. 'How—?'

'I'll explain later,' said Sophie.

'Do you know each other?' said her friend. She was a thin petite girl, with golden-brown hair that draped below her shoulders, and wore a pale green sweater.

Before Sophie could answer, more thugs piled out. The Aquilacry was charged up. Scott blew. The cry incapacitated the thugs and almost his friends too.

Scott took to the air then, and the others watched dumbfounded as he took their attackers down. Sophie was the most gobsmacked of all. She stared at him as if she'd been struck in the face.

'How—?' she began.

'I'll explain later,' said Scott.

They heard more footsteps – more thugs. Scott blew, but there were more than before. He dispatched all except five. He'd used up the Aquilacry's power again.

Bullets blazed – the thugs fell down dead. Scott and the others stared, and in came the SWAT team.

'You kids stand down now,' said their commander. He was fully kitted out in body armour, his eyes communicating a seriousness they couldn't argue with.

A helicopter could be heard from afar, making its way towards the school. The unmistakable noise of its rotating blades was getting closer. They cheered; this had to be the backup they needed, though Scott couldn't see an identifiable label of 'Police' on its metal flanks.

It descended to the height of the school – and then it produced a particularly devastating weapon. From either side of its cockpit slid two miniguns, each with six revolving barrels of death that could dispense hundreds of rounds in one minute flat! They let loose. The SWAT commander's men were cut down like grass. The rest of them ran for shelter behind a brick wall, the blaze missing them by millimetres. The brickwork burst all around them. The commander had managed to escape death but only just; he'd been hit in the back and was now dragging himself across the tarmac one agonising inch at a time.

'We're really done for now,' said Wayne. 'They were our last hope.'

Scott stared wildly. Anyone in that open space must be dead or close to it. He spotted the commander's M16 rifle; he was barely keeping a hold of it.

'Stay here!' he cried.

'What?' said the others.

But Scott was off, shooting across the ground to snatch up the commander's rifle. The helicopter saw him and pressed home the attack. Scott returned fire. The rifle punched through the glass and the helicopter went down in a plume of smoke. The others seized the chance to pull the wounded commander to safety.

Teachers and pupils emerged from the school. Their mouths were open, speechless with what must have been amazement but also apprehension.

Then the army turned up – rather too late. A company of troops had appeared, dropping down from helicopters, instinctively spreading out to surround the school. Out of nowhere, three tanks thundered into the schoolyard and so did five Humvees, each with a gunner stationed on their machine guns.

What looked like a commanding officer stepped out of one of the Humvees. Scott was expecting him to be praising, but he disliked him instantly. He had a cold and blank look on his face that radiated indifference. He was the kind of person everyone was reluctant to obey, but obliged to out of fear.

'What the hell?' one of his troops spoke in sheer astonishment.

The commanding officer examined the row of students lined up in front of him with a calculating stare.

'Well?' he said adamantly. 'Who did all this? *Who?*'

He was a hard-looking man who'd probably seen lots of military action in life, and he was clearly prepared to belittle them. His troops stood by him in stunned silence; no one else from his company dared to speak out of turn again.

Scott felt Sophie tap him, then with audacious strides he stepped out of the crowd, staring that commanding officer in the eye with malevolence –without fear of the dozens of guns held by the men in green. Everyone fell silent.

He lifted himself into the air, just a few feet, and all the troops, including the commanding officer, shrank back, drawing their weapons out of fright. He dropped to the ground again with a thud that wasn't that heavy but seemed to reverberate through the concrete.

Scott could see the commander biting back the urge to jump out of fright, or even to shiver.

He stared him straight in the eye; like everyone else, he wanted them to back off – now!

The commanding officer had seen enough.

'Return to base!' he barked at his troops.

A convoy of *yes-sirs* followed, then without any more comments, the troops were whisked back onto their helicopters, the armoured vehicles driving away. The commanding officer however stayed a little longer, the look of contempt growing across his hardened face. He was clearly used to being more powerful. Perhaps they were having this staring contest because he was struggling to come to terms with his own inferiority in the face of such technology. He reserved his last contemptuous look for Scott before grudgingly wandering away to join his company.

Everyone stared at Scott with apprehension, clearly torn between being thankful for his help and unnerved by the unorthodoxy of the victory – that it had been achieved by a stranger who they knew nothing about and who'd stared the United States Army in the face without fear.

He was surprised to see Sophie making her way unhesitatingly towards him. The crowd held its breath.

'Well everyone,' she said uncomfortably, noticing everyone's reaction, 'meet my new friend Scott.'

He bowed like an eagle spreading his wings, causing a few people to shrink back in fear.

'What is that thing you fly with?' said Nigel.

'This,' said Scott, 'is my most prized possession and I call it the micro-flyer. You saw earlier that it allows me to fly. But it's flight without the power of any fuel except your mind.'

'How does that work?' asked Nigel.

'I have no idea,' Scott replied. 'Except, you put this helmet on your head and you can do it. I call it the mindshield.'

'Can I try it?' asked Nigel. He came out of the crowd.

'You're Nigel, right?' said Scott. He knew this already but introductions before had been rather rushed.

Nigel nodded. 'Can someone look after Hyliana for me?' he asked.

He carefully took the little girl and handed her to Sophie. Hyliana looking bemused.

'Here's a hint for you, Nigel,' said Scott. 'The key to mastering this thing overnight is to imagine that you're a graceful bird in the air, like an eagle or an albatross. Because it's powered by your mind, imagining that will make it go a lot smoother. Good luck!'

Nigel closed his eyes, as if trying to grasp this incredible concept. Then the extraordinary happened. He hovered slightly, just a few inches off the ground. It wasn't much, but already people were gaping. Some were rubbing their eyes as if refusing to believe them.

Something in his head must have changed though, because within seconds he rose so high into the air that he became a dark hovering speck in a sea of cloud.

Everyone cheered, daring him to do something bolder. He flew back to the ground, spinning like a spitfire, then landed rather awkwardly, taking a while to cancel his momentum. Certain other people had a go and within minutes all of them were flying, albeit clumsily.

Then at once the majority crowded in like nosy journalists to ask questions, but Scott was more than happy to answer them. They were usually repetitive questions, things he'd actually already told them, but he answered them over and over again without tiring of it.

It was the first time Scott had ever experienced treatment like this. These cool American high-school kids wanted to know about him. Big lads came over and showered him with praise, giving him high fives and openly offering him their friendship. Scott could barely believe what was happening. He'd never made friends as easily as this. They'd only met him a few minutes ago, but they were crowding round as if he were a celebrity.

Sophie was the most gobsmacked of them all. So far she'd been relatively reserved compared to everyone else, but the excitement was finally getting too much for her too.

She was rapidly ushering another girl towards him. So many people were competing for his attention, it was difficult to tell who to respond to.

'Scott, this is Samantha, my best friend since elementary school,' said Sophie.

She offered a hesitant handshake, which he took, followed by a courteous half-hearted nod.

'So you're Scott then?' said Samantha shyly.

'That's right.'

'Sophie told me about you on the bus. You're not from here, are you?'

'I'm from Scotland – from Aberdeen.'

Samantha studied him for a moment, as if she was looking for something. 'Do you not have a kilt?' she asked.

How typical, he thought, but even *he* wasn't immune to being influenced by stereotypes.

'Uh no,' he said, chuckling. 'People in Scotland usually only wear kilts for traditional events.'

Samantha seemed lost for words, and her eye contact wavered. Scott glanced at her brunette friend, who was standing a few metres away, looking rather zoned out.

'Is that the Scottish boy over there?' came an ominous shout from across the playground.

An adult approached the gathering, his face gloating.

'Hi,' said Scott, raising his hand for a handshake.

The guy batted it away. Scott frowned. This guy's social skills seemed even worse than his own.

'Who are you?' asked Scott defensively.

'He's Mr Hockley, my math teacher,' said Sophie gloomily.

'I see,' said Scott.

Her disdain was clearly appropriate.

'You're the Scottish boy,' said Mr Hockley. 'The one that I've been hearing about non-stop all day. How can you be a true Scot? Your hair's brown, and where's your kilt? I thought Scots didn't wear trousers.'

Unlike Samantha's ignorance, Scott wasn't laughing at this one. It was one thing for one of his peers to make an awkward comment, especially without meaning offence. But this was an adult, who should have known better. It wasn't only stereotyped but very rude.

'I apologise for this, Scott, but he's a racist bully,' said Sophie. 'He belittles anyone who doesn't have a mathematical career in mind and he's been doing it for years – even to me.'

'Is that true?' Scott asked him.

Unlike the teachers Scott knew at home, this man had no power over him. He could say whatever he wanted.

'Absolute rubbish,' said Mr Hockley. 'Kids these days say anything to make you look bad.'

'But you've just proven to me that you *are* bad,' said Scott.

There was a collective 'ooh' from the onlookers. No one had ever spoken to their most feared teacher like that before.

'Excuse me?' said Mr Hockley.

'Maths isn't my best subject either,' said Scott. 'In fact it's one of my worst ones. But a good teacher should be inspired to teach to the best of their ability, especially to those who struggle at their subject. But you're not a good teacher.'

'What insolence, boy. How old are you?'

'Fifteen,' Scott replied. 'And how old are *you*?'

Somebody in the audience laughed loudly.

'Shut it!' he shouted at whoever did it.

'He's fifty-seven!' shouted Dave.

Spontaneous laughter.

'Why you—' Mr Hockley began, then looked around, realising he was outnumbered.

'That's not the worst of it, Scott,' said Sophie. 'As well as being a bully, he's also a predator. He's even tried it on with me.'

Even more spontaneous laughter.

'Mr Hockley!'

Everyone spun round.

He was only one man yet now it felt like *they* were outnumbered. He wore a black suit and tie, over a white shirt, and his shoes were a shiny black without laces: the principal. He stormed up to the gathered crowd. Scott wasn't quite sure who he was mad at, and he began to wonder if his teasing had been such a good idea.

The principal took a look around at the crowd of students assembled and the wreckage of the helicopter, then at him, showing no emotion. Everyone had fallen silent, expecting to be berated.

As fast as lighting, he marched up to face Mr Hockley, and a split second later, Mr Hockley cried out in pain. It caused everyone to laugh uproariously.

Scott wasn't sure what the principal had done at first. Then he saw Mr Hockley clutch the side of his obese chest, and when the bodies parted, Scott saw his shirt bore a hole the size of a tennis ball, exposing a hairy nipple. The principal had Mr Hockley's ID badge. He raised it up for all to see then threw it away. As a bonus, it fell down a drain.

'This is the last straw, James,' he said. 'Miss Patterson has perfectly summarised your inane tendencies. You're struck off with immediate effect!'

'But, sir!' said Mr Hockley, the arrogance in his voice reduced to a whimper.

'I'll write a formal dismissal later,' said the principal. 'And the appropriate charges will be brought I'm sure.'

'But—' Mr Hockley protested.

'Go now,' he said calmly, though thunder rumbled in his voice.

Mr Hockley was helpless to do anything.

The principal gave him his briefcase.

'I have something to give you too,' said Scott.

He flew away, then a few seconds later dumped a garbage bag at Mr Hockley's feet.

'Here's *the sack*.'

Mr Hockley barely looked at him. He left, and didn't take the bag. His authority meant nothing and now everyone had even more reason to feel triumphant.

The principal watched his employee leave, smiling discreetly to himself. But he soon got serious and to everyone's delight he abruptly announced that the school day was now officially over and that they were free to go.

Scott was about to board the bus with the others when the principal called to him.

'You there, young man,' he said. 'I'm curious to talk to you. Mind if you stay behind?'

Scott frowned.

'What about transport home?' he asked.

'I think you've already got that covered,' the principal said, eyeing the micro-flyer.

'Aren't you coming, Scott?' called Sophie.

'I have to stay; I'll meet you back at the house.'

With a hiss the bus doors closed and it drove off down the road. Scott watched them go, wishing he was traveling with them. It would have been a great bonding opportunity.

He turned to the principal who stood patiently, studying him. Scott was nervous. He seemed very serious, yet dryly humorous at the same time. He didn't know what to make of him.

Scott came closer, as if awaiting a tirade.

'Who are you?' he asked.

He wasn't angry, just intrigued.

'I'm Scott Wallace,' he said. 'From Scotland.'

The principal raised his eyebrows. 'Well that explains it then,' he said. 'It must be in your blood to fight like a warrior; considering the many Scottish soldiers that fought the English for independence, centuries before this country was even known.'

He too seemed influenced by stereotypes.

'I've never thought of it that way,' said Scott humbly, not knowing how else to respond.

'How did you do that?' the principal asked softly. 'Do you do some sort of martial art?'

'It's complicated,' Scott replied.

'In what way?'

Scott sighed. 'If I told you, you might find it disturbing.'

The principal frowned uncomfortably. 'Tell me about your machine,' he asked. 'Where did you get it from? I've never seen anything like it.'

'I call it the micro-flyer,' said Scott. 'It's powered by my thoughts, though I have no idea how.'

'But where did you get it from?' he asked, noticing that Scott had avoided the question.

'I found it,' Scott replied. 'A weird capsule washed ashore. I went to it when it was unguarded and found it inside.'

That probably created more questions than it answered.

'So you've had it a while?'

'Yes,' said Scott.

It wasn't that he was short of words, he just wasn't sure he wanted to dispel everything to this man.

'I'm new to the area,' he said hastily. 'I've only been here for a few days birdwatching and hanging out with Sophie.'

'Speaking of which, is she any relation to you? You seem to be quite friendly.'

'We're just friends,' Scott replied. 'We met at the Sea Marshes Reserve; she likes birds too.'

'I see.'

Scott piped up. 'She's the best friend I've ever had. It's a great privilege to spend time with her. I don't have any friends at home.'

'From the way I saw it, it looks like everyone in the school wants to be your friend,' said the principal. For the first time Scott saw him smile fully.

'I run a good school, Scott,' said the principal. 'I've seen many strong friendships develop between so many different people, but I get the impression you're not so fortunate in that regard.'

'I used to have friendships,' said Scott, 'back when I lived in the Highlands. But I had to move to Aberdeen and since then it's been terrible. I don't know why.'

'You might be pleased to know that Sophie is at least partly the reason for our success. Every year in America we hold an anti-bullying day at school. It's a legal requirement, you see, and I think it goes some way to dealing with what I think is wrong with society. Too many deaths are associated with bullying. I hear of too many shootings in schools, many related to victims out for revenge. I never thought I'd ever see such a massacre in my own school; we've never had one until today.'

He steered himself back on track.

'I'm impressed by how strongly Sophie puts across her anti-bullying messages. She's very confident, and people follow suit with that and join her. There's been precious little bullying reported here since she enrolled four years ago. She adopts people with all manner of issues into her social circle, and as far as I'm aware they seem to get on fine. If someone needs help with exam revision, or is being bullied or has any issue at all, anyone can come to her for help. She's an angel, Scott; I don't think the place will be the same without her.'

'Wow.' Scott didn't know what else to say.

'Her popularity isn't even restricted to the school – she's popular with the community as a whole. She's done volunteering at homeless shelters, given money to some notable charities, sponsored children in the Third World, and is campaigning to end cetacean captivity. At the end of the day, she inspires us all to give more to the world.'

Scott was still lost for words – it was a lot to take in and a lot to come to terms with. But he felt as if he'd heard enough. He wanted to fly away and be with Sophie and all her friends.

The principal saw his restlessness. 'Do you want to go home?'

Scott nodded and thanked him for his information. He flew off into the afternoon sky, the wind rushing by like an invisible icy river across his cheeks, which very soon were going to be warmed up again when he was reunited with his best friend.

He descended onto Fisher Street, automatically folding his wings up out of sight, and was greeted with a flurry of enthusiasm and laughter from Sophie and her friends, who'd clearly been waiting for him.

Despite the fact he'd finally been accepted into a social circle, he nonetheless felt a twinge of envy. He found it amazing that Sophie could be popular so easily and have so many *meaningful* friends as a result. But to enjoy the thrill of acceptance, he pushed these thoughts aside – those days were behind him. Now he was being brought into a social circle he would cherish forever!

CHAPTER 9
The Fair

'You never told me you could fly!' said Sophie. The amazement of today's events had hit her hard.

'And *you* never told me you were going to school today and were able to do karate for that matter!' Scott was awaiting an explanation from her.

Sophie hung her head sheepishly. 'Well… we were having fun remember?'

He smiled. 'Sure.'

There was an awkward pause.

'So what happens now? Are we all just hanging out?' he asked.

'Yeah, there's no school now so we can do whatever we want,' she said.

'You didn't lose anyone you knew, did you… back at the school?' he asked. Although he was happy Sophie and her friends were alive, many hadn't been so lucky. The death toll had been at least fifty.

'I don't think so,' she said, 'but thank you for asking.'

She sighed, her blue eyes shimmering as she gazed at him. She threw a hug around him which took him by surprise. He shuddered initially but soon relaxed and awkwardly returned the affection.

'Thank you for coming to get me,' she whispered.

'That's OK,' said Scott, not knowing what else to say.

She released him. 'If it hadn't been for you, we would have lost more,' she said.

Samantha came in. 'Sophie, your parents are here and they want to have a word with you.'

'Can't it wait?' Sophie asked.

'They're quite angry'

Sophie sighed again. 'I gotta go, Scott; I'll come back.'

Then she was off.

But Scott wasn't alone for long.

'Hi.'

He turned. 'Oh hi,' he said, trying to sound polite.

'You're Scott, right?'

He nodded.

She sounded painfully shy. Scott soon recognised her. She was the girl from the playground – alongside Sophie and Samantha she'd helped them out when Scott and the boys had been surrounded. She'd been looking away most of the time, and he was actually quite surprised now he was able to examine her appearance properly.

She wore glasses just like him and had brown hair, a thin mouth and a thin body. Her face was pitted with spots and blackheads. He tried not to grimace.

'And your name was Sara right?'

'Yeah.'

She looked down at the floor, avoiding all eye contact. There was a long silence.

'I thought you were very brave back there,' she said at last.

'Thank you,' Scott replied.

Another long silence. Neither of them were very good at this.

'So you're friends with Sophie as well?' Scott asked.

'Uh yes, not as long as Samantha's been though.'

'Uh, right.'

She kept staring at the floor, then she flapped her hands. 'I need some air.'

She ran off outside.

Scott blinked repeatedly, wondering what had just happened.

'Scott?'

Samantha had reappeared.

'There's some people outside saying they're your parents. They want to see you.'

Oh crikey, he thought, he'd forgotten all about them.

To his surprise and absolute horror, both Sophie's parents and his own were assembled outside the house. Scott waited for the axe to fall on his now exposed neck.

'OK, Scott,' said Mary, 'let me tell you what we've discussed here. We're not happy with you disappearing again, not least when a siege has been reported.'

'But Scott helped—' Sophie began.

'*No!*' Scott hissed hysterically.

She stared at him.

He felt bad. He couldn't articulate the fact that any questioning of his involvement would lead to them discovering the micro-flyer, but he hated to be so sharp.

'But we want you to know we've reached an agreement about something,' she said. 'We feel in hindsight that we've been too hard on you. It's obvious that you want to be social and you've developed a good friendship with this girl, so we're not going to stop you from hanging out – just don't get into any more trouble, OK?'

'It's early days of our holiday, Scott,' said Sean. 'We noticed you've been lonely and we want you to have a good time, and if this is the way you want to do it, then we have no right to stop you.'

'Thanks,' said Scott.

'I think you'd be a very good influence for Sophie,' said Sally. 'I don't think there can be that many people with your shared interests around.'

Her father said nothing.

'Now go and rejoin the party,' said Sally.

And so they did.

Scott didn't know how she came to know about it, but Sophie suddenly started: 'The fair's on tonight everyone!'

An uproarious cheer resounded around the room.

'The fair?' asked Scott.

'A monthly traveling one,' said Sophie. 'There's rides, stalls – everything. It's going to be tonnes of fun. Interested in coming? It'll take our minds off what happened earlier, and I'm sure lots of people will be thinking the same.'

Scott nodded profusely.

'Awesome,' said Nigel. He shot outside like a hare, and to Scott's astonishment started scaling a coconut palm. With Hyliana clinging to his back like an infant, Scott watched him climb with apprehension – the palm tree must have been at least ten metres in height, and he had no safety gear. Scott was very worried about the girl clinging to him and couldn't help but raise his concern with Sophie.

'It's OK, Scott,' she said. 'It's something they do together all the time.'

Scott had had a chance to examine Nigel properly during the party. He was quite small for his age, and Scott had a hard time believing he was really fifteen like himself. He looked closer to eight.

One thing that Scott immediately found distinctive about Nigel was his face, which was full of attitude and animation. He could never seem to keep still. If he wasn't bounding about like a chimpanzee, he was always twitching, as if at least one part of him always had to be one hundred percent mobile.

He wrapped his legs around the trunk and hung like a giant bat, making plenty of noise. Hyliana was upside down with him, grinning with exhilaration. Scott found it amazing that he was agile enough to accomplish that but couldn't help but cringe at what could best be described as expert recklessness. Everyone waved up at him, praising him for his daring mission. He was as nimble as a monkey – in fact he did almost everything like a monkey, hence his nickname: the Monkey Man.

Nigel climbed down from the tree and gave people high fives. The strange thing was that they looked at his odd habits as if they were perfectly normal. Perhaps Sophie had imposed that they should be accepted. If Nigel's behaviour was accepted by all then perhaps they wouldn't scrutinize Scott's own true character.

He remembered then that there was one thing he hadn't yet told Sophie about himself. He hadn't told her about his Asperger's syndrome, a condition that affected the cognitive abilities of a person, especially with regards to learning and social interaction. It was a condition he had a love-hate relationship with.

On the one hand, it helped him focus on his passions, but on the other it made making friends hard and forming relationships even harder; being out of tune with people was an all-too-common problem.

Watching Nigel be himself gave Scott reassurance though.

'How do you do that?' he asked.

'Do what?' asked Nigel.

'Climb like that?'

'Through practice,' he said.

Scott found it rather difficult to keep him engaged. Scott wasn't the best with eye contact, but Nigel barely gave him any. He was still looking around like the conversation didn't matter. The little girl had to prod him to return Scott's gaze.

'Sorry, I have ADHD,' said Nigel. 'That's why I'm restless.'

Suddenly it all made sense. ADHD – or attention deficit hyperactivity disorder – was a condition involving intense hyperactive behaviour, coupled with difficulties with impulse control and attentiveness.

'Who's the girl on your back?' asked Scott.

'This is my sister Hyliana,' said Nigel. 'My adoptive sister at least.'

'Adoptive sister?' Scott asked.

'My parents do charity work in Brazil. Her family were murdered by drug dealers and they rescued her, brought her here and gave me someone to look after.'

He ruffled her hair and she grinned.

'How old is she?' Scott asked. 'Four? Five?'

Hyliana gave him a rather venomous look, her dark-skinned face contorting.

'I'm fifteen!' she said sharply.

Scott looked from him to her in surprise. Up until now he wasn't sure she could speak. He knew he'd said something wrong and was looking to Nigel for an explanation.

'She suffers from primordial dwarfism, and because she can't walk for very long, I have to carry her everywhere.'

She giggled.

Scott tried to relax.

'I'm sorry about what I said. Are you OK?' Scott asked.

Hyliana frowned, not really giving him an answer. She looked away.

'It's OK,' said Nigel. 'She just takes a while to get used to new people.'

It was 3 p.m. and the fair was still at least three hours away, so Sophie felt that a walk was in order. The sun boiled the suburbs; cracks appeared in the road and on the 'sidewalk'. Everything either sweated or cracked. Looking back, Scott saw someone lagging behind. He thought he wasn't one of their group to begin with but soon remembered that he'd seem him at the party and dropped his pace to meet his.

'Hi there,' he said, the awkwardness of his social skills causing his voice to shake.

'Hello,' he replied, not quite with an American accent. It sounded deep, with a slight raggedness that took him by surprise.

'I'm Scott, the saviour,' Scott joked.

The boy tried to smile. 'My name is Olav,' he replied. 'Olav Jensen.'

They shook hands, albeit awkwardly.

'How are you feeling after today?' he asked.

'Shaken,' Olav admitted, 'but not stirred I believe is the English saying.'

Scott grinned. 'Where about do you come from?'

'I am an American citizen now,' he said rather abruptly, 'but I am originally from Norway. Which means as you can probably tell, the heat here doesn't agree with me.'

Scott hadn't been examining anyone's perspiration levels that closely, but Olav definitely seemed to sweat a lot. His white T-shirt bore sweat holes under his armpits. Scott quickly took the opportunity to examine him: about his age, fifteen maybe sixteen at most. His cinnamon-coloured hair looked woolly and dishevelled, and his face was broad, with a large Roman nose and an unshaven chin.

'Where about in Norway do you come from?' Scott asked.

'A small village called Korsnes at the head of Tysfjord. That was where I spent most of my days. I had a great childhood back home. I went to a small school with the best teacher I could ask for. It was a small neighbourhood, everyone knew everyone, and I was friends with nearly every child my age.

'I was encouraged to use my father's sailing boat, and at the weekends me and my friends used to camp on the nearby islands or on the far shore next to the forest. If we had time, we would sail across the fjord to Lofoten – but that was usually a much longer, more difficult trip.'

Now that Olav had begun speaking, the words poured out him. 'My father was a fisherman. He would fish for cod, haddock and ling amongst other things, and I thank him for developing my interest in the sea, and the outdoors in general. When I was nine, he took me on a very exciting trip to Svalbard. It was so much fun. I had more friends to play with, and we'd sail around seeing seals, walruses, whales, reindeer and polar bears.'

'Sounds amazing,' Scott commented. 'What made you move here?'

'Ah,' said Olav, 'that happened because of the death of my father.'

Scott gaped.

'He was on a trawler somewhere off the northern coast in the middle of January, a storm picked up and he was thrown overboard. His body was never recovered. I was only eight years old.'

'I'm so sorry.'

'My mother worked at the local church, but without the income from my father's job, she struggled to make ends to meet. Norway is an expensive country to live in, you understand, and there were too few other jobs for her to take.

'I was too young to understand what would become of me. I did suggest that we move to Trondheim or Oslo – it would have meant the loss of my playgrounds, but at least my mother could have found a job. It was bad timing that my aunt and uncle had decided to emigrate to Miami – apparently fancying the sun – and they made the decision that I would stay with them.

'I didn't want to go, but I was unruly, and I suppose that made my mother's decision easier. My aunt and uncle are kind, but this place was so alien to me. I hated the heat, the blasting sunshine. I had to be enrolled in a new school. I had been taught English in Korsnes, but it became a necessity once I came here. I lacked any friends, and I was bullied because of my accent.

'Things are better now, but I still miss home very dearly. I lost contact with the friends I knew, though I still keep in touch with my mother obviously.'

Olav sighed.

'But at least I've made friends here,' he continued. 'And my English is better than ever. I keep an Oxford dictionary on my bedside table, just in case I want to learn any new words.'

Scott had to remember that Olav too was in a culture shock just like him, and appreciated that he needed to do these things in order to find his feet.

Loud slurred whistling interrupted the conversation. Scott quickly turned to see a small brilliantly red bird alight on the uneven roof of one of the villas. It was so loud that everyone turned to look at it.

Olav grinned. 'I heard that you like birds. Can you tell us what this one is?'

Sophie, who was walking alongside them, would of course know the answer to this but she clearly wanted to see how well Scott knew North American birds. Scott knew the answer too but he couldn't believe he was seeing one properly for the first time. He had seen them in the Sea Marshes Reserve, yet the views of them hadn't been all that satisfactory.

'That's a cardinal,' Scott replied. 'A northern cardinal.'

The cardinal descended onto the lawn to the left of the house, picking off insects with its red finch-like bill. It foraged quickly, raising its head every few seconds to scan for a threat, then flew up and perched on the low chain-link fence, sticking its face outward as if suspicious.

They found more birds. Scott and Sophie were busy pointing them out, but although the others were initially curious, their interest soon fizzled out, with Wayne the first to switch off. Out of all of them, it seemed as though Scott, Sophie and Olav were the most nature-oriented of them all.

Nigel and Hyliana seemed to enjoy climbing trees though, and Scott supposed that counted. Now and then he would also catch sight of Samantha pausing to examine plants and shrubs, giving some of the more aromatic species a sniff.

Rickey seemed to shun the forest cover for some reason, hanging back from it as if it were a dark web. Sara seemed ambivalent to it all, showing a polite curiosity at best. While Wayne had great trouble sustaining any curiosity. No wonder he'd switched off so quickly.

◆ ◆ ◆

They waited until nightfall before heading out to the fair. The short walk there was merrily wonderful. It was almost beyond belief that Scott was here, with a group of people more or less his own age, accepting him as one of their own. Wayne would banter with other young passers-by, while Nigel raced ahead, climbing on anything he could.

In the midst of all this activity, Scott truly saw what he'd been missing out on. It almost saddened him how so much time in his life had passed without anything like this. He was best friends with Sophie for crying out loud, the most popular girl in school, who ensured everyone was treated justly and equally. Not only that but he'd won the respect of the entire group. He was euphoric.

They practically ran into the fair. People were pouring in from all sides, the atmosphere lively. There was the soothing electric sounds of arcades; the dodgems smashing into each other; the screams and shouts of dizzy youngsters spinning crazily on a wheel behind the shooting stands; a carousel playing its music, its plastic horses rising and falling to the rhythm. The excitement had been so intense that no one else in their party was anywhere to be seen; as soon as they'd got inside, everyone had dispersed without discussing a plan of action, rushing excitedly over to different attractions.

Sophie glanced at him. 'Looks like it's just you and me, Scott,' she said. 'What would you like to do first?'

He considered. There were some attractions here he definitely wanted to avoid, the spinning wheel being the main one. He'd never been a fan of spinning rides or rollercoasters; fear would usually stop him going on them, and even if it didn't, he would always feel sick and dizzy afterwards. Then he looked at the attraction closest to them: the dodgems, a floodlit ring buzzing with tension. Scott had always enjoyed dodgems – they gave him a friendly feeling of being in a battle with other people. He made a decision.

The cars powered up, and Sophie and Scott sat in one together, eagerly awaiting the moment they were given the signal to go and bash the others.

'Who shall I go for?' Scott asked.

'Anybody you like,' said Sophie. 'Anyone who takes us on.'

The signal was given and the cars began to move.

Scott pushed down on the pedal with all his strength and they shot forward, slamming into the side of somebody else's car. It slid sideways, momentarily stuck. Scott drove around for another attack but another car slammed into them.

He momentarily lost control and received another smashing hit; the people responsible were another couple, both grinning competitively.

You'll regret that, thought Scott, but he wasn't upset. It had taken him time to learn not to treat games too seriously.

They drove forward for the next attack and Scott instinctively drove out of the way, making a sharp turn, then crashed into their side. He pushed the car into the middle of the ring and three more cars hit it with a bump. They looked truly stuck. Sophie gave him a high five and turned around to see them better.

'That's what you get when you mess with us!' she shouted.

Now all the cars in the ring were after them, coming at them in a blockade of lights and metal. Scott shot forward through the closing gap of the cars, only just making it! The other cars hit each other head-on, causing the passengers to shudder in their seats. Since there was no reverse gear, they took longer to get out of this entanglement.

Scott turned the car around and sat for a moment, preparing to mount a counter-attack. The other cars tried to take action, but he weaved in and around them, and once again they crashed into each other. They looked in even more of a pickle than before.

Scott had to bite his tongue to stop himself from jeering. Then when the fun seemed to be at its best, it was time to stop.

Scott took Sophie to the shooting stands next, with their characteristic oversized soft toys sitting at the back, waiting for the improbable moment that someone would win them. They browsed the stands until they came to one with an air rifle lying chained to the counter. The man at the stall saw their curiosity and went to greet them.

'Would you like to win a prize for your girlfriend?' he said, staring hopefully at Scott.

He blushed. 'Oh we're not actually—' Sophie began.

'My apologies,' said the stall owner.

Scott tried not to droop. He recovered swiftly.

'How much will that be?' he asked.

'Five bucks.'

Scott gave him the money and the air rifle was his. He loaded it tenderly and aimed for the tiny ringed gold bottle at the top.

Scott had three shots to win something for Sophie, just three. He was going to go for the gold bottle in the background, but then he changed his mind and went for an easier target.

He hit one of the green bottles and it toppled, though the ring on it stayed put. The man looked somewhat furious – he was evidently someone who got in a bad mood when someone was winning at his game. The speed at which the cork travelled was astonishing; it could probably take an eye out.

Scott aimed for the gold one again. A flicker of lightning from the black sky took his eye off the game and he fired it by accident. It missed by a centimetre. The bottle shook a little but didn't fall over.

With his last cork he took aim for the gold one for the last time – he held the gun as still as he could and fired. The cork hit the neck of the bottle and it toppled – the ring still intact.

'We have a winner!' he said, pretending to sound triumphant. 'Since you hit a gold bottle, that makes you lucky; there's a hundred-dollar note in there and that's yours.'

Scott took the hundred dollars and stashed it in his wallet.

'Since you also hit the green bottle, you now get to take away one of these.' He gestured to the giant soft toys hanging on the wall.

'Which one would you like, Sophie?' he asked. 'It's your choice; I played this game for you.'

Sophie made an effort to choose, though it took her a while – they were all equally adorable.

'I'll take that big polar bear,' she said finally.

He took the polar bear off the wall and handed it to her. It was enormous, almost as big as her.

'Thank you, Scott,' she said, hugging him with the polar bear.

She carried it on her back like a youngster that had long outgrown piggyback rides. When they reunited with Samantha, the other girl stared in astonishment at it. Sophie waved the polar bear's paw in greeting.

'Did Scott get you that?' Samantha squeaked.

'Yeah.'

'Can I hold him?' she asked.

Sophie handed the massive soft toy over. Samantha stroked it, eyeing the huge bear enviously.

'Scott must be some shot to win you something this big.'

'Oh he is,' said Sophie. 'I find that a fascinating ability.' She then changed the subject. 'So what have you all been doing while we were away?'

'Well the boys have gone to play on the arcade games. Personally I think it's a rip-off, but they don't seem to care.'

'Where's Nigel?' asked Scott.

'He's on the climbing frame as usual. Hyliana's with him.'

Sure enough Nigel was there, and it was clear that he was the best climber out of all of them. He could have reached the top several times over without any safety ropes. While everyone else struggled, he raced to the top of the twenty-foot frame and was in the hardest section, clambering over and around obstacles that had defeated the others with ease. Very soon he was at the top for a third time in a row, scrutinising the other climbers.

When Nigel eventually decided to come down, he did so in style, bouncing on and off the wall until he hit the ground.

People gaped at him – it was something they'd all be afraid to do. Scott wondered which he'd be better at: being a climber or a stuntman! People applauded him – it was an absolutely amazing method of attracting attention.

The instructors looked somewhat in shock. Their climbing frame had been carefully designed with dispersed hand and foot holds, steep overhangs and a dizzying height from bottom to top, and it had all been defeated three times in a row by this small, hyperactive kid.

'You're one of a kind!' said Sophie. 'I wonder what

you'll scale next?'

'Well I see a flagpole over there; I'll try that next!' said Nigel excitedly.

Before Scott could speak to him, he was off towards to the flagpole and humping his way up with tremendous speed, Hyliana doing nothing to stop him.

'Why don't we leave him to do that?' Scott said to Sophie.

'Would you like to go on the arcade games?' she asked.

'Yeah sure. How much money have you got?' he asked. 'I've got my hundred.'

'And I've got twenty bucks.'

The arcade-game section was enormous, a shimmering cabin of multi-coloured lights and electric sounds, something Scott found quite a draw. With undivided attention, the kids played their games, eager to win to the end. There were racing-car games, shooting games, gambling machines (not for them as they were too young) and air hockey, which Sara and Rickey were playing together. Wayne was playing a game that seemed to be about football, while Olav was on a sort of pirate-ship game, nuking all the other ships with his plastic canon. They whiled away the next few hours there, until the fair was nearing closing time.

However no one had forgotten the atrocities of earlier today. They were all seated on foldable plastic chairs as the fair owner took the stand.

'Good evening, our fine young boys and girls,' he began. 'Our fair is an annual tradition, one that we are very proud to support, for it provides our youth a place in which to unwind, enjoy our gloriously hot summers and make memories with friends and family alike.

We're gathered here tonight to honour the fifty boys and girls from the South Dade High School who I'm sure planned on being here tonight but could not do so because of a truly tragic invasion. There are no answers as to why this happened, but leads will continue to be followed for as long as it takes to find the justice they deserve.'

He read out the names of all those that had perished at the school. The highly jovial mood had turned sombre.

'Too many die in this city,' he said afterwards. 'I can only ever wonder when they will end?'

For some reason he said 'they'.

After that, everyone made to leave, the sobering punch of the fair owner's words still smarting. Scott glimpsed something on the beach, half hidden by the palm trees. He excused himself by saying to the others that he was thirsty and wanted a Coke and went to investigate the trees.

Once he was close, he shivered. Dark hooded figures stood there like terracotta warriors waiting to be resurrected.

For a while nothing happened – the figures simply stared, and Scott wasn't sure whether to get out of there or stay put. Had they seen him? Of course they had – his silhouette was obvious enough against the light of the fair, so why this staring contest?

The moonlight streamed down from the starry sky, illuminating the faces of everyone there – and Scott realised there were far more than he'd thought – around twenty of them!

He heard Sophie calling his name and looked wildly back. Then his heart leaped when he saw all of them move. Simultaneously, all the hooded figures had put their hands in their left pockets as if to take something out.

Scott braced himself, fearing the worst.

There were blinding flashes, the bullets finding their marks in a group of teenagers heading out of the fair. The crowd screamed in terror and panic erupted, everyone pushing and shoving to get out of the firing range.

◆ ◆ ◆

Meanwhile Sophie and the others had heard the shots and were already trying to get the other teens out.

'Where's Scott?' shouted Samantha above the chaos.

'He said he needed a Coke!' said Sophie.

Another barrage of bullets brought down five more, narrowly missing Nigel and Hyliana.

'I'm going to find him,' said Rickey.

'You'll be killed!' said Samantha.

'I'll go too!' said Olav.

'Sophie, Samantha, Sara, stay here and look after the crowd!' said Rickey. 'Nigel, are you coming too?'

'Absolutely,' he replied.

'Let us take Hyliana,' said Sophie.

Nigel handed her over.

'Wayne?' asked Rickey.

'I'll stay here.' He looked sheepish.

Another barrage claimed six casualties this time. Sophie hesitated. They were her friends – they were no good to her dead – but what else could she do? This couldn't go on. She sighed and reluctantly let them go and find Scott.

◆ ◆ ◆

The boys ran into the chaos. The stall owner from the shooting range where Sophie and Scott had won their prizes lay on the ground, three bullet wounds blossoming red on his chest.

Olav took the air rifles from the stand and gathered as many corks as he could find. Rickey had a second rifle, which he was now loading. He couldn't help but wonder whether they might be too late? The last thing they'd want to see was Scott's dead body lying on the grass, brought down by a shower of bullets. Sophie would be distraught.

There was a flicker of movement in the palm trees. Rickey saw it and fired. The cork hit the hooded figure in the eye and he fell down, blinded. There was another at a much closer range; Olav saw it this time and his shot hit the guy in the groin, and he crumpled. Nigel kicked him in the head and he passed out.

They came under fire as they progressed. A guy flew at Dave with a knife, but he swerved and finished him with a knock-out punch.

More thugs surged in. With a smash, a Molotov cocktail hit a stall and it went up in flames.

Suddenly Scott flew in on the micro-flyer. Seeing them under attack made him fly to the rescue. He swooped down and neatly removed one of the thugs, dropping him into the sea.

The last of the thugs seemed to have been taken out, so Rickey promptly put out the fire in the stall.

'Where the hell have you been?' asked Nigel.

'I tried to check out who they were!' said Scott.

'Never mind, it looks like all these guys are down,' said Rickey.

'Where's Sophie?' Scott asked.

'She's near the entrance, with Samantha and Sara,' Rickey replied.

'Nigel, are you OK?'

'Yeah, thanks for helping us out,' said Nigel.

'We should get back to the girls!' said Rickey, dashing off into the ruins of the fair.

Scott was pleased to know that the girls had rescued the vast majority of the people. Even so, the shootings here had claimed twenty-six lives. Their bodies lay strewn on the grass. Scott instantly recognised three of them – the first two were the couple they'd battled on the dodgems, the other was the fair owner earlier.

That couple had been their rivals, but friendly rivals, and the guy giving the speech had talked about this very thing. Like many, he wanted peace, but his life had been claimed by violence. It angered Scott to his bones. He was shocked at the carnage, but he felt relieved that his friends were still alive – and more importantly, Sophie was still alive too!

But he was also amazed. How was it that his friends could stand firm in the face of death and show calm and courage and be able to fight well? Twice today?

Tonight's battle had left him badly shaken, but Scott had a small atom of security to kindle. From then on he felt confident and reasonably secure that if anything else happened, they would fight alongside him.

CHAPTER 10
Undercover

Sophie had another part to her personality that took Scott completely by surprise: her activism. There was no school the next day, so that clean-up operations could take place, so she'd taken him and Olav downtown to the Miami Sea Aquarium. She eyed the entrance contemptuously.

'We need to get inside,' she said.

'How much is it to get in?' asked Scott.

'I don't mean that way,' she said rather sharply. 'There's gotta to be a side entrance.'

She looked around. The fence was taller than them, with sharp corrugated points curved forwards to discourage intruders. Then her face lit up.

'Fly us in, Scott.'

'Um...' he replied. He wasn't one to go around breaking rules and trespassing. Even though there were times he'd made exceptions.

'Don't worry,' she said, 'once I show you what this is about, you won't want to pay a cent towards this place.'

'But...'

'What is it?' said Sophie. 'Is it just breaking and entering that's the problem? We'll be alright. After today, hopefully your respect for this place will go down to zero.'

He hesitated still.

'I trust her to the end of the Earth, Scott,' said Olav.

'We'll be OK.'

Sophie tried to smile warmly. 'Please.'

Her eyes sparkled.

Scott nodded. 'OK.'

It took only minutes to get the three of them inside and no one seemed to notice.

'What if we run into any locked doors or codes?' Scott asked.

'I've got that covered too,' she said. 'Samantha works here as a cleaner, but she's also an undercover activist, but be careful who you say that to. If people knew about that, she might be eaten alive. Let's just wait here. We need her to escort us through the park, just so that the people behind the CCTV don't get suspicious.'

They stood in a dark corridor, between two brick buildings of unknown usage. Sophie's reassuring words did little to calm Scott down. Anyone could come along, see them and wonder what they were doing there. They could fight, argue or whatever, but it would probably get them in more trouble.

Sophie glanced at her watch. 'I did tell her we were coming,' she said, seeing Scott's displeasure.

A figure suddenly appeared. Scott tensed. It came closer.

'Samantha?' Sophie called.

The figure paused.

Scott was so tense; he was so averse to causing trouble that he might have just flown out. The others could come if they wanted, but he would be gone.

'Sophie,' said Samantha. The two embraced. 'How are you doing?' she asked.

'Great,' said Sophie. She took a moment to check they were alone, inspecting the surrounding corridors for staff and cameras.

'You said you wanted to come over today?' said Samantha. 'Any particular reason?'

'I wanted to show Scott what we're objecting to,' she replied. 'Without you we wouldn't have inside access, at least not for free. How's Lolita doing today?'

'Surviving as always,' she said. 'She's a fighter that one; it makes me hopeful every time.'

As they walked through the Sea Aquarium, all Scott could feel was wonder. He didn't share Sophie's contempt for this place. It seemed very social, with hundreds of people walking up and down wearing caps, sleeveless shirts and shorts in a variety of colours. Parents pushed prams and guided children of all ages around the endless facilities of the aquarium, including food and drink stalls, each painted the red and white stripes of the American flag handing out hotdogs, burgers, fries and soft drinks to the hungry visitors.

There were chain-link exhibits of parrots from all over the world – in a rusted exhibit, about the size of a small bedroom, Scott recognised one of them as a St Vincent parrot – blue headed with white spots near its eyes giving way to a brown body tinged orange – eyeing him beadily as he passed by.

Sophie had said that manatees and dolphins were kept here, but it wasn't them that they were there to see.

Samantha had taken this part-time cleaning job to help pay for university fees, as she was keen to study medicine. Sophie hadn't approved at first, but Samantha had suggested she help keep an eye on Lolita and take whatever chances she could to document their cause.

When they finally got to their destination, they sat down overlooking a large water tank, about the same size as a hotel swimming pool with a concrete work island in the middle. There was a series of concrete grandstands to the side with deep blue seats, circling the tank like a colosseum, nearly all filled by the dense audience that had gathered.

'Who or what is Lolita?' Scott asked.

'You'll see,' said Sophie.

A PA sounded. 'Ladies and gentlemen, meet Lolita, the killer whale!'

Loud music started up, and from an adjoining tank, in came a majestic creature. She must have been at least seven metres long, with an unmistakable white eye patch, lower jaw and underbody, but otherwise she was black all over.

Lolita breached, stunning everyone. She flipped a trainer up in the air. She dived. More cheers. More splashing. The trainer rode her like a surfboard, at least four times around the tank.

To Scott it looked bizarre yet enthralling. Sophie, Olav and Samantha looked on joylessly. Lolita beached herself up on the tank's concrete island, her fins splayed in a ta-dah pose, and the music stopped. The show ended, the audience departed and so did the trainer.

Lolita floated there.

Scott frowned. 'I don't understand,' he said. It wasn't that he didn't want to understand – to him the problem just wasn't obvious.

'Keep looking,' said Sophie.

Lolita swam round her tank, over and over again. There was nowhere else she could go.

'She's been here for over thirty years,' she said. 'She was taken from the wild in the 1970s during the Puget Sound captures. She was just a calf when it happened; her capturers used seal bombs to scare her and her family into a cul-de-sac. Many orcas died during that capture. But her mother is still out there in the wild, in her native Washington. If we don't free her, she'll never see her family again, and she'll die alone in this tank.'

Scott's expression changed to one of bewilderment.

'The tank she's in is illegal by government standards,' said Samantha, 'It's only thirty-five feet long instead of the minimum forty-eight feet required by law. I've heard scientists say that they're used to travelling hundreds of miles a day in search of food and social activity. They say two things matter most to an orca's well-being: family and the world of sound. She has no other orcas here, and because she lives in this box, she doesn't use her sound, so she feels constant sensory deprivation. It would be like asking you to cover your eyes for your whole life. But there's a whole movement dedicated to freeing Lolita and it's our job to put pressure on the owners for her release. That's why I'm here.'

'If the tank isn't big enough, why haven't they done it already?' asked Scott.

'I've wondered that for a long time,' said Samantha, 'Other activists say the regulatory agencies don't come here very often, and when they do, they pretend there's nothing wrong. It's like they don't want to find anything wrong, but how they would deal with it I don't know. I don't think anybody knows.'

Olav broke his silence. 'It's a disgrace to humanity to allow such a beautiful creature to remain here in a hotel swimming pool,' he said. 'In Norway, me and my friends saw them many times on our sailing trips. She reminds me of just how much I'd like to go home; I want to help her go home too.'

What a reaction, thought Scott, and looking now, his heart and empathy reached out to Lolita.

'It's important you don't tell anyone about my role in the movement,' said Samantha, 'otherwise I'll lose my job and my prospects of studying medicine. Money's tight in my household because my mother runs a corner shop single-handedly, and my father doesn't work at all because he's got cerebral palsy. I may not get to study medicine at all, even with this job. To be honest, I think a miracle would have to happen for my dream to come true.'

Samantha became glum and stared at the concrete tiles with a pout on her face. Scott didn't know what to say. It was dramatic and completely off topic.

Sophie broke the silence. 'Not to mention our ability to document this would be ruined forever,' she said. 'Some members of the movement have an idea to raise a million dollars for her release, make a film about it and use the proceeds to modernise the park. An IMAX theatre would be built to provide education to visitors; something they claim to offer but they really don't. These places don't contribute to education or science, they don't help conservation and they probably make the orcas more endangered, as family groups have been ripped apart by those hunters. But this isn't the only one,' said Sophie. 'There are others in the US and around the world whose animals need to be released, and we won't rest until they are.'

It was a sobering speech.

'I see,' Scott didn't know what else to say but he was thinking plenty, and suddenly he felt as committed to the cause as if he'd been with it from day one.

They left the Sea Aquarium, walking discreetly past the thousands of protesters all shouting and waving placards demanding Lolita's release. Police cars embossed with golden badges had gathered, their blue-uniformed owners forming blockades just outside the entrance, aggressively keeping them back.

They made a speedy get away.

CHAPTER 11
Dennis Murphy

Dennis Murphy wasn't born an evil child. No child is. But factors beyond his control were influencing him otherwise. He was too young to know why things were happening to him, and certain adult figures in his life completely failed to provide any kind of stability.

Dennis's dad, James Murphy, had seldom been on the right side of the law, constantly shoplifting food, alcohol and the occasional electronic item from local grocery stores. Even before Dennis was born, he'd been in and out of prison several times for similar offences. Dennis and his fraternal twin Lorenzo had been born some time between stints.

His longest sentence had been for six years, for hiding in a clothing store after closing time and attempting to make off with $6,000-worth of clothes, cash and jewellery. But the burglary had gone wrong. James hadn't expected anyone to be in the store at this time, and a female employee by the name of Stephanie Bradley caught him. Panicking, he'd tried to escape the store via its fire-exit staircase. She'd tried to stop him, but he'd run past her and she'd fallen, hurting herself.

When the case went to court, the prosecution wanted to have him charged with robbery, citing the fact that Stephanie had been hurt. However, James insisted on being convicted of the lesser charge of burglary. He hadn't come armed and he hadn't wanted to hurt anyone – he'd tried to time it when no one would be around. The judge accepted his guilty plea to a lesser sentence and he was sent down for six years. James did his time respectfully without incident, hoping to get on the straight and narrow when he got out and be a real father to his two sons, not just in an hour's visitation every week.

However one cop with a racist streak thought his sentence wasn't satisfactory. John Bradley was Stephanie's husband and he was an infamously nasty piece of work. He was always accosting people, usually black males, asking for ID and frisking them for weapons. These encounters would go on for hours, and it was quite clear they were racially motivated. The worst thing he'd ever done was shoot a black man that had fled from him when questioned. But being the practised liar that John was, he'd always avoided disciplinary action, and in the latter case the jury took his side, believing he'd acted in self-defence.

The day it happened – a hot summer's day in June 1996 – looked to all intents and purposes like any other. The main difference was that Dennis and Lorenzo were celebrating their eighth birthday. They should have been in school, but to Dennis that didn't seem fair given that it was his birthday – not that either of them spent much time in school anyway. Truanting was Dennis's favourite thing, and Lorenzo always followed along. Today, in this shithole of a neighbourhood, with few jobs and run-down terraced housing, with burglaries and homicides virtually every week, often committed by the epidemic of gang members in the city, Dennis couldn't care less about multiplication tables and Shakespearean literature.

The two brothers sat there in the courtyard, a desolate space of cracked concrete just twenty metres from their apartment block, home to very little except a few rusted benches and a lonely cabbage palm grown into an earthy space, having turned ash grey in the decades since its death.

'Lucky escape, wasn't it, Lorenzo?' said Dennis as he ate a chocolate biscuit, one of dozens in the three packets he and Lorenzo had pilfered from a local convenience store just an hour earlier.

'The guy couldn't run,' said Lorenzo. 'Too many hamburgers and fries, you know?'

'Did you see the sweat that came off him?' said Dennis. 'I can still smell it now. The way I see it, it's a win-win, brother. We got three packets of cookies just to ourselves – Mom never gets us these – plus we had some exercise running from that guard. And *he* got some exercise too; he must have burned plenty chasing us out down the street, so it's all good. Oh and that's another thing,' Dennis added. 'He probably doesn't get out much so I feel happy that he got to enjoy some fresh air, before he lugged his whale's ass back inside.'

Lorenzo laughed, exposing his biscuit-blackened teeth.

'As long as we keep running, I don't think we'll ever get fat,' said Dennis.

He lifted his red T-shirt, which was embossed with a giant skateboard, above his chest, revealing his slim, emaciated body. Not that Lorenzo realised that was what it was.

'Cool,' he said, helping himself to another biscuit.

Dennis shaded his blue eyes, pushing aside a cowlick of his greasy brown hair. He looked back the way they'd run, across at least a hundred metres of cracked concrete, with a turn through some dark alleyways shadowed by the apartment blocks, past haphazard trash cans and dumpsters, round another turn to where a few sparse shops and barbers eked what business they could in this dangerous neighbourhood. Another hundred metres more of the same and then there was the beach itself, with its boulevard of fancy hotels, casinos, clubs and penthouses, all heavily frequented by the one percent.

Even at the age of eight, Dennis felt the divide.

'Can I ask you a question?' Dennis asked his brother.

'Sure.'

'Have you ever wondered why those people over there seem to have more money than us?' He nodded in the direction of the beach.

'Not really,' said Lorenzo. He had another biscuit, the crumbs trickling down his red-and-white-striped baseball shirt, down his tattered blue shorts to the foot of his torn white trainers.

Dennis grunted, annoyed that his brother seemed virtually oblivious to their situation.

'I see it every day,' said Dennis. 'The way they walk about with their fancy clothes, cameras, make-up and drive their fancy cars. Do you not wonder why they have those things and not us?'

'They've got more money?' his brother suggested. He had another biscuit, then pressed his hand on his red-and-white baseball cap, as a slight breeze nearly took it off his head.

'I believe it's because they're born lucky,' said Dennis. 'They just have what they want; everything in life is laid out for them, while the rest of us are born to have nothing.'

Lorenzo frowned, unsure how to respond.

'Let's face it, Lorenzo,' said Dennis, 'neither of us are that interested in school, and Mom and Dad don't make much money. Even if we got straight A's the way that Sophie Patterson does, how could we have enough money for college or university? I say we make our own way, and get what we can – like these cookies.'

Lorenzo noticed his brother had already eaten his packet. He felt conscious that he'd nearly eaten two out of the three packets they'd pilfered and shook his own in offering.

'You have them, brother,' said Dennis. 'We can always get more.'

Dennis patted his brother's shoulder affectionately. Lorenzo smiled and finished the rest off.

'Some day things will change,' said Dennis. 'We'll *make* them change.'

Lorenzo glanced at his brother, as if trying to grasp the significance of his words, but he couldn't.

Dennis tensed, then he stood up.

'What is it?' said Lorenzo.

'Cops.'

One solitary policeman came from the alleyway.

'Get down, get down!' said Dennis hastily.

'Is he looking for us?' said Lorenzo.

'It looks like it.'

'What do we do?' said Lorenzo. He was suddenly terrified and shedding tears. He looked to his brother for reassurance.

'We'll make a break for our place,' said Dennis. 'Lock the door behind us.'

He made a move to leave but Lorenzo lay there frozen.

'Come on!' hissed Dennis.

Lorenzo shook his head in a flurry.

'The longer we stay here, the more chance we have of getting caught.'

Lorenzo's face reddened with tears.

'Come on, that's it,' said Dennis comfortingly.

The policeman was about fifty metres away, distracted by the windows in the apartment blocks.

Crouching low, they headed to the flaky blue door of their apartment and were about to try to open it when they saw the handle turn. Dennis yanked his brother out of the way and a tall black man with thick black sideburns streaming down to his chin came out.

He wore a large white shirt with the word 'Miami' streaked in black across its width, at least a size forty to accommodate his burgeoning belly.

His blue jeans were tatty, and even more damaged than Lorenzo's shorts, with conspicuous tears that made it look as though they might fall apart at any moment. They were the best clothes he had.

'What's Dad doing here?' asked Lorenzo.

'I don't know,' said Dennis. He noticed that he was carrying a piece of paper in his right hand, though what it was, Dennis had no idea.

'James Murphy!' called the cop.

'Yeah?' he replied, his brown eyes wide with exasperation.

James hadn't long been released from prison, and

he'd done nothing illegal since then. He'd promised the family they'd make a new start and that's exactly where he was heading. Unbeknownst to his two sons, that piece of paper he held in his hand was his CV, which he'd handwritten the night before. He was on his way to a job interview for a barman position at one of the casinos near the beach.

Without warning, the policeman sprang at him, trying to hold him down.

'What the fuck, man?' cried James. 'What did I do?'

The policeman didn't answer the question, and even in his panic-stricken state, James knew this was odd. When he'd been arrested in the past, they'd always said right from the get-go what he was being arrested for and stated his right to an attorney.

'Ow!' cried James. His head was shoved into the concrete. He clenched his cheeks and gritted his white teeth. 'What did I do?' he repeated. It came out like a howl.

◆ ◆ ◆

From behind the dead palm tree, Dennis and Lorenzo watched in horror as the policeman shoved a taser into his back. James screamed like an animal, then struggled ferociously, demanding to know what he'd done wrong. The policeman had an inane grin spread across his pierced mouth.

Dennis couldn't take any more. He searched the ground for a stone he could chuck at the policeman when something fell out of his pocket with a clatter. Dennis gasped – despite the bulk of it in his pocket, he'd forgotten that he had his camera with him. It hadn't fallen too hard. Dennis whipped into action. He wound the wheel. Click. That was one picture. He wound the wheel a second time. Click. That was a second picture. Dennis paused and saw that James had managed to get to his feet and was attempting to run away.

The moment seemed to happen in slow motion. Dennis and Lorenzo watched as the policeman reached for his belt.

He drew something, black and pointed. There was a flash of yellow and James fell to the ground.

'NO!' cried Dennis. He was shedding tears. He gritted his teeth, his camera clicking away five more times.

Dennis thought quickly and winding the wheel as he ran over, he took a perfect mugshot of the cop. The policeman's expression turned venomous.

'Hey, come back here, you kids!' He chased them down the street.

♦ ♦ ♦

Dennis and Lorenzo had been caught by other policemen and persuaded to come to the station. Their mother Vera had to take the nightshift off to go and see James. He'd been rushed to the hospital and was in intensive care. The doctors had been working for four hours straight to save him and now he was in a coma. But her hospital visit had been short-lived and she'd soon been ushered away by detectives to join her sons at the station.

At the station they met their lawyer. He wore a navy-blue jacket and tie, with a white shirt and polished black shoes. He had a thickset face, covered in stubble, and greying dark hair. He put down the stack of papers he'd been reading on his desk and looked at them grimly with brown eyes.

'Hello,' he said, 'I'm Joseph Statton. I'm tasked with aiding you through the legal process. I'm here to get justice for James and answer any questions you might have about the case.' He cleared his throat. 'I can't imagine how you must all be feeling so I'm going to get straight to the point and tell you how the situation stands at present. John alleges that James assaulted him with a firearm—'

'Wait just a minute!' cried Dennis. He was outraged – beyond outraged. He pointed a finger at the lawyer. 'Dad didn't do anything. He was set up.'

'I understand you're upset—' Joseph began.

'I saw it!' cried Dennis. 'Me and Lorenzo were there when it happened. He stopped him as he came out of our apartment and attacked him.'

'You were there?' cried Vera. 'You skipped school?'

Dennis ignored that. 'I've got proof,' he said, holding up his camera.

Joseph blinked. 'No way! This could reveal everything we need to know. We'll get it developed right away. I'll meet with the prosecutor and let them know of this development. Thank you, Dennis, and well done for getting that.

'If you ask me,' he said, dropping his voice to a whisper, 'I think part of this incident was racially motivated; I've seen it before. This particular cop has a record for this kind of thing, and he got away with it last time. I have a copy of James's CV and yes, this should mean your story checks out, Dennis. This should all get sorted in no time. Justice will be done.'

Everyone was optimistic. The photos would show exactly what Dennis and Lorenzo knew to be the truth. Why else would this guy have chased them if only to cover up his revenge-filled, racially aggravated crime? This cop would be thrown in prison and preyed upon by the same animals he targeted. For Dennis, it was second best to a death sentence.

When James came round, he would hopefully get his job at the casino, and the family finances would be better than they'd ever been. Perhaps they would save up enough to move away from their shithole neighbourhood and move somewhere cleaner and safer, where more opportunities for jobs and education would exist. If that happened, Dennis and Lorenzo might even persuade themselves to stop truanting and commit properly to their lives ahead. The family would get justice; they *should* have got justice. But they didn't.

James never recovered from his injuries and he was pronounced dead the following morning. The news was devastating, and the family's grief made it hard for them to function, whether it be to work, go to school or even get groceries. All they could do was hunger and pray for a favourable trial.

When the incident went to court six months later, the photos that Dennis had taken mysteriously never came to light. There were no pictures to be shown to the jury, and the prosecutors had a field day mocking poor James, digging up every aspect of his criminal history for scrutiny, and the jury quickly ruled that James had been lawfully killed and that John Bradley was to be acquitted.

There'd been pandemonium in the courtroom,

the prosecutors and some of the policemen celebrating with cheers and handshakes, though the defence and some members of the public gallery were in uproar, some of whom were relatives of the black man John had killed before.

The celebrations didn't last, and things turned violent, with several black members of the public leaping over the bars to attack the cops. They responded with pepper spray and truncheons, and one person ended up being shot dead in the courtroom. It did nothing to sway the judge's decision.

John walked free. His wife Stephanie finally saw sense and filed for divorce, but Dennis had been inconsolable, and the family was now on the verge of breaking point. The stress of it all made Vera so ill her ability to work as a cleaner rapidly deteriorated, and it led to her dismissal. With no income, their ability to pay their rent diminished. They were served multiple notices to pay, and the amount owed rapidly increased in the following year to over $10,000. It was recovered by the bailiffs. They took their TV, stereo and almost everything of value that they owned, but that still didn't cover it.

They were in $5,000 dollars in debt, homeless, frightened and alone. They spent many nights roughing it on the street, sheltering from the torrential downpours with only trash-can lids and cardboard boxes for protection. They endured sleepless nights, threatened by the many gangs that roamed the streets. Vera had resorted to petty theft to keep them afloat, and they eventually found an abandoned, half-demolished property to stay in. But even there they were far from safe. Gangs and crack addicts visited the place daily, and

they would hide under the floorboards whenever they came to visit. To Dennis and Lorenzo, life was on a knife edge. It was almost unbearable. And every day the hatred and resentment grew within Dennis.
One vision kept him going. He would fight back. He would turn the tables. He would take back everything that had been stolen from him by the corrupt arm of the law. He would do whatever he had to do, for however long, to have revenge. Every night before he went to sleep he would say to himself that he would annihilate them all.

CHAPTER 12
Lake Okeechobee

The remaining days of Sophie's school term flew by. Scott had barely seen her during this time. She'd just finished her exams, but with the term coming to an end, he'd be able to see her any time.

She'd recently had a row with her father. Scott's role in the last two battles had only made him hate Scott even more. He cited his autistic behaviour and latest victories as proof of his 'evil'.

It made her angry and despondent. Why couldn't her father see that he was different from other boys? Why couldn't she reason with him? Being friends with Scott gave her joy in ways she'd never felt before. Didn't he want her to be happy?

◆ ◆ ◆

The next time Scott saw her, she'd called him over for what she called a special chat. Scott's heart had leaped, excited by what this could mean he went to see her.

Sophie invited him to sit down on her double bed. It had an ocean-blue duvet cover with a diving orca spread diagonally across its width. Scott felt his stomach tickle as he did so. Sophie sat next to him, and he waited with palpable anticipation.

◆ ◆ ◆

'We're going away for the weekend, for a mini vacation,' said Sophie. 'Just to clear our heads. We're all shaken up by the attacks at the school and the fair. It's a favourite place of mine. Almost as much as the Sea Marshes Reserve. Well, second favourite.'

'Where are you going?' he asked.

Sophie was trying to be happy, but her arguments had left her feeling glum and despondent. Scott didn't seem to notice.

'We're going to Merritt Island for two days,' she said.

'Awesome,' said Scott. 'Have a good time.'

Sophie chuckled. Somehow she sensed he hadn't read between the lines.

'However,' she added, 'Mom and I are inviting you to come with us.'

'To Merritt Island?' said Scott. 'That wildlife refuge?'

Sophie had shown him a pamphlet for it a few weeks ago.

'Yes,' she said. 'We'll go and see some more birds. There might be some interesting mammals too. I love the manatees the most.'

'Manatees? They've been on my wish list for ages!'

◆ ◆ ◆

They set off early on Saturday morning into the dawn twilight of the tropics.

Their car was more like a van. There was enough

room to seat about eight passengers.

Scott sat next to Sophie. She'd kindly given him the window seat to make it easier for him to appreciate the rolling countryside. Even though it would take at least three hours to get to Merritt Island, Scott loved every minute of the journey.

The countryside was indeed breathtaking. Scott gazed out at vast plains of scrubland, intermixed with jack-pine forests and wetlands. There were huge bridges and vast highways – so vast they stretched over 670 miles from Miami in the south to Pensacola in the west, on the border of Alabama.

They would follow the Florida Turnpike, the highway that connected Miami to Orlando, then, from there, they'd cross a bridge into the water world of Merritt Island.

Sometimes Scott couldn't believe this was happening. Now and then he stopped to wonder whether any of it was real – it had to be a dream, one so fantastic he'd never want to wake up from it. Even having Sophie as a friend felt somehow unreal. He wondered how fate had allowed them to come together.

He had a habit of believing that him mixing with someone as popular as her would be a blasphemy to the social system they were a part of. But if it was a blasphemy, it was one he was happy to make. It felt like the social rules that kept hierarchies apart had been smashed purely by their friendship. He hated the class system in every way; he felt he'd been at its mercy just for being himself, but now it was payback time.

After nearly two hours of driving, Sophie's dad wanted a break so they decided to stop at Lake Okeechobee, one of the largest lakes in Florida. Lake Okeechobee was so huge that one might mistake it for the sea, yet the lake was as far inland as you could possibly be in Florida. They had lunch at a small café in Pahokee, one of the towns close to the lake. When they'd finished, Sophie thought she ought to show him around the place.

The two young friends visited the Pahokee Pier, which was stuffed with fishermen eager to haul something sizeable out of the fresh water. Beautiful white yachts floated on the water, all of them crowded round by thirsty tourists. Some brown-feathered mottled ducks floated lazily, and a large black double crested cormorant stood poised on a water meter.

When they'd finished looking, Scott took Sophie for a flight, her first ever on the micro-flyer, where they stopped at another town called Taylor Creek. It felt embarrassing to be flying over a civilized area; he couldn't avoid the thought that most people weren't accustomed to somebody flying on wings – and with a girl strapped underneath! But it was worth the embarrassment. Certainly people gaped at his unorthodox method of arrival at their peaceful town, but he shrugged it off.

The land on which Taylor Creek was built was extraordinary. The town was actually divided into islands by canal-like rivers that flowed into the lake. He'd never been anywhere like it – it seemed such an amphibious place to live he almost likened it to an American version of Venice.

'So, are there any particular species to see here?' he asked.

'Snail kites are the star attraction as far as I'm concerned,' said Sophie. 'I've seen them here several times but not always. Their numbers vary depending on the water level – they need a high water level for their diet of apple snails. It's been dry this year which is a bit concerning; it could mean there are fewer around but we'll keep looking. This subspecies is only found in Florida so I don't want to let the opportunity pass.'

In the meantime she pointed out a few more things: a great blue heron – a tall wading bird with reddish blue feathers, head bent down in hunting mode. There was a diminutive Carolina wren skulking in the bushes, occasionally emerging for a closer look, and swallow-like purple martins zipped overhead, their white bellies contrasting with iridescent purple backs.

'Um, Sophie?' said Scott. 'What's that raptor?'

Scott pointed to a bird soaring high above the lake. His scope was on it in an instant, but he strained to capture the detail because its silhouette was so dark.

When Sophie had a look at it, the answer came in a split second: 'That's a snail kite! Keep following it and see what it does.'

Scott had no idea how she'd managed to identify it in these conditions.

There was an anxious wait. The bird was still tantalisingly distant, and he couldn't see any detail on it. Scott might have dismissed it as an osprey (which is far more common here) if Sophie hadn't known otherwise.

The kite flew down and, to their joyous relief, perched on a tree, staring at the water. Far from the brown-and-white plumage of an osprey, it was mostly dark grey, but its talons and long meat-hooking bill were bright red. Scott was too stunned to say anything. He stared in awe at the rare raptor that had landed not more than thirty metres from their position.

The kite didn't settle there for long before it was in the air again, swooping into the reeds talons first. Up it came with a snail then flew back to its perch to eat it.

Scott was enthralled already.

'Congratulations, Scott: you've just seen one of Florida's rarest birds – already!' Sophie beamed.

The snail kite prised flesh from shell and gulped it down, then sat there for a few minutes until something caught its gaze and it flew away.

She glanced at her watch.

'We should go back to the car now.'

◆ ◆ ◆

Now they were all fed, rested and had been to the toilet, they were ready to cover the last leg of their journey. It took another hour and a half before they reached Cape Canaveral, but it was a scenic journey at least.

Fields were packed together with exotic hedgerows cutting through them like leafy streams. They gave way to yet more wetlands, and even at high speed Scott saw that most of them held alligators.

Titusville appeared. Then before Scott knew what was happening, they were crossing a causeway to the island, carrying them stylishly over the brackish water into its swampy world.

Their accommodation was a beautiful white villa, about two storeys high, almost right outside Cocoa Beach. The sun was beginning to leave the sky, preparing for its night-long sleep until dawn. The ocean lapped at the sandy shore, miniature waves breaking.

A single Wilson's plover could be seen probing the mudflats. This tiny pied wader looked rather lonely.

It momentarily stopped foraging, staring at them as if hopeful for companionship.

Scott and Sophie sat on the fine white sands of Cocoa Beach and stared wistfully across the ocean. It was beautiful. Nothing would want to be lonely in a setting like this. At least the brown pelicans flying overhead were together. There was no one else here, only the seabirds.

'You have a knack for taking me to beautiful places,' said Scott.

'Do I?' said Sophie.

'What are we going to look for tomorrow?' Scott asked. 'What about the manatees?'

'We've got a trip for them booked for the day after tomorrow,' said Sophie. 'I thought what we would do is look for the Florida scrub jay – the only endemic bird to Florida.'

'Didn't you say the Cape Sable sparrow was endemic too?' Scott asked.

'It is,' said Sophie, 'but it's not recognised as a full species. They consider it a subspecies of seaside sparrow. The scrub jay, however, is.'

'Are they difficult to find?' asked Scott.

'If you know where to look, it's not too difficult. They seldom move further than a few kilometres from their territories,' said Sophie. 'The Scrub Ridge Trail is our best bet. We'll go there tomorrow.'

'Great,' said Scott. 'I'm really looking forward to it. There'll be so much more to see, and I get to see it with my best friend.'

Sophie laughed and playfully rubbed his shoulder. 'Thanks.'

An hour later the darkness came, and they went to

their separate rooms.

As Scott lay in bed, the stillness of the night soothed his senses. His eyes grew accustomed to the gloom, and he could hear the wind blowing softly outside, the ring of crickets and the reassuring hum of the air conditioner.

Scott had never felt so happy in his life. Tomorrow their visit to Merritt Island would begin, and Sophie would be his guide, showing him all those awesome creatures. It was the companionship and fun that he'd dreamed of for years. He fell asleep, shedding happy tears.

CHAPTER 13
Merritt Island

Scott was woken early the next morning by Sophie's alarm clock. He leaped up thinking there was an intruder.

She knocked on his door.

'Sorry, Scott, my bad,' she said. 'Good morning.'

'Morning,' he mumbled, dumbfounded.

Sally appeared at the door.

'Morning, you two. Breakfast will be ready in five minutes.'

Sophie went back to her room to get dressed, while Scott went to the breakfast table. He poured bran flakes into his bowl and wolfed them down with a glass of milk.

'You two seem to have become quite close haven't you?' Sally said.

'She's been a great friend,' said Scott hesitantly.

He poured some more milk into his glass.

'People have taken advantage of her before.'

Scott abruptly stopped drinking. 'What?'

'I said people have taken advantage of her before.'

'In what way?' he asked.

'One of Sophie's weaknesses is that…' She paused. 'She's rather trusting, you see.'

'I don't.'

'She likes to see the best in people, Scott; it helps her make lots of friends, but it hasn't always ended well.'

'Do you share your husband's view?' he asked. 'I know he doesn't like me.'

'Not at all. I'd say you're one of the safest people I know.'

She sighed. 'There's a reason why I encouraged Sophie's interest in wildlife,' she said. 'When I was her age, all the boys liked me, but looking back, I feel as if I had hardly any individuality. That was when I met her father at high school. He was a football player back then, very fit and handsome, a high-school girl's dream. But like many of the other popular boys, he was cocky, arrogant and wild. He wasn't always as serious and mature as he is now. My friends warned me that he'd cheated on other partners, and in time he cheated on me too. I think we only stayed together because I became pregnant with Sophie. I only want to encourage her to do more and give her something to set herself apart from the others. Something that would contribute to her future. Then perhaps one day she'd meet someone who's not like her dad.'

Scott was stunned by Sally's speech.

As if on cue, Sophie's dad came in and took a seat at the table. He looked moody, taking care not to make any eye contact with Scott. That was mutual.

'I'm going to check on Sophie,' said Sally. 'I'll be right back. And, David, please be nice.'

David grunted an acknowledgement.

When Sally left, David made eye contact for the first time.

'I'll tell you now,' he said. 'When this trip is over,

you're to leave her alone!'

'Why?' asked Scott, unsure how to react.

'Because you're dangerous,' he said. 'Don't try to deny it. You may have fooled the others, but I know better. Look at what happened earlier – you brought down that chopper with that *thing* you fly with. I knew things were bad but I never thought it would be *this* bad.'

Scott tried to pay no attention.

'Hey, look at me when I'm talking to you!' he snarled. 'I see it in your eyes – your mind is full of evil and death. She's had boys ruin her before, one who brought her nothing but misery and fear. I won't let you do the same. When we get home, you stay the hell away from my daughter!'

He stood up abruptly, rolling up his sleeves.

'I don't want to fight you,' said Scott.

David raised his eyebrows like an angry baboon and Scott knew someone was going to get hurt. He made a move to leave.

'Hey, don't you walk away from me!' he shouted. 'I'm not done with you yet!'

He charged after him, and Scott almost broke into a run. Sophie and Sally appeared in the lobby.

'Scott, what's happening?' asked Sophie.

'Your dad wants to kill me,' said Scott, hiding behind her back.

'Sophie, step aside,' said David angrily.

Sophie refused to obey. David looked as if he was ready to kill. Sally intervened.

'Now, dear,' she said. 'We've got an exciting day ahead; don't spoil it.'

David looked about, realising he wasn't going to win. He gritted his teeth.

'This is not over,' he growled.

They went straight to the Scrub Trail, about twenty minutes' drive away. They walked along the trail, walled in on both sides by dense thickets of bushes and trees, crowding in like an overgrown hedgerow. Common yellowthroats – unseen in the vegetation – uttered their whistling *wichity-witchity* calls and the metallic *wiaack-wiaack* of red-winged blackbirds filled the morning atmosphere.

It wasn't long before they found what they were after. Perched on a bush like sentinels were a pair of Florida scrub jays. Naturally, being an endemic species, Scott took the opportunity to examine them in detail. They were about the size of thrushes and had blue heads topped with snow-white crowns, white throats which gave way to greyish white breasts, azure wings and long tails. One of the jays took off and landed on the path in front of them, as if blocking their way. Sophie laughed.

'They're quite tame,' she said. 'Tame enough to take food from your hand, but the trouble with that is that it tempts them to breed earlier in the year than they should, and their chicks die if they're not fed caterpillars.'

Scott felt a little disappointed. He'd have jumped at the chance to feed them by hand; he'd done it at home, but of course that was a different situation with a different species involved. If this bird disappeared here, then other places within its narrow range would have to take on a heavier burden.

The jay fluttered and Scott grimaced, feeling a slight weight on top of his head. He let out a loud chuckle. Sophie and Sally laughed too, while David looked bemused. The jay pirouetted on top of Scott's head, tussling his brown hair. Scott reached up awkwardly, as if tempting the jay to settle on his hand, chuckling again as the jay accepted his offer. It sat there on his palm, cocking its head from side to side and locking its amber grey gaze with his own.

Scott raised his other hand. The others watched, a look of edginess on their faces as if they wondered if that might be a little too much. Scott's finger was only able to gently brush the jay's milky grey breast before it flew over towards David and sat on *his* head.

David wasn't amused. 'Get off!' He swatted at it like a fly.

'Dear!' Sally began.

The jay shot away. David touched his head and felt something wet and squishy. He looked at his fingers – they were creamy white with a yolk of yellow.

'Oh for fuck's sake!' cried David. 'Come near me again and I'll crush you like a grape.'

Sophie and Sally fell silent. Scott tried unsuccessfully to stifle a giggle.

'You find that funny, do you?' David growled.

Scott said nothing.

'Come on, dear,' said Sally. 'Let's move on. We'll get some water to wash it out.'

David raised a finger towards Scott. 'I'm watching you.'

They then drove along the well-known Black Point Wildlife Drive, in the north of the island. It was like the Sea Marshes Reserve only much bigger; a mosaic world of brackish lagoons and scrubland. The great white egrets flapped their angelic wings and preened themselves with yellow dagger bills, their ashy webbed feet clinging to the interwoven branches of the mangroves. They paused in a lay-by overlooking the egret roost.

Sophie tugged Scott's shirt and pointed towards something else of interest. An alligator had emerged from the reeds and was plodding awkwardly across the dirt road. It didn't look like a creature designed for walking but then he'd heard that alligators can run at ten miles an hour if they want to. Scott admired its reptilian beauty: the dark grey scales, arrayed like a set of tiles, the lemon-yellow belly below and the sharp conical teeth hanging from its jaws that seemed to smile menacingly at you.

The alligator paused and eyed the van for a moment then locked eyes with Scott. He trained his scope on the creature, zooming in on the black vertical eyes. He could see it in perfect detail, down to the smallest scales on its toes.

The alligator soon lost interest and slumped head first into the water. It soundlessly submerged itself and was gone.

They saw another car that had pulled over to watch something, and being nosy they crept up behind it. The man in the car was armed with a pair of expensive binoculars and was viewing a reddish egret, with its gingery head and mauve body, and a small flock of attractive roseate spoonbills, pink as flamingoes, that stood in the background.

They pulled over from behind, blocking the road, but they could easily move if someone else came.

A flock of black, ultraviolet birds alighted on the bush above the car, but before Scott could identify what they were, the vehicle jerked backwards, Sophie's dad abruptly moving them on. He was so keen to get out of there that he nearly hit the other car. The man's horned blared, and he said something that none of them heard, but David just drove away.

Scott's subjects had flown away, the reddish egret had dived into the reeds and the spoonbills had taken flight into a fading wall of red and pink.

'Hey, I saw some grackles back there. Can we go back?' asked Scott.

'Too late, they're probably gone,' Sophie's dad muttered.

Scott spun round to see that they'd descended onto the road.

'No they're not; they're still there!' Scott protested.

'Too late, moving on,' he replied.

'What did you see?' asked Sophie.

'A couple of grackles possibly boat-tailed grackles. Do you want to look?'

Sophie twisted round and trained her binoculars on the birds; it was difficult with the constant bumping up and down of the vehicle but she confirmed his identification.

Scott lost his cool.

'Your dad's trying to sabotage this trip for me.' His voiced had dropped to a whisper. 'I know it. I mean, what's he got against me? What have I done to upset him?'

'I don't know,' said Sophie, 'but don't worry about it, Scott. I won't let him get away with it. Just relax and enjoy the rest of the day. Leave my dad to me.'

The morning had been swallowed up rather quickly in Scott's opinion and his species list for the trip had risen to a hundred. Later that afternoon, they paid a visit to the Kennedy Space Centre, the site from where the fabled mission to the moon had launched. They'd seen a life-sized replica of the Atlantis Space Shuttle – hanging lopsided like a jet in a dogfight – and enjoyed a shuttle launch experience, the closest thing most people got to feeling like they were lifting off into space. They'd been able to touch an actual moon rock brought back by the Apollo 17 mission in 1972, the final landing ever made on the moon. The bus tour had also taken them to see the space company SpaceX, and their tour guide had explained to them their ultimate aspirations for colonising Mars.

Their next and last day dawned. It started off great as they saw many different things on the car journey out of the house, however their early start produced some brand-new highlights. There'd been a pair of northern flickers (a kind of greyish spotted woodpecker) which they'd seen attending a nest hole in a large, twisted oak tree. The male had a pink breast with black spots, a brown back – also black spotted, with a peachy coloured face, grey crown, red nape and a black moustache either side of its long grey bill. The female was similar, but without the black moustaches. The flickers themselves were agitated – they flashed the yellow streaks in their tails as they flew, piping a rapid *wicka-wicka-wicka-wicka*.

Scott and Sophie hadn't been able to figure out why until they saw the great horned owl, complete with its yellowish buff barring, ash-grey face, sharp ear tufts and piercing yellow eyes only open about a crack to the commotion around it.

Three white-tailed deer ran across the road, one

of the bucks stopping to give them a wary look. As it did, they admired its brown hide, grey face with white spectacles and black nose. Adorning its head were a pair of antlers, spanning half a metre wide.

Only minutes later, after the deer had run off, they had to stop again.

A small, unidentified mouse had scurried onto the road, then a second later something big sprang out of the bushes.

'Oh my God!' cried Sophie.

The mouse got away. The creature that had been chasing it froze when it saw the vehicle. It hunched its shoulders as if trying to hide, but it was in plain sight of everyone.

'It's a bobcat,' said Sophie. She sprang for her camera.

Everyone admired its pale chestnut coat. The spots on its back were chestnut while the underbelly was white, with extensions of it just visible on the back of its legs, with black spots. Its reddish face bore pointed ears tipped with short tufts, only just visible, and its green eyes stared back at them, expectant of trouble. Sophie had just about taken enough pictures when the bobcat plucked up the courage to dash away, back into cover.

A good start – a very good start! Was it about to get even better?

Well yes it was. Because they were heading to Titusville, and despite being delayed constantly by wildlife sightings, they arrived in good time for their manatee boat trip.

Scott loved the journey; this boat moved so deliberately slowly, it allowed him to see everything – the scenery, all the other wildlife on offer – and of course their speed was for the benefit of the manatees.

There was virtually no way of not being aware of their presence, as there were warning signs everywhere saying: **MANATEES IN AREA, PLEASE SLOW DOWN!** That shouting text would be accompanied by a drawing of the giant sirenian, with separate speed-limit signs next to them. Complimenting those were rangers in airboats, reminding people of the rules if need be. If somebody didn't follow them, then one of these rare, special, gentle animals could risk serious injury or death.

Like all the other passengers, they were constantly straining to see under the water for one. It was hard though – the water only allowed glimpses to the depths of this half-fresh, half-salty environment. Though they often saw fish and there were some strange ones – like pike only bigger – the manatees weren't there – at least not yet.

They were momentarily distracted from their search when the boatman pointed out a few American white pelicans upending like oversized ducks to catch fish, some double-crested cormorants and grey-and-white American royal terns, adorned with jet-black caps, hovering and striking for fish with carrot-coloured bills. Also drawn to the frenzy were black skimmers, similar in build to the terns, trawling the water for any stragglers outside the main frenzy.

But fish weren't going to draw manatees because they were vegetarian, and so the search continued.

Three quarters of an hour passed, and they could see another airboat coming towards them. One of the patrols warned them through a megaphone: 'Manatees in the area – please slow down!'

'Manatees!' Scott exclaimed, leaning over the side. He couldn't see anything at first. Then in front of the airboat, he noticed small discharges of vapour, bursting into soft attention-grabbing 'whiffs'.

They'd come to a complete stop; the boatman didn't dare start up the engine. They were so close now, large, graceful grey forms cruising next to the airboat.

Everyone was taking pictures of them, the atmosphere buzzing with camera clicks and excited murmuring.

Scott studied the manatees. They were huge, bore small flippers and stubbly faces that could have belonged to a walrus or even a burly drunk person. Their backs were encrusted with algae and their tails shaped like gigantic spades, used to propel themselves through the shallow waters they called home.

Scott could soon see why such trouble had been taken to warn boat users. Far from being swift and agile like dolphins, these animals were very slow, gracious creatures. Even when making haste, they still looked like they moved in slow motion. With that lack of speed, how could they possibly take evasive action if an oncoming boat was speeding their way? But they were magnificent creatures – they made up for it by being big and gentle.

Scott glanced at Sophie, who gave him a reciprocal grin. She'd told him that she'd experienced this multiple times on her trips to Merritt Island but never tired of it. How could you tire of it? There was something original about a close encounter with animals that were large and harmless, and there was virtually nothing these animals could do to hurt a human being.

They seemed to almost trust humans completely, but according to the boatman they could be stressed when touched, chased or harassed. Hence there were laws against those things. Whatever humans did to these animals, by accident or otherwise, they somehow saw the best in people, otherwise they wouldn't interact this way.

The manatees hung around for over an hour, and only when they'd moved a safe distance away did the boatman restart the engine.

The rest of the tour yielded a handsome belted kingfisher – a grey-and-white banded bird the size of a crow with a patch of chestnut on its breast; some dark-grey eastern kingbirds – about the same size as the kingfisher – and a green heron, complete with its namesake green feathers and chestnut belly, sitting on the jutting branch of a submerged tree. They visited a three-metre tangle of sticks, the nest site of a pair of bald eagles – brown-bodied with their namesake bald white heads, their corn-yellow bills tearing up a fish and handing titbits to their greyish eaglet, perhaps only a month old yet it would be ready to leave the nest within the next month or two.

The final delight was a family of North American river otters: a female heading three pups, perhaps teaching them how to fish.

She'd dived beneath the surface and a few minutes later came back with a small olive-green catfish. She tried to get her pups to chase the fish, simulating the skills they would need in later life. Two of them took to the challenge, but the other hung back, unsure of itself. Size-wise they were each at least half a metre long; the pups were more or less fully grown but they wouldn't try to fend for themselves until the coming autumn.

It was early evening by the time the tour finished, and in the car park in Titusville a party of five raccoons were scavenging for scraps. They were a curious sight, their ringed tails and black up-to-no-good masks peering up at the spectators watching them with interest.

The dark-bodied, red-headed turkey vultures that had been soaring over the car park earlier had quietly vacated the skies, but they spotted a stout great crested flycatcher flying into a hole in a nearby building to settle down for the night.

They'd had a very exciting day without a doubt, but there was one last opportunity to spot things. They found an amazing nine-banded armadillo foraging at the side of the road; caught in the headlights of the van, it was a half-armoured, half-hairy curiosity.

Its shell was a reddish purple, bearing its namesake nine bands that flexed like an accordion. From the shell extended a ringed hard tail. The armadillo was equipped with a long nose, long tongue, sharp claws and tough leathery skin, the perfect tools for dealing with a diet of ants and termites.

The evening also yielded common nighthawks (a kind of nightjar) fluttering in the night sky uttering their nasal '*peent*' calls, generally offering only glimpses of their cryptic brown plumages, and various bats and moths, all unidentifiable, were already on the wing.

When Scott could take no more, he retired to his room, but a combination of fear and restlessness set in.

It was a beautiful night, with crickets ringing and the lapping of the waves on Cocoa Beach. They were leaving tomorrow, and Scott felt philosophical about all that had happened, all the sightings and all the time spent with his best friend. There was something he needed to discuss and he felt it couldn't wait till morning. He got up and knocked on the door of Sophie's room. Thankfully, she wasn't already asleep.

She was in bed reading her field guide to North American birds but put it to one side.

'Hi, Scott. Is everything alright?' she asked. Her voice was as soft as ever, but it failed to ease his unease.

'I'm just thinking about your dad's attitude to me. Why does he hate me so much?'

Sophie sighed. 'Have a seat.'

His heart skipped a beat. She hadn't indicated where to sit, and not wanting to be presumptuous, he pulled a blue-cushioned chair from across the room.

'I don't think he hates you; he's just nervous about my welfare is all. He can be overprotective. He's the only one who thinks that way – no one else does.'

Scott felt a lump in his stomach, there'd been something about himself that he'd been keeping from her. He trusted almost no one else with this secret.

'There's something else,' said Scott. 'I should have said this earlier. I wasn't sure how you were going to react. I've got a learning difficulty that makes social interaction difficult. I struggle to read people sometimes. I've got Asperger's syndrome.'

'I know.'

Scott was taken by surprise – he was half expecting a negative reaction or even one of pure perplexity.

'How do *you* know?'

'I can spot Asperger's from a mile away!'

'You can?'

'I've met plenty of people with it at school, and I've seen how nice they are, even if they have trouble talking to you. It's really no big deal. In fact, most people in my group have got something that affects them and they're the best friends ever.'

Scott felt a huge surge of relief. He instantly felt closer to her than ever. He'd never felt such warmth.

'May I ask you something?' he asked.

'Yes?' she said. She began to quiver.

'Your dad mentioned that someone hurt you before. Do you want to tell me about that?'

Sophie frowned. 'Yes, I had a bad boyfriend. Out of all the boyfriends I've ever had, I wish I'd never met this one.'

Scott frowned. 'Why?'

Sophie met his eyes.

'I trusted him – and then he—' She hesitated.

'His name was Jack Robinson,' she continued. 'He was from Sydney, but he'd moved with his dad to Miami. We got on great for a while, but now I see what he wanted from me. It took me a while to see what a truly awful guy he was. He would drink heavily and sometimes take drugs. He would often lose his temper at the slightest things. On one occasion, I remember someone bumped into him in a club, and he got angry and punched him repeatedly. He got into many fights over things like that. When a night out was over, I'd often find out that he'd been arrested and had spent the night in a cell. When I tried to reason with him, he became violent towards me. He hit me, pushed me and the last straw was when he tied me to my bed. I would have been raped if my dad hadn't saved me. For my own safety, I had to say goodbye to the relationship, and I don't regret it either – good riddance!'

Scott was overwhelmed and shocked. He'd

suffered sexual abuse too, but it had only involved having rude pictures thrust into his face. What Sophie had experienced completely dwarfed that.

'I'm sorry.'

Sophie nodded. She was on the verge of being emotional, and even Scott could see it.

'I can't understand anyone who'd want to treat a girl like that,' he said. 'I've always supported women's rights, and it appals me to hear what you've suffered at the hands of this individual. Why can't some people realise that girls and women aren't objects? There may be some boys out there that won't change, but if they won't then personally I think they need to seriously rethink their lives. If they want to judge me for respecting you the way I do, then they can. I'm an individual free from the influence of magazines and lad culture. I believe that girls and women should be cared for, and misogyny crushed!'

Sophie smiled. Then she patted his arm, causing him to jump.

'Thanks, Scott,' she said. 'That really cheers me up.'

'But you know what?' he said, changing the subject. 'About what your dad said about me being dangerous, I suppose he's right in a way.'

'What do you mean?'

'I have a sort of inner fury that I'm afraid to express. It's the part of me that gives me the courage to feel that I can take on almost any opponent. The fire of combat goes through me all the time. All the time I hear the clanging of swords, shields and spears. The sound of gunfire, bombs, screaming casualties, tanks and half-tracks and missiles. It's the sort of thing that comes on when I'm being picked on and I get enraged so much I want to take them out. I'm always ready for a war, but I can find it hard to control that anger sometimes. I can manage it most of the time, but I have that fear at the back of my mind of it going out of control. That's why I think that.'

Scott tried to think what to say next, suddenly conscious of the fact he might have dominated the conversation too much.

'The principal told me a lot about you and I have to say I'm impressed – charities, activism, being good with the community. How did that all start?' he asked.

Sophie smiled. 'When I was about five, Mom told me rightfully that you should treat people equally and above all accept and protect everyone who's different from yourself – so inevitably autistic people and so on fall into that category. When I was a little bit older I had a habit of going round and befriending loners; I even helped them with their work when they were stuck, and everyone said what a kind, helpful young lady I was. I wasn't just helpful, I was also acceptant – that was why so-called dorks and nerds liked me. To be honest I don't like those terms – they sound like labels. But one incident stayed with me.'

❖ ❖ ❖

Ten years ago Sophie Patterson was a very innocent child. She was enjoying yet another day at elementary school, enjoying her lunch hour in the playground with Samantha. They would play tag, go skipping and even catch the flies, beetles and other insects drawn into the playground's bushes. Samantha voraciously collected whatever flowers and leaves she could find. Plants were more her thing – they didn't move or fly away like Sophie's insects.

But today would be different. Today Dennis Murphy had had a bad day and he would deal with it in his most dramatic way ever.

Sophie and Samantha were skipping when an anguished shout came from the opposite side of the playground.

'Did you hear that, Samantha?' asked Sophie.

'Hear what?'

'That scream?'

Samantha frowned. 'I don't hear anything.'

'Listen.'

The scream became louder, and a guffawing laughter accompanied it.

'Come on,' said Sophie. 'We have to see.'

'Even if it's Dennis?' said Samantha.

'Especially if it's Dennis,' Sophie replied. 'Now come on.'

They ran to the other end of the playground, the full hundred metres of it, and found a group of about six boys gathered in a ring. All of them were attacking something, or someone. Sophie guessed what was happening, but there was no way she could take them on herself.

'Samantha, stay here,' said Sophie. 'I'll go and get Mrs Greg. Keep an eye on them for me.'

Sophie ran to fetch her favourite teacher. She was the one who had always motivated her to learn. It was a big reason why she liked school. It hadn't been an easy transition from preschool to elementary, but it would have been so much harder if it weren't for Mrs Greg. She wouldn't turn down the cry for help from her favourite student.

Technically no children were allowed inside the school during the lunch hour, except for the toilet block. Usually anyone would be challenged and either told to get out or face detention, but Sophie didn't worry about the fact she was running through the corridors – she had a very good reason to be running. It was a bonus that no one was there to tell her not to.

'Mrs Greg!' Sophie banged hard on the door. 'Mrs Greg! We need you!'

The door opened. 'Sophie, what are you doing here?'

Favourite as Sophie might be, Mrs Greg had adopted her patronising professional tone.

'You need to come quickly. Dennis and his friends are hurting someone in the playground.'

'Who?' asked Mrs Greg.

'I don't know; they were in the way. Please come quickly!'

'Come with me.'

The boys had fled the scene. Samantha was there trying to bandage the victim – a boy about Sophie's own age – with some leaves and her school uniform. He was barely moving; he'd lost a lot of blood, but Samantha had somehow managed to stay strong despite her inexperience.

'Dave!' cried Mrs Greg. 'Are you OK?'

He could only manage a mumble.

'I'll call an ambulance,' said Mrs Greg. 'Can you two stay with him?'

She ran off.

'How are you doing, Dave?' asked Sophie.

He coughed.

'What happened?' she asked.

Dave coughed again; he was trying to say something.

'I think we should let him rest,' said Samantha. 'I'm not sure if he can talk.'

Dave pulled out an inhaler from his pocket and took a blast of it.

'Dennis...' Dave rasped, 'Dennis attacked me.'

'Why?' said Sophie.

'I don't know,' he said throatily. 'He just did.'

The two girls glanced at one another.

'I'm angry,' he mumbled. He started to cry and the girls patted him reassuringly.

'Don't worry,' said Sophie. 'An ambulance is coming.'

'What about Dennis?' he rasped.

'They'll find him,' said Sophie. 'I'll make sure of

◆ ◆ ◆

'So Dave recovered?' said Scott.

'Yes he did,' said Sophie, 'But they decided to move him to a different school – they thought mine was too dangerous.'

'But they expelled him though, didn't they?' asked Scott.

'Yes,' she said, 'but his other friends were allowed to stay. Dave's parents were afraid of reprisals from them so they thought it would be safer to move. I never saw him again until seven years later, when I started high school. By then he'd changed a lot: he'd shaved his hair, put on weight, taken up smoking, got a few piercings, used a lot more swear words and just tried to do anything to show the world he wasn't weak. He was always getting into fights with other boys, usually people much bigger than him over minor things like being bumped in the corridor, presumably on purpose.'

'So what changed? How come he's good friends with you now?'

'I took him aside,' she said. 'I reminded him who I was, and when that happened he became easier to talk to. I explained to him that I would help him change, though he was stubborn at first. He denied that he had a problem and said I was wasting my time and that he could handle everything himself. But eventually he acknowledged where his behaviour might land him and that he didn't want Dennis's actions to spoil his life. He's a great friend now; he always helps us out when we need him and he's good company, and even though he still smokes and swears, I can safely say he's good now.'

She sighed. 'When I asked my mom why Dennis was so cruel, she told me that bullies often came from bad backgrounds. When she explained the concept to me, I began to feel differently about him. I began wondering whether I could have helped him abandon his cruelty, and maybe so much could have been avoided.'

Sophie fell silent. She looked glum, but Scott didn't notice.

'How do you remember all this?' he asked, intrigued.

'They're the sort of adventures you never forget, like you're the hero of the story. A seven-year-old hero – that's something you don't see every day.'

Scott laughed.

'And presumably this is what inspired Samantha

to want to study medicine,' said Scott. 'I remember what she said at the Sea Aquarium. Is it true?'

'Yes,' said Sophie. 'What she didn't say at the time is that she's dyslexic. I have to help her with a lot of things – reading and writing assignments. Expressing herself on paper has never been her strong point. She thinks it condemns her to failure, and I try to tell her it doesn't have to be that way. She has a rather sour attitude to money, just because she lacks the amount she needs.'

Sophie craned her neck as if trying to see what was outside. She felt a warmth course through her and a nervous tingling excitement. She'd been waiting for this moment for days. She'd discussed it at length with Uncle Wilson, and he seemed happy enough that she'd got it covered.

'Do you want to go back onto the beach?' she asked suddenly. 'The view's breathtaking at night.'

'Um, sure,' Scott said.

'We'll go out quietly; I don't want Mom and Dad seeing this,' she said.

They snuck out of the house and moved down the beach till they were out of sight, then sat down on the sand. There was barely any light pollution in the sky tonight, and the sky was so clear that the Milky Way shone in a thick band across the sky. Ursa Major and Ursa Minor, the two celestial bears, arched across the sky, marking the way north. To the east, Ophiuchus draped Serpens over his neck to the east, while the massive water snake Hydra dominated the west and to the south the great figure of Centaurus impaled Lupus the wolf.

Scott explained how all of these odd squares and

lines had been imagined into the shapes of mythical beings, but to Sophie there were no shapes or figures, just a kaleidoscope of light.

❖ ❖ ❖

Jack Robinson had been looking forward to this day for a very long time. He wasn't used to failing in getting what he wanted, least of all with the ladies. They'd had two different raids on two different places, both with the target there and hadn't managed to take her.

His boss was getting impatient, but Jack's lust made his impatience insufferable. He'd absorbed his father's misogyny and he lacked the introspection to challenge it.

Next to him was his second in command, and another former high-school rival of Sophie's. Her name was Natasha Smith, a black-haired, petite girl three years older than her rival. She was proud to follow her superior – whether it was keeping new prostitutes in line or giving him the full treatment, Natasha would oblige. Jack's misogyny, which most women would have found obnoxious, was what had attracted Natasha to him in the first place.

She'd left school about a year ago, with no qualifications and an unsavoury reputation for sex and dominance. Like Jack, she had no interest in introspection. She'd been inspired by her pompous mother to become a gold-digger, sleeping with students and four high-school teachers and extorting money out of them. She didn't care about their job losses or their divorces, or their children growing up without their fathers around. To Natasha it was all worth it because of the money, a million dollars between them. She would have gotten more, if only that impertinent, usurping blonde hadn't exposed her 'relationships' to the principal.

Now they came with a team of six others to pursue the prize they wanted.

◆ ◆ ◆

'Isn't it beautiful?' said Sophie softly.

'Uh yes,' Scott said, not quite knowing where this sudden enthusiasm was coming from.

Then Scott saw something, but he couldn't quite be sure what it was. A rustling of the bushes, but no more. He felt fearful. Everything that had happened suddenly came flooding back to him: fear, paranoia, and an impending sense of doom, like something ominous was coming.

'Is something wrong?'

Sophie had to prod him quite hard to remind him she was still there.

Her hand was on his shoulder.

'I just thought I saw something,' he said.

'What?'

'I don't know, something unsettling. In those bushes.'

'I don't see anything.'

'It was there a moment ago; the bushes were rustling.'

'Lots of things can make bushes rustle,' said Sophie. 'Like wind and animals...'

She became curious. 'If it's an animal, why don't we see what it is?'

'No, please don't,' said Scott. 'I thought it was a person.'

'Well why don't you come with me and we'll find out.'

'No, please...'

'Just a look?'

'Please don't.'

'I'll go myself then.'

'No!'

Sophie stared at him as if he'd slapped her, then she composed herself.

'I think you're stressed, Scott. What with my dad having a go at you and the attack on the fair and my school. I've felt it too; just let me calm you down.'

'Sorry.'

Scott put his hands on his head. 'I can't stay here,' he said. 'Can we go inside?'

'What? *Why*, Scott? We're perfectly safe.'

'No, I don't *feel* safe. Can we go inside?'

Sophie held him. 'Scott, stay here with me. The night's beautiful – let's enjoy it.'

Scott saw a shape moving, and another, and another. All too brief.

'I'm sorry, Sophie, I can't stay here.' He got up.

'Where are you going?' she asked.

'Back inside. I just need somewhere to feel safe.'

'But you're safe here,' said Sophie.

'Please...'

Sophie was visibly dismayed; she clearly couldn't understand why she couldn't calm him down. Scott wanted to stay, he really did; he just felt compromised, and he didn't want to go over there and find out if his fears were true, especially not without the micro-flyer.

'Come with me,' he said.

Sophie gaped. 'What? Scott, I'm not going anywhere. There's nothing wrong; we're safe. Just stay here!'

She frowned. 'OK, just do what you want!' she said, and she turned away.

'But, Sophie—' he began.

'Do what you want!' she cried. 'Go inside if that's where you'd rather be! Go inside!'

He tried to comfort her.

'Leave me alone!'

Bewildered, Scott did as she asked. But he didn't feel safe even when he was inside, and he also felt terrible for leaving her out there by herself. He couldn't convince her of what he'd seen, and he couldn't prove it either.

◆ ◆ ◆

Sophie sat there for a while, the stars lighting up her tears. Her eyes sparkled, reflecting the heavens above. After everything she'd shown him, this was how it ended? Without Scott here, what was the point of staying outside? She huffed, and walked back to the house. She locked the door, put on the burglar alarm and left a light on. Just in case.

◆ ◆ ◆

Two police cars appeared and six officers began to patrol the beach, looking for something they'd been called to investigate.

Jack Robinson ground his teeth. They could have

achieved this snatch tonight. In actual fact, police had been called out to look for them, not because of their planned abduction, but because a few concerned residents had noticed their large group moving on foot through the darkness.

They'd also been spotted partying loudly around a massive fire, something that was prohibited on the reserve, as it upset the tranquillity of the waterways and swamps.

It was his own fault they'd messed up, but Jack didn't equate tonight's failure with his impulsive partying. He knew that if they tried anything now so close to the cops, things were bound to go wrong.

CHAPTER 14
The Meeting

Dennis Murphy had met his punishment. He'd been sentenced to fourteen years in a correctional facility, and for the first five years it had been hell. He'd been mercilessly targeted by the other inmates – he'd been intimidated, punched, kicked, head butted, put in hospital and nearly killed.

Then there were the guards. Every morning they would clang their truncheons on his cell bars, handcuff him and take him to breakfast wearing an orange jumpsuit in a queue of others, as armed guards and vicious snapping Alsatians looked on.

Breakfast was always a very short, rushed affair. They were served mouldy bread, watery scrambled eggs and some disgusting stew with the odd maggot wriggling inside.

When that was over, there was usually a stint in the exercise yard, home to some monkey bars, a football field and a racetrack – one that he would run round for the thousandth time screamed on by drill instructors. There were no weights in this outdoor gym – nothing big and heavy that could be used as weapons.

Then there was the contraband – usually mobile phones, drugs and weapons. It regularly snuck in one way or another, either through visitors or by bribed staff.

Fights broke out every day over the smallest things. There were stabbings every week from smuggled blades, as well as little bags of cocaine and heroin that would send inmates into berserker rages. Takedown teams were summoned virtually every day, and the inmates would be split apart using everything from brute force and pepper spray to barking dogs and truncheons. Even live bullets on more occasions than Dennis cared to remember.

Dennis rarely got peace of mind and so developed severe anxiety and depression. Every week or so the guards would ask for a urine sample. He'd never taken any drugs. He was intelligent enough to know that they wouldn't do him any good, but the guards made it increasingly difficult for him to provide a specimen till eventually he could no longer do it. He would be thrown into solitary confinement more and more regularly.

He would lose his mind in there from the endless boredom and isolation – hardly any light penetrated through the slit they called a window. Escaping the torture of the system sanctioned by the world's most powerful government was virtually impossible, and the years had taken their toll on Dennis Murphy. He was almost spent. Almost.

But inside him was a hope. One so audacious that if successful he'd change everything.

❖ ❖ ❖

For Dr Sally Patterson he was a regular and rather unique client. She would drive nearly an hour twice a week just to see him, though it wasn't ideal. Her daughter had therapeutic needs of her own that needed even more attention. But Dennis Murphy wasn't going to be committed here for life.

By now he'd served thirteen years and eleven months. In just a month's time, he would be eligible for release, and despite misgivings from some, there was no real reason why it couldn't happen. He'd had a very rough time of it. He'd been controlled, coerced and told what to do and when to do it every single day since he'd arrived.

And yet to everyone who wasn't a staff member, he was considered a legend, a man who brought people together. As time wore on, his relationship with the other inmates improved. There were still some who tried to bully him, calling him names and beating him up, but they were dealt with by the other inmates, and were now isolated for their own protection.

To Sally this was surprising. Promising even. If she was successful in rehabilitating Dennis, he could do really well, perhaps even give back to the world in some way. Her superiors had advised against working with him, given her daughter's history with him, but she went ahead with it anyway. For Sally it would be a chance to show herself that she wasn't just the simple pretty face everyone had thought she was in high school.

Dennis was brought into the meeting room, which contained a table with several chairs circled around it and a projector screen. Two guards stationed themselves outside.

'How are you today, Dennis?' asked Sally.

'I'm good, thank you,' said Dennis. 'What about

you?'

'Good thanks,' said Sally, then she sighed.

'The parole board is looking to release you in the next month and I wanted to assess you again to see how you were doing. Tell me how this week has gone for you.'

'My friends have been excellent,' said Dennis. 'They're all keen to support me in a special project on the outside.'

'A special project?' said Sally. 'Tell me about it.'

'We're proposing a humanitarian scheme to bring the people of the world together,' said Dennis. 'I figure that division is at the heart of most conflict on Earth – the fact the police effectively killed my father for being black is proof. I want to change things so that we can all live together in peace.'

'Interesting,' said Sally. 'And how do you plan to implement this?'

'I've sent some people on the outside to spread the word.'

'To where?' said Sally.

'All over the world,' said Dennis. 'People of all nationalities are answering my call. My followers have already found some great people. One of them used to be in the Congolese army; he called himself Nganda. He'd been living in the bush for nearly a decade after fleeing the fighting of the Rwanda genocide in 1994. He was rather tired of roughing it, so we offered him a place to take care of our African operations.'

'African operations?'

'He's there spreading the word amongst everyone in Africa and taking care of all logistical arrangements so anyone can join. It doesn't matter who they are or what qualifications they have, if any – we're finding a use for them.'

'What sort of uses?'

'We're arranging that as we speak,' said Dennis. 'It's all very new so far.'

Sally raised an eyebrow. Normally Dennis was rather reticent during their appointments; his cheerful optimism seemed an odd change of character.

'Great,' said Sally. 'So who else is involved?'

'We have a guy from Japan called Hanzo Takeshi – he's my bodyguard. There's also a biopharmaceutical expert from Brazil called Gavier Munoz, who's looking to manufacture the drugs we need to bring the world the healthcare it desperately needs. We have several other people who I won't name, but the point is I've got generals and we're all working together to make our group take shape. As I said, it's very new. We don't know how we'll organise ourselves in the end. But I'm sure we'll get something sorted out. It's all about getting these skills to work in a vision that will benefit all.'

'It does sound rather ambitious,' said Sally.

'I know,' said Dennis, 'but I'm sure more will be accomplished by the time I'm out. Otherwise I'm doing just fine.'

He smiled.

Sally frowned.

'What do you mean by generals?' she asked.

She didn't mean to burst his bubble, but it seemed a rather odd choice of word.

'Leaders,' said Dennis. 'Leaders who are reliable and ready to do what's necessary to make this project work. There's far too much violence in the world; I don't want to add any more.'

Sally paused, wondering if she had more to ask. She was encouraged and at the same time troubled by Dennis's change in character. There was a part of her that had trouble believing Dennis had changed, and yet he'd done nothing to suggest he hadn't. He'd been almost angelic these past few years – the inmates adored him and even the staff had to admit that he'd been no cause for concern.

'Will that be all, Dennis?' asked Sally.

'I think so,' said Dennis.

'Then it was a pleasure seeing you today,' she said.

They shook hands.

'Goodbye, Doctor,' said Dennis.

'Goodbye.'

She left the room.

◆ ◆ ◆

Dennis smiled to himself. Everything was going as planned.

CHAPTER 15
A Difficult Day

On the long drive back to Miami, Sophie's father made one last effort to have Scott removed from the Pattersons' lives. It turned out that he'd overheard the argument last night and saw it as a perfect excuse to get rid of Scott once and for all. It was clever and cunning. He'd tricked him by saying that there was a wounded alligator by the roadside and that he should 'go and help'. He'd accompanied him into this small patch of forest where a muddy swamp lay, fringed with reeds and algae. Then, without warning, he'd pushed him into the swamp, then ran back and told the others the alligator had got him.

◆ ◆ ◆

Sophie wasn't happy with how things had ended between her and Scott last night, but her moral integrity held fast. She saw through her father's lies and threw a barrage of demands to go back for him, but he drove on regardless. He just wouldn't listen – as long as this 'threat' was removed, he was happy.

◆ ◆ ◆

Scott was soaking wet and muddy. He staggered around trying to get his bearings and made it to some dry land, still blinded by the stagnant water. Nothing came to attack him, so he felt lucky in a way. He'd seen an alligator in almost every body of water regardless of size or innocence, except this one.

On impulse he fumbled around his body, checking to see if he'd lost anything. When his hands came to his back, he breathed a sigh of relief – the micro-flyer was still there. If Sophie's dad had thought he could just leave Scott behind in the middle of nowhere then he was completely mistaken.

Scott had simply followed them all the way back. One or two people in hot air balloons had stared in astonishment at him, but he was too determined to keep up to care. He didn't suppose David would think of looking up and behind either. Not while he was driving.

Surprisingly, given his experiences, Scott wasn't interested in revenge.

When he returned to Miami, he tried to apologise to Sophie for the night before. She said she accepted his apology, but even Scott could tell that she hadn't really. Her father, furious that Scott hadn't been eaten, ordered him away.

Scott gave it two days, but Sophie didn't contact him again, so he knew he had to put things right and plucked up the courage to go and see her.

As he made his way over to see her, he noticed Wayne was standing at her door. He was holding something that looked like a box of chocolates. Sophie opened the door and the two greeted one another with a hug, then a kiss. They embraced tighter and then went inside, hand in hand. Scott watched in disbelief – he wanted to go over there and stop them, but what good would that do?

Suddenly all the joy he'd felt over the past few weeks became a distant memory. Had he waited too long? Had she thought that he wasn't interested? Had she ever been interested in him at all? He had trouble grasping what had just happened. They'd found out how much in common they had. They'd been on a cruise, a shark dive – she'd saved his life. He'd saved her life and the lives of so many others and they'd even been on holiday together. What had changed in the last few days? Was it the other night's argument? That alone? Or had anything changed at all?

Scott was horrified. He flew away in a tempest.

A short while later, he descended into the Sea Marshes Reserve, causing the white ibises and roseate spoonbills to scatter. He didn't care. He was hurt, upset and angry; he felt used! He kicked a bush, disturbing some six-lined racerunners (a kind of lizard) taking shelter in it.

More questions raged through his mind. Had she been with Wayne all this time? When she was spending time with him one on one, was she viewing him only as a friend? Or something less? Had she meant to deceive him? He thought it unlikely.

Had he bought way too much into everything that had happened? Had it all meant anything? To him it had. He knew that much.

After his anger burned away, he broke into torrential sobs. Wayne had won her over – *how typical*, he thought. No matter how nice he was, no matter how much he had in common with them, the jocks always won the girls he liked. School had taught him that. Life had taught him that, and now it was teaching him again! Was this how it was always meant to be? Was he always to be led on, only to see natural selection take its same, sad predictable course? It was the Asperger's, wasn't it? She would only want someone normal. Not like him; never like him. His chance from day one had been zero.

He knew he would never meet another girl like her. No girl he ever liked had reciprocated his feelings. He knew in his heart that he would be alone, unloved, forever. Society would continue to step on him until he died, the order of the universe dictated by the 'normal' minded!

He lost track of time. The sun began to set.

'Scott, are you OK?'

He looked up in astonishment, his spirits lifted. But it wasn't Sophie.

'Sara, right?' he asked.

'Yeah,' she replied, looking at the floor, not seeming to notice his tear-stained face.

'What are you doing here?' he asked.

'I came here just to see what this place was like,' she said.

'You like birds too?' he asked.

'Not really,' she replied. 'I just wanted to figure out what the attraction was.'

'I see.'

Scott didn't know what else to say.

'What are you doing out here?' she asked. 'Are you birdwatching?'

Scott realised he didn't have any optical equipment to back that kind of story.

'I came here to think and be at peace is all,' he said.

'Why's that? Is something bothering you?'

Scott barely knew Sara so he wasn't willing to share what had happened.

'Not really,' he said. 'Sometimes I just need to think.'

'I do that too,' she said. 'There's lots going on that I need to think about.'

'Such as?' he asked.

Unlike himself, she didn't hold back.

'I hate my life,' she said abruptly. 'There's always problems at home, I'm struggling through schoolwork as it is and I've got chronic acne. That probably explains why the boys keep away from me. Sophie can have any guy she wants just because she's pretty – that's all there is to it.'

Scott was taken aback. This sudden unprovoked barrage of negativity wasn't what he'd expected.

'But she's also very nice,' he said. 'The principal said she gives to charity and gives people like ourselves a refuge.'

'I am grateful for that,' Sara admitted. 'Samantha, Sophie and the boys have all given me a sanctuary. I've asked for their advice repeatedly on talking to guys. They give me the same old advice and I really do try it, but no one ever seems to notice me. Whilst those two, I feel like they unconsciously make fun of me with their success.'

'That can't be true,' said Scott. 'Sophie wouldn't knowingly make fun of anyone.' Though as he said that, he wondered if it was really true.

'Do you mind if I walk with you?' Sara asked. 'I've got a lot on my mind; years of it have just built up and

I need someone to talk to. Sophie says she's too busy to talk to me.'

'Um... sure,' said Scott hesitantly.

Sara spilled more of the beans. 'For years I've felt as if who I am is somehow already predetermined. I don't know if you noticed but I'm not exactly the prettiest girl around. In fact, I think I'm the ugliest.'

Scott looked at her acne. It was indeed very severe, with extensive scarring where she'd either picked at spots or they'd left a mark after their departure. He frowned, knowing exactly how she was feeling.

'No matter what I use, these spots still keep coming – like I've got chicken pox or something. My hair is naturally greasy and no amount of washing or conditioner seems to help it. The way I see it, Sophie seems to have her pick of the guys; she's beautiful enough to get anyone she wants and I feel like I can never have that. I mean, I quite like Wayne as well. But I just expect her to win because someone like her always does.'

Scott wasn't getting much of a chance to reply.

'But the worst part is that even though I get good grades and work hard, it just feels as though the system doesn't care. Even the people who say they care about you, I feel don't actually. I feel like Sophie is making excuses not to talk to me; she always says she's busy. She keeps talking about psychiatric appointments she needs to attend for all that's happening, like she can't cope with her greatness or something. She'll do the same for you: make excuses, offer you sanctuary and then give you no real friendship.'

Scott wasn't in the best mood with Sophie, but even he felt Sara was overreacting.

'I don't believe that's the case,' he said. 'Like I said

before, I'm sure she doesn't do these things on purpose.'

Suddenly he stopped and asked: 'What's wrong, Sara – really?'

She stopped too.

'Did you really come in here to look at the birds if you're not that interested?' he asked.

Sara said nothing.

'Tell me what's wrong and I might be able to help you,' he said.

Sara's face contracted. Scott wondered why she was coming out with this now. He'd learned from experience that when he ranted this way, it was because of a bigger underlying problem. Tears flowed from Sara's eyes.

'This time last year, my parents were shot dead.'

'*What?*' He'd heard what she'd said; he just couldn't believe it. 'Shot dead?' he said. 'How?'

'My parents were both cops,' she said. 'They and a team of others were investigating a criminal gang. They were parked outside a building thought to be their hideout, keeping surveillance on them. They had a well-planned operation, but something went wrong. There was an ambush, as though the criminals were waiting for them. There were no survivors. To this day, their killers have never been found. It's like they don't exist, even when evidence suggests they do.'

'I'm so sorry,' said Scott softly.

He put an arm around her, just to comfort her. Nothing more. Sara tried to smile.

'I just can't cope without them,' she said. 'Since the day I was taken into care, life has been hell: bullying, bureaucracy, deprivation—'

They'd come to the edge of the boardwalk overlooking the vast pool of tidal currents whipped into frenzies by the wind. Sara's tears intensified and she held onto him like a child. Scott was overwhelmed. He didn't know what to say or do other than to just let her hold on.

Suddenly she let go of him and walked up to the railings.

'I can't cope,' she said. 'Things just don't change.'

She took a step onto the railings. Scott frowned. She took another step onto the railings, completely off the ground now.

'What are you doing?' he asked.

She climbed to the top of the railings, the raging water rushing beneath. Sara looked back at him, her red tear-stained face quivering with fear.

'Goodbye, Scott,' she said. Then she cast herself into the water.

Scott took to the air in a heartbeat. Sara floundered. He swooped in to grab her, but she went under. He was horrified, powerless.

'Sara!'

The water raged past in a torrent. On impulse he looked around, wondering if anything predatory had taken any notice. He was desperately worried.

'No, no, no, no!' he cried. 'Sara!'

He scoured the water. 'Sara!'

There was no response. He kept shouting for her.

'Scott?'

He turned and saw that she'd travelled underwater for at least fifty metres.

'Hold on, Sara; I'm coming!'

Sara struggled to stay above water, coughing and spluttering. She wasn't swimming, she was drowning.

How she managed to get to the surface in these conditions Scott didn't know.

'Take my hand!' he cried.

But he couldn't get low enough. His wings were far too wide, and the water kept lapping up and down to the point where the risk of immersion was very possible. Then Scott would need rescuing too.

He saw a stick floating downstream.

'Grab on!' he cried desperately.

Sara grabbed it. She was only just managing to keep her head above water. The stick snapped!

'Lie on your back!' he cried.

'What?' she coughed.

'Lie on your back!' he repeated. 'Now!'

Sara still didn't hear. She nearly collided with a log the size of a canoe. Scott was relieved to see she didn't hit it. He had an idea. He pushed the log towards her.

'Grab on!' he shouted. 'Take it!'

Sara managed to wrap her arms round it, gasping for breath. But the problems didn't end. Within a heartbeat, the ocean loomed and a fierce riptide tore her away from the log. No amount of kicking seemed to stop her from being taken out into the ocean.

The waves crashed in, some about six metres high. Scott spun wildly out of the way, and while he could ascend out of their reach, it became increasingly difficult to spot Sara. Several waves crashed over her. She'd probably swallowed water. She would have difficulty breathing right now – how much longer could she last? There was no easy way to grab her now. The waves made it impossible to get close enough without putting himself at risk. He just had to hope that she'd make it past the surf zone.

Miraculously, Sara came up again. Scott thought quickly. *Come on*, he berated himself, *I've got to have another plan.* She was still in terrible danger. Worst still, the current was rapidly taking her to the Deep Drop where he'd faced both a great white shark and a sperm whale. Even if the water wasn't cold like he was used to at home, there were other things out there to contend with.

Sara seemed to stop moving. She lay on her front, face down in the water, fatigued from trying to stay afloat. She would have only minutes before she drowned.

He ascended to a greater height. He remembered the brown boobies he'd seen on the cruise, the way they'd dived like missiles into the water. A precise vertical drop was his only chance.

He shot down and grabbed Sara's waist. Somehow, very awkwardly, he managed to reverse backwards, only just managing to miss the incoming swell. No sharks had come. That was a relief.

Sara was unconscious so it was straight to the hospital, where she was instantly given CPR.

Scott's eyes turned even redder. A bad day had turned even worse.

Four hours passed before Sara came round.

'Are you OK?' he asked her.

'Yes thank you, Scott,' she said. She grabbed hold of him for a hug. 'I'm glad I've got someone who loves me.'

Scott felt so awkward. What had he got himself into?

CHAPTER 16
Hurricane Patricia

Scott had to find Sara. He had to tell her the truth. That there was nothing between them; they weren't in a relationship – they were just friends.

The first Scott knew of a new threat was an envelope posted through the letter box. His parents had taken it in with the intention of opening it later, but Scott was curious and decided to open it himself, given that it was addressed 'to the residents of 22 Fisher Street'.

When he unfolded the letter, his heart raced. It was advising all residents to take urgent preparatory action. He read through a list of at least twenty precautions and recommendations. All of these had to be completed within twenty-four to thirty-six hours – before the hurricane hit. When he showed the letter to his parents, they reacted with no more calm than himself.

Scott stuck to his plan to find Sara, and almost as soon as he set out, he noticed a potent difference in the atmosphere. There was bright flawless sunshine, but the fine weather was lost on the hundreds if not thousands of people that were already out. He passed several houses where the occupants were nailing planks of wood over the windows. Some were piling sandbags against the doors, while others had clearly decided to leave.

'Scott!'

He turned and saw Samantha there.

'Have you heard?' she asked hurriedly.

'Yes,' he said, holding up the letter.

He changed the subject. 'Do you know where Sara is?'

'Sara?' she said. 'She's gone away to Alabama with her carers – they left this morning.'

Scott ground his teeth.

'Is something wrong?' she asked. It was a rather rhetorical question.

'What about Sophie?' he asked.

'She's out shopping,' she said. 'Her parents have decided to stay.'

'What about you?' he asked.

'I'm staying as well.'

'And the others?'

'I'm not sure.'

Scott could hardly take it in.

'Maybe when Sophie comes back, her parents can help you make arrangements?' Samantha suggested.

Scott's mind slowed ever so slightly.

'Sure,' he replied.

In the hours that followed, so much happened. Half the residents had fled. From the air, Scott could see hundreds of cars gridlocked on the highways. He'd wondered why the others weren't doing the same thing. He'd even suggested going back to the house in Cocoa Beach, but Sophie told him that being a holiday home in peak season, it had been booked by someone else.

When he asked why they were making no attempt to leave at all, the universal reply was that everywhere they could go was either full or too far away. Scott was so worried even the reconciliation he longed to have with Sophie wasn't at the forefront of his mind. They worked together to make preparations and Scott figured she must be over it, though he certainly wasn't. But the urgency of the present was at the sole forefront of his mind. With windows boarded over, and extra food, fuel and water to last the next three days stored away, all they could do was watch and wait.

◆ ◆ ◆

Two thousand four hundred miles into the Atlantic Ocean, the monster roared. There was nothing out here, nothing that would want to be out here. Nothing except sea, sky and storm. Over the following days, she sucked violently from the sea's surface, her clouds doubling in size, spinning anti-clockwise in a swirling mass of cloud, rain and wind. Her scale would only have been appreciable from either the air or from space. With a loud ominous moan, she edged westwards, passing over miles of open ocean.

Brown boobies and magnificent frigate birds struggled against her winds. Bottlenose dolphins – sensing the change in the water – shot away to safety, while a humpback whale felt what was coming and dived below the surface, trying to find some temporary sanctuary from the wind.

The week before the warning was issued to Florida, she'd already done damage to many Caribbean nations: the flat sandy, touristy island of Antigua, the volcanic rainforests of Montserrat, Guadeloupe, Dominica, Martinique, St Vincent and Grenada and westwards still to the Greater Antilles: Puerto Rico, the Dominican Republic, Haiti, Jamaica and Cuba. About 621 miles of devastation, all in the space of a week. And Florida would be next.

◆ ◆ ◆

From atop his abandoned block, Dennis Murphy pondered over the blackening clouds above the ocean. He wouldn't have admitted it, not even to himself, but he was nervous. Who wouldn't be if they saw a hurricane approaching?

Yet he was ambivalent at the same time. This storm could make his plans easier in some ways, but harder in others. On the one hand, it could mean more cover for their activities, especially if law enforcement found themselves stretched. It could also mean more allies if he wasn't too paranoid to appear publicly. But on the other hand, the eyes of the world would be on Miami. Aid workers and soldiers would more than likely pour in to deal with the aftermath, and that could make future operations more dangerous.

The wind picked up suddenly, and Dennis nearly lost his footing. He took it as a cue to head underground, quickly descending the steps where a shutter door opened to an underground parking lot. The door shut behind him, cutting out the wind.

'How is it up there, my lord?' asked Hanzo, bowing courteously.

Dennis turned to his calm, collected Japanese colleague.

'Getting worse. Is everyone accounted for?'

'Yes, my lord.'

'Did Jack pile the sandbags like I asked him?'

Hanzo didn't answer, yet he probably knew the answer.

'Jack!' said Dennis. 'Come here!'

A scrawny young man hurried over.

'My lord?' he asked, his Australian accent thick.

'Are the sandbags piled?' said Dennis.

'Natasha's doin' 'em,' he muttered.

'Why is Natasha doing them?' said Dennis. 'I specifically asked you.'

Jack pouted like a little child about to throw a tantrum.

'I asked Natasha and her girls to entertain the boys tonight,' said Dennis. He put a hand on Jack's shoulder. 'Don't worry – you'll get your first choice of the lot without question. I'll ensure it.'

Jack managed to grin, though his insecurity didn't make it look sincere.

Dennis sighed. 'Now go on – the storm's coming!'

Jack's pout returned but he went away. They watched him go.

'I don't know why I put up with him sometimes,' said Dennis. 'I suppose he was one of my first allies back in the facility. Enthusiastic, keen to make the others bow to me. But he also keeps the girls in line better than any of them. He has the raw strength that Natasha doesn't, plus he's pretty good with a knife.'

He sighed. 'Go and join him and make sure he does it this time, Hanzo. I do apologise. Your true talents are wasted on keeping him in line.'

'I'll do whatever you command, my lord.'

'I wish I had a hundred more like you,' said Dennis. 'See to it.'

'Yes, my lord.'

Hanzo went away.

'Nganda!' called Dennis.

A tall, well-built African man came to his call. 'My lord?'

'Do the animals have sufficient food and water to last this storm?'

'Yes, my lord,' said Nganda. 'My men imported at least a hundred tonnes of meat, grass and hay for them just yesterday.'

They perused the stable-like complex. The jackals snarled, the lions roared and the hyenas laughed, while the two rhinos grunted, the steam from their nostrils billowing like chimneys. Green lights blinked from their ears.

'Makasi especially needs it,' said Nganda.

They paused outside an enclosure much larger than the others. The huge elephant trumpeted a greeting upon hearing his name. He extended his trunk as if to shake hands.

Nganda gently grasped it.

'My strongest solider,' he purred. 'You come first above all else.'

The elephant rumbled, as if ingratiated.

Lightning cracked and Makasi jolted, swaying in his pen.

Dennis squinted. 'Now it begins!'

◆ ◆ ◆

Mary and Sean were in their house, watching the TV for updates. But Scott was preoccupied with the sky. He couldn't believe what had happened to it. Where there was usually a cloudless blue expanse and sun, there was now a vast wall of grey and black clouds. The wind had picked up, so strong that the palm trees bent like catapults ready for launch.

Scott was struggling to digest the situation. He felt overwhelmed and helpless. He ran to find Sophie, getting away before his parents could shout an objection.

'Sophie!'

The wind was furious. Debris flew in his face. He grew more desperate.

'Sophie!'

Scott was in an anguished state of fear. It felt like the whole world was actively ending around him.

'Up here!' Sophie shouted.

She was on the rooftop of the house. He flew up to join her.

'Sophie! Are you alright?' He was breathing hard.

Sophie nodded. 'It's alright; I'm OK,' she reassured him.

Scott soon saw the view that was captivating her. Over the ocean was a barrage of swirling cloud that spread as far as the eye could see.

Hurricane Patricia bore down on the land; she clearly had everything she needed to pulverise everything in her path. Her 150mph winds had the power to rip houses from their foundations; trees and bushes from their roots and whip the ocean into a colossal battering ram. Inside her heart was a rich supply of heat and humidity, creating enough rain to overwhelm every drain around. All the time her loud thunder and lightning pierced the atmosphere, illuminating the chaos that their beloved mistress caused.

The wind accelerated!

'Scott, get down!' shouted Sophie.

She pulled him to the ground just in time to avoid an incoming mail box. It flew over their heads and smashed into the house opposite.

'Scott!' shouted Mary. 'A neighbour has offered to take us in – come with us!'

Sean stood there too, just as incredulous.

'We need to get to the basement!' Sophie shouted. 'Follow me!'

Scott delayed, torn between who to go with.

'Come on!' his parents shouted.

'Watch out!' cried Sophie.

A lamp post toppled and smashed, exploding in sparks. Scott's parents nearly didn't see it, and with the sight of similarly sized debris blowing across the street, a decision was made.

Sophie took Scott's hand and pulled him into the house, leading him down the stairs to the basement.

Sophie's parents were already there and ran to greet them.

'Are you two OK?' asked Sally urgently.

'We're fine,' said Sophie.

'What do we do now?' asked Scott.

'We have to sit it out, Scott; it's the only thing we can do,' said Sally.

'Are we safe here though?'

'I don't know,' she replied, 'but we have to stay here – it's our only chance.'

Scott was hyperventilating. He paced around all over the place in a panic.

'Scott?' Sophie called.

He wasn't listening. His hands were on his head; he

wished he was anywhere else but here.

'Scott? Stop. Listen to me.'

Sophie took hold of him.

'Listen, I know you're scared – we *all* are. But we can't afford to lose our heads; we *have* to stay here – it's our best chance.'

Tears streamed from his eyes. Her grip tightened.

'Hey, Scott,' she said softly. 'It's OK – we're together. Your family will be hiding somewhere. I know they will.'

Scott met her eyes.

'We've done this several times before. We *are* going to get through this, I promise. Come on – let's sit it out together.'

They sat still on the floor in complete silence, listening to Patricia venting her fury above. This wind was so unusually loud, like the roar of a freight train. The rain pelted down, lashing everything as lightning cracked and thunder growled. The lights inside the basement went on and off constantly, but didn't switch off altogether.

Scott dreaded being here in total darkness. He dreaded being here at all even though it was the safest possible place he could be right now. Sophie had tried to start up conversation, just to take their minds off it. But despite her best efforts, Sophie couldn't take his mind off it. Scott felt so alone. The others were afraid – they'd said so – but he felt as though none of them really understood *his* fear. He'd never experienced anything like this. For once it was something he couldn't fight, and he felt truly helpless.

The others finally managed to sustain some conversation, but he didn't want to join in. He got up at that point, and Sophie looked up at him in surprise.

'Where are you going?' she asked.

'Just over here,' he mumbled vaguely.

He parked himself well away from the others and stared into space like he was in a world of his own, desperately pretending this wasn't happening. He really got to examine the basement: it was a vast room; the floor was wooden and creaky, with old disused household objects standing forgotten in the gloom, and the lighting was appalling. It cast deep shadows across the room – the only source of illumination from a little light bulb dangling from the ceiling by a thin thread of wire.

Sophie came over to comfort him, sitting down beside him and wrapping her arms around his shoulders. He glanced up at her but said nothing. There was no point complaining – she knew exactly what was on his mind.

'Scott, it's going to pass,' she whispered. 'I know it will.'

He said nothing; he was hardly convinced of that at all.

'There's no point thinking about it all the time,' she continued. 'We have to make the best of it while we're here. Besides, we're two metres below sea level, the sandbags are going to prevent us from being flooded and we're going to be fine. Right?'

He nodded pessimistically.

'Why don't you come over and join us? It's the least you can do.'

Scott met her eyes and nodded.

He tried to reason things with himself. She was right – this place was two metres below sea level with every possible entrance barred. With that in mind, they were safe, right?

A while later, he'd managed to get deep into conversation with the others, but during that conversation he heard a new sound that he liked far less than the others he'd heard so far. It sounded like a river was flowing up above. He could hear the distinct roar of flowing water, and he didn't like it one bit.

Then they heard a new sound, a quieter sound but closer! Scott spun round and saw a steady trickle of water coming down the stairs. As it flowed onto the floor, it spread out, embracing every surface it could.

That was when they all saw the bigger picture. What became a steady trickle started to intensify into a rapid gush. They were mortified. The sandbags had failed, and the room was beginning to flood. It was Patricia's will. She was merciless – she wanted to eradicate everyone here, right down to the stubborn survivors.

Sophie's father hurried up to the door with three more sandbags and dumped them there, pressing them hard against the door. That should have held the water back, but it kept coming! Patricia wasn't going to give up so easily.

On top of that, Scott sensed that the water level was beginning to rise ever more rapidly.

He thought quickly; they might be able to fly out to safety – no, maybe not, not while Patricia was looking for them. But then if they stayed down here then they'd surely all drown.

Scott considered the door that lead upstairs to the house – no that wouldn't do either; the wind and floodwater would take them. Floodwater was coming from there too, and he somehow doubted that the upper levels would be safe to stand on (if they were still there).

Scott had no courage earlier on, and he barely had it *now*, but all Sophie's reassurances about their basement's defences were no longer valid. She was no better than himself now.

That was when he noticed another small staircase in a dark corner, leading up to what looked like a small panic room. The water was up to their waists now, and this roof was fairly low. If the water level rose any higher they'd lose all hope of escape. This was their only option.

'Everyone I have an idea – follow me!'

He waded through the deepening water and gestured to the stairs. 'Come on!'

Sally stood there dumbfounded. 'Have you ever seen that room before David?'

'Well I remember having it set up years ago, but I don't remember anyone using it. Oh what the hell – we've got no choice anyway!'

They followed Scott up the stairs into the room. It was just big enough to accommodate all four of them. Soon they were locked inside, her dad securing the several different bolts on the door, and together they waited for whatever happened next. Scott held tightly onto Sophie, both of them quivering with fright.

Scott heard both basement doors burst open then, overwhelmed with water. Torrents came in, flooding the room to its highest extent. In no time it rose up the stairs so it was lapping at the room's feet.

They didn't dare open the door now. The only way they could see anything at all was by the thin window at the top, but all they could see through that was water. The door had held – that was the main thing. They just had to wait for help. But was Patricia gone yet? Scott could hear even from this sound-insulated room that the winds had subsided, but he had the feeling that this was one of Patricia's tricks – that this was only the eye, the calmest part of a hurricane. So calm that people may assume the storm was over. Even the sun comes out in the eye, but whether they could go outside or not, the storm wasn't over – as some first-timers would find out. There was still the second half to pass by.

It came again very suddenly, and then they could only hear episode two of Patricia's rage.

With death surrounding them all, Scott couldn't help but wonder whether retreating to this room might have protected them too well, and that they'd eventually suffer a different kind of death – of dehydration or starvation.

There was no way out, and Scott could see defeat. But there was a comforting thought to be had whilst he sat there: if he was going to die here then at least he was with the one person who had made his life happy and fulfilling. They'd die together, like that couple from the dodgems.

Finally though, the wind subsided, Patricia wailing in her passing. They were still trapped, and for Miami the actual hurricane was only half the ordeal. The other half was cleaning up the mess she made: draining the floodwater, repairing and rebuilding homes and businesses, caring for the sick and injured, providing fresh supplies, temporary shelter etc., etc. – and preventing looting too!

There was another reason that stopped them from opening the door right away though. With the sea defences breached, and seawater running freely through the streets, the flooding offered ease of travel for some of the area's dangerous residents. It was even more terrifying to think that rescue wasn't likely to come until tomorrow, so that meant that they were going to spend the night here too! No tea, no comfortable bed – pure discomfort.

Sophie screamed.

'What is it?' Scott asked.

'Th-Th-Th-That!' she stuttered, pointing at the window.

Scott peered out, then jumped backwards with a start. It was an alligator. Scott wondered if it would break the window. If bulletproof glass was so tough that bullets couldn't break it then surely an alligator couldn't? Only an alligator was significantly bigger than a bullet – what then?

But the alligator seemed to prefer watching them, at least for the moment. It made him think though – if an alligator could get through to them, what else could? What about sharks?

Even if Scott had thought about swimming to safety now that the hurricane was over, there was now an alligator outside to contend with (and it didn't look as if it was intending to leave at all) – and even if they did somehow get past it, there'd be the problem of getting to dry land.

Then there was the question that had revolved in his mind ever since he'd found the micro-flyer: could it work underwater and could he take off from the water too? He didn't know, and it felt too risky to try now, especially when their lives were at stake; if he got it wrong they'd certainly go to a watery grave.

His mind continued to debate what to do. He kept on thinking about the alligator, the water, the insurmountable swim to safety. Meanwhile, the ceiling began to crumble. He glanced up at it and was showered with flakes of paint.

He felt something trickling along his trousers then and dabbed at them, wondering why they were wet. He stared at the glass in horror.

'Guys, we have another problem,' he said.

'What?' said Sophie's father.

Scott pointed at the crack spiderwebbing slowly across the glass. The alligator saw it and took a bash at it, and the cracks grew wider. Again came the alligator. They all screamed, and something fell from the roof – a chunk of plaster that slammed into Scott's back. He stared up; there was a hole in the roof.

'That's it!' he shouted. 'The ceiling! We'll climb out!'

The alligator rammed the glass again, breaking a hole wide enough for its snout to fit through. Scott leaped for the ledge and struggled, the water offering no purchase, then braced his feet against the wall and with an awkward effort managed to pull himself up.

'Come on!' Scott cried. He reached for them, grasping Sophie's arms and hauling her up. The alligator now had its whole head through the window and David was wrestling with it, trying to keep its jaws shut.

'Go, Sally!' cried David. 'Go now. I've got a hold of him!'

Scott and Sophie pulled Sally onto the ledge. David was the last to get away. He kicked the alligator in the face and made a break for the others.

They struggled frantically to pull him up. It was made harder when the alligator clamped hold of a trouser cuff and was unwilling to let go.

They yanked harder and harder. The trouser ripped, and the alligator swallowed only a wet rag as David was pulled to safety. They were able to find somewhere dry and from there Scott took them to the roof. The storm was over. The house still stood, but Sophie and her parents stared in horror at the residence that had been their home for so long. The sandbags had kept out the worst of the water, but the ornaments and wallpaper were still damaged beyond repair.

Helicopters were flying overhead searching for survivors, and they all waved their arms in the air, desperate to be seen. Until the house was refurbished, the street drained and all the nearby services back to normal, they would have to stay elsewhere.

As it turned out, they had to stay in a camp, built like a refugee centre. Sophie's house wasn't going to be inhabitable for a long time to come, perhaps years.

When Scott flew over the vast suburbs later that day, he could appreciate just how high the waiting list was. There were plenty more streets to be drained, plenty of shops out of service; some houses had been reduced to rubble while others were too dilapidated and unstable to live in – inevitably there'd be ferocious competition for survival. Patricia had made a mess of this place, big time.

Scott could visualise riots breaking out and tense disputes that all too often ended in violence. Patricia had claimed a lot of lives all on her own; now some dangerous, selfish individuals would do the same.

Scott eventually got to see his parents again, but it was clear by now who he preferred to be with. The emergency camp was very big and crowded, and after just two days living there it became too much to bear, so they opted to stay in a rather dilapidated brick block that no one was officially supposed to live in.

It was a very jealous and desperate gang of thugs that discovered that there were people around better off than them. They found this place, dilapidated as it was, and from their demeanour it was clear they were in no mood for negotiation.

One of them banged on the rusty metal door, demanding to be let in. Looking out of the window, Scott could see about thirty of them hanging around the door, most of them boys but some girls too. He could tell from the way they cradled their pistols that they were quite prepared to gun down whoever was inside so they could take the apartment block; there was no sharing with these guys.

'Yo, you in there!' one shouted, evidently their leader. 'Give up the block. If you don't open the door, we'll gun ye all!'

Despite his grammar issues, he'd made his intentions clear.

One of them took a crack shot at the door; his bullet shot into the metal and hit the foot of the stairs. An act that was meant to scare them into complying, but the lead thug didn't see it like that.

'You idiot, that's gonna be our home. What ye shootin' it for?'

'Whoa, whoa, whoa,' said the other thug. 'Be cool, man – I was just wanting to show 'em we mean business.'

'*I'll* show 'em we mean business thank you very much; I don't need *you* for that.'

In a swift motion he shot him in the head; the other thug crumpled to the ground and lay still.

'This is yer last warnin', man,' he demanded. 'Open the goddamn door!'

Scott knew from Sophie's face that there was only one thing to do.

'This is yer last chance!' shouted the lead thug from outside.

They didn't stir; they wouldn't surrender.

'There ain't anyone answerin' the freakin' door,' said another one. 'It's time we bust 'em outta there!'

'You people, we're comin' in!'

The lead thug gave the door a loud kick, causing it to shake. Scott's heart was pounding. Kick, kick, kick – and then the door was down.

'Eviction notice!' called the lead thug.

There was a collective roar of jeering as the twenty-nine other thugs poured in, all of them spilling out onto the ground floor.

'You there!' said the lead thug. 'Stand guard! We'll check upstairs after we've searched all these rooms.'

This thug did as he was told, but it meant that now somebody was watching the stairs.

He was on his own but they didn't dare open fire. Sophie's father reached down, slipped his hand through the banister and grabbed the thug's mouth to stop him from screaming. In a split second, he dealt a punch so hard that the thug passed out and fell unconscious against the stairs, his nose bleeding hard.

'Well done, dear!' whispered Sally triumphantly.

No one else seemed to have heard what had happened, but they were sure that someone would check up on him at any moment and find he was down. To keep it ambiguous, they dragged the body up the stairs and dumped it in Sophie's room. Scott frisked him of any weapons and tied him up.

One down, twenty-nine more to go. Their victim had given him a knife, a pistol and, to his surprise, a baseball bat. He grinned – this would cause devastation for sure.

Scott saw two more thugs out the window, searching the back of the apartment block. He opened a window and silently dropped down with his micro-flyer, sneaking up from behind and swiftly knocking both of them out with a smash to the back of their heads.

Scott then flew up to the window carrying one body at a time and dumped them in Sophie's equally musty room before tying them up.

'Excellent work, Scott!' whispered Sally. 'They've lost three of their guys and they still haven't found us!'

But their joy was short-lived; they could hear footsteps coming towards the stairs. There were too many of them to be taken out silently. They stood by.

'Anythin' on the ground floor?' the lead thug demanded.

'No, nothin' down 'ere,' said one of them.

'Speaking of which,' said another, 'wasn't there someone 'ere guarding the stairs? I can't see 'im anywhere.'

The lead thug pondered that, then a grin spread across his face.

'So that just leaves up the stairs then, ain't it?' he said.

They were about to go upstairs when Sally swiftly

appeared out of nowhere and fired her jackhammer. A barrage of bullets took another four of them out, but she narrowly missed the lead thug.

'There they are!' he shouted.

They piled upstairs and in that instance Sophie did a commando roll, blasting some of them. The remaining thugs fired, but she rolled away.

'Awright, I've had enough o' this. I'm gonna shoot ye myself!' warned the lead thug, and he charged up the stairs, a Desert Eagle in one hand.

Before he could take a shot at anyone, Sophie lashed out, disarming him, then she held him like a human shield, his body taking the impact of the gang's bullets.

When the shooting had ceased, she chucked his body down the stairs. It crashed into the thugs, knocking some of them down, which in turn knocked some others over, creating an almost domino effect. They all lay in a mangled heap at the foot of the stairs, kicking and trailing their arms defencelessly in the air. One or two managed to fire some shots, but Scott and the others took them all out on the spot.

Scott flew up on top of the roof about to release his joy to the world – but he stopped short! There was another army of thugs heading this way, presumably after the same thing. There were at least fifty of them this time. This was more serious – some were armed with Alsatians ready to be let loose; others were waving Molotov cocktails in a threatening manner.

It wasn't over yet!

'OK, everyone, I've got some bad news,' said Scott. 'There's another group on the way and they look better armed.'

The others stopped cheering and stared.
'What? How many of them?' asked Sally.
'At least fifty!'
Sophie gaped.
Scott walked up to David.
'Are you good with cars by any chance?' he asked.
'Yeah, why?'
'Do you think you could hot-wire one?'
Her father raised his eyebrows, suddenly excited at the idea.
'Yes, I can actually; I learned to do it in the force.'
'Excellent,' said Scott. 'We three will keep them busy, but while their attention is focused on us you need to find a vehicle that still works, then when I give the signal, I want you to rev that engine and run them down. They shouldn't persist after this victory.'

Sophie stared at him worriedly. 'But...'

'I'll look after you, Sophie,' Scott assured her. 'I'll look after all of you – no one in this family is going to die today. You Americans are warriors, just like us Scots. Believe in yourself; have faith in your skill. Trust that this strategy will work and we'll all live to fight another day!'

There was an almighty cheer, but Scott quickly silenced it. 'Now make haste!'

Her father went away, leaving the others on their own. Thugs shot at the windows, glass shattering all around. They fired at them, but didn't manage to hit anyone. They were ducking for cover all the time, there were so many guns that could kill them. Finally Scott flew up onto the roof and gunned some down from there, dodging and weaving around the bullets just as he'd done at the school.

He inwardly urged her father to find a vehicle fast then realised he hadn't thought this plan through. What if there was no vehicle around or if there was, would it even be operable?

More bullets came his way. As he dodged them, he saw Sophie's father running past the horde of thugs. He couldn't let them see him. Scott blew on the Aquilacry, and the thugs covered their ears, screaming loudly in pain. Scott returned fire, taking out two more.

A short while later he saw a van nearing the thugs. It was only three metres from them.

Scott gave the order to charge, his shrill eagle cry piercing the battlefield. Dogs leaped up, barking loudly, and then David revved the van, before it charged forward, crashing into the gang of thugs in the middle of the road and sending them flying in all directions. In that one move, he'd taken out at least ten of them, driving away the rest by driving around and revving the engine aggressively. The survivors dragged their fallen peers away.

It was all over. They'd succeeded in defending the apartment block, and it remained their property. Sophie stared at him, apparently stupefied by the spectacular results of his strategy. Her father came back to the apartment.

'Scott, you are by far one of the craziest people I've ever met, but the greatest commander I've ever met too.'

'Cheers,' he muttered, not knowing what else to say.

'This isn't even your family, and yet you risked everything for us.'

Scott tried to be modest and it seemed to work.

'I'd do it for anyone,' he muttered.

Sophie glanced at her father and in the silence that followed, she wondered what this meant.

'Dad, I think you owe Scott an apology.'

Scott swallowed.

'Well,' her father started, 'I, uh—'

He was interrupted. They could hear footsteps outside.

They were automatically suspicious.

'Who is it?' called Sophie nervously.

There was no answer.

'Hold on – I'll be right back,' Scott muttered. He went upstairs and checked out a window.

'Sophie, it's your friends!' he called down the stairs.

'Is it?' said Sophie. 'I better let them in.'

She threw open the door to find Rickey standing there, looking desperate.

'Sorry to bother you,' he said apologetically, 'but I was wondering if we could stay with you. We haven't been allowed back to our houses, and we heard that you might be here.'

Scott glanced at Sophie. It was going to a tough arrangement, but Sophie nodded.

'Alright, come on in. We'll lay mattresses out in the living room. We'll make sure you're all as comfortable as possible.'

Scott was surprised to see Uncle Wilson amongst them.

Dutifully, Scott helped Sophie lay out the mattresses in the main room. They'd come up with the idea of converting the three couches into beds as well, but who would take them? Dave and Olav decided to take the offer, whilst Nigel and Hyliana opted for the floor beside them.

Out of everyone, Hyliana seemed to complain the least often; she seemed to be happy in most circumstances as long as her brother was with her, preferring his company almost to the exclusion of the others.

Samantha was put in a room two floors up – apparently she wanted her privacy. Her parents were given a room of their own, and Uncle Wilson decided to take the last room. Sophie and Wayne were apparently sharing, much to Scott's horror.

The thought of what they might do with one another didn't sit well with Scott. He'd decided to use the main room as well, alongside Rickey, Dave, Olav, Nigel and Hyliana.

He found Rickey lying alone in deep contemplation.

'Do you like your bed?' Scott asked.

'It's OK.'

'I know it seems a bit makeshift but it's the best we can do,' he said.

'It's better than the camp, where you're constantly waiting to be ticked off the waiting list and the wind's bothering you all the time. I've slept in worse conditions anyway – back in the Congo I was made to sleep on a hard musty floor, back when I was trained to be a soldier.'

Scott gaped. '*You* were a soldier!'

'Yes,' said Rickey. 'Me and my seven brothers were abducted from my home when I was only five years old by a warlord called Nganda. We all feared him. I was thrown into a world of war and violence and trained how to use a gun. I'm sorry to say that I killed people.'

'I'm sure you didn't want to do it,' said Scott.

'I was sent to kill people in Hutu villages. I terrified people and killed them because I was told to. When we weren't fighting, we were guarded by adults, which made escape at any time of the day very difficult. But one day we came under attack, and in the confusion and chaos I slipped away. I was forced to leave my brothers behind because they were ahead of me, fighting alongside the adults. There was no time to rescue them. I ran as far I could – I must have been running for at least a day. But I collapsed in the forest and I was very ill with malaria. Luckily I was found by UN peacekeepers. I told them where Nganda was, hoping that they would save my brothers. They found him but he escaped, and they didn't come back with my brothers. They couldn't say whether they were alive or dead, and no one ever did manage to catch Nganda. Part of me wishes he died in the forest; another part hopes he's alive so he can face justice.'

Scott sighed. It made the issues he'd faced in his life sound trivial.

'So I was adopted by an American family who worked for the UN and that was how I came to Miami,' said Rickey. 'I attended the same elementary school as Sophie, but I had to learn English and learn to read and write, which I was slow in doing. I converted to Christianity to move past some of my sins. And when I moved to high school, Dave suggested I adopt a more Western look to help me feel like a different person. As well as these clothes, I chose this plaited hairstyle, that as you can see I take great care to maintain. Olav's been very supportive too. He knows my story and he's always been there to reassure me on bad days.'

Rickey chuckled. Scott reciprocated.

'And here am I today,' said Rickey. 'So trust me, I've seen worse.'

He smiled. 'I might just go to bed now, Scott, if that's OK?'

'Sure,' he replied. 'And, Rickey?'

'Hmm?'

'I'm glad you told me. You're extremely brave.'

'Thank you,' said Rickey. 'Goodnight, Scott.'

'Goodnight.'

The horror and grief of Rickey's story was powerful enough to make Scott forget everything he'd been feeling. In deepest darkest Africa, Rickey had been brutalised to a degree even Scott could barely imagine. Yet here he was, thriving and making a good name for himself. If Rickey was disinclined to become a monster, if Rickey was still keen to engage and protect the world after all this, then surely there was hope for Scott.

But Rickey wasn't feeling exactly what Scott was feeling.

Night was already upon them; soon everyone was asleep. Except Sophie, Wayne and, because of those two, Scott. He could hear them laughing and giggling next door. He couldn't hear what they were saying, but that was less of a concern than the amorous sounds they were making. There was nothing sexual – in the eyes of the law they were still children – but he could clearly hear hugging and kissing. This was too cruel.

Suddenly Scott wished he'd accepted his parent's request to go with them. If he'd known he was going to end up sleeping in a dilapidated apartment block with so many other people, listening to the jock of the high school getting together with the girl he loved then he wouldn't have chosen to go with her.

He hadn't even heard from them in days. He didn't know how they were coping. They were alive, he'd seen that, but were they healthy, well fed and hydrated? All of these aspects of their welfare had simply not occurred to Scott until now.

How long was this arrangement going to last? How many more nights was he condemned to listen to natural selection in action? He felt worse than all the nights he'd spent in his aunt and uncle's flat in Aberdeen. He'd have rather had their lodger smoking weed well into the night, the smoke wafting into his face, than this. He wished he'd died after being stabbed by Blake Mitchell. Out of all the bullying he'd received, this was the worst ever, from the one person he'd least expected it from.

He wished he'd drowned at the Deep Drop. He wished he'd been shot and killed either at the school or the fair.

He wished an alligator had been in that pool to devour him. He wished the hurricane had either drowned him or the other alligator had feasted on his flesh.

Scott filled his grief-stricken lungs and tried to sleep, and just as on the ward in that hospital, he would have welcomed it lasting forever.

CHAPTER 17
An Awkward Meeting

Scott had only about two and a half weeks of vacation left in Miami. His parents had wanted to go home, but they couldn't afford the cost of changing their flight.

Under normal circumstances Scott would have been dreading returning to Aberdeen, but this time home time couldn't come soon enough. He was literally counting the nights till then.

Wayne and Sophie were exercising all that Scott despised about the social structure of today's youth, but he couldn't let it go. It was like he was obsessed, not willing to walk away from his chance of romance lightly.

Night had come again and Scott was out trying to find owls and nighthawks, hoping to at least temporarily shelve his resentment. He'd managed to slip out unseen by the others and went to work trying to do the one thing that gave his life meaning in the face of chaos.

He would try the Sea Marshes Reserve, assuming it was still standing.

He passed the emergency camp, went down the recently drained Fisher Street and past Sophie's house, and although it was still too dilapidated to live in, Scott heard a voice coming from her garden.

It pricked his curiosity and he stood at the gate

listening, wondering who could possibly be in there, given that her house was uninhabitable and the garden must have been full of debris. He wondered briefly if it was a gang.

He must have made a noise or something because footsteps approached and her gate opened.

Scott tensed.

'Hey, Scott. Do you want to come in?'

He stared. Sophie stood there wearing her blue swimwear.

'Hey, Scott.'

It was worse than he thought. Wayne stepped out from behind her, wearing only trunks, his six-pack goading him. The pair of them stood there smiling at him quite innocently, unaware of his real frame of mind.

'Sure,' he said nervously, totally bereft of any feelings of enthusiasm.

Sophie's smile faded slightly.

'So what brings you here, Scott?' said Wayne.

'Just looking for owls again. Maybe some nighthawks. What about you guys?'

'Just fooling around,' said Wayne. 'Sophie was feeling bored and wanted some company.' He pulled her in and rubbed her shoulder affectionately.

She giggled.

'Her pool's not too bad – a little dirty but I cleaned out the worst of it.'

Scott wondered what he really meant by fooling around. 'Yeah.'

Sophie bowed her head, smiling politely but clearly unsure how to carry on the conversation. In his awkwardness, Scott stared at the moon, illuminated by the sun shining down elsewhere in the world. It was pleasantly quiet, with only the ringing of crickets breaking the silence.

'It's a beautiful night, isn't it?' said Scott. 'Do you guys like stars?'

'Do you want to go in the pool?' Sophie asked. 'And you can point them out to us while we swim?'

'I haven't got swimming trunks,' said Scott.

'That's a shame,' said Sophie.

Despite him not being able to join them, they moved to the pool. Scott frowned – this was becoming more and more awkward.

'So here we have Cassiopeia – sometimes known as the Double U, or in this case an M...'

Scott chuckled, noting that at this latitude some constellations appeared upside down or much lower in the sky than at home. 'Cassiopeia was a queen who'd helped co-run a kingdom known as Aethiopia – not to be confused with the African country of course, this was a kingdom in what is now North Africa.'

Sophie raised her eyebrows.

'Looking left, there's her husband Cepheus. The constellation's supposed to depict a king but I think of it more as a garden shed,' said Scott.

Wayne squinted up at it, but he seemed only mildly interested.

'Cool,' he said. It appeared he didn't know what else to say.

'Up above you can see the Square of Pegasus and Andromeda coming off of it,' Scott continued.

He went through all the constellations he could recognise and pointed out Mars, Jupiter and Saturn. Sophie seemed to be loving his knowledge, but while

Wayne listened, it was clear it was without enthusiasm.

They stayed up all night, and when dawn broke, Sophie and Wayne made a move to go back to the apartment.

'Well I'll see you around, Scott,' said Sophie.

'You too,' said Scott. 'And you, Wayne.'

'Sure,' he replied.

Scott looked from her to him, at least twice over. Sophie frowned at him quizzically, apparently wondering if he had more to say. In the awkward silence that often accompanied a sudden departure, Scott was desperate to find some modicum of doubt in her decision. Sophie's quizzical frown intensified.

'Well see you,' he said shakily.

He could have accompanied both of them back to the apartment, but he didn't. Instead he watched them go away together. He felt sad, angry and deflated; part of him had thought that his presentation in astronomy might have helped change her mind.

But he was wrong. She'd moved on. She'd gone with Wayne, the jock, the classic cool dude who always got the girl.

Scott sighed. It was time for him to move on too. He took to the air to blot out his broken heart.

CHAPTER 18
Revealing the Enemy

What Scott had witnessed last night had left him in a world of hurt. A hurt that trumped all that came before it, because what he wanted had been dangled in front of him like a piece of meat, shaken enough to attract his attention and then withdrawn at the last second.

But he knew that the only thing to do was carry on enjoying this trip as best as he could.

He now flew over the several hundred keys near the tip of Florida, all of them with a ring of shallow turquoise water harbouring the jungles of the sea.

On some of the larger ones there were small villages, but most of them were shrouded in palm trees – the classic image of a desert island, with pirates, parrots and treasure; enormous ships armed with banging cannons and large sails harnessing the wind to its maximum. His imagination was really vivid even at fifteen, and there was always a story to be pictured wherever he went.

Scott decided he wanted to fly somewhere else, and with the power and freedom that came from being in charge of a flying machine that no one else possessed, came wild excitement.

He had several options: he could fly to the north overland or over the sea to Jacksonville or Tallahassee, both close to the border of Georgia. Or he could go east of Miami, which would take him to the Bahamas and their beautiful coral reefs and sandbanks that extended as far as the eye could see.

If he was feeling more adventurous, he could fly west and see the coasts of the other states like Louisiana – or Texas! Or he could take a more exotic option and go to Cuba or some of the other Greater Antilles. But surely they were all recovering after the hurricane?

He decided he would go back to the Everglades in search of the one creature that had eluded him so far – the Florida panther. Though they were rare and finding one wasn't guaranteed, Scott decided to try it anyway, and descended into some jack pine forest to begin his search. The forest was strangely quiet, with very little stirring. The hours stretched on and his thoughts about last night came flooding back to him.

It was because he was different, wasn't it? Scott had seen from several movies that this bad attitude to people who were different hadn't eased completely in these slightly more tolerant times. Smart people like him (though he often didn't view himself as smart in many contexts) were still labelled as nerds or dorks, enforcing the forged class hierarchy that prevented nerd and jock from mixing.

Sophie, at least, practically loved difference, but perhaps not enough to want him as anything more than a friend. Which in the grand scheme of things was alright and better than nothing – after all, everyone had free will to choose who and what they wanted.

Arguably, Scott shouldn't have taken it personally – rejection was a fact of life for virtually everyone in some shape or form. No one was obliged to date you, let alone spend the rest of their lives with you, or even notice you at all, Scott thought radically.

She was still his friend, but as accepting and angelic a figure as Scott viewed her, perhaps when it came to dating, even she subscribed to high-school politics. Perhaps his Asperger's was the deciding factor after all.

When he flew back to Miami, it took him more than twice as long as his journey out. He didn't see any panthers.

Feeling like flying wasn't stoking the flame as well as it had before, he thought some food might help, as it was nearing dinner time. He hadn't had any lunch and was truly starving by the time he landed.

◆ ◆ ◆

Hanzo Takeshi had been searching for weeks for the lead he sought. He'd never seen this lead himself, but he knew others who had. He was growing impatient, a trait that wasn't like him at all. He'd never had so much difficulty finding what he sought, not since his relatively humble beginnings in a city on the other side of the planet.

What he sought would have been easily attainable if only other people's caution had been employed on earlier occasions. Since then, he'd become better informed about this lead and was glad that the position of responsibility had shifted. At least Jack Robinson wasn't in charge anymore – as far as Hanzo was concerned, that beast was barely a man, let alone a leader.

From the sand on which he stood, he saw something akin to a huge bird alight up ahead. But it looked bigger than any bird he'd ever seen. His heart began to race. He took out a phone.

'Hello, my lord. I think I've spotted the target, but I'd like to request backup. The subject is potentially dangerous.'

◆ ◆ ◆

In the partial darkness of the beach, Scott ordered a small hamburger with chips, a portion of nachos and a Coke from a nearby hotdog stand and chose to sit on the most open stretch of sand he could find that still retained a decent view of the ocean. As he tucked in, he stared out across the shimmering, moonlit water and considered his surroundings, knowing that they wouldn't always be around him. The palm trees blew in the breeze, the ocean lapped lightly at the shore and behind him there was only a busy road and white business blocks. He looked left and right. There was a lifeguard tower to the left; a party of boys playing volleyball on the right. Normality.

Then Scott turned back to the sea. His thoughts of Sophie resurfaced as he remembered the stars he'd shown her on his last attempt to win her back. The moon shone brilliantly, so low it almost sat on the horizon as if it were solid ground. With the street lights all around, the view was nowhere near the same quality as in Sophie's backyard, but he could still make out the Summer Triangle of Vega, Altair and Deneb from the constellations Lyra, Aquila and Cygnus respectively. He looked right and saw the yellowish glow of Saturn over the teapot-shaped pattern of Sagittarius. The smaller constellations that remained in between them were outshone by the street lighting.

After finishing his meal, he made a move to leave, but when he looked up, he noticed several dark figures slightly hunched over as if they were creeping towards him. He looked left and right and saw that a line of people covered virtually every exit. Then one nodded to another and they moved in swiftly.

Scott stood there not knowing what to do, and when he saw that they weren't stopping to register his alarm, his terror grew. One of them came too close, and he felt something sharp against his shoulder.

'Come!' the man said, in a brusque accent that wasn't American.

Scott looked about him, cornered.

'Come!' repeated the assailant. 'Right now!'

'Who are you?' Scott asked with an effort.

'I am Hanzo Takeshi.'

Scott's heart pumped madly. He would not go with them.

In a split second, he shot skywards and away.

❖ ❖ ❖

Some of the thugs raised their guns but Hanzo Takeshi stopped them, discipline restoring his calm. 'Target has escaped; surround their residence. We'll be there shortly.'

❖ ❖ ❖

'Scott what's happening?' Sophie asked nervously as she let him through her bedroom window.

He didn't answer immediately, slumping on her mattress and staring at the floor as if in denial.

'I was on the beach,' he said finally. 'Some people encircled me.'

'Who?' asked Sophie.

'I don't know,' he replied, 'but this one guy called himself Hanzo Takeshi.'

'He's come back,' she said, in a voice that didn't sound like her own.

'What?' Scott said suddenly.

Sophie didn't answer.

'Who's come back?' he demanded. 'If you know something about this then please, for all our sakes, tell me! Who's Hanzo Takeshi?'

Sophie stared at the ground. 'I can't,' she said.

Scott was bewildered. 'Sophie, if this is in any way related to what we've faced before, don't you want to benefit everyone by telling me what this is all about. If you do then maybe I can help?'

'It won't benefit anyone,' Sophie muttered pessimistically.

Scott almost lost it. 'And *why* not?'

Sophie hung her head. 'Because—' She broke off, afraid to say it.

He sighed. He didn't understand why it was so difficult.

'Sophie,' he said softly, 'whatever it is you're afraid to tell me, I'll be there to help you.'

Sophie sighed.

'Are the others here?' he asked, wondering whether they'd be overheard.

'They're all out,' she said. 'It's just me here. I needed some time to think.'

Scott didn't ask about the contents of those thoughts.

There was a very long pause as Sophie considered. She stared at the floor with more intensity than ever, then stood up as if in preparation.

'OK,' she muttered, 'on one condition.'

'Which is?' he asked.

'You can't tell this to another soul. I wasn't even supposed to know this myself.'

Scott braced himself, breathing hard. 'OK,' he said at last.

Scott was often poor at deciphering other people's emotions, but even he could see that she was struggling to muster her courage. She closed the curtains, locked her bedroom door, locked the window, locked everything that could be locked.

Sophie swallowed. 'Please don't be mad at me, Scott,' she said.

'Be mad at you?' He was incredulous – despite everything, all he felt was love and compassion.

'I know who's behind the attack at the school and the fair,' she said. 'I've known for a long time.'

Scott looked at her hard.

'There's a reason why I've been getting so much therapy over the years,' she said. 'Do you remember what I told you about Dennis Murphy?'

Scott remembered. He was the kid that Sophie had helped to expel from school for nearly beating Dave to death in the playground.

'My therapy was initially about certain development and school issues I was having,' she said, 'but it got extended, because of Dennis.'

'Was it the trauma of what he did?' Scott asked.

Sophie shook her head. 'I regret not stepping in to help him sooner,' she said, 'now that I know what he's become.'

Scott frowned.

'My mom's a social worker,' she said. 'I was in her office this one time during therapy. I went snooping and found a file with Dennis's name on it. When I opened it, everything changed. To this day I wish I'd never read it.'

'What did it say?' Scott asked.

'It said that during his time in the correctional facility he'd devised a plan that no one at the time took seriously. To form a humanitarian group.'

'A humanitarian group?' said Scott.

'Yes. But it was a lie. It became a criminal group, whose ultimate ambition was to rule the world. Dennis is the leader of that group. The media called it the CCC, or the Criminal Culture Club. The file detailed others that work for him. Hanzo Takeshi is an ex-Yakuza assassin.'

Scott was horrified.

'The CCC are involved in virtually every illegal activity you can think of around the world. They've become so powerful that the entire world now fears them. I see them constantly coming up in the news – that's how I know what they're capable of, but what no one knows is that I had a pivotal opportunity to stop this from happening and I didn't. That's what's made this so hard to deal with. I feel responsible.'

'How can you responsible?' said Scott. 'You were only five years old at the time.'

'I know,' said Sophie, 'but still...' She paused. 'They're here now. I've known all this time and now I've put you and your family at risk.'

'Why?' said Scott.

'That file I read was confidential,' said Sophie. 'My mom was furious with me and demanded I never speak of it to anyone except my therapist. If that information became public, Dennis would tighten his grip harder – he might even have destroyed the city just to make an example of everyone; he's that powerful. When my mom's not around, I really struggle to hide the truth from my friends. I'm one of the few people in the world who knows who he really is, because publicly everyone knows him by a different name – the Annihilator.'

Scott gaped. 'So what happens now? Could those thugs that surrounded me today be from the CCC?' he asked.

'Probably,' said Sophie. 'Now that they know who you are and what you've done to sabotage them, they'll try to come for you. For all I know, we're *all* in terrible danger.'

Scott was speechless. His thoughts raced.

Suddenly everything seemed louder. The wind blew at the window, the floor creaked and the door shuddered violently. Even the atmosphere didn't like the CCC being discussed aloud.

Scott heard what sounded like the opening of the door downstairs and footsteps slowly coming up the stairs. After a while he noticed their shadows underneath the gap appear; stop, and stay there.

'Mom?' Sophie called. 'Dad?'

There was no answer. Goosebumps rippled through Scott's body.

'Wayne, Dave, Samantha – anybody?' Sophie called.

Still no response.

Scott felt a sharp touch. He turned – and nearly

screamed! A Japanese man held a katana to his throat.

Her bedroom door burst open and presumably the same thugs that had attempted to close in on him earlier piled inside, encircling them and blocking off all manner of escape, guns raised!

'You will come with me, or I'll behead the both of you!' said Hanzo Takeshi.

CHAPTER 19
The CCC

Nigel and Hyliana were enjoying yet another arboreal view across the city. It was still a mess of junk and debris, but a least a few palm trees remained for them to live as close as possible to normality.

Hyliana was used to so much crap from either people's ignorance or malice, and ascending to heights like this was her idea of unwinding.

But this evening something was amiss. Hyliana noticed a large group of people heading down the street – at least twenty of them. She lifted her pair of binoculars, something she'd wanted after having seen Scott's telescope. A scope had been too expensive for her, so she sufficed with binoculars.

Hyliana focused and saw what looked like two people with bags over their heads in the midst of the group. She lowered the binoculars.

'I think something's wrong,' she said. 'We need to follow them. Now!'

'Follow who?' said Nigel – he hadn't noticed the crowd, his attention elsewhere.

'Down there,' she said.

Nigel looked, failing to share her concern.

'What about them?' he said.

She passed him the binoculars. He looked through

them at the crowd below.

'I still don't see the problem,' he said. It wasn't that he didn't care; his eye just wasn't in the right place.

'There's two people with bags on their heads,' said Hyliana. 'They might be hostages.'

Nigel suddenly understood. 'Shouldn't we call the police?' he asked.

'We don't have a phone,' said Hyliana. 'We don't want to lose them.'

'OK,' said Nigel. 'We'll go carefully; we don't know who they are.'

The duo crept behind them until they came to a huge ominous building in the centre of town. An office block, though it was perhaps not used that way anymore.

'Come on, Nigel,' she said. 'We need to go in.'

'Are you sure?' he asked. His attention was wavering. All his impulses begged him to retreat.

'Yes,' said Hyliana bluntly. 'Now come on. I'll look after you – as usual.'

Despite his tics, Nigel smiled at her. Despite everything that had ever happened to her, her iron will was a force to be reckoned with.

Little did they know this place's history.

They crept in behind the group, but it was a slow, tedious process for Nigel, and his fidgeting became increasingly worse as he followed them up the stairs. The group went into a room and locked the door.

'They've gone,' Nigel whispered. 'We can't see who's in there.'

'There must be a window on the other side,' said Hyliana. 'Go to the other side of the building – see if we can open a window and scale round till we see this room from the other side.'

'There might not be any footholds,' said Nigel.

He was right but Hyliana wasn't quitting.

'Let's just see if it's doable first,' she said. 'I have to know who's in there. Those people with the bags over their heads look like hostages to me, and I can't just sit here and do nothing.'

They followed a corridor. Although it wasn't too difficult to open a window, scaling the wall would be a challenge. There was a stone ledge only about two inches wide and it sloped diagonally, which would make it difficult to keep a firm grip.

'I think we can do this,' said Nigel, but Hyliana could tell he was still unsure. It was at least a hundred metres to the room in question.

'You're the most sure-footed person I know, brother,' she said. 'If anyone can do it, it's you – just try not to fidget.'

Nigel considered, but though she was sure his impulses were telling him to do different things, Hyliana's will prevailed again.

About four storeys below was a solid tarmac pavement. Nigel was used to rapid ascents up trees and cliffs, not slowly edging along the ledges of buildings, so despite his head for heights, even this was out of his comfort zone.

'Just move slowly,' said Hyliana. 'I'll keep watch.'

Hyliana had never seen her brother so focused, but even that was far from perfect. The adrenaline meant his fidgeting became fiercer and he wobbled, and however many times Hyliana told him to focus on the route ahead, he couldn't help but keep watches of his own.

'Stop,' said Hyliana suddenly.

Nigel was slow to react.

'Stop,' she repeated. 'I see someone.'

At the same window they were heading for, someone was also keeping watch, his head jutting out.

'Stay still,' she whispered.

She knew it was going to be a near impossible request to make of her brother, but at least he no longer tried to proceed.

Hyliana trained her binoculars and saw that the sentinel was dark skinned like she was, chubby faced, dark haired, perhaps also Brazilian. She began to wonder if she recognised the person, but she didn't dare ask Nigel to take a closer look, in case he did so incautiously. She couldn't quite see his face well enough. Little did she know how relevant this person was to her life history.

They kept as still as they possibly could, but Nigel rocking to and fro didn't help their concealment. He grunted a little too loudly.

'Shhh!' she whispered brusquely. 'He's right there.' She knew Nigel really was trying his best – that he couldn't help it.

The sentinel withdrew his head from the window and Hyliana took it as a cue to come closer, mindful of course that he might come back. They made it to the window and saw a big gang of people gathered round the two hostages – indeed that was exactly what they were. The bags over their heads weren't just a joke – this was a real-life emergency.

The sacks were removed and both reacted in horror when they saw the hostages' faces.

'Go back,' said Hyliana. 'We need to tell the others – fast!'

❖ ❖ ❖

Scott and Sophie knelt with their hands behind their heads in a surrendering position. They were surrounded by a large group of people – strong, loud, intimidating and lethal.

Scott looked up to see Hanzo standing guard over him, feeling his blade resting on his back. He saw another guy standing over Sophie; he was pressing a knife to her throat, grinning excessively.

His first thoughts were for her.

'Hey, leave her alone!'

He strained to get at him, but Hanzo stopped him.

The guy looked up in curiosity.

'Who's that you're playin' with, Hanzo?' he called in an Australian accent.

'He's my prisoner,' said Hanzo. Apart from a Japanese accent, his English was perfect, and his voice was quiet. He didn't need to shout; he imposed obedience only with that sword.

'Can I have him too?' pleaded the Australian greedily.

'No, Jack, you can't,' replied Hanzo softly.

He was impossible to intimidate; he was perfectly calm; he never panicked – he never raised his voice; he never ever lost control.

'I wan' him too!' Jack argued.

'You can't – he has to be unspoiled for the lord,' said Hanzo.

He said that with such calm.

'Aw, it's always for the almighty, eh!' scoffed Jack.

'You would be unwise to blaspheme him,' said

Hanzo. He was still calm, but there was a trace of sincerity in his voice.

Certain thugs gathered round to see them, pointing and jeering. It was as if they'd become some sort of tourist attraction, with them all gathering round and taking pictures.

Suddenly Scott was curious; Sophie had mentioned an Australian before.

'Are you Jack Robinson?' he asked the Australian.

He turned his stubbly, unkempt face sharply, eyeing him with disgust.

'O' course I am, you fucker; everyone knows who I am! If you've got nothing great to say about me, then you can shut yer fuckin' face!'

Even Scott picked up on his mannerisms: his constant sniggering, his unkemptness, his horrid teeth and immaturity.

'I can see why you dumped him,' said Scott.

Sophie managed to grin.

'What did you say?' Jack growled.

'Nothing!' said Scott, his terror returning.

Jack pressed the serrated blade of his knife to his throat, almost right next to his Adam's apple.

'You better watch it, Poindexter,' said Jack. 'If you make one more step outta line, I'll be knoyfing you right where I'm pointin', got it?'

'OK,' Scott muttered hastily in an attempt to massage his ego. 'You're the man. The man with the power.'

'Good,' Jack muttered. 'Now *you* just keep tellin' yerself that because ye know that I am.' He thought that was the end of it. 'And no funny business, alright?'

'Sure, Jack,' Scott chuckled nervously. 'Anyway, why don't you go and do something else now that you've seen me and this great exhibition?'

Jack thought for a moment. 'Yeah alright – Hanzo guard 'im, *I'll* deal with this one.'

He grabbed Sophie from the waist and hauled her to her feet. Sophie struggled, saying that had been a terrible mistake!

'Get off me!' Sophie screamed, 'Get off! Ahh, you're hurting me! Let me go! Leave me alone! Scott, HELP!'

Jack clamped his hand over her mouth and shoved her hard against the wall.

'*Now* for the fun part!' Jack grinned sadistically.

Some other thugs restrained her as Sophie struggled frantically. He ripped her T-shirt off and was seconds away from doing so with her underwear! This was very bad.

For a few seconds, Sophie broke free of his hand. 'SCOTT, DO SOMETHING!'

Scott took two seconds to make a decision.

He did a backwards head butt into Hanzo's crotch then quickly grabbed the sword and shoved him against the wall, his own blade sitting on his neck.

'RAPE HER AND HE DIES!' he shouted.

The CCC thugs stopped and turned. Scott was intent; he had no fear. Even Jack turned, but disconcertingly he looked more amused than alarmed.

'Ye really don't know what yer getting yerself into.' He grinned mockingly. 'Hanzo is one of our best assassins.'

'All the more reason to keep him alive. Now release her!' he shouted. 'DO IT NOW!'

Jack was undeterred. 'Ye do know that he's just faking it?'

'Faking it?' Scott was confused.

'Show 'im, Hanzo,' Jack muttered.

Suddenly Scott felt his arms twisted round behind his back, then Hanzo threw him over his shoulder and Scott hit his head hard on the ground. Hanzo picked up his sword and now it was back where it had been before.

'Scott!' Sophie shouted. She strained to get to him but the other thugs held her back.

'Ye really have balls, don't ye?' sneered Jack, leaning close to him, his eyes bloodshot.

'Fuck you, Jack!' Scott snarled and spat right in his face.

Jack was blinded for a moment, flecks of saliva dripping from his teeth. He punched Scott right in the face with a sharp knuckle-duster.

'Gavier!' he called raucously. 'Give this Scottie boy something to shut 'im up!'

A black, chubby man came forward and thrust something powdery towards his face – cocaine. He wanted him to sniff it. No chance! He headbutted the bag and the illegal white powder rained down on the floor like snow.

'I've had enough of this!' shouted Jack. 'I'll kill ye!'

'Leave him!'

A few figures had appeared at the door – two men and a girl. But one man in particular seemed to have an air of authority.

The ground trembled; his feet were clad in stout black boots; his trousers were navy, blending into a huge black jumper giving way to a thick determined face. His presence seemed to have an effect on all of these thugs; they bowed their heads as if they worshipped him – like he was a god!

Scott truly felt at his mercy now; as soon as he

gave the order, it would be all over. He didn't want to look up at him; he didn't want to give him the satisfaction of showing him he was afraid.

The Annihilator knelt down to his level, face to face with the one person who could stand in his way.

'So you're Scott Wallace, the one who seeks to defy me?' His voice was terrifyingly calm and sly. Unlike a lot of the others, his vocabulary was perfect, useful if he was to make it clear to him just how his life was going to end.

Scott didn't answer; he just stared into his hard, emotionless face.

'I've heard a lot about you, Scott. You're one difficult person to capture.'

Scott said nothing; he didn't even look up.

'You're not speaking?' he said. 'In that case, let me first introduce myself – I call myself the Annihilator, but you must address me as my lord. I'm the one who runs the so-called CCC. But we can come back to me later. These are my colleagues: Hanzo Takeshi, my best assassin – he was born in Tokyo, grandson of a sword maker and a revered member of the Yakuza.'

He gestured.

'This is Jack Robinson from Sydney – he runs the sexual business of the CCC, and he loves it too.'

He introduced a black-haired girl, with blood-red lips, dressed in a revealing black dress, with a black leather jacket over the top.

'This is Natasha Smith, also an ex-student of South Dade High, she works as his second in command. Sophie didn't get on too well with her either.'

'I was the prom queen until Sophie came along,' said Natasha. Her voice had a sly, cat-like quality, devoid of warmth and compassion.

'Tables are turning, aren't they, Sophie?' She cackled like a hyena.

The Annihilator moved on.

'Life of course would be unbearable without my friend Gavier Munoz from Brazil; he's an expert on drugs and pharmaceuticals. Any drugs or poisons you want, ask him. He used to come from Rio de Janeiro, doing business with the local drug gangs until he offered his allegiance to us.'

The Annihilator turned.

'And I almost left out my wonderful comrade Vladimir Pedrolvski. He's from Moscow; he's our war director who heads our European and Russian operations.

'But let's not forget our main African representative,' said the Annihilator. 'Meet Nganda, a veteran of the ethnic wars in the Congo. Wanted for genocide, after being ambushed, he lived in the bush for ten years fighting gorillas, lions and elephants just to maintain his strength. A powerful addition to our team.'

Nganda eyed Scott contemptuously. Scott was horrified; he didn't know what Rickey would do if he knew his worst enemy was here.

The Annihilator named more and more members of the CCC until he came to the one that surprised Scott the most.

'And finally we're down to our newest member: James Hockley!'

Scott recognised him at once; he was the terrible maths teacher at Sophie's high school!

'You surprised to see me?' he bellowed. He glowered down at Scott, his face contorted with rage.

'Do you seriously not know how much humiliation you caused me that day?' he demanded. 'I'm on the run from the law now, they want to bring me to account for what they called "gross misconduct". My conduct was perfectly natural! They wanted a hearing and a court case. I'd be jailed for who knows how long and I'd never get a teaching position again. If Jack and Natasha hadn't found me and offered me a position here, I'd have nowhere to stay.'

He then turned on Sophie. 'But *you*, the worst of them all! The insolent young lady that you are, that you will always be! You have no idea how badly I want to bust you up!'

He punched her in the nose so hard that it bled. Scott strained to get at him, but Hanzo barred his way.

Sophie's nose bled furiously, but there was nothing she could do about it – she could only look up angrily at her abuser. Jack would stop her if she tried to hurt him, and now Natasha had joined in guard duty.

There was silence. The Annihilator spoke again.

'We have a few issues to settle, don't we, Sophie?'

Sophie hesitated.

'What issues?' said Scott.

'Did she tell you that she had me expelled and sent to the Miami Correctional Facility?' said the Annihilator.

'Yes,' said Scott, 'because you and your friends nearly beat Dave Tate to death.'

'Correct,' said the Annihilator.

'But why?' said Scott. 'Why did you target him?'

'He was disrespecting me,' said the Annihilator. 'He insulted me. He said that "it was about time you were punished" – that was a clear reference to my dad's death not being punished and us being homeless. I couldn't take that and walk away. We took him down, and I don't regret it either. I wish I'd killed that boy for what he said to me.'

'Dave is very much alive,' said Scott. 'He's a much better person than you are.'

'Shut your fucking mouth!' snapped the Annihilator. 'Don't ever tell me that anyone is better than me. There's no one in history, recorded or otherwise, that's better than me. I have a destiny to fulfil. We came after you in the name of vengeance, Scott. *Why* you might ask – because you ruined everything for us. Let me start at the beginning: you foiled my invasion of Sophie's school. I was furious. We suspected that you would go to the fair, and we failed – again! But I didn't have to wait long for a new opportunity. We followed you to Merritt Island and Jack was all ready to commence the snatch, but that failed as well.'

Scott snorted. 'Why?'

'Jack was very irresponsible,' said the Annihilator. 'Some of the others told me they had a bonfire and some drinks, which drew the attention of the cops. So when they later primed themselves for the task at hand, the cops were already there looking for them. With the cops so close to the house, Jack had to abort, didn't you, Jack?'

Jack said nothing.

'I rather enjoyed hearing about your little fight,' the Annihilator continued, 'but you gave them the impression that they'd been spotted. If the plan failed and you'd called for backup, Jack's team would have been too small to deal with it. I couldn't send a bigger team – people would have asked too many questions and there would have been more cops than my followers could handle. At least that was my logic before Jack screwed it up.'

He chuckled.

'Then the hurricane came of course, as if nature herself obeys my wishes. I didn't seriously count on it to finish you off, though that would have been nice, but the aftermath of it did allow law-enforcement resources to be diverted elsewhere, and gave us a chance to regroup and rearm, so that the time would come when we could seize this city and you along with it. But with the eyes of the world on Miami now, you have to be careful what you do. I decided not to risk doing any more operations like we'd done before. We would bide our time, then take over when the media coverage had died down. This brings us to now. It was pure chance that Hanzo found you at the beach, and thanks to a little stealth and espionage on his behalf, I have the two of you right where I want you.'

Scott's understanding wasn't complete.

'Why did you invade the school?' he asked.

The Annihilator's reason wasn't complex yet very hard to understand.

'For business – you see, we were organising our homecoming to mark the fourteenth anniversary of the club. The girls there were supposed to be our entertainment; afterwards we would have put them into Jack and Natasha's brothel business,' he replied, smiling like a lunatic, 'They're relatively new to the business, you see. They knew the ins and outs of the place, and besides Jack desperately wanted his plaything back. But most importantly, it's because I'm a god, and I have to prove it by defeating all who may threaten me.'

'But why?' Scott demanded. 'Why are you doing this? Don't you care about all those you hurt?'

The Annihilator knelt down only inches from his face.

'Don't you tell me about getting hurt,' he hissed. 'Don't tell me that I can't have what I rightly deserve. Do you have any idea how hard life is when you're stuck in poverty, with no respect from anyone, not even the law, which you and all those other insects uphold? I deserve everything I get, and the law deserves everything we give them. I am a god. I always have been. I just had to have the courage to take action. To commune with all those in the world, millions of them, whom society suppresses without a scrap of compassion. From nothing I built my legions on the people of this world. I realised there are about six or seven billion people on this planet, all united by issues that you top one percent wouldn't understand the way we do: hunger, thirst, persecution, poverty—' he paused. 'Deprivation, deceit, destruction!'

He swivelled his gaze.

'That's a lot of weapons,' he said, 'and I'm the one who primed them. I saw the world as it really was, a graveyard for those too weak to make it. I decided there and then that I wouldn't let the system beat me. I realised that if you want to change things, you'd have to go to war, and for that, year after year, I built up the army you see behind me – and that's only a fraction of my forces scattered across the world. My vision may not have taken hold if it weren't for a very special ally that myself and my generals met shortly after forming our group. They gave us new technology, weapons and science, and all they wanted in return was something that

I believe is a big part of your life. Biodiversity itself!'

Scott gaped. '*Who* is this ally?' he asked in a combination of curiosity and exasperation.

'Wouldn't you like to know?' said the Annihilator mockingly. 'Even *we* don't know who they really are. But they gave us the chance we needed, ample evidence of my divine right to rule.'

'You're insane,' said Scott.

'Perhaps,' said the Annihilator, 'but I got the chance, didn't I? It's because of them that your wretched law enforcement and government fear us. They're afraid to lay a finger on us in case our ally gets involved. We may not have heard from them for some time, but I know they'll be back, and when they are, nothing will stand in our way.'

'What technology, what weapons, what science?' asked Scott, backtracking. 'What did they give you?'

'Jack, will you do the honours?' asked the Annihilator.

Jack grinned, then pressed a button on some kind of device, a green screen lighting up his face. Something came surging down the corridor outside. When someone opened the door, Scott was stupefied.

A cloud of birds flocked in. Scott only recognised three species: kingfisher-like grey kingbirds – the very first bird Scott had seen on day one in Miami; rufous-sided towhees with black heads and white and orange breasts, and scarlet northern cardinals. Each bore a tiny green light adjacent to their right cheeks, as though they were wearing some kind of headset.

'Stop,' said the Annihilator. 'Stay.'

They obeyed as if they were dogs, though some were still chirping away.

'Biotechnology,' said the Annihilator. 'These birds respond to our commands thanks to the device Jack has in his hand. If we want them to go somewhere, they go there; if we want them to attack then they attack. Though these ones aren't much use in that department – they tend to die quickly.'

Jack pointed the device at the wall and the birds flew in to strike it, each crashing and injuring themselves beyond recovery. The flutter of feathers stopped, and each bird lay dead or dying. Scott noticed one towhee twitching its leg feebly.

The Annihilator and most of the generals laughed, Jack the hardest of all, till he was on the floor.

'That's not funny,' cried Sophie. 'Why did you do that? Couldn't you have set them free?'

'We could have,' said the Annihilator, 'but we've already got those species in the bank. They're not much use, and we can get more any time we like. Besides it was rather hilarious.'

'What bank?' Scott asked.

'Our allies have insisted we store the DNA of each species we catch; we've already got enough for those ones. We don't need any more.'

'You're sick,' said Scott.

'Thank you,' said the Annihilator, as if it were a compliment. 'With this technology, these weapons, this science, we have everything we need.'

'Don't think it's going to last forever, *my lord*,' said Scott courageously. 'You were talking about vengeance earlier, well consider this: for all that you've done, all your victims will come after you for it, and I guarantee you, they won't stop until the Club is destroyed – and *you* with it.'

'We have so many enemies, Scott,' the Annihilator continued, 'but I expect that. Even if I'm gone, someone else will take over – and the Club will continue forever more.'

He waited a few seconds for a response. Scott suddenly thought of something else.

'Did you have anything to do with the death of Sara Mallory's parents?' Scott asked.

Sophie gaped.

The Annihilator scratched his head, as if trying to remember.

'Ah yes,' he said, 'Sara Mallory. I'd never met her, but I met her parents. You see, word was coming to me that my base was going to be raided. In fact, you could say I was tipped off.'

'By whom?' said Scott.

'You may have heard of him,' said the Annihilator. 'He used to be a cop and now he's a businessman, working with real estate, thanks to us.'

Sophie was horrified. 'Richard Kennedy?'

As if on cue, the man himself appeared. He looked almost exactly the same as when he'd visited Sophie's house – well dressed, in a black suit and tie, and black shoes. He smiled toothily at Sophie.

'Hello, Sophie; long time no see.' He sounded almost like a gloating child, with a bleating voice that reminded Scott of a sheep. 'I thought you'd have given up on that pathetic little nature reserve of yours by now. We just want to build a nice residence, and the lord Annihilator has paid me handsomely for the job.'

'But why?' said Sophie.

'Because it's going to be his house,' said Richard. 'Well, everyone's, including myself. When this city is taken properly, it will be the best fuck you I've ever given to society. It was a lucrative deal: we get to harvest the biodiversity for our gain and create a place of residence our lord has wanted to exact vengeance upon this society. There's nothing sweeter than to use money and power to get what you want, especially slap bang next to the people who purposefully reduced your opportunities. Now we get to do the same to them.'

'Who's they?' said Sophie.

'In my case,' said the Annihilator, 'it was the background I came from. Me and my family grew up in poverty, in an apartment frequented by junkies. Jobs were scarce, and they paid so poorly I could only assume it was done deliberately. My mother used to be a cleaner in a fast-food restaurant, but the pay was dreadful; seven dollars per hour I believe it was. My father was locked up for armed robbery, and when he got out, he was hoping to get a position as a barman at a casino. But one cop felt his sentence wasn't long enough and tried to create a situation in which he'd be recalled to prison. He was a racist, and I believe he targeted him because he was black. Police have persecuted us, stolen from us and ultimately limited our opportunities. When I was put into that correctional facility, I swore that me and my twin brother Lorenzo would turn the tables and control society the way it controlled us. It's taken many years, but now we do. This development that Richard has so kindly agreed to help me with is my monument – the ultimate symbol of our wealth, success and domination.'

'And for me,' said Richard, 'the pay was more than I ever dreamed – two billion dollars. Money like that is irresistible when the police have paid you poorly – not that much better than the lord's mother's cleaning job. I was initially tasked to spy on the CCC, but I became interested in our lord's business practices and the money he could offer. So I switched sides.'

'And Sara's parents?' said Sophie. 'What does this have to do with them?'

'They put together a team to take us down,' said Richard. 'I knew what they were planning, I knew their tactics and to safeguard my pay cheque and my lord's organisation, I let him know. The ambush was quick and successful.'

'I came out myself to personally finish them off,' said the Annihilator.

'By which point I knew they'd be onto me,' said Richard, 'so being my lord's business advisor became my full-time job and I've never looked back.'

Sophie was outraged. 'My dad trusted you,' she cried. 'First my nature reserve and now this.'

'It's business,' said Richard. 'Capitalism is how the world works, Sophie. Those with can do whatever they want to those without. That's what society taught us, and now it's a lesson we reciprocate.' He paused to let the reverberation of his words be felt.

Sophie was speechless.

'Anything else you want to know?' asked the Annihilator.

Neither Scott or Sophie gave him any response. Sophie's head was bent down. The Annihilator moved on.

'Fine then. Jack, take Sophie away from him. She's *yours* now!'

'That's what I loyk to hear. Come wi' me, sweetheart; yer mine now – no more Scottie to disrupt it.

We're gonna get on just fine you and me, *aren't* we?' He pinched her cheek and shook it, trying his hardest to tease her.

Sophie shook herself free.

'Get your fucking hands off me,' she snapped.

'Come on, sweetheart; yer coming with me,' sneered Jack. 'Guys, can you give me a hand 'ere?'

Sophie was dragged away out of sight. Jack laughed and swaggered after them, looking to enjoy his new prostitute.

'You better not hurt her,' Scott snarled. 'That is the number-one way to piss me off, my lord!'

The Annihilator chuckled. 'I have no control over what people own here, Scott – don't think there's anything you can do about it.'

'Let her go – please!'

The Annihilator paused as if contemplating his offer, then he grinned.

'No deal, Scott.'

'LET HER GO!'

'You know I can't do that, Scott; you're both accountable for your actions against me. Besides, Sophie will make an excellent source of entertainment for us all. I might just join in myself. I'll ask Jack about it later – once he's taken the first sample.'

Scott burst forward but was thrown aside and kicked in the head by a thickset boot. He curled into a ball, his hands clasped over his head. He felt so helpless; there was nothing he could do.

'Finally, Scott,' said the Annihilator, 'I have you where I want you. I've found you so difficult to track down. It's been an arduous journey, but now it's about to come to an end. So let's finish this business – once

and for all!'
　　He raised his gun to Scott's head.
　　Scott stared at the ground, closing his eyes as he waited for the inevitable end.
　　'Did you honestly think,' the Annihilator whispered, 'that an amateur such as yourself could defeat a god like me? Let me put you in hell where you belong!'

CHAPTER 20
The Rebellion

Bullets spattered everywhere. Scott looked up and saw that some of the thugs had been taken out. He couldn't see who had fired the shots.

The Annihilator was thunderous.

'Get outside and fight!' he shouted. 'Hanzo, Nganda, take them out!'

The Annihilator's most deadly warriors charged out of the room to engage the mysterious assailants.

Meanwhile, shots came from the window, felling more thugs. All the generals were able to flee, and Scott – and then Sophie – were suddenly without the supervision of any thugs. In seconds they were both freed.

'Take these.'

Scott stared.

'Nigel! Hyliana!'

'Thank us later,' said Hyliana abruptly. 'After they're defeated!'

Scott smiled; she made it sound like a foregone conclusion.

'Sara's leading a force to storm the building,' said Nigel, 'but Hyliana thought it would be best to help make that easier. The police were slow to respond.'

'Sara's here?' said Scott.

'Yes,' said Nigel, unaware of Scott's thoughts. 'We

need to do what we can until she gets here.'

❖ ❖ ❖

Sara's mission had never been clearer. Her time in Alabama had given her a sense of autonomy that she'd never had before, and as far she was concerned she had Scott to thank. Upon hearing the call that Scott and Sophie had been taken to a building she knew only too well, this mission had become personal. She had assembled an assault team of at least twenty people, mostly girls. Despite heavy fire and heavy losses, Sara was able to get inside. She wasn't the kind to take prisoners.

With her own AK47, she opened fire on every CCC thug that tried to stop her. Far from being emotionally collected and composed, Sara shed tears by the bucketload – not for the thugs she gunned down but the power she was taking back, the vengeance, the fact that the Annihilator would finally be at her mercy. But Sara's ultimate aim of the assault was even more radical than just killing the Annihilator.

Sara and her team were moving along the last corridor, engaging with yet more resistance. She was struggling with this one; some of her team were shot dead, and it only came to an end when Scott, Sophie, Nigel and Hyliana intervened to finish them off.

She stared at Scott, overjoyed to see him after so long.

'Are you guys, alright?' asked Sara.

'The generals have escaped,' said Nigel. 'Rickey and the others are engaging them.'

'We'll catch you up,' said Sara. 'I've got something important I need to do – now go.'

One of her followers tossed her something and Sara grinned – today she would obliterate this symbol that had haunted her thoughts for so long. She drenched the place in gasoline, then one flick of the lighter was all it took.

◆ ◆ ◆

Whilst most of the CCC were retreating, Hanzo and Nganda were standing firm.

On seeing them standing there, Rickey, Dave and Wayne concentrated their fire – then the impossible hit them.

Hanzo leaped in front of his comrades and with impossible speed and judgement started deflecting them. Bullets struck Hanzo's sword, the steel ringing with every impact, sparks flying, and soon all were deflected harmlessly to the ground like coins.

Hanzo then made a titanic jump towards them. Rickey rolled out of the way just in time.

Another CCC thug came to help by throwing a knife at him. It missed by half a centimetre. Scott ran to retrieve it just in time, before Hanzo stepped in front of him, sword raised. They fought.

He was very fast with his sword, faster than Scott could have imagined. He dodged slash after slash, trying to get around him for a stab at his hip. His weapon was considerably bigger than Scott's – this was hardly a fair fight.

In the end, Scott threw his knife at him, desperately trying to take him out. But it was hopeless – in a split second he raised the flat of his blade to intercept it, knocking it away.

Scott's eyes widened; he was weaponless. Frozen to the spot, he had no idea what to do! Then, in one gigantic leap, he kicked Hanzo, sending him flying onto the grass. Dave leaped in, driving his full body weight into Hanzo's prone form.

'Thanks for that,' gasped Scott.

'Don't mention it,' said Dave. 'I'm not alone either.'

Sophie and Scott's parents, Uncle Wilson, and a whole army of others Scott had never met before appeared – all armed to the teeth! A formidable force of manpower, guns, knives, slingshots, barbed baseball bats, steel rods, BB guns and mopeds – all were in their possession. So formidable that even Hanzo, fighting free of Dave, was forced to retreat. They were at full-scale war now, everyone fighting to defeat the enemy.

Alongside all his comrades Scott charged full tilt into the battle – shooting, knifing, punching and kicking foes as they came. From the corner of his eye, he saw Nigel abruptly drop from a tree, felling someone to the ground, then taking some others out with his slingshot. What he lacked in size, he made up for with uncanny skill.

◆ ◆ ◆

Jack Robinson was in the heat of the battle, knifing several people who tried to challenge him then tossing them aside. When one of his opponents was a girl, he grabbed her and shoved her against a wall. She struggled and screamed, and Sophie ran to intervene.

'That'll be the last person you violate tonight,' she shouted.

He threw the girl away, suddenly disinterested.

She ran away.

'I wouldn't be so sure.' Jack grinned, licking the blood from his blade.

'Come on then, Jack, finish your sick fantasy.' She squared herself. 'It's why you've gone to such trouble.'

Suddenly a dingo charged, barking and snapping as it ran. Sophie had no idea where it came from, but as it leaped, she sidestepped, striking out with her heel. It hit the dingo in the jaw. The animal yowled and staggered away, unable to fight any more.

Jack wasn't done yet – he pressed a button similar to what he'd used to control the birds and from across the battlefield, a saltwater crocodile stomped towards Sophie.

Sophie trembled.

It ran towards her and snapped at her heel. Sophie cartwheeled over it to land behind it, but the tail of the animal struck her on the leg and she stumbled. The crocodile twisted round and snapped again, and this time she fell over. It came on top of her, its jaws just millimetres from her head.

She swung her legs round then, pulling herself onto its back, and the crocodile spun frantically, trying to shake her off.

Jack saw an opportunity and flung his knife at her, but with all her strength she exposed its neck and Jack's knife found its mark in its throat. Sophie pressed down on the hilt harder until it went limp.

Jack looked stunned and suddenly fearful – without a shadow of a doubt, the tables had turned. In a mixture of fear and anger, he shot a punch at her face which missed; instead, she grabbed it and twisted his arm behind his back. Jack struggled, crying out in pain, and she shoved him away. Jack tried to run, his cowardice all too clear.

'Good riddance!' she muttered hotly.

❖ ❖ ❖

Then Olav arrived in style; this part of the street hadn't been completely drained of water since Patricia, so he was able to come by boat with yet another garrison of troops awaiting battle – a huge gang of big boys.

There were casualties on both sides. Some desperately tried to retrieve them and treat them as best they could. CCC thug and good guy alike lay sprawled on the street dead and dying. Samantha had been on it instantly, but the numbers in need of care were overwhelming, and she only had a handful of other helpers.

❖ ❖ ❖

The Annihilator himself had distanced himself from the battle, watching his own guys fall without a care.

'We can't hold 'em much longer, my lord!' protested a thug, 'There's too many of 'em!'

The Annihilator spat on him.

'What do you mean you can't hold them much longer? They're smaller in numbers than we are. Get in there!'

'I'm sorry, my lord,' shouted the thug. 'I'm gettin' out of 'ere!'

The thug ran off, but the Annihilator raised his gun and pulled the trigger. Then he took his leave.

❖ ❖ ❖

It looked as if victory was going to happen already. As the CCC thugs fled, some of Scott's side cheered uproariously, thinking the war was over. Was it? Nope. Hanzo Takeshi had appeared once again.

For everyone else, he looked like an easy target so they opened fire, but once again their bullets were deflected away, striking tough steel instead of soft flesh.

Olav opened fire then, but Hanzo deflected it. At the same time he was struck on the cheek by a stone – one of Nigel's.

Hanzo grimaced.

Some of Olav's group tried to get behind him.

'No, *don't!*' Olav shouted.

To his horror, Hanzo recovered swiftly. He grabbed one of them and drove his sword into his stomach. The three others were terrified. Hanzo moved swiftly towards them, slashing all three of them across the chest.

Olav fired again. More deflection. They were all terrified now. He'd killed four of his guys and now the rest of them were next!

Hanzo leaped, sword raised high above his head, and felled more youths that tried to attack. He slashed and slashed, until Olav motioned at everyone to retreat. He was just too powerful.

Olav fled, with Hanzo in swift pursuit.

◆ ◆ ◆

'MG CREW!' shouted Dave.

'TAKE IT OUT!' cried Scott.

There was an incredible burst of gunfire; the other

lads beside him were going down like flies.

'KEEP FIRING!' shouted Scott. 'OPEN FIRE!'

The intensity increased until the crew was down. It wasn't over yet, more shots were coming from the dark. Some of the guys charged with their mopeds; in horror, Scott watched them buckle and fall with bullets in them – one burst into flames!

This was a bad place to stay! They couldn't see where they were hiding. Scott gave a new order.

'FALL BACK. DRAW THEM INTO THE STREETS!'

'YOU HEARD HIM!' Sophie shouted, 'COME ON!'

They fled back into the more public area, firing back at the CCC thugs as they ran. Scott quickly snatched up a machine gun, keen to make use of it. But even as they ran, some were being picked off; Scott would often turn to see someone beside him falling down dead.

Scott was running so fast that he never saw the gap sandwiched between the kerb and the dumpster – he tripped!

The others were already a good five metres on, but when they heard his cry, they stopped short, horrified.

'Guys, *help*!' shouted Scott desperately.

'Give him covering fire!' Sophie shouted. 'Someone pull him out of there!'

Dave ran back and dived behind the dumpster, rapidly struggling to get him on his feet.

'Come on, Scott – we have to go!' he said pleadingly. 'Come on.'

He pushed the front of the dumpster wide enough to free him.

'This way!'

Dave was able to get him back with the group, but

whilst the others ran on, Scott remembered that there was still ammo in the machine gun.

'Scott, what are you doing?' shouted Dave.

Scott ran back the way and let it loose. As the CCC advanced out of the dark, they toppled and fell, but still they kept coming. Scott spent every last bullet before they were forced to run on.

'Police must be on their way,' said Scott. 'We need to diverge our forces and remove the blockade so they can advance.'

❖ ❖ ❖

Gavier Munoz led his two jaguars with the reverence of dogs. One yellow, one black. To Nigel and Hyliana it was a terrifying sight.

'Gavier!' Hyliana shouted over to the drug lord.

His jaguars tensed, loading their weight onto their hind legs.

The two stared across at one another.

'Who are you?' shouted Gavier. 'Why do you cling to his back like an infant?'

To his surprise, and to Nigel's as well, Hyliana slipped off his back and stood unaided.

'You're just an infant?' said Gavier.

'I was once,' she said. 'At that time your men killed my parents and left me for dead.'

'I don't remember,' said Gavier. 'Perhaps they didn't pay their debts. It's something we all do to people who don't pay their debts; it's nothing personal.'

'Well it was to me,' she said. 'Now come and fight me!'

Gavier laughed. 'You'll fight me? How do you plan on doing that?'

'My brother will help me,' she said.

'Your brother?' Gavier was mocking her. 'You don't look anything alike – how can he be your brother?'

'After what you did, his parents adopted me and made me one of their own. Perhaps we're not biological siblings, but in heart and spirit we are. Now come at me!'

'Very well,' said Gavier and gestured to the jaguars. 'Take her!'

The two jaguars charged, kicking up dust and dirt, snarling ferociously.

Nigel opened fire, but it failed to stop the cats. He whisked Hyliana onto his back and in a split second they jumped up a palm tree. The black one clawed at them, and Nigel had to work double time to stay ahead of them. The jaguars pursued them up the tree, and no matter how fast Nigel climbed, he couldn't stay more than a few millimetres ahead of them. He reached the top of the tree and leaped like a monkey onto the roof of a nearby house.

The jaguars joined them. He leaped to the next one, but it was too far for him to land on it completely. He caught the gutter with a shudder, nearly tearing it off, but recovered swiftly, swinging his body so his feet would catch the gutter. He pulled himself up, Hyliana clinging on for dear life.

The two jaguars split up, the yellow one chasing them from behind. Nigel was about to jump over to another house when he saw the black one already there. Nigel shuddered to a stop, almost falling off the roof. He looked behind to see the yellow one growling at them, then the black one leaped over to join them. Nigel and Hyliana were cornered. On either side, the roof sloped steeply to the bottom. Hyliana's faced intensified with terror.

'Brother!' she cried.

The yellow one leaped. Nigel looked round to see the black one doing the same thing. He and Hyliana rolled out of the way and they almost smashed into each other, denting the roof, but even their combined weight didn't make it collapse. Nigel slid on his bottom down the slope, but he could barely control his landing. His bottom strafed the gutter and he landed on his stomach, almost hurling Hyliana into the wall of another house.

Nigel was winded and bruised.

'Come on, brother,' said Hyliana frantically. 'We need to get moving – hurry!'

Nigel grimaced as he came to his feet, glancing down at his knees which were swelling to a dark shade of purple.

'Make for a tree,' said Hyliana. 'Come on – we can ditch them.'

Nigel was about to move but froze in the same instant. The yellow jaguar stood in front of them, snarling. Nigel ran the other way, but the black one was there waiting. They were in the middle of the street, far from any trees or houses to climb. They were trapped!

Nigel shot at the black one, but the bullets only bounced off its armour. It swung its paw, gashing Nigel in the belly. Nigel collapsed to his knees. Then the yellow one leaped and knocked Hyliana from his back, pouncing on her. Hyliana screamed and shot at it. The same outcome followed. The cat roared. She crawled over to her brother, grasping his knee.

Some more shots came their way, and the jaguars roared. Rickey was there and a large group of his fired more shots. A well-aimed bullet hit the yellow one in the paw. Crying out in pain, it fled. The black one, seeing the situation, followed.

'Are you guys OK?' asked Rickey.

'I think so,' said Nigel. 'Hyliana?'

'I'm alright.' She breathed heavily.

'You guys hang back and recover,' said Rickey. A few of his guys ushered them away.

◆ ◆ ◆

Nganda was relentless. Nearly two decades of military training and exile in the jungle came to a head. Police were already en route to the battle, but Nganda's red-beret force of guerrillas and animal army kept them at bay. From behind him, two rhinos, ten lions and a huge pack of hyenas and jackals charged into battle. Nganda himself rode an elephant. All of them were wearing armour, very light armour – so light it looked like Lycra but more transparent.

When police opened fire on these animals, many of them didn't crumple immediately, for the armour itself was not only light but bulletproof. The largest animals seemed almost impervious to their shots, and many vehicles and personnel were tossed and flipped into the air, with a number being crushed, gored and savaged.

Rickey was terrified of the task he'd volunteered for, but this was mitigated by the fact that he couldn't believe his worst enemy had returned. The monster that had stolen his childhood was here, and he led a ridiculous yet formidable army that had to be stopped.

He and some others opened fire on a group of hyenas, lions and jackals that went for them. The animals took about ten shots each before they went down.

Nganda rode high and mighty on top of his elephant. Some police were already there, opening fire as he charged straight into their ranks. The elephant's tusks had been customised with barbs which tossed some police sky-high and impaled others. Rickey couldn't watch him take any more lives.

'Nganda!' shouted Rickey.

He motioned at the others to cease fire for the moment.

Nganda strode forward, his elephant bellowing ominously as it reared on its hind legs and collapsed with a thud. This display went right through the others, but Rickey stood there unflinchingly.

'So it's you!' said Nganda. His voice had a heavy African accent and sounded almost as threatening as his elephant.

'Yes,' said Rickey, 'I'm here, and so are you.'

The battle raged in the background.

'You've grown,' said Nganda.

'No thanks to you,' said Rickey.

'Do you know how long I've waited for this moment?' said Nganda. 'I lost everything that day you ran away and told the UN where we were. I fled into the jungle. I left my men to die. I was wanted by every authority and never went anywhere near civilisation in case I was recognised. All I could do was scratch meaning out of every day by fighting the animals of the bush, just to prove that I was still strong.'

'*You* lost everything?' said Rickey thunderously. 'What about me? What about my brothers? Are they still alive?'

Nganda didn't answer.

'What about all those children you kidnapped from their houses and made to fight in an ethnic war? I've killed people because of you, Nganda; I see their faces every moment I'm awake and when I'm asleep. You tortured me; you used me for your sick entertainment. I'm glad I disobeyed you that day. It must have really hurt realising just how weak you really were.'

'I am a hero,' said Nganda. 'A hero of the Congo.'

'You're a coward,' said Rickey. He couldn't restrain the angry tears forming in his eyes. 'You think you're strong, but there's more than one way to be strong, and I'm stronger than you will ever be, because of friendship, because of love from my new family and all who've helped me along the way. I've got a life worth living because of it. That's something that you will never ever have! That's all I have to say to you!'

'Enough!' roared Nganda. The elephant bellowed again, raising its trunk. 'Today I crush you!'

The elephant charged. They opened fire, but it didn't do anything. They dodged, then Nganda came at them again, this time smashing into three of Rickey's group and sending them flying. Rickey attempted to shoot at Nganda himself, but the African warlord produced his minigun and let it blaze.

Rickey quickly took evasive action, ducking behind houses. The rate of fire was so intense the stonework splintered like wood, providing no protection.

Rickey returned fire again, and Nganda gasped in

pain, clutching his arm. Rickey had hit him in the bicep, thick and muscled from years of conditioning. Nganda cursed, pulled the trigger on the minigun and, when no more ammo came out, charged at Rickey in a tantrum.

The elephant bulldozed through houses as it chased him, and Rickey wheeled round, avoiding a swing of its head. He kept running, avoiding the attention of some lions before Nganda headed him off from the front.

Rickey was hurled into the air, flying across the tarmac. To the left of him, there was a body, and from its belt hung a knife. Rickey scrabbled for it.

The elephant bore its head down to stab him with its tusks. Rickey grabbed them but was in no way strong enough to keep them back. Then a stray shot hit the elephant, causing it to double back.

It was enough: Rickey jabbed the beast in the face and it staggered backwards. It took another swing, and he felt the wind of it as it missed him. Then he took a daring slash at its leg, and to his astonishment the armour on it tore. Nganda was thrown off and his elephant cantered away.

Rickey closed in on him, stopping suddenly upon seeing Nganda rising to his feet. Rickey was suddenly seized with terror, realising there was no way he was a physical match for the man who had ruined his life. Rickey fired some shots, but despite the short range, he somehow managed to miss, and then Nganda hurled himself at him, pinning him to the ground. Rickey felt a machete blade at his throat.

'All those years ago,' said Nganda, 'you were mine, and I did whatever I wanted with you. Fate has us tied together – how else can you explain the coincidence of meeting you here? The one I never thought I would see again.'

'I'd rather you killed me than used me again,' said Rickey.

'That can be arranged,' said Nganda.

'But I've lived life to the full every day since I left the Congo,' said Rickey, 'thanks to my friends. You'll never have friends like mine. I own my past, and I don't care whether you take responsibility for your choices.'

Nganda gritted his teeth, then more shots came their way. Nganda averted his gaze. Rickey spat at him and resisted fiercely. Nganda pinned him down again, but seconds later Olav appeared and opened fire. Nganda returned fire with his pistols, but Olav hit him in the chest and he staggered away. He motioned at some hyenas and jackals to take them, but Olav felled them in the nick of time.

'Are you OK?' asked Olav.

'Yes,' said Rickey. 'Where's Nganda?'

'He got away.'

Rickey tried to run after him.

'Leave him,' said Olav. 'He's not worth it.'

Rickey gritted his teeth.

'Help me take down his blockade so the police can get in,' said Olav.

Rickey hesitated.

'Come on – it'll prove his team aren't as strong as he thinks,' said Olav.

❖ ❖ ❖

Scott edged over to Sophie.

'Sophie, cover me. I'm going after the big boss!'

'He'll kill you!' Sophie protested.
'I have to try – this war ends if he's gone!'
'But you'll die!'
'Sophie, I have to; I've got no choice! This is only happening because of him!'
Sophie stared at him, wild with fear.
'Don't worry, Sophie; you'll see me again. I'll come back for you!'
She nodded hesitantly.
Scott hugged her before he reluctantly let her go. Then he hitched into the air and sped after the Annihilator!

◆ ◆ ◆

The Annihilator was having a fierce argument with another one of his attendants.
'That Scotch boy has wiped us all out, man!' he protested. 'We gotta give up while we still can and run away! He's just unstoppable, my lord!'
The Annihilator stared at him despicably.
'Unstoppable? We outnumber him a hundred to one, or we used to until you wasted our forces!'
'We must run away, my lord! It's our only hope!' insisted the attendant.
The Annihilator made up his mind.
'Yes, it is,' said the Annihilator. 'But there's no hope for *you!*'
He drew his pistol and shot him in the head. The attendant fell. The Annihilator didn't care.
'Soon,' he muttered. 'Soon Miami and eventually the world will be under my control!'

◆ ◆ ◆

Scott ran after him, but more thugs poured in, blocking the way.

'Scott!'

Sara charged into the battle, felling opponent after opponent. They stood back to back, hacking away at them. The Annihilator himself, hearing her battle cries, stepped towards them.

An animal instinct pricked Sara's attention.

'Is that him?' she cried.

'Listen, Sara, be careful.' But he couldn't stop her. Sara's face ignited and she sprang towards him.

Though her antics took him by surprise, the Annihilator quickly relaxed.

'You must be Sara,' said the Annihilator. 'Ready to join your mom and dad?'

'I'm going to make you pay!' screamed Sara.

'Before that happens,' he said, grinning, 'would like me to tell you why they had to go?'

'Don't you dare,' said Sara, but at the same time she wanted to know.

'If I'd let them live, our organisation would have ended,' he said. 'They're the cops, the worst people on Earth alongside soldiers and politicians. I'm sorry if you feel bad, but that's business. Our wills collided and I came out on top – it was just natural selection at work.'

Sara squared herself.

'That's it!' she cried.

She leaped in with a jumping kick, but the Annihilator merely stepped to one side. Sara threw a barrage of punches, yet he barely seemed to feel them.

'You amuse me, Sara,' he said slyly.

Sara gritted her teeth and threw her strongest punch. The Annihilator grabbed her fist and twisted her wrist almost to breaking point.

'But I think now I'll make you join them!'

He grabbed her by the throat and lifted her off the ground.

'No!' Scott cried, charging in to rescue her.

The Annihilator thrust a knife into Sara's chest. She made an ominous gasp, her shocked eyes wide open. Then the Annihilator threw her to the ground, leaving the knife embedded.

◆ ◆ ◆

'You!' Scott cried. He flew in at the Annihilator, but Hanzo quickly blocked his path and he backed off.

'I'm leaving now,' said the Annihilator. 'Save her if you can, but if you want me, you'll have to leave her.'

Scott gritted his teeth in anger. He was right. He was getting away, quite calmly, but he couldn't leave Sara; he had to save her. Saving her came before capturing him.

'Sara!' he cried.

'Scott,' she croaked wearily.

'Hold still; I'm right here. You're going to be OK. Just stay with me.'

'It's over for me, Scott,' she said.

'No it isn't,' he said. 'I saved your life before; I can do it again.'

She was losing blood fast. The battle raged behind him.

'Not this time,' she said.

Scott stared at her.

'Don't say that!' he said. 'Samantha!'

He stared frantically around for anyone who could help.

'Scott, don't worry about me.'

'Wha—?'

'My time has come,' she said.

'What are you talking about?' he cried.

'Part of me has wanted this for a long time.'

'Why?'

'Ever since my parents died, I've often dreamed about being able to pass on with dignity. I'll get to be with them again. But I'm grateful for so much now. First there was Sophie. Then you.'

'Sara, I...'

'I want to thank you for giving me another chance at life. To at least let me know what it was like to feel loved again.'

Scott felt her hand clasp his.

'Thank you.'

'Sara, I...'

'Thank you.'

It was fainter this time.

She wouldn't let him say it. He felt her grip relax, and her head fell to one side, her eyes transfixed in a stare.

'Sara?'

He shook her shoulder.

'Come on – help's on the way. Sara?'

She didn't respond.

'Sara?'

He tried to resuscitate her. He kept at it for what

felt like an eternity – until he ran out of breath. But Sara didn't move. He realised then, so bitterly, that there was nothing more he could do.

He closed her eyes and cried, rocking her back and forth like a baby. He'd failed her; he'd saved her life before only for her to lose it now. Worst of all, he hadn't had a chance to tell her the truth. That he did like her. At least as a friend, someone vulnerable to watch out for. Someone whose life he could have made better.

He turned in the direction the Annihilator had gone. He ground his teeth hard and ran!

◆ ◆ ◆

Hanzo Takeshi and his employer walked together as if they were best friends. There was an almost leisurely pace to their walk, as if they were walking towards a sunny horizon, where a bright future lay decked out before them. One in which they would be in charge, using force and terror to have the world exactly as they wanted it. The Annihilator had almost completed what he'd started: his dream of global supremacy. Authority figures from police to politicians would one day bow down to him, now that they saw that their beacon of hope was crushed.

'DENNIS!'

The Annihilator spun round, affronted at the use of his real name. A brave figure stood before them.

Hanzo's stance was primed for action.

'Will you excuse us, Hanzo?' said the Annihilator.

'Are you sure, my lord?' said Hanzo calmly, yet with an atom of concern.

'I am a god, Hanzo,' said the Annihilator. 'I must

prove it by defeating him alone.'

Hanzo bowed, glancing at Scott one last time before walking away.

◆ ◆ ◆

'Don't think you can just walk away,' said Scott. 'Not after that; not after all this. The cops are on their way.'

'Then let them come,' said the Annihilator. 'We'll spill their blood before the night is out. When I'm victorious, I will simply get more of my troops scattered across the globe into Miami; with my overwhelming numbers, our careers will continue – minus the irritating interlopers like you! When all is calm I will take everything that this world owes me. *Everything*!'

'You're insane,' said Scott.

'Perhaps we all are. Even you.'

'What do you mean?'

'How is it that a mere boy like yourself with no formal training save some karate and fencing has the courage to face me? To risk literally everything – his friends, his family and the world ahead of him? Is there something you're trying to prove?'

Scott flinched. The Annihilator saw it and laughed.

'I know what it is,' he said. 'It's Sophie, isn't it? You want to defeat me to prove to her that you're worthy. You love her, even though she's way outside of your league, even though she would much rather have a handsome, blonde jock instead of you. Even though you're too inferior to even stand next to her as an equal, you want to do this. Why else would you risk so much?'

Scott locked gazes with him. He would tell his

worst enemy something he had never told anyone.

'I don't fear death, my lord,' he said levelly. 'Since the day I took my landlord to court and moved to Aberdeen, I've been looking forward to fighting to the death for a cause I know to be worthwhile. I've grown strong and bitter in those years. I've had multiple disasters – socially and academically – but when such impossibility is against you, you wonder what the point of carrying on with life is.'

The Annihilator flinched.

'But if I must die tonight, know that I've never been stronger. For all I know, Sophie may never love me; for all I know I'll never be good enough for her. Perhaps there's no hope at all. But there's even less hope for you – and your ambitions. Because such impossibility is against you and it always will be!'

The Annihilator chuckled. 'Bravo,' he said mockingly. 'Just what I wanted to hear.'

'I will stop you!' Scott exclaimed. 'If I must, I'll give my life to do so!'

The Annihilator paused, then a grin spread across his broad face as if in slow motion.

'Very well.'

Without warning, he fired a shot at him. Scott took to the air.

'What's the matter?' taunted the Annihilator. 'Afraid to face me on the *ground*?'

He fired more shots and this time Scott was really kept busy dodging them. Many flew wide of the mark and soon Scott's turn to taunt had come.

The Annihilator's anger skyrocketed – no longer was he a calm divine presence.

Scott blew on the Aquilacry and the Annihilator

grimaced before spinning round for another attack. His bullet found its mark in the right wing of the micro-flyer.

Scott hit the ground hard. He hadn't fallen far enough to break any bones, but the impact was overwhelming. He was gasping for breath, the fight momentarily knocked out of him. The Annihilator ripped the micro-flyer from his back.

Scott stared.

'I think this belongs to me,' said the Annihilator. 'I don't know why this came to you and not me.' He cast it aside. 'But let's finish this the old-fashioned way!' He threw his pistol away and clenched his fists, taking a distance of about ten paces. Scott only just had time to get to his feet before he charged.

Despite his bulk, the Annihilator moved with extraordinary speed and knocked Scott to the ground. Then Scott felt his strong hand pick him up by the throat. Desperate to be free, Scott lashed out with his fist. It missed. The Annihilator's jeer returned.

Scott had come close to death so many times. But perhaps today might be the day he'd go.

As the oxygen drained from him, visions of all that could be enveloped him.

Sophie was wailing for him. The pain of losing someone she'd bonded so well with was tearing her apart. He saw the two of them walking hand in hand along the beach into the sunset. New images of travel and marriage morphed and vanished. Whatever he was to her, he had someone in his life that was worth living for. He had a promising social outlook for the first time in his life.

He thought of all the love interests he'd once had.

He thought about how he'd lost miserably every time, how they'd laughed him off, how their suitors had turned up on cue to take them away. The Annihilator would take her away, and he, Jack and God knows how many others would exploit her for their sick amusement.

A powerful, otherworldly voice inside his head yelled: DON'T GIVE UP!

Scott felt adrenaline flow through him. With his newfound strength, he grabbed the Annihilator by the face and clenched his fist over his nose and mouth with great force. The Annihilator gave a muffled cry and, in doing so, released him. Scott fell to the ground, but he quickly came back at him and delivered a savage punch to the neck, making the Annihilator fall back.

The Annihilator picked up a large rock. Thinking rapidly, Scott tore a stick off a sturdy low-lying palm and whacked him over the head with it.

He recovered swiftly and threw the rock at Scott; it flew over his head and hit a lamp post, splitting in two. Then Scott was barraged by punches. His nose was bleeding hard, and his head was reeling. The Annihilator clamped down on him one last time, and this time he had no intention of taking his time.

With a heave, Scott grasped some rock fragments and slammed them both into the Annihilator's head. He crumpled to the ground with a thud.

Scott contemplated what had just happened. They'd just taken on the CCC, and he'd just taken down their leader – a worldwide criminal organisation had now been defeated. Scott felt like a hero, like he'd made everyone safe. He'd never felt so proud of himself.

'Scott?'

He turned.

Sophie appeared in the distance, beaming her smile across what had been only moments ago a battlefield. He couldn't believe it; he felt even more proud. Here she was still alive.

'You did it!' she called, full of relief. 'We won! It's over!'

Scott grinned, the euphoria taking him by storm.

They ran towards each other, spreading their arms out for an embrace.

Blindly Scott ran on, smiling, calling out reassurances, his arms open.

Then he saw Sophie's smile fade.

'Scott – LOOK OUT!'

It happened too fast. Scott turned to see the Annihilator rising groggily to his feet. He'd taken up his pistol and weakly fired a single shot.

Scott felt a sudden searing pain in his right leg, tearing the flesh from his calf bone.

He collapsed to the ground, clutching his wounded leg and crying out in agony.

'Scott!'

Mr Hockley stepped in.

'I've been waiting a long time for this!' he said eagerly. 'Now we're even!'

Sophie was horrified. 'NO!'

She took aim and fired; Mr Hockley crumpled and lay still. Then she turned to the Annihilator and pulled the trigger – but it was empty! Sophie roared and tried to grapple with him, but the Annihilator grabbed her by the throat and threw her into a wall.

Then he loaded his pistol with a fresh magazine and walked unhurriedly over to Scott's sprawling body, aiming the gun at his head with an unmerciful satisfaction.

'You're stubborn, I'll give you that! But congratulations, you finally outmatched yourself, Scott – your school would have been proud. All that you did today shows how far you've come in your life, Scott; you clearly know more than I think you do, and for a moment there I thought you had me. I think I've seriously underestimated your power – you're clearly more than just a typical fifteen-year-old. But it's OK, you tried your hardest – isn't that what counts?'

Scott looked past his standing legs.

'But too bad it wasn't enough. Because at the end of the day, Scott, everyone bows down to me. Oh and about Sophie, let's just say you're right – *you have no hope* – but don't worry, Jack will take good care of her! How about I spare you the pain of living a life unloved? She's out of your league after all.'

Scott shed angry tears as he stared into that hollow black hole – then he closed his eyes.

All of a sudden, he heard a smack. He opened his eyes and checked himself. Then he saw the Annihilator lying unconscious on the ground, having been clobbered with a brick.

Sophie had saved him once again, hadn't she?

Scott looked at his wound; his leg was still bleeding. He began to convulse. He felt so weak, he could barely lift his head.

'Scott, are you alright?' she asked, desperately trying to keep him awake.

'I don't think so,' he replied stiffly. 'He shot me in the leg.'

'Don't worry, we'll get help – we'll get you to the

hospital! You're going to be OK!'

Scott gave a worrying convulsion as if about to vomit. Sophie's strength lapsed.

'Please stay with me,' she pleaded desperately, her eyes filling with tears.

It was the most sorrowful sound Scott had ever heard in his life and he knew it would be the last he ever heard.

◆ ◆ ◆

Sirens wailed in the distant twilight, screaming towards the aftermath, police and ambulances all ready to help out. The Annihilator was roused by his generals and, with Hanzo and Nganda covering him, beat a hasty retreat into the shadows.

◆ ◆ ◆

'Please, Scott!' she begged. 'Don't go. I need you here – you're going to be fine, right?'

Scott stared into her grief-contorted face with great sympathy, but he gave her no promises.

An ambulance pulled up beside them; paramedics leaped out at the double and precariously lifted him onto a stretcher, carrying him limply into the ambulance.

'Are you his girlfriend or something?' asked a paramedic.

Sophie hesitated.

'Do you want to come onboard and keep him company?'

'Thank you,' she sniffed.

An oxygen mask was secured over Scott's mouth and another paramedic was crouching next to him, keeping an eye on his heartbeat, with Sophie beside him. Scott was scared as well as upset. He heard the sounds of arrests being made from outside, the banging on the police cars, and grew restless with fear.

'It's alright, Scott,' Sophie repeated. 'I'm here.'

Scott tried to lose himself in her caressing strokes, but he had to be careful not to let them lull him to sleep. He might not wake up again, and it'd be like a kind of euthanasia caused by her.

The road was bumpy all the way, the sirens were ringing in his ears and his vision was blurring, the life support machine beeping all the time.

After what felt like forever, they arrived at the hospital. On his stretcher, Scott was pushed through the double doors of the A&E department and blinded by the lighting. In his dying state, he was disorientated and confused, and wondered why he wasn't being taken straight into an operating theatre. From the shouting and arguing he could hear behind him, there appeared to be some sort of delay going on – all the operating theatres were somehow all full. The paramedic was close to breaking point, stress and frustration consuming his voice.

'I'll deal with this,' he snapped. 'Could you look after him until I get things straight?'

'How are you doing?' asked Sophie.

'I don't know,' said Scott dreamily. 'I feel like I'm leaving.'

'Don't do this, Scott – *please*!'

'I just want you to know that – if I don't make it – over the past several weeks you've been the best friend anyone could have asked for.' He sighed. 'It seems so soon; there was so much I wanted to do in life, and because of you I – I had something to live for. So many people love me – I didn't realise that until now. I know I'll be missed.'

'I know *I* will miss you,' said Sophie inaudibly.

'I'm sorry,' said Scott. 'I wish I'd acted earlier.'

'It's not your fault,' she whispered. 'It's mine.'

Sophie wiped her tears. 'Tell me, Scott, are you mad at me for keeping this from you?'

Scott stared at her, but stars were forming in his vision.

'Of course not,' he replied.

Sophie had another spasm of grief, then something else happened. She clutched her chest in agony.

'Oh please, Sophie, not *you* as well. If you go down then I will too.'

Sophie visibly tried to recover her strength, but it was fading fast. Now it seemed that their roles had been reversed – Scott needed to reassure her.

'You've got to be strong, Sophie, but I know you can do it. You're braver than me in many respects – you can deal with things in life that I'd struggle with.'

Scott tried to smile reassuringly, but it clearly wasn't working.

'They're coming back,' said Sophie.

The paramedic had returned looking very much relieved.

'OK, young lady, I'll have to ask you to scoot now,' he said.

'You have to let me go if I'm to stand any chance of being saved, Sophie,' said Scott softly.

Sophie hesitated, then she bent down and placed a

kiss on his forehead, slowly loosening her hand – then he was carted away down the corridor towards the operating theatre.

Scott raised his head and stared helplessly at the disappearing figure at the end of the corridor as she sank to her knees and sobbed, as if she'd never before experienced a feeling of loss like this.

Scott was taken into the operating theatre and lifted onto a board. A nurse came to check his blood pressure; she looked grim.

Hoarsely Scott said to her: 'If I don't survive, then could you tell her that I—?'

'That blonde girl outside?' she queried.

Scott nodded weakly.

'I will. Now we're just about to give you the anaesthetic. You've done very well, Scott – keep it up. You want to see her again, don't you?'

'Yeah,' he replied. And it immediately gave him new strength. The thought of seeing Sophie again sounded so wonderful – yet unlikely.

The mask came down over his face.

'There we go, Scott – just lie back and relax,' said the nurse. 'We'll take care of things now. It will all be over soon.'

His mind became heavy, and he could feel himself lapsing into unconsciousness.

'Go to sleep now,' said the nurse softly. 'Sleep.'

Scott had no strength left in him, and without knowing he did so, he passed out.

CHAPTER 21

A Miraculous Turn

Sophie's grief was incapacitating. She'd never cried like this before, not to the point where her body hurt and she felt sick to her stomach. Her face was bright red, tears streaming from her eyes. She curled herself into a ball, rocking to and fro. Her heart ached and eventually she lost the strength to remain conscious.

If this was a dream, Sophie was desperate to wake from it, but when she woke up again, her grief didn't dissipate.

Even if Scott was gone, Sophie was far from lonely – she had plenty of friends, and her kind nature encouraged them.

She stared at the stars twinkling outside, Cassiopeia shining light years away, and her grief swelled again. That's what Sophie would miss if Scott died – sharing lovely natural spectacles like those starry nights they'd spent together. Whatever was beautiful out there, Scott wasn't going to be with her to enjoy it.

She heard the sound of someone coming down the desolate corridor; she turned and saw a nurse walking towards her. It was 4.30 a.m., nearly sunrise.

'Sophie Patterson?' said the nurse.

'Yes?'

'I've got a note saying that you've got to go to the

Fisher Hilltop.'

Sophie frowned.

'But why?' she asked.

'You'll find out soon enough.'

Sophie left the hospital and went to the Fisher Hilltop. It was a quiet night, though Sophie felt weird going there on her own; her grief had temporarily gone, replaced by an increasing curiosity. It was safe to wander at night now that the CCC no longer stalked the streets, all thanks to everyone involved.

The Fisher Hilltop wasn't much more than a small green hill – there was nothing too special about it except its exceptional views over the Atlantic. Today the Atlantic was in an unusual state of calm, rare in any ocean.

Curiously Sophie waited, wondering what was about to happen next.

The sun was beginning to rise; red and pink light lubricated the sky. In the twilight, Sophie could make out a figure standing at the hill's edge. Then the sun began to rise from the horizon, a huge golden ball of fire, illuminating the morning sky.

The figure walked towards her, silhouetted against the rising sun, and only then did Sophie see who it was. She could hardly believe her eyes. The sun shone on his hair, turning it as gold as hers, and every part of him seemed to glow like the sun.

It was like coming back from the dead. The brightness Scott radiated was like that of an angel – a golden angel. He was very close to Sophie now, close enough to be examined thoroughly. Sophie shook her head.

'No,' she muttered. 'No, Scott, you can't be real – you died.'

'Sophie, it's me,' said Scott softly, though his voice had a ghostly lilting tone.

Her eyes filled with tears. 'No, it's not. I'd like to think you're real but you're not! You're just an apparition!'

'Sophie,' Scott repeated, 'I'm right here with you – that's what's making me feel so alive.'

Scott looked at her chest where her heart would be, as if he sensed its aching sadness; its frantic beating.

'Let me fix that for you.'

He slowly reached out and rested his hand over it, and as he did, its beat began to slow.

'You're... you're warm,' she said.

'Yes. If I was a ghost, I'd be cold and my hand would go straight through you.'

'Scott?'

Happiness and relief flooded through her, and to deliver the final blow to the pain and the heartbreak, he gave her the biggest hug he could give.

'I was so worried about you,' she said. 'I thought you were—'

'I thought I was too,' said Scott. 'I admit I did look rather like a ghost there.'

'How did you know I'd come up here?'

'Well, after my operation I woke up without any problems. I was told that I could walk normally again but that for the next few weeks I should take it easy. But I arranged this surprise – I told the nurse to tell you to come up here, and now look at us, back together again as always!'

Scott spread his wings then and his face lit up, as if he'd just had a great idea. 'Sophie Patterson, here's a question for you.'

'And what's that?'

'How about a flight?' he asked, spreading his arms as if he wanted a hug.

Sophie stared, but she took the offer without hesitation, trembling with excitement as he strapped the belt around her waist.

'Ready?' he said.

Sophie nodded, and with that he shot vertically upwards into the awakening sky.

'Is this too scary for you?' Scott shouted above the deafening rush of air. 'Do you want to go faster?'

'Faster!' Sophie shouted.

'Faster? Alright, down we go!'

Sophie screamed with exhilaration as they plummeted downwards like a peregrine falcon. Then Scott spun sideways like a swift, somersaulting backwards and forwards in a dizzying pattern.

'Scott!' Sophie shouted, 'we're heading for the sea!'

'Ha ha – that's the fun part!'

The glistening sea loomed; they were so close to it that they could have dived into its blue depths.

'Scott, pull up!' Sophie shouted.

They were just about to hit the water when he rapidly swerved upwards; now they were gliding across the sunlit water, the gentle waves of the Atlantic lapping below.

'Do you want to touch the water?' he shouted.

'Yes!'

Scott steadily descended towards the sea, and Sophie reached out, skimming her hand across the water, white sparks of foam erupting as her hand sliced its way along. Sophie had transformed during this flight – one moment it had been the worst day of her life and now she was hooting at the top of her lungs, not in grief but in sheer joy.

◆ ◆ ◆

Scott pulled up, and together they soared over the city, weaving in and around huge business blocks. The wind rushed past them, cooling their orangey faces, Scott's wings glimmering in the dawn sky.

Glancing down at Sophie, he saw that due to the richness of the light that her face was a colourful blend of reds, oranges, yellows and pinks. The sun seemed to convey spectacularly that Sophie was beaming out her happiness to the world!

People in the streets shouted and pointed as they soared across the city, crowds gathered, people took pictures, policemen looked on in total awe, and traffic stopped completely, determined to watch this spectacle of spectacles.

Scott saw Dave, Rickey, Wayne and the others running towards the scene and yelling in triumph: 'Yes – he did it!'

'Everyone!' said Dave. 'I know that guy – he's Scott Wallace. He can fly like a bird, he can take on the most formidable opponents, he's exceptionally brave, he's one of our best friends and – above all – the Annihilator has been defeated because of *him*!'

'Three cheers for Scott!' shouted Rickey.

Scott and Sophie descended onto the street.

'Rickey!' exclaimed Scott, giving him a hug.

'I thought you were dead,' said Rickey, grinning.

'I thought so too,' he replied, 'but I woke up in the end, back in this life where I belong.'

'How's Sophie?' he asked.
He glanced at Sophie, who was talking animatedly to Samantha.
'She's fine; she was very upset earlier but look at her now.'
'You're quite a stubborn survivor, you know that? You took a bullet in the leg and you're still OK.'
Scott chuckled. 'I didn't think I had it in me. If a battle can't stop us then nothing can stand in our way – not as long as we've got each other.'
'Now that's what I'm talking about,' said Rickey, giving him a fist bump.
Police sirens sounded and several of them surrounded Scott and his friends, guns raised.
'Hands behind your head!' they shouted.
Everyone reacted with shock and confusion.
'Get down on the ground!' they shouted.
Nobody resisted, not even Scott. He felt the tight grip of handcuffs.
'You're all under arrest for arson, murder and the disturbance of public order!'

CHAPTER 22
In Custody

Scott couldn't believe this was happening. They'd saved the day, each other and countless others. The CCC had been defeated, their headquarters burned down, and whilst the Annihilator and his generals had got away, everyone had applauded them – all except law and order, the one body that should have achieved all this and didn't, perhaps out of scorn and disbelief that amateurs had achieved what they couldn't. Many had argued that what Scott and his friends had achieved today was a long overdue service to the city. But whatever the opinion of the masses, it was the opinion of the law that mattered at the end of the day.

Scott and his friends were taken to the cells. Whilst the others had to share, Scott had one to himself, not that it was much of a blessing. He would have rather been in with Sophie at least.

He lay hunched into a ball on a blue mattress, with no duvet cover, more aggrieved and terrified than he'd ever been. He'd just fought the CCC, many had died including Sara, but many more had probably been saved, people whose names he would probably never know. They may have had no idea this was happening, but he'd saved hundreds, thousands, millions, perhaps billions.

He'd nearly died himself; he'd given Sophie a ride that should have cleared the cobwebs from his soul and it had, until this happened.

A hatch opened with a harsh clang and a tray of food was pushed hastily through.

'Come back!' cried Scott. 'Do you know what's happening?'

The guard that had delivered the food stopped short. 'How the hell should I know?' he snorted. He stank of cynicism and indifference. 'I don't know what they're talking about in there.' He narrowed his eyes. 'But I did hear them say that you kids are going to go away for a long time.'

'How long?' asked Scott.

'I've dealt with thugs like you for twenty years. I know guys who've been given five hundred years for less than what you all did last night.'

'Five hundred years!' Scott could barely grasp how people could be given sentences that long. He'd have to live his entire life and die at least five times over for that to pass.

'You ain't going home ever,' said the guard coldly. 'You have plans – travel, people, marriage, retirement? Forget all about them. My guess is you'll go to a high security prison. The cells there are full of the most violent, despicable people you can imagine. You'll be there for life I imagine, but I bet you won't survive a day. There's plenty of CCC in there that will rip you to pieces.'

Scott was horrified. He burst into uncontrollable sobbing.

'There's no point doing that,' said the guard callously. He chuckled. 'You haven't been here twenty-four hours and you're already making yourself look like a three-course meal.' He gestured to Scott's food. 'Eat yours while it's still hot.'

He slammed the hatch down and walked away.

Laden with grief, Scott did as he suggested, even though he was too sick to stomach it. He had his steak, his cheese, his salad but the tomatoes looked disgusting. He left them alone. He drank his water, a small cup that didn't quench his thirst. He went over to the sink to fill the cup again, but when he tried to drink the water, it tasted warm, almost dirty.

He couldn't drink any more, even though he was still thirsty.

He heard a bang on the door.

'You have visitors,' said the guard.

Scott jumped up, wondering who it could be. He hoped it was his lawyer; surely he would get him out of this madness.

The heavy door opened and Sean and Mary Wallace stood there, both red in the face with grief.

'Scott!' His mother threw a hug around him and his father joined in. 'How are you?'

A redundant question.

'Terrible.' He grew agitated. 'Do you know what's happening? Where's my lawyer?'

'We've met him,' said Mary. 'He's coming to see you tomorrow.'

'Tomorrow?' To Scott that felt like an eternity away.

'Yes,' she said, 'but at least he's coming, and we'll be here for you. We have to because you're a minor – it's your legal right.'

'Have you heard about the others?' Scott asked.

'Sophie's fine,' said Sean. 'In fact all your friends have got lawyers fighting their cases.'

'Are we going to be alright?' asked Scott. 'Am *I* going to be alright?'

'It's too early to say for certain,' said Sean, 'but from what we gathered they feel that while your case is very strong, it's still going to be an immense challenge. But they've assured me they're going to fight your charges as hard as they possibly can. They say that tomorrow you'll be transferred to a correctional facility till your trial, but your lawyer will discuss the circumstances with you further.'

'Do you think everything will be OK?' asked Scott. His angst had made him ask this question repeatedly.

'I hope so,' said Mary.

The guard came back.

'You have to leave now,' he said.

'Why?' said Mary crossly.

'Your time is up,' he said.

'According to *who*?'

He didn't answer the question. 'Time's up.'

Mary was furious. Sean had to restrain himself.

'We'll be back,' said Mary.

'You're not staying here?' asked Scott.

'We can't stay in the station overnight,' she said. 'There's nowhere to sleep. There's a hotel nearby – we're staying there.'

'So I'm spending the night here?' said Scott. He was genuinely frightened of the idea of being left alone in this cell.

'We'll be back first thing tomorrow,' said Mary. 'Just go to sleep; things will be sorted I promise.'

Scott's tears welled up again. 'OK,' he sniffed.

'You have to leave,' the guard reminded them.

'Yeah, yeah,' said Sean dismissively, giving him a venomous stare.

'It'll be OK, Scott,' said Mary as they were escorted back along the corridor. 'It'll be OK.'

Scott fell apart. He desperately wanted his parents to be in the room with him. He wanted Sophie, Rickey, Dave, anyone. He didn't want to be alone. The Annihilator should have been in this cell, being treated like this; all Scott had tried to do was stop him and this was his reward. Perhaps the Annihilator had been right about law and order – its persecution, its corruptness, its hubris. If this was how they treated him, for saving lives from thugs, for doing their job for them…

Scott jolted himself out of it in an instant. What was he thinking? He'd never thought of the law that way. He knew it as a body that anybody could go to for help, protection – almost anything you wanted. He'd known as much back home. He wondered how much of the Annihilator's words had influenced him. How was it that this evil crime lord had swayed Scott's view on all that he believed was right in this world?

Yet Scott found himself agreeing with at least some aspects of what he'd said: that the world was a graveyard for those too weak or unlucky to make it. Did the world deserve to be razed to the ground to reverse that pattern? No. Whatever logic he could see from it, Scott could never accept that that should be the way.

Scott's mind turned to darkness, and through an automated switch so did his cell. He was in for a *long, long* night!

CHAPTER 23
On Remand

His parents came to see him first thing in the morning, but their visit was short-lived. Scott was handcuffed and bundled onto the black prison bus that would take him to the Miami Correctional Facility, the same correctional facility that the Annihilator himself had once been admitted. Scott was surprised to discover that the others were coming aboard too, and he was even more stunned to see Sophie, Samantha and Hyliana. He'd tried calling out to Sophie but was silenced by last night's guard.

They were driven for miles into some wide grassy countryside – in fact along the same road that Scott and Sophie had walked along so many weeks before, as they'd bonded through birding. It seemed like an eternity ago now, a different era, from a life that was no longer his own. He was sitting next to a complete stranger, whilst the others were otherwise seated next to one another. He tried to catch Sophie's eye. She'd turned to look behind her once and managed to give him a faint smile, but otherwise she'd been facing the front, unable to easily look at him.

When they came through the wired gates of the facility, Scott felt as though he would never leave this place alive. They were bundled in single file through the gates, and as soon as they entered, guards screamed in their faces; dogs barked and snapped, straining on their leashes; men in gun towers scrutinised the line below. Everyone was visibly scared, with only Dave putting on a brave face.

They were made to put on orange jumpsuits and given a stern briefing by the warden, advising all of them without sympathy that their lives were virtually over.

Then they were taken to their cells. Scott was put on his own. He'd only been here a few hours and already it was horrendous. If this was what the rest of his life was going to be like, his will to live would evaporate.

His cell door opened and a man dressed in a suit and tie introduced himself.

'John Stanley,' he said. 'I'm your lawyer. Your parents were advised that I was your best hope.'

'Are my parents coming too?' Scott asked.

'They should be,' said John, 'but I don't know when they'll be allowed.'

Scott sighed. 'What can you do for me? I'm facing life in this horrible place,' he said gloomily.

'My colleagues and I believe you have an excellent case to appeal,' said John. He took a seat on Scott's bed, a metal tray attached to the brick wall.

'Appeal it in what way?' Scott asked.

'We could easily look at getting your sentence reduced,' said John, 'but I have another idea – it's radical but it could work.'

'I'm listening.'

'The CCC are a controversial group. There have been a number of societal complaints about governments, including our own, not doing enough to tackle them. I have some friends in high places that may be interested to hear your case.'

'Who?'

'The CIA for one, but I can't release the details for you. However, if we get them involved, if we play our cards right, we could do even better than reducing your sentence. We could make sure there was no sentence, immunity if you like.'

'Immunity?' Scott found the whole concept difficult to believe.

'Yes,' said John, 'but I have to contact them first, and they might make me wait.'

'For how long?' Scott asked.

'Days, weeks, months, years at most.'

'Years?' Scott could barely imagine being here for a day.

'It's our best chance,' he said.

'What about the others?' said Scott. 'My friends? Sophie?'

'I can't help them, Scott,' he said, 'but we might have a chance for you.'

Scott felt torn, but if there was any chance for him, he had to take it. He couldn't stand the thought of being here for the rest of his life. He thought of what it would be like to be free, out enjoying his life, completing school, going to college, living life as he wanted to. But he also thought of how lonely it would be without Sophie, and also the friends that he'd made here. Yet it was the only chance he had.

'Then I'll take it,' said Scott. 'Whatever you have to do.'

John made a move to leave; he was just about out the door when Scott called his name.

The lawyer paused.

'What will happen to me in the meantime?'

John sighed. 'You'll have to stay here,' he said. 'I can't do anything more for now.'

Scott collapsed and curled up on his bed, drowning in grief and uncertainty.

◆ ◆ ◆

John Stanley was a very professional, experienced lawyer. He'd argued and won many cases, even to the point of exonerating people from the worst charges imaginable. He did so expertly, skilfully and impartially. But in this one he was struggling to stay impartial. Even *he* hadn't been successful in adequately compensating victims of the CCC and was convinced there was some corruption afield. The state consistently refused to give details, to the point where citizens well and truly despised the legal system, almost as much as the Annihilator did.

He'd had no choice but to exercise a degree of corruption of his own, not exactly illegal but so controversial it had to be conducted clandestinely. He'd tried his best to reassure Scott that he would obtain this incredible outcome, but in his heart he wasn't so sure. If the state had its way again, as it did with any case relating to the CCC, then Scott Wallace really would be condemned for life. But hearing news of Scott's feats *and* the fact that they'd been publicly applauded gave him a fierce spark of hope that perhaps this trend could be ended.

Even his frequent consultations with the CIA hadn't influenced the course of trials the way he'd wanted. But today he had an idea so audacious it might just work. It would all depend on whether his favourite CIA official Quantay Jackson would take his call. He was often busy with other assignments, sometimes for years, and even if he did, would he take it in time to spare Scott Wallace a life behind bars?

A few hours later, someone knocked on the door of his office.

'Come in.'

He was relieved to see Quantay Jackson standing there, wearing a brown leather jacket and brown trousers, like rough beaver skin. His thick face was broad and stubbly; despite shaving frequently, his grey stubble hairs were still showing.

'You wished to see me?' said Quantay.

'Yes,' said John. 'Have a seat.'

The CIA agent pulled out a big heavy chair and sat there, curiously studying the lawyer.

'We have another CCC case,' said John.

'Another one?' said Quantay. 'Aren't you fed up with the same outcome over and over again?'

'I called you here because I honestly believe this one could have a different outcome.'

'I'm curious to hear what this incredible idea of yours is.'

'I read some classified files on the CCC and—'

Quantay interrupted him. 'What were you doing reading classified files?' he demanded.

'I'm a lawyer,' said John. 'I'm not prone to spreading news like wildfire. But I did want to discuss one aspect of it with you, if I may?'

Quantay frowned. 'Well you're down the rabbit hole now,' he replied. 'What is it you'd like to discuss?'

'As you know, the Annihilator is a threat to world as well as national security.'

'Of course,' said Quantay. 'He's got millions of followers from around the world, all ready to fight for him in a heartbeat.'

'Not to mention his biotech,' said John. 'Some of my clients have described the most outrageous stories of his use of animals, each fitted with some sort of green chip that works akin to mind control. Plus the use of body armour lighter and stronger than anything we have in our nation's arsenal. I've wondered for years how they could obtain such technology, until I came across what I assume to be a code name – Enemy A.'

'Enemy A,' said Quantay. 'You *have* been busy.'

'My question to you is who is Enemy A? The file doesn't say.'

'That's because no one knows,' said Quantay, 'but whoever they are, some sort of exchange between them has been witnessed, the nature of which we can only guess. All we know is that because of them, the CCC has grown tenfold, yet we're terrified to do anything about them *because* of Enemy A.'

'Why is that?' said John.

'From CCC members that have been interrogated on the subject, the pattern we've ascertained is that they've never heard from them since their last exchange,' said Quantay. 'They haven't been seen again. If Enemy A are indeed allies with the CCC as many of us think and they turn out to be more dangerous, then the results for our nation – and the world for that matter – could be catastrophic.'

'I thought exactly the same,' said John, 'so here is my proposal. If Enemy A returned and were willing to communicate with us—'

'That's a big if,' said Quantay.

'Indeed it is,' said John, 'but you've heard about what Scott Wallace did? How he used that flying machine of his to despatch the CCC. He nearly got the Annihilator once and for all. He defeated them three times, he's brave and ferocious, and I think it would be wise to recruit him in case Enemy A returned. If they were to engage with him instead of us then perhaps there's a chance, albeit a slim one, that we could be spared another world war. I call the idea Operation Cetus.'

Quantay chuckled. 'How exactly are you going to convince others that this is a good idea?'

'There's only *one* other I think we need to convince,' said John. 'The President himself.'

Quantay found that hilarious. 'Are you honestly suggesting that the President would authorise such a plan, this Operation Cetus? Especially one that involves overruling every other authority there is?'

'If he has any care for world security, I think he will.'

Quantay sighed. 'I've seen you exonerate people for the worst of charges,' he said, 'but do you think you're going too far in this case?'

'Perhaps,' said John, 'but as a public servant with a duty to know the law, work with it as well as criticise it, I have to do what I can for my clients. When it comes to the CCC, I get the sense that there's no consistency, other than to let people down, in ways that I feel wouldn't be the case if it were anyone else. I must work within my brief of course – it's been my job for twenty years – but as a critic I feel I must highlight the flaws in our reasoning and adopt new ways to deal with circumstances as they unfold.'

'With all due respect, John,' said Quantay, 'hasn't our legal system always sought to improve wherever it can? Is that not the essence of our democratic society?'

'It is,' said John, 'and in many other areas, I feel that we respond as well as we can. But with the CCC, I feel that's not the case.'

Quantay didn't voice it, but John was sure even he agreed on that point.

'Put it to the President,' said John. 'Get back to me as soon as you can. Operation Cetus may be our best hope.'

❖ ❖ ❖

Scott had been having a dreadful time. He'd been here for three days, usually in his cell, but when he had to be out of it, he was dining with the others. He'd seen his parents only once. The rest of the time he was made to do assault courses and run round a racetrack, forced on by the screeching staff. He couldn't stand them. He couldn't stand the way they screeched commands like drill sergeants or the way they got right in his face and screamed in his ear. This was a hellhole, a thousand times worse than his school.

Almost everyone except his friends was a bully, fights broke out virtually every hour and takedown teams equipped with armour, truncheons and shields would storm in to break them up.

Just today one person had snapped and stabbed another with a smuggled blade. The perpetrator nearly broke into a stabbing rampage and when a takedown team was summoned, he resisted violently and died a few hours later from the injurious blows of their truncheons. Scott was afraid of being stabbed, bludgeoned or shot, but at least it would be a ticket out of here.

In fact no one was having a better time of it than he was. Sophie and Samantha had already experienced sexual harassment by some of the other boys. This ranged from catcalling to physical assault. More serious things would have happened had it not been for their resistance and the prompt intervention of the guards.

Rickey had been shadowed by a group of black men wanting him to join their gang, but suspecting their motives he'd refused, only to be harassed about it again and again.

Olav stayed in his cell most of the time. Out of everyone he was the quietest and most timid, which led him to be taunted by the other inmates. He'd had his few belongings stolen from him and otherwise had no peace of mind.

Nigel had had his head shoved into a toilet and flushed by a group of inmates, whilst at the same time Hyliana had been ripped from his back and tossed around, and when Dave and Wayne got involved, the inmates led them on a chase around the facility.

The guards didn't do anything other than look on and laugh, especially when Dave's asthma got the better of him. Hyliana had struggled frantically but all her shouts to be put down were laughed at. She'd managed to sink her teeth into her captor's hand, but he still hadn't released her.

This went on for about three hours, until Wayne was eventually able to ambush the person carrying her and knock him to the ground. Nigel and Hyliana were from then on guarded by the two of them at all times.

Scott didn't think anybody could take another day here.

'Scott Wallace!' said a guard. 'Your lawyer's here to see you.'

Scott stood up to accompany John back to his cell, his friends looking on with hope.

'I've spoken with the CIA,' said John. 'There's good news.'

'OK,' said Scott.

'The good news is that your case was passed on to the President himself.'

'The President – in the White House?' Scott was astonished.

'Yes,' said John. 'He's one of the highest authorities in our country and he's agreed to my plan that would exonerate you of all charges.'

Scott felt as though a concrete block had been lifted from his shoulders. The relief was so overwhelming it hurt.

'In fact, given the situation with the CCC,' said John, 'he's actually desperate for you to accept his offer.'

'What about my friends?' said Scott.

'He didn't mention them,' said John.

'Why not? They helped me all this way. I can't abandon them here.'

'The President insists you take the offer as it is; he says it's vital for world security.'

Scott cleared his throat. 'Well then, if that's the case, he'll agree to whatever I wish.'

John stared. 'Scott, I know your loyalties are strong, but if this deal isn't agreed by all the parties concerned then there's not much else I can do for you.

Do you really want to stay here, await trial, then eventually move to an adult prison where you'll eat garbage and piss in a basin for the rest of your life?'

'If I went and my friends didn't, I would have trouble living with myself. The guilt would stay with me for life, and it wouldn't be a life worth living, especially without Sophie.'

John sighed. 'I know you love her,' he said.

Scott suddenly felt self-conscious. 'Please don't tell her that,' he said. 'I haven't told her myself yet.'

'OK,' said John. He scratched his chin, letting the awkwardness settle down. 'But just think about this. If you were to stay here, if things deteriorated between you, who's to say that she would necessarily stay with you? The nature of this place means that you'd see her every day. If she chose someone else, you'd have to endure that day in and day out. You'd never get away from it. Not until you were old enough to be transferred, by which stage you'd have thrown away your chance at freedom. Is that really a risk you want to take?'

Scott thought about how she'd got together with Wayne, the pool party they'd had and the noises he'd heard in the apartment. It made his heart sink.

'If you speak to the President again, put that condition to him,' said Scott.

'That's if I get to speak to him again; he's very busy, you know.'

'But do it if you can,' said Scott.

John sighed. 'OK.'

He stood up and left the room. Scott wondered what he'd just done; he'd been wanting to leave all this time and now he was effectively choosing to stay. But the reason was simple: he simply couldn't walk out of here and leave Sophie and her friends to rot, not after everything they'd done for him. They were the people – besides his parents – that meant the most to him in the entire world, that oasis of sociality that he'd always dreamed of and, better still, had come true.

Scott would face a new day here. But he would hold his head high knowing that in spite of the overwhelming injustice he felt in his heart, for the first time ever in his life, that with his heroism, his morality, his honour, his love and society on his side, he had a power to rival the system itself.

CHAPTER 24
Renegotiations

Scott sat with his friends in the cafeteria tucking into yet another meal of chlorinated chicken, rice and salad. It pleased him that they were a large enough group to take up entire tables to themselves, meaning they didn't have to sit next to volatile strangers. What was more, he was discussing the ramifications of his deal and didn't want to be overheard.

'You decided to do *what*?' said Sophie incredulously.

'I could have taken the deal as it was,' said Scott, 'but it would have involved leaving you all here and I knew I couldn't do that.'

'That's noble,' said Dave, giving Scott such a heavy pat on the shoulder that he winced.

'If he agrees,' Scott continued, 'we could all be out. The only trouble is I don't know when – it could be years. But he said the President himself was desperate for me to accept it, and that offers us our best chance.'

'You're brave,' said Wayne. 'Most other people would have taken it and gone.'

'Well I believe that Scott has worked on our behalf,' said Olav.

'Agreed,' said the others in unison.

Some inmates looked in their direction – it was

the ones who'd kidnapped Hyliana yesterday. Dave's middle finger shot up to ward them off. If Dave was going to slip back into his old ways, this was the best place to do it. In a place like this, so finely tuned to torture you, he didn't care if he started a fight as long as those punks backed down.

'Scott Wallace!' A guard approached them. 'Your lawyer's here.'

He looked at his friends.

'I hope he has some good news for me,' Scott said.

'He wants all of you to come,' said the guard.

The others began to murmur excitedly.

'Us?' said Dave.

'Yes,' said the guard. 'Now move!'

He and his friends followed the guard, but rather than going to Scott's cell, they were instead led into what looked like a conference room, with a projector screen at the head of a large table. John was there already, consulting his notes.

'Leave us,' he said to the guard.

The guard didn't say a word and closed the door, though Scott could see that he hadn't actually gone but was just standing discretely outside the door.

John looked at them all, studying their expectant faces and hoping in his heart that he wouldn't disappoint them.

'There's someone very important that wishes to speak to you all,' said John. He took a remote control and pressed a button, bringing the screen to life.

'Mr Vice President,' said John, 'meet Scott Wallace and his friends.'

Everyone gaped.

'I'm afraid the President himself couldn't be here

with you today,' said the Vice President. 'He's been called away on urgent business, but I will relay the news of this meeting to him later. I'm pleased to tell you that he has agreed to Scott's deal, and he's convinced the law enforcement involved to clear you of all charges.'

There was an uproarious cheer, and hugs and handshakes all around.

'There is, however, one thing that the judge wanted,' said the Vice President. Everyone fell silent. 'He still wants you all to come to court for a formal trial.'

That really wiped the smile off everyone's faces.

'How come?' said Dave. 'You just said we were free to go.'

'They won't do anything more to you,' said the Vice President. 'They merely want an official word about your case and to provide some closure to the public. I suggest you accept the deal.'

'It's more than fair,' said John. 'I know it's not ideal and you all wanted out today, but it will please both parties.'

Scott considered. 'If we go, will I get my microflyer back?' he asked.

'Yes,' said the Vice President.

'Can I request one more thing?'

The Vice President frowned, then leaned forward on his chair, eyes narrowed. The others, including John, stared at him incredulously.

'Shut this place down!'

The Vice President gaped. 'They're never going to agree to that.'

The others ground their teeth.

'Scott, what are you doing?' said Dave, his cool edge now lost.

'This was where the Annihilator came in his former years, yes?' said Scott.

'That's correct,' said the Vice President.

'Did it not occur to you that maybe the treatment he had in this place is the reason he's public enemy number one today?'

'I'm sure that's probable,' said the Vice President.

'Scott, don't do this,' said John. 'Please. I beg you. Don't complicate this further – think of your friends.'

Scott looked round the table at the confused, shocked faces of his friends. Seeing Sophie's hurt most of all.

'Think of *their* families; think about *yours* too,' said John.

Scott reconsidered. 'OK,' said Scott, 'but let me just say…'

The others shook their heads; Sophie cupped her face in her hands.

'These places destroy people psychologically,' said Scott. 'This place could produce another Annihilator, and I feel like this is no place for people to get better. Think about that, for the future at least.'

The Vice President nodded.

'But I accept the deal,' said Scott. 'I'll say nothing more.'

Everyone breathed a sigh of relief. They should have been happy, and they were, though Scott knew he'd tainted their joy. The others departed, not looking at him, but Sophie pulled him aside.

'What were you thinking?' she demanded. 'Did you not think this deal was good enough? We're getting off literally scot-free!'

'It was just a stupid thought is all,' said Scott.

'Don't you understand that you could have risked everything back there?'

'I know,' said Scott. 'I was just angry and it was... déjà vu.'

Sophie frowned. 'What do you mean?'

'This place is worse than school, and if school can be brutal enough to change people then this place—' He stopped short.

'That's not up to you,' she said. 'You can't play god with these things. They're not our issue.'

'But they are,' said Scott. 'The Annihilator exists because of this place.'

'Are you blaming me?' she said angrily.

'Absolutely not,' said Scott. 'I would never blame you for anything. You did the right thing; he had to be stopped. It's just...' He faltered. 'You were very young,' he said. 'No one could have predicted what happened. You're being far too hard on yourself.'

'It's the one time I didn't do enough,' she said. 'How am I supposed to do anything other than be hard on myself?'

'There was nothing you could have done. I told you: you did the right thing. If he'd stayed at school, justice wouldn't have been delivered. His victim would have been let down, he may have done something similar again and who's to stay he'd have even listened to your attempts to help. If I've learned anything about people I've met before, it's that not everyone *wants* to be good. I found that concept so hard to accept, but sadly it's true. If people don't want to be good, if people don't want to live the right way, then no amount of compassion can make them.'

Sophie sighed. 'We're out at least anyway,' she said. 'I'm tired. I just need some time alone.'

'Can we talk about this?'

'We already have!' Sophie snapped. 'Please. Let's just leave it!'

'OK,' said Scott.

He felt so stupid. He began to wonder if he'd blown it with her, and the worry stuck to him like Velcro as he lay in bed that night. He was told there was nothing to worry about, but even if everything went well, he knew that once on the outside, he and everyone he knew would be hunted forever. The Annihilator was a god. And like other gods, he wouldn't tolerate blasphemers.

CHAPTER 25
The Trial

Everyone who meant anything to Scott and his friends were assembled in that courtroom. The 'defendants' themselves all sat together in the dock guarded by five policemen. The agitation in the atmosphere was overwhelming; the judge knew that everyone in the public gallery was *not* on his side.

'We are gathered here,' he began, 'not for a trial by jury, but merely to offer the words of the law on the proceedings that have taken place. First of all, I want to emphasise as agreed by the President of the United States of America that you are cleared of all charges, the deal of which takes immediate effect. But I have some things to say to you on the subject.

'This is most likely the first case in the world that has offered complete immunity to charges as serious as these, but the circumstances surrounding this case are extraordinary indeed. We wouldn't normally congratulate individuals this way and the ramifications of this decision are yet to be seen, and I'm not completely happy with it. But the President has gone a step further and wishes you to be properly rewarded for your efforts. As such we have decided to reward you, Scott Wallace, two hundred million dollars!'

Scott gaped.

A cheque was handed to him by one of the policemen. Scott took it with both hands, spreading it with his fingers as if it were a lottery ticket – well, it was really.

'What you do with this money is up to you,' said the judge, 'but use it wisely.'

Scott continued to stare at the cheque, his mind struggling to encompass all the possibilities this could grant him.

Once he was of legal age, he would leave the hellhole that was his home and his school. He could travel anywhere, at any time, disappear for as long as he wished. No one would ever have to see him again, no one would harass him – not his bullies, not his teachers, not the dope-smoking lodger, nor the love interests that had laughed in his face. He wouldn't have to deal with anyone who failed miserably to return his affections. He would have no need for anyone ever again!

Something made Scott stop there. The others were happy for him, despite all that had happened. But as Scott returned their gaze, he felt a prickling sense of conflict, of obligation, of devotion. They were his friends, all eight of them, and without them, nothing about his stay in Miami would have changed anything about his life. He had the best friends he'd had since living in the Highlands – maybe ever.

Even if Sophie could never see him as anything more than a friend, at least she was the best friend he could have possibly asked for. If he'd had more people like her earlier in life, then perhaps so much self-degeneration could have been prevented; perhaps his mind could have taken a very different turn. But he realised too that it was the path he'd had that had led him here at all.

Many Scots had once emigrated to the New World looking for better, and Scott had been lucky enough to find it here. He smiled and filled his lungs.

'I think I'll split it with my friends,' he said. 'Ten million each, and I'll donate twenty million to freeing Lolita the orca and returning her to her family. The rest I'll keep for myself and my family.'

The others gave the most ecstatic cheer, so authentic and heart-warming that the judge didn't even call for silence. The public gallery was on its feet cheering, hugs were exchanged left, right and centre, and even the judge was smiling, albeit with professional restraint.

'You are free to go, Scott Wallace,' said the judge, 'but be aware that the Annihilator will hunt you for as long as he lives.'

'I understand, Your Honour,' said Scott.

'There is one more thing,' said the judge. 'The President himself would like to speak to you.'

'The President?' said Scott.

The cheering had died down, and now a new hushed awe had descended upon the courtroom. Some people glanced at the court entrance, expecting that at any moment, the most powerful man in the world would walk in.

To their disappointment, however, the judge took a remote control and pointed it at a screen. No, it wasn't the Vice President that appeared this time; it really was him, dressed in a dark suit and tie.

'Scott Wallace, we owe you an immense debt of gratitude,' the President began. 'You are one of the bravest people our planet has ever known. This fight will be long and arduous, but with you as our secret weapon, we have our best chance to triumph. But things will be on your terms. You are still free to do as you wish, but we hope you will fight alongside us when the time is right.'

'I will, sir,' said Scott.

He left the courtroom with his friends in tow. The guard that had been cruel to Scott at the start was in the courtroom looking on in bewilderment. Sean couldn't resist getting even, barking something loud and animalistic that made the guard jump. No attempt was made to discipline him, and Sean made no attempt to hide his laughter.

'Congratulations, Scott,' said John. 'This is a better outcome than I dared hope for. We're all immensely proud of you.'

'I'm proud that you could make such a thing possible,' said Scott.

They shook hands.

'Good luck,' said John.

So everything was sorted, and it had all worked out better than Scott had ever imagined.

In the days that followed, Scott learned that preparations were underway to move Lolita back to her home in the Puget Sound, a film was being produced to cover the story of her departure and the proceeds would fund an educational IMAX theatre for the aquarium. The orca was going home – after over thirty years in captivity, she was going home.

There was more good news still. The demolition work on the Sea Marshes Reserve had been stopped completely. Richard Kennedy was now a wanted man, his links to the CCC finally exposed. There were already talks underway about replanting what had been lost.

Sophie beamed the whole time. Scott was happy to see *her* happy, but it reminded him that he had something left to do. He took his friends aside that evening.

'I want to apologise to you all,' he said, 'for getting you into this situation and for nearly prolonging it too. I was feeling angry when I asked the Vice President if the correctional facility could be shut down. I was picturing my school as I did so. I hope you can forgive me and we can put this whole episode to bed.'

The others had cheered, Dave being the most vocal in telling him not to worry. He glanced at Sophie; she was still smiling warmly at him and it was in that moment that he felt that she needed an apology just for her.

He took her aside and spoke his mind.

'I want to apologise for earlier,' he said humbly. 'I just thought that the awareness of what these places could do to people wasn't well known. I thought I could do something that would tell authority once and for all that it's something that needs to be dealt with alternatively. I didn't mean to make things worse for you.'

'It's OK,' she said.

'I don't blame you for any of it,' Scott reiterated. 'I just wanted them to know that the system is partly responsible.'

'I understand,' she said.

'Are we OK?' he asked.

Sophie smiled expansively, then spread her arms for an embrace. 'Of course we are.'

CHAPTER 26
A Birthday and a Celebration

On the dawn of her sixteenth birthday, Sophie was the first to rise. As she got dressed she heard a slight knock at the bedroom door and drowsily went to answer it.

As soon as she opened it, a great cheer erupted which woke her up completely. There was the loud banging of party poppers, and each of her friends carried an armful of presents.

They all sat down in the living room of the apartment, still bare of any proper furniture, and from there the parcel opening began.

◆ ◆ ◆

'So, guys,' Sophie beamed. 'Whose presents should I open first?'

She glanced at Scott.

'Maybe you should leave mine till last,' he suggested.

'Does this mean it's something good?'

'Maybe,' he replied mysteriously.

'Can I go first?' said Nigel.

'Go ahead,' said Sophie.

Nigel produced quite a small parcel beautifully wrapped in green paper decorated with jaguars.

'A bird guide to Britain and Europe!' she said. 'This could be really useful in the not too distant future – thank you, Nigel.'

Scott frowned; he wondered why Sophie would need it so soon.

Hyliana brought out another parcel which contained six rectangular boxes of chocolate – all for Sophie.

This occasion had only just begun but Sophie already looked wildly impressed.

'Do you want to see mine next, Sophie?' asked Olav.

'Come on then.'

Olav's present was the most amusing so far. It was an alarm clock but it had a baby penguin with a bass guitar in its hands with shades over its eyes.

Olav pressed a button, then at once the penguin began to sing, jumping about and swaying to its rock music.

Sophie burst out laughing – compared to the old alarm clock that had rudely awoken Scott on Merritt Island, this one sounded a lot more tuneful.

Samantha had given Sophie new clothes, while Dave gave her a warm-looking white jacket that was rather too big for her, explaining that she'd grow into it. Again Scott wondered about that – why would she need a thick jacket in a place like this?

Rickey presented his gift next. It was another bird guide, this one for birds of Sub-Saharan Africa. Then Wayne brought forward his present – some hairspray. Sophie thanked him, despite the fact it still had its price tag of $1.20 on.

Sophie's dad came forward with his ones – each

roughly the size of two disk cases. When Sophie opened them she gasped. They were wireless camera traps, traps that were triggered by movement, with monitors which could show you live images from both camera traps at once. It was the sort of thing scientists would use when they wanted to monitor places for animal activity. He also gave her a night scope, an electronic device that could see in the dark.

With present opening over, it was time to go onto the next phase of their day. For this, Olav welcomed them aboard his beautiful white yacht, and in leisurely style he took them out to sea.

Scott could see instantly how proud he was to be captain of his boat; he had the feeling that Olav would strive to become a sailor, or have some sea-based career at least.

Scott loved this yacht. It was quite a big one with a cabin below and a wide observation deck with a beautiful white sail hoisted above, the wind animating its orca emblem. She sliced the water with ease, showering salty spray at them in friendly torrents.

As the day wore on, they all ended up on deck, admiring the natural beauty and talking to each other at the same time in animated loudness. But Sophie eventually silenced the conversation by asking one big question: 'What was *your* present, Scott?'

There was a suspenseful hush amongst everyone.

'I'll go and get it for you, shall I?' said Scott.

Scott descended below deck and appeared with something fairly large, wrapped not in paper but in some fancy cloth material.

'Close your eyes,' he said softly.

Scott then approached her from behind and

strapped something to her back, tightening a belt around her waist, before finally securing a helmet to her head.

'Imagine you can fly,' he said, as if hypnotising her. 'Imagine you're an eagle or an albatross gliding effortlessly through the air.'

Suddenly two wings stretched outwards and she hovered slightly.

'Sophie, this is your very own micro-flyer!'

Sophie opened her eyes in astonishment. 'My *own* micro-flyer!'

'Correct.'

'Can I hover again?' she asked.

'Whatever you want,' said Scott enthusiastically.

Sophie gently took off again, this time going much higher.

'See if you can touch the top of the mast!' he called up to her.

Her beginner's flight was slow and careful, then the breeze caught her and she wobbled precariously. But she'd done it – she wasn't nearly as good as him, but that would change with practice.

'That was the weirdest feeling I've ever had in my whole life,' she said breathlessly. 'I *flew!*'

'It's wonderful, isn't it?'

'Do I have one of those whistles?'

'Yes,' said Scott, 'but I would be careful how you use it – it's pretty powerful.'

Scott gave her a whistle and she blew on it.

It came out as a loud crescendo of squeaks and clicks, one that sounded so familiar.

'It's a dolphin call!' said Sophie.

'I knew you'd like it.'

'Guys!' called Olav. 'Dolphins!'

They all tensed as the water boiled, then at least two thousand of them leaped simultaneously from the sea, each in a distinct flashing of grey and yellow – common dolphin! They could see their shimmering bodies beneath the surface; they could see mothers and calves swimming together in unmatched unison.

A dolphin leaped at head height next to Dave and he gave a delighted start. Its splash had showered him in foamy water, causing him to whoop with laughter. Sophie played her dolphin noise again, and then simultaneously the dolphins began to sing. That amazed Scott more than anything; all the wildlife seemed to love her. It was as if that dolphin whistle could summon dolphins – like some mystical talent.

Scott had always known that Sophie had a strong love for nature, but until now he hadn't fully understood the extent of that. She treated the wild as if it were her home – as if she was born there and would one day die there.

When the dolphins departed, the light became so poor that Olav decided it was best to return to shore – that was when the final event of the day took place.

◆ ◆ ◆

The atmosphere was loud but soothing. Music throbbed in Scott's ears and everything looked purple. People danced and leaped to the music; the air was humid and smelled of sweat.

Scott sat at a stool near the bar feeling somewhat distant in the purple gloom of this disco. It was something about him that most people didn't know – he liked to think. Not just to entertain himself, but because he was a naturally deep person.

The music and the shouts from the crowds all seemed blurred, and as he looked into the future, he smiled with a kind of tired happiness. He and Sophie were still great friends; they'd watch a bit of TV, go to bed, but then – that was when it hit him – it would almost be time for his departure.

He would have to leave soon, and that sad truth was only three short days away. The shock of that realisation was overwhelming; he stood up abruptly, as if feeling the need to make the most of his time here. It was strange – not that long ago he'd been counting down the days to his departure, and now he felt differently.

Scott looked about him. The real world seemed muted and far away as he took in the last images of a world that he might never come back to.

He stared in the direction of an open door at the far end of the room and caught a glimpse of the outside world; he went over and stepped out into the open air. This disco was some distance away from the main city, with a swathe of scrub outside of it. He looked from left to right along the floodlit road, then up at the tops of each of the palm trees that edged it. The breeze blew through their expansive leaves and they swayed softly.

From beyond the light, crickets rang and bullfrogs croaked. There was the distant hoot of a great horned owl hidden in the scrub. And above that scrub was the starlit sky – he was giving it all one last look before he returned home to the relative cold, rain, school and loneliness of Scotland.

He didn't want to leave. He didn't want to leave Sophie behind. He truly wished that he could stay here forever and leave behind everything else at home – but at the same time he knew he couldn't!

He had a future to consider back there, three thousand miles across the water. He had a family, he had a way of life and he had a home – sort of. Could he leave it all behind for this? Besides he had the rest of school to finish – no, maybe not now.

Scott returned to his friends inside, eager to spend the next seventy-two hours with *them*!

CHAPTER 27
Making Amends

Scott's sorrow deepened as the end of his holiday loomed. He thought about it all the time – even when he was with Sophie and the others. Fun just didn't seem like fun anymore – it was like going away to relax knowing that you still had lots of homework to do and time was nearing the last minute.

He found Sophie experimenting with her favourite present and everyone had crowded round to watch. At first Sophie had had difficulty adjusting to the idea that this machine required mind power instead of gas, and now and then her suspended belief would lapse, causing her to drop.

'How's she getting on?' asked Scott.

'You should have seen her before – she was doing backflips and everything,' said Samantha.

Seeing her with the micro-flyer gave him another idea, one that he'd completely forgotten about until now.

'Oh and I almost forgot!' he said. 'There's perhaps one more thing I should give you all. I know I've given you lots of money, but there's one more thing.'

Scott quickly ran back to the apartment, and when he returned brought out his surprises.

'I think you deserve these too!'

Samantha gaped as he handed out *more* micro-flyers from spare parts that Scott had assembled yesterday.

'Hey, look everyone!' she called. 'Scott has got micro-flyers for us too!'

Her friends crowded in and soon they were already flying with them, gaining height with ease. Even Uncle Wilson had a try.

'How did you make these?' asked Samantha.

'I have spares,' he replied.

Samantha ran off to try hers out again, and although Scott was happy to watch them fly, inwardly a resentment was building inside of him. Another day had passed and that resentment intensified. One more day, he thought, one more day of happiness and he would be back to that hell that they called a school, and this day was ending too.

Sally Patterson looked on, laughing at their antics.

'Are they getting better?' Sally asked him.

'I think so,' said Scott. 'They'll be professionals with it before they know it.'

Scott bowed his head, suddenly troubled by their happiness.

Sally turned to look at him. 'Are you alright?'

'I'm fine,' said Scott, recovering swiftly.

'I hear Sophie told you about Dennis,' she said. 'Is that true?'

'Yes,' said Scott. 'I know she wasn't supposed to tell anyone, but things kind of escalated and I needed to know the truth.'

'Don't worry,' said Sally, 'I understand. It was eating away at her, knowing who he was and what he'd done. She felt responsible for him in a way – that was why her therapy got extended. She needed therapy when she was younger because she had delays in her speech and motor skills that needed addressing.'

Scott was surprised; he didn't think she was delayed in any respect.

'I used to work with Dennis, as a therapist, but I was juggling Sophie's needs with his, and I'm part of the reason he was let out.'

Scott stared. 'How come?'

'He was coming to the end of his sentence,' said Sally, 'and I was tasked with finding out if he was suitable for release. He even told me about his ideas once – he said he was going to form a humanitarian group. He was vague about it. I just thought that was because he was just starting it up and didn't know where it was going to lead. But I think he knew exactly where it was going to lead.'

'And you were never suspicious about it?' Scott asked.

'I had my doubts,' Sally admitted, 'but since his incident with Sophie he hadn't caused any trouble in a while, and no one took his claims seriously.'

'I don't see it as your fault,' he said. 'He was just cunning enough to take advantage of the system.'

She sighed. 'Thank you. I've been waiting for someone to say that to me for years.'

Then she smiled.

'Scott?'

He looked round and saw Sophie's father standing behind him, staring as if he was seeing him in a completely new light. In the weeks that had passed since Scott had first met him, he was now a totally different person. The frown he used to wear when Scott was around was nowhere to be seen, his expression no longer distrusting, no longer suspicious, just one of pure openness.

'Can we go for a walk? I'd like to talk to you.'

They strolled along the friendly neighbourhood street for the last time. The birds were singing, children in their gardens were laughing and playing, and the air was warm and humid but otherwise tropically tame.

'I...' he said hesitantly, 'I never really thanked you for helping us get out of the tight spots during the hurricane. We might not be here otherwise, but most of all I'm sorry for my behaviour earlier. I realise now that you *are* safe to be around, and I was wrong to think that you were anything like Jack Robinson. I feel so stupid now that I realise that.'

'That's quite alright,' said Scott.

'You can call me David,' he said.

'Pleased to meet you, David,' said Scott, shaking his hand enthusiastically.

David looked at him as if in awe. 'I'm not sure what to say.'

He laughed, then David cleared his mind and said: 'Thank you, Scott, for all that you've done for us. You saved our lives – *everyone's* lives!'

'It feels good,' he said, 'particularly when it's Sophie's life I've saved.'

David smiled. 'I see why Sophie likes you – she knew there was something about you that was unique. Wilson was right; I just couldn't see it until now.'

'She's an incredible person,' said Scott. 'The best there is.'

'I know,' said David. 'She's my daughter – the best daughter I could have hoped for. She has her own interests, her own path, her own self. I feel guilty now for trying to protect her too much. I wasn't always a very good husband you see.'

Scott remembered what Sally had told him.

'At high school, I cheated on Sally quite a lot. I saw my life as some superficial front that had to be maintained at all times. I wanted to appear glamorous, popular, the guy who had everything. In doing so, I neglected the value of what I had. I feel like Sophie was something of a miracle – without her I feel as though I would never have had the second chance I needed to be a better husband, and be a father. It's only because she was born that we stayed together, and I desperately wanted to make it up to my wife and prove that I could be the father Sophie needed. When Jack Robinson nearly ruined her, I went into overdrive, and in overprotecting her, I feel like I interfered with the fabric of who she is. She had her own decisions and risks to take that had nothing to do with me. I see that now, and you're the proof.'

Scott looked away, his sadness coming back.

'Are you alright?' David asked.

'I was earlier,' Scott replied, 'but now I'm not sure. My time is upon me.'

'You have to go home tomorrow, don't you?' David said sadly.

'Yeah.' He had to restrain himself from crying, but he was failing.

'You can still be the best of friends even when you're home,' David said.

'It's not just that,' said Scott.

David frowned sympathetically.

'I love her.'

David put a hand on his shoulder, his look of sympathy trebling.

'And I think she loves you too, Scott; I just don't think she's had a chance to say it yet.'

'But what about Wayne?' Scott asked. 'Aren't they still together?'

'I'm not sure,' he said. 'But talk to her, Scott – find a moment with just the two of you. It's a risk, I know, but if Wayne's not with her anymore just tell her how you feel. She'll understand.'

'I don't want to leave!' said Scott vehemently. 'I wish I could stay here; I wish I could stay here forever.'

David thought for a moment.

'Go home first, finish your exams; do everything that needs doing at home first. Then you could get engaged maybe.'

That put a smile on Scott's face. 'Marriage? You think I'm good enough for that?'

'Maybe. I could imagine you two getting married. Lots of flowers, big dress, fancy car, you know what I mean?' he said, though he stopped when he saw he was embarrassing Scott.

'I always thought that young couples never last,' Scott muttered.

'There might even be a baby next.'

Scott cringed. Then laughed. Momentarily he felt his sadness chased away.

'What else can you imagine?' he asked.

'Well, in two years' time I can imagine something,' said David.

'And what's that?'

'It's a surprise – one that we'd been planning for a very long time. We wondered whether we'd manage it, but thanks to all that reward money you gave us, it's going to happen and we'd like *you* to be part of it.'

'What is it?' Scott asked.

'Sophie will tell you soon.'

That was all he would say.

When the end of the last day came, Scott's sadness returned in waves. It was already night time; tomorrow was almost upon him.

Scott was in Sophie's room, keen to spend this last night with her, but he was alone – Sophie was elsewhere in the apartment. He didn't understand himself. How come he was here in her room and it wasn't making him feel any better?

He'd managed to suppress it all day, even when he'd come into the apartment and spoken to Sophie – even though his departure had been discussed, he'd still managed to suppress it.

Now that he was here, with a moment to himself all alone, he couldn't suppress it any longer. An emotional heaviness descended upon him. His face contorted in one last attempt to hold it back, but it was useless. The tears flooded out in torrents – once he started he couldn't stop.

The door opened and Sophie came in soundlessly, her pyjamas a ghostly white. If there was such a thing as an angel, he thought, it would be Sophie.

Scott still cried – somehow it felt worse when she was close to him. She sat down, and he felt her bare smooth arms being wrapped comfortingly around him. He wanted to look at her, but emotionally he couldn't do it.

'Are you alright?' she asked.

'No,' he said with full honesty. There was a long

pause. He tried to collect himself. 'I'm going to miss you, you know?'

She sighed. 'So will I,' she sniffed.

'I'm going to miss all of you,' said Scott, 'but at the same time there's some things that have happened here that I really regret. So many people died because I chose to stand up to the CCC, including—'

He could barely say her name.

Sophie knew who he meant. 'Scott, I'm sorry about Sara; I got the impression you really liked her.'

He paused.

'That's just it,' he said.

Sophie frowned.

'After our argument on Merritt Island, I went to the Sea Marshes Reserve to do some thinking and I came across Sara. She told me what she was going through, and what had happened to her. No one ever mentioned that she had no parents. She started despairing and I tried to comfort her, and then she tried to drown herself.'

Sophie stared. 'When did that happen?'

'Just before the hurricane,' said Scott.

Sophie was furious. 'Why didn't you tell me?'

'She pleaded with me not to say anything about it to you – she kept going on about how you didn't want to see her and that you somehow wouldn't help her. She hugged me and told me how great it was that there was someone out there that loved her and she obviously meant me. I didn't know what to do; I didn't know what to say. I didn't love her; I wasn't into her at all. I liked her as a friend and only rescued her because I didn't want her to die. I didn't say it at the time because she was in such a fragile state. It was in the forefront of my mind to tell her that there was nothing between us, but because she went away during the hurricane, I couldn't contact her – no one knew how to get in touch with her. She only came back when the battle happened, and when I tried to say it then, she was dying. The thing that really kills me now is that I always intended to let her down as gently as I could, but I didn't get the opportunity to and now she's gone to her grave believing I loved her, and I'll never get the chance to tell her the truth. She had a long life ahead of her – I was hopeful that perhaps she would pick herself up and be strong on her own. But the Annihilator completed what he started and wiped out her whole family.'

Sophie's frown vanished, her expression turning soft. 'There was nothing you could have done, Scott.'

'I tried to help her,' he said.

'I know you did,' said Sophie.

She shook her head. 'I should have told you about her,' she said. 'She was the most emotionally fragile person I've ever dealt with. We didn't always see eye to eye – we kept having arguments about what she saw as my popularity with the boys.'

'But you are popular with the boys,' said Scott.

'That's true; I don't deny that. But very often I don't draw the right ones. She was happy to just jump into any relationship available to her. She was clingy and quick to form emotional attachments to people she barely knew, even before her parents died. I know from experience that that's not what you should do. My mom knew that, and looking back I think she wanted me to be different. She encouraged my interest in nature, and I think that's why I desire something different in a guy. Not just the typical jock that everyone wants – what my mom got.'

'So are you and Wayne like…?' he asked cautiously, trying not to look at her.

'I thought about it,' she said. 'Wayne's a really nice guy, fit and athletic – but I feel like he doesn't really get my interest in nature. He's not into it the way you are.'

Scott's heart pounded.

'He likes me,' she said, 'but even he admits that we're not compatible on that level. We both want different things. I ultimately want someone I can enjoy spending time with who likes the things that I do.'

She looked at him.

Scott didn't dare look back.

There was another long pause.

'What was the surprise your dad was talking about?' asked Scott.

Sophie sighed. 'Do you remember on that beautiful cruise you took me on – the sweetest thing that anyone's ever done for me? I said that someday I wished I could travel the world, and thanks to the money you gave us, that dream is now a reality. My parents share my ambition, and they want you to come with us.'

'The whole world?' said Scott.

'Europe, North America, Africa, Central and South America, Asia, Oceania and Antarctica.' She spelled out a huge list of possible places around the world, and his tears vanished, replaced by sheer wonder. Scott was rather breathless by the time she'd finished.

'Can we really go to all those places?' he asked.

'We can, now that we've got wings!' she said, smiling. 'I think that our micro-flyers are going to make this vacation a lot more interesting, don't you?'

Scott had had the micro-flyer for so long that

sometimes he forgot its potential – perhaps he'd taken it for granted long enough.

'Think about it, Scott – the places we can fly to! Untouched by man, hanging out in unspoiled wildernesses with no other people! It would just be the two of us and the wildlife for company, and that backed up with my camera traps will double our chances of finding rare things.'

Overwhelming potential had settled its expansive embrace on Scott. Sophie was one hundred percent right – they could see much more than any other average holidaymaker now that they could fly.

Scott felt excited; he was sure the green light had been given but wanted to be extra sure. He knew who to talk to. He excused himself from Sophie for a few moments.

'Uncle Wilson, can I speak to you privately for a moment?' he asked, realising with a pang of irony the déjà vu of this meeting.

'Sure,' he said, smiling. They found a room in the apartment block to talk privately. 'So what's up?'

He was as kind and approachable as he'd been since the beginning. Scott realised how little he'd seen of him, yet he'd been the most instrumental in advising Scott about his feelings for Sophie.

'As you know, the end is drawing near,' said Scott.

'I know,' said Uncle Wilson, 'but you've enjoyed it, yes?'

'Yes – well most of it,' said Scott. 'Do you remember the last time we spoke – that night when Richard Kennedy came round?'

'I do indeed,' said Uncle Wilson.

'Now that I'm leaving tomorrow,' said Scott, 'I'm

wondering if I should – you know?'

'I know,' said Uncle Wilson. 'Well since the last time we spoke, I've seen a lot develop between you two. I can tell that she likes you, Scott; I don't think she's met anyone like you.'

'She's shown me so much and been a friend to me like no one ever has. I love her – I love her to pieces. I love her like every bird, mammal, fish, reptile, amphibian, invertebrate, plant and fungus there is on planet Earth. I love her like every star, planet and comet in the night sky. It's so intense I can hardly bear it.'

'I understand,' said Uncle Wilson. 'I've spoken to David and Sally quite a lot on the subject, and I think they very much approve. Has she told you about your world tour?'

'Yes,' said Scott. 'She told me that I was the ideal companion for it. I'm really excited.'

'I can imagine you are,' said Uncle Wilson. 'The best stroke of luck you could have had.'

'Have you spoken to Sophie?' he asked. 'Has she ever said anything to you?'

'As a matter of fact she has,' said Uncle Wilson.

'What?' Scott asked, almost pleadingly.

'She says you're the best companion she's ever had,' said Uncle Wilson. He tactfully didn't say any more.

'Is that it? Does this mean I should ask her tomorrow? She said that she's broken up with Wayne. Apparently he doesn't get her interest in nature.'

'She was with *Wayne*?' said Uncle Wilson. 'Now she never said anything to me about that. Well if she's quite clearly said they're not together anymore, and that you have the more compatible interests, then I think you should go for it. The odds of success are much higher than they were when you last spoke to me.'

'I don't hate Wayne,' said Scott. 'I think he's a really nice guy.' He backtracked. 'I just get the message that people like him: athletic, muscled, a football captain and prom king win all the time with the ladies. Especially all the ones I've liked, and it almost seems satisfying to see that kind of person lose for once.' He checked himself. 'I shouldn't gloat, Wayne's a good friend, but it feels good to finally smash the stupid rules that drive these high school politics – if you know what I mean?'

'I know exactly what you mean,' said Uncle Wilson, then laughed. 'High school politics – now that's the best term I've ever heard to describe school dynamics.' He laughed louder this time, but soon composed himself.

'It's probably an overgeneralisation,' he said. 'Look at what happened – it hasn't gone that way this time. Scott, there are girls who are attracted to guys like that. That's OK I suppose, but there are some who only like that kind of person because of a desire to be popular. They might not care about the person they really are, just as long as their peers see them as being at the top. But there are also girls who are attracted to people for who they are inside. There'll be girls who are attracted to guys who like birds, and Sophie happens to be that kind of person.'

'I hope Wayne finds someone else who's right for him anyway,' said Scott.

'I'm quite certain he will,' said Uncle Wilson.

'I always believed rejection was a form of natural selection,' said Scott, 'and that through natural selection I was just destined to be alone, pigeon-holed into a group I felt I didn't belong to. But I'd much rather decide where I belong. It's taken me so long to realise that I'm not an abomination for asking out who I like.'

Uncle Wilson gasped.

'Where on Earth did you get that idea?' he asked. 'You're not an abomination – you're quite unapologetically who you are. I hear you have Asperger's,' said Uncle Wilson.

Scott frowned.

'Don't worry – Sophie told me.'

'She told you?' Scott asked, taken by surprise.

'Yes,' he said, 'but don't worry. I guess that's probably made it harder for you to find someone. I imagine you must have difficulty relating to your peers; you must feel as though everyone without it is better than you. But that's not the case, Scott. You and all those with your condition have as much chance as anyone else of finding a partner who's right for you. You talked about natural selection earlier, but even in that there are many exceptions. Anyone can be an exception if they want to – you just have to use what you have and develop yourself as best as you can.' He smiled. 'Just tell her how you feel Scott; something good will come out of it.'

'But do you know if she likes me?' asked Scott. 'Yes or no?'

'Wait and see,' said Uncle Wilson.

He couldn't get a straight answer.

CHAPTER 28
The Tearful Goodbye

Scott's dreams took him into a world of happiness. He saw Sophie, himself and the whole world in an idyllic sort of way, as though it were the Garden of Eden.

'It's just us now, Scott,' said Sophie, in a dreamy voice. 'Nothing can pull us apart now; let's stay here forever.'

The colours were just too bright, animals were everywhere, reality seemed so distant.

But something disturbed his sleep – suddenly this idyllic world vanished and he awoke into his harsh reality.

It was two in the morning, and even though the day hadn't yet dawned, it still didn't change the fact that he was going to be leaving today. Leaving this place with its palm trees, its sun, its sea, its reefs, its wildlife, its friends and not to mention its girls. Scott had loved Miami. In the past month or so, all his dreams had come true here: he'd met the perfect girl, he'd gained some new friends, he'd seen an extra part of the world... It had outweighed all his expectations – far more than a good getaway from the stresses of reality.

But reality didn't bring only negative thoughts. The biggest reality out of all of them was the promise of traveling the globe with what he could only describe as his ideal companion. What better result could he have asked for? And yet he felt despondent.

Still with his pyjamas on, he got out of bed, and went onto the roof of the apartment. The only light around was from the lamp posts below, the lights of the city and the stars and the moon.

Scott didn't feel cold though; the air had retained its pleasant warmth. He wanted to bask in it one more time, for as long as he could.

A moth settled on his arm, and he studied its furry body and its dull wings. He had no idea what kind it was. He gently brushed it away and it fluttered over to a light, which it batted itself against continuously.

He saw a nine-banded armadillo foraging on one of the lawns below, then watched a raccoon dashing across the road to join it. Together the two animals foraged. The wildlife of the suburbs must have been saying its farewells too.

Scott tried to digest it all.

Silence loomed – that was until he glanced round, hearing light footsteps coming up the stairs, and Sophie appeared in the doorway. She was also still in her pyjamas, looking at him with great sympathy. He tried to smile, but it just didn't happen.

'What are you doing up here?' she asked softly. She didn't seem annoyed, just confused.

'I just wanted to enjoy the night; it seems so short.'

Sophie could clearly tell that wasn't the real reason. 'We're going to travel the world soon, so why are you feeling so despondent?'

He stared at the floor, trying to suppress another flood of grief.

'Because nothing seems fair. I'm certain I'll experience more loneliness till the world tour begins, another two years of it, back to a world of indifference, exams...'

Sophie sighed. 'There's nothing you can do about exams,' she said, quite realistically. 'They're there and we have to do them, in our own countries. That's just the way the world is. No one can bend the laws of education into their favour and certainly not in ours. I'm afraid.'

Scott looked away sharply.

'Look I'm sorry, but I can't do anything to change that. Life is cruel—'

'Particularly in my case,' he muttered. 'I had to leave my home in the Highlands and live in a flat with a drug-dealing, gun-toting lodger, and go to school with thugs that have beaten me to within an inch of my life without punishment.'

'But you've got the money now,' she said. 'You can move away to a better school, just as you said before.'

'It's still school though,' he said pessimistically.

Sophie sighed. 'I know. But, Scott, look how things have changed. Haven't you noticed what great things have happened to you since you got here? I remember when we first met, I could tell how shy you were. You've got past so much, and now you've got me and a whole load of other things to look forward to. That's very generous, I think. But then I suppose at the same time, there has to be a compromise. There has to be some price to pay for this reward, and going back to school *is* that price, I'm afraid.'

'I wish it wasn't,' Scott muttered. His anger didn't dissipate. 'I'd do anything to bring down that place. The one place I'm legally condemned to go to, the one place I can't escape their negativity, the one place that seems to find my individuality so offensive it makes me suffer for it. The one place where equality is completely lost on everyone I interact with. They demand the utmost loyalty and respect whilst giving none back.'

'*Scott*,' Sophie muttered, 'that's not helping.' She sighed. 'Listen, I understand completely why you don't like school. I've had a lot of crap in it myself; it might not look that way to you, but I have.'

She tried a more cosmopolitan approach.

'Think about it, Scott. I'm sure there are plenty people in the world that aren't nearly as lucky as you or me – billions of them! The Annihilator himself said so. There are people out there that are more hopeless at finding a date than you are; there are poor, impoverished people like the favelas in Sao Paulo and Rio de Janeiro – believe me, I've given them donations all my life! They barely have enough money to support themselves, let alone travel the world – and don't forget that there are people out there who are born with far worse struggles than you. So I think life has been quite kind to you actually.'

'I can't really say the same for my past,' Scott muttered.

'My past wasn't quite kind to me either. I had Jack Robinson as a boyfriend; I suffered his abuse – that's quite a shadow over my past, just as bullying and inequality casts a shadow over yours. I missed a chance to help Dennis before he could become what he is today, and I have to live with that every day for the rest of my life.'

'So we're the same?'

'Maybe we are.'

He sighed. She was right about that at least, though his negativity switched itself on again.

'I just find it unfair, how everyone liked you and respected you right at the start of your life. I was still an outcast even when I was unaware of my Asperger's. People ostracised me and to begin with I didn't even know it, let alone why. I had this belief that because you don't have a disability, you can sail through life while I'm struggling.'

Sophie shifted. 'Nobody can sail through life, Scott, not even me. It's just certain hardships we face along the way that are a little different. The worst hardship I had to endure through elementary school was everyone relying on me to help them with their work. Then there was Dennis Murphy; his classmates were looking up to me for protection from him – they all said that I stood between him and death. I had to protect everyone, Scott; if I didn't then someone could have died – it was that extreme. Imagine what a responsibility that is to carry at such a young age. It's the sort of responsibility that the military take on. I was a straight-A student, but having that duty on my shoulders wasn't fun – it may have made me feel good, but it was usually a round-the-clock job, in the playground, but most especially after school. I had no backup – I did this virtually on my own, and it could have risked *my* life too!'

'So you've had just as hard a time as I have?'

'Yeah, I would say it was even worse, but still, I managed to get over it. But there's something else to this story too. Do you remember when I told you that I had therapy when I was younger?'

'For dealing with the guilt at what the Annihilator did?' said Scott.

'Before that,' she said, 'I was having problems, developmental anomalies.' She took a deep breath. 'They said I had Asperger's syndrome too.'

Scott was amazed. He would never have guessed it, and yet at the same time it made sense.

'Maybe that's why you like nature so much,' he said, 'and why you relate so well to some of the others, and why you relate to me.'

Sophie was taken aback, as if she was surprised he'd taken it so well.

'So we're cool about it?' she asked.

Scott smiled and nodded.

He suddenly changed the subject.

'I'm not going to see you for a long time,' he said.

'That's true, but we'll keep in touch by e-mail. You've got my address and I've got yours.'

'Still, it won't be the same talking to you through a machine as it is in person.'

'That's true, but it's better than nothing and you *will* see me again. If we don't manage to meet up during the school holidays, it may be a long time till that happens, but at least it *will* happen Scott!'

Scott felt too tired to argue any more, but just as he was about to make his move to go back to bed, a spectacle of natural fireworks took place in front of their eyes. Meteorites from high in the mesosphere began to burn up; pinpricks of white light in the night sky falling to Earth.

'Why don't we enjoy this together?' Scott suggested.

Hundreds of them were entering the atmosphere,

bursting into beautiful displays of light, making wishes come true from all around.

But that moment never lasted long, and reality came in again!

◆ ◆ ◆

Scott was told that morning that their flight back home was at four in the afternoon, so that meant that he at least had the morning to spend with his beloved friends.

They mostly chatted and laughed, but there were plenty of references to his departure later on.

As their deadline neared, everyone gathered on the street, eager to bid Scott farewell.

'You're a legend, Scott!' said Wayne. 'I'm a millionaire now!'

'What do you think you'll do with all that money?' Scott asked.

'I'm not sure. There's plenty of things I *could* do. I could have a big fancy house, servants perhaps, my own snooker table, private yacht – who needs a private plane now that I've got wings! But I'd still love to play for the Miami Dolphins most of all.'

It seemed extraordinary to Scott that Wayne would pursue a career even with all his money.

'Right up your street,' said Scott. 'Wayne, you've been a pal to me from day one.' Scott said that with rather an effort. 'You deserve it all! All that you want, it's all yours now.'

He was secretly pleased that that didn't include Sophie.

Wayne grinned. 'Thanks a lot.'

Scott turned to Dave. 'Dave, you were brilliant

too,' he said, fist- bumping the wannabe tough guy. 'Thanks for pushing Hanzo off of me.' Dave nodded. 'What will you do?'

'Me?' Dave chuckled. 'I was thinking I could become a wrestler. I've got good muscles and thanks to all the excitement that's happened, I think they've improved! It depends on the asthma though.'

'You've never let that stop you,' said Scott. 'Sophie told me that after Dennis beat you up in the playground, you tried to toughen yourself up so that people wouldn't bully you again. I think you've already succeeded, and I think you're tougher in spirit than in muscle.'

Quite out of his normally restrained, polite social manner, Scott clamped a firm hand on Dave's shoulder and gave him a playful shake. Dave grabbed him and Scott was lifted to head height. It wasn't the kind of camaraderie he was used to, but he laughed it off.

Dave put him down.

'Scott Wallace out to travel the world and kick some more CCC ass,' Dave proclaimed. 'The Annihilator better beware – there's a new warrior in the world.' His eyes suddenly gleamed as if he'd thought of a brilliant idea. 'The World Warrior has arrived.'

Scott fell silent as he tossed the title in his head, then he smiled gleefully. He somehow realised there were still others to speak to and snapped out of his trance.

He looked at Olav – out of everyone, he seemed to have rejuvenated the most.

'Olav, feel free to go back to Norway whenever you like.'

Olav grinned. 'It's been many years since I last saw

Norway – my home village of Korsnes. The fjords, the Northern Lights, the islands and forests, the orcas, my friends, my mother – I'll see them again soon!'

'What do you want to do when you leave school?' Scott asked. 'Apart from going back to Norway? You've got ten million dollars – you can do whatever you want.'

'I've been thinking about that and I figured that because I like the sea and because I found myself coping well with all that war and excitement, I think I have just the idea to fulfil both of them!' There was a slight pause. 'I want to join the navy!'

'The navy?' Even Sophie hadn't anticipated this.

'Really, Olav, I think you'd be a good captain. You know lots about the sea – more than anyone I reckon. Which navy would you join?' Scott asked.

'I've been wondering about that; I haven't decided yet.'

Scott nodded.

'But uh, can I really do it – I mean go back to Norway?'

'What do you mean?' Sophie asked.

'Well, even though America isn't the same as Norway, I've lived here for at least five years and I'll miss it because I've been given a home here – thanks to you, Sophie.'

She grinned.

'Olav, we all love you,' she said. They crowded in to give him a group hug.

Then Scott got to Rickey.

'I want to return to the Congo, but the only thing that stops me is that when I was a soldier I was ordered against my will to slaughter entire neighbourhoods – I have a feeling I won't be accepted.'

This was a hard question to answer, but Scott came up with one anyway.

'Why don't you vow to educate other people about war and protect their communities? You could become a preacher.'

'I hadn't thought of that,' said Rickey.

'You've seen horrors, Rickey,' said Scott. 'Mentally that must have been difficult to deal with, but I think preaching would be a great avenue to let it all out. Before all this happened, I didn't have a chance to translate my past for good, but there's always a better option than the way the Annihilator did it. A better way than Nganda.'

Rickey nodded.

'I know he got away,' said Scott, 'but however much he preaches his strength, you will always be stronger than him. You have a constructive direction in life, Rickey – that's something he will never have.'

Rickey had tears in his eyes and reached out to shake Scott's hand.

'What about you, Samantha?' said Scott.

'I'd still like to study medicine,' said Samantha. 'And thanks to you, I don't have to worry about where the money for that is going to come from now.'

'I know we haven't spoken much,' said Scott, 'but I think you'll be very good at it – you saved hundreds of people during the battle. I'm sure if you need a reference, you'll have plenty of patients to vouch for you.'

Samantha's answering smile was full of joy.

'What about you, Nigel?' said Scott.

'Well my parents and Hyliana have told me many stories about the Amazon jungle,' said Nigel. 'It's made me want to go there. I thought I would travel, climb trees, see some wildlife. I might even decide to live there.'

Hyliana affectionately clasped her brother's hair. 'I'll be going with him,' she said. 'We belong together. Mom and Dad have always talked about showing me where I grew up. I don't remember it.'

To Scott's surprise, Hyliana dropped down from her brother's back and clasped Scott's hand with her own.

'I know I'm stubborn and difficult sometimes,' she said, 'but I don't hold your initial insensitivity against you.'

'Thank you,' he replied.

Hyliana grinned, and to Scott's further surprise, she didn't climb back onto her brother's back – she just stood there next to him, beaming.

Scott felt the deadline to departure nearing.

'And, Sophie, can I just say that you've been the best companion I've ever had in my life – more than I'll ever have with anyone else. There's something I want to give you; a parting gift.'

Scott reached into his pocket and took out a necklace with a beautiful blue dolphin attached to it.

'I made this for you, just so you remember me. I wanted to give it to the person that made the most difference to me. It'll give you good luck!'

'Won't *you* need it?' Sophie asked.

Scott grinned. 'I've already had my good luck. I met you, I got new friends, I had fun and now I'm going to achieve my ambition of traveling the world. I defeated the CCC, survived the Annihilator's bullet and secured the release of Lolita – a decades-long battle you thought you'd never win, and the Sea Marshes Reserve was saved from development. What more good luck could I ask for?'

He put it around her swan-like neck and she examined it with an expression of warmth on her beautiful face.

'I love it, Scott,' she said. 'Thank you.'

'I'm giving this to you because you're the best person I've ever met. You saw through my Asperger's and you've given me the promise of traveling the world. If I'd met people like you earlier in life, perhaps I'd have turned out differently.'

Sophie beamed. 'If you'd turned out any differently, you might not have had the heart and bravery to defeat the Annihilator,' she said. 'Or dare to challenge an empire that everyone was afraid of.' She paused. 'But I want you to know that even if all those events with the CCC never happened, I would have still chosen you to hang out with. It's not about accomplishing heroic feats to look impressive; it's not about proving your worth by risking your life. A lot of the time things like that don't happen. It's about the qualities that you have as a person, in the context of a normal day-to-day life that matters more: trust, kindness, honesty, authenticity, supportiveness and, most of all, compatibility. It was your interest in nature that drew me to hang out with you, and the rest just took care of itself. You seek acceptance, Scott, and you were willing to do anything to get it. You came from a world that didn't fully appreciate you, but whatever they made you think, you had the tools for acceptance all along. You just needed the right group of people to recognise it.'

Scott didn't say a word. He was stunned at just

how well Sophie understood his mind.

He'd visualised this moment countless times, and now that it was actually happening, he felt as though a spotlight had been shone on him. Everyone was watching him. He looked just beyond where his friends were standing and saw that David, Sally and Uncle Wilson were also watching.

'I have one more thing to say,' said Scott tentatively.

Sophie craned her neck in slightly.

'You've been the best friend I've ever had,' he said.

Sophie smiled, and he heard the others laugh.

'But there's more.'

Sophie jerked her head. The others fell completely silent.

'There's something I've wanted to say since the moment I met you,' he said.

He took a few steps closer to her, so they were standing only centimetres apart. Sophie went very quiet. Scott's heart raced – he'd been told off so many times before for standing too close to people. But Sophie didn't back away. He reached out with both hands to clasp hers.

Her friends gasped. Sophie's smile was completely gone; she stared at Scott as if breathless, and didn't let go.

'I want to be with you, Sophie,' he said. 'I love you!'

Sophie's breathing accelerated. 'And I do too!'

In a swift movement, she grabbed his shirt and kissed him. The others applauded and cheered. Dave wolf-whistled.

Wayne bowed his head.

They held onto one another, reluctant to let go;

if it was to end, the world would have to forcibly tear them apart. Life itself had never felt so sweet; there was everything to live for. With Sophie in it, life was the best thing ever.

Scott heard a clock strike in his head and opened his eyes, aware of the most awful feeling that was coming next.

He'd run out of time. The van was waiting for him, and he knew all too well what would happen. It would take him to the airport and onto a plane that would take ten hours to get to Amsterdam; then a two-hour flight back to Aberdeen and a half-hour drive at most to get to his aunt and uncle's flat. Scott saw the stare of urgency in his family; he saw the van's doors inviting him back to its colourless dominion where loneliness, rain, darkness and uncertainty reigned king.

Scott stood between the two worlds – the cold white van that would ultimately take him home to reality and the gleaming faces and colourful T-shirts of his new girlfriend, friends and paradise.

Scott went and hugged his beloved friends one more time – but he hugged Sophie hardest of all, and they shared another long kiss before he reluctantly released her. Scott's tears trickled, his face reddened, and Sophie stroked his face, smiling consolingly at him. *It's OK to cry.*

Finally, his face now red with grief, he turned away.

But at the door of the van, he stopped abruptly and looked back at the world that had adored him – his friends, Sophie, paradise, wildlife vast beyond imagining – then he looked towards reality – to the prospect of loneliness, rain, school, exams, uncertainty and darkness – and hesitated, before taking that first step inside. He twisted round in his seat and waved. Everyone waved back at him, the uproarious cheering like the deafening crash of a waterfall.

'Farewell, World Warrior!' they shouted in unison. Scott's tears intensified, and he grinned widely.

With every inch the van moved, his lovely world fell further and further away, and the figures in the distance grew smaller. Then the van turned a corner and they were lost, for now anyway.

He lay with his head against the van window simply daydreaming and contemplating the extraordinary things he'd been through. He was so lost in thought he didn't even hear his parents debate through the rush-hour traffic the best way to get back to the airport. The journey took over an hour, but to Scott it seemed like only a minute had passed since they'd left.

He saw the airport looming, and as he walked through its revolving doors minutes later, he took one last look around. It felt like an eternity had passed since he'd last seen this place; it looked the same yet felt different. But it had been him that had changed, not the airport.

They went through security without a hitch and sat in the departure lounge, awaiting the announcement of their flight.

Mary and Sean Wallace, his beloved parents who had given him a home and the means to have this adventure, took a break from their reading, sensing Scott's mood. Scott hadn't said a word to them since leaving; indeed, he'd barely returned their gaze.

'Don't worry, son,' said Sean, clasping his hand. 'You'll see her again very soon.'

Scott smiled weakly.

Mary put an arm around him. 'Thanks to your reward money, we'll be looking for a new place to live and a new school. You have to understand, Scott, that neither of us wanted to move to Balnagask – things were very different then and we were struggling. But now we can move to wherever we want and you won't have to put up with your aunt and uncle's lodger anymore, nor your classmates and terrible teachers. We could move back to the country, where there'll be more nice, supportive people, just like you had in Speyside. Who knows where we'll end up, but I hope from now on everything will be just right for us all.'

Mary had summarised it perfectly. What happened next was anyone's guess, but one thing was certain: Scott and his family had never had a brighter future. There would be plenty of financial security, and if they didn't like the first place they chose to settle, they had plenty of means to move to another, until everything was as it should be. Then, in time, Scott would begin the adventure of a lifetime.

Their flight was called out and, armed with their hand luggage, they made their way across the gangway to board the plane. Scott entered the cabin and saw that plenty of people had already been seated. It looked jam-packed, but they soon found their seats and wearily sat down in them. Scott had a window seat; his head was already pressed against the glass, gazing out at the view. He was in no hurry to get away; he wanted to enjoy his last images of Miami with its grassy runways littered with lakes, its egrets and alligators, its palm trees and endless skies.

'Good evening, ladies and gentlemen, this is your

hostess speaking. The flight to Amsterdam should take approximately ten hours; the weather tomorrow will have light showers with sunny intervals. As for the weather across the Atlantic, we've had an unusually large high-pressure system over the last few days so we hope that it will linger long enough for you to enjoy a very starry night. We'd also like to address the following safety issues...'

She went through the usual instructions, then the plane began to make its way to the runway. Scott glimpsed an orange sock blowing in the breeze, and the plane stopped momentarily. He stared out of the window again – his very last look at Miami. The plane revved its engines and shot across the runway, and he let the thrill of the speed take him before the plane eventually left the ground.

From this height he could see the beach, the main city and the open ocean, but every second took him further away from them, and at that realisation, Scott's lovesickness seized him in its intoxicating web. The beauty of it all was astounding; it was the perfect scene for romance – if he had any right now.

The hours passed and it became dark, though the stars and moonlight lit the Atlantic below like a lantern. He looked on between sea and horizon, as if trying to sense the future that lay ahead.

He felt so sad. As if a switch had been flipped, he found himself missing Sophie even more terribly than before, and his heart sagged as if suddenly weighted. He longed for the soft touch of Sophie's hand in his own. He missed her warming presence, her soft voice, her chattiness, her hugs, her kisses and her expert ability to show him the wonders of nature.

Then an idea snapped him out of his sorrow.

He came up with another warm thought, a metaphor, one from Mother Nature herself.

The way Sophie kept him warm was like how the Gulf Stream kept the seas of Britain free of ice all year round, always providing warmth even from afar.

Scott stayed awake for as long as he could. The pilot had long ago turned the seat-belt sign off and refreshments had been served. Most people were asleep by now.

That was how he liked it. That also meant there were no crying babies or toddlers to contend with.

The cabin was dimly lit, though one or two seats still had their reading lights on. No more stewards or hostesses came to serve refreshments.

Scott's mind cleared one more time. He had nothing to be afraid of – why would he? School, bullying and exams were nothing compared to what he'd taken on and defeated. In fact, now that they had the money to go anywhere they wanted, perhaps bullying would never be a problem again. And even if it was, Scott's combat skills had increased quite markedly during his time in Miami. If people wanted to take him on, they wouldn't stand a chance.

His friends' last chant replayed in his head like a remix. 'Farewell, World Warrior.'

His friends couldn't have come up with a better name for him. Dave was right. He was going to travel the world, taking on a foe the world feared and he could be a benefactor for anyone. He liked it. He would embrace it. It would be woven into his destiny. As World Warrior he would explore the world, fight its enemies and enjoy the vast array of wildlife it had to offer –

everything that was endemic to Earth.

Printed in Great Britain
by Amazon